THE MAN I MET ON HOLIDAY

Fiona was born in a youth hostel in Yorkshire. She started working on teen magazine *Jackie* at age seventeen, then went on to join *Just Seventeen* and *more!* Fiona has three grown-up children, writes for many newspapers and magazines and lives in Glasgow with her husband Jimmy.

For more info, visit www.fionagibson.com. You can follow Fiona on Instagram @fiona_gib.

FIONA GIBSON

The MAN I Met on HOLIDAY

Published by AVON
A division of HarperCollins*Publishers*
1 London Bridge Street
London SE1 9GF

www.harpercollins.co.uk

HarperCollins*Publishers*
Macken House,
39/40 Mayor Street Upper,
Dublin 1
D01 C9W8
Ireland

A Paperback Original 2023
1
First published in Great Britain by HarperCollins*Publishers* 2023

Typeset in Sabon LT by Palimpsest Book Production Limited, Falkirk, Stirlingshire

Printed and Bound in the UK using 100% Renewable Electricity
at CPI Group (UK) Ltd

This book is produced from independently certified FSC™ paper to ensure
responsible forest management.

For more information visit: www.harpercollins.co.uk/green

For Michelle with love

PART ONE

A Taste of Corsica

A perfectly ripe apricot and a sliver of creamy goat's cheese. There you have it – sunshine on a plate

CHAPTER ONE

LAUREN

There's something odd on the beach. At first, from a distance, I'm not sure what it is. It's just some kind of shape with what looks like a towel draped over it. But as I make my way towards it I recognise the towel as belonging to Mum and Dad; or rather Mum and Dad's dog, Minnie: pongy of breath, farty of bum and beloved by all of us.

Closer now, I can see it's definitely the towel that's reserved for rubbing her down after a swim. But what's it doing here, draped over something? The shape flinches and the towel falls away from its face. I see now that not only is it an actual human – but my son.

On the island of Corsica – 'the scented isle', as it's known – Charlie has plonked himself next to a litter bin swarming with wasps. I'm interpreting this as a sign that this isn't his best-ever holiday. It's as if he's *asking* to be stung, parking himself here. Then he can be even more miserable and have a tangible reason for it.

I approach with caution as if he's a neighbourhood cat, prone to lashing out when provoked. 'Here you are,' I

3

venture, trying to sound sunny and bright. 'I wondered where you'd got to.'

'Hmm,' comes Charlie's grunted response. He grabs the book from his side, flips it open randomly and focuses hard on the page.

'What're you doing here?'

'Reading?' Recently his tone has developed an upward lilt.

'Isn't there somewhere nicer you could sit?'

'I'm all right here.'

Sure, it's recommended in all the guidebooks: Unmissable Bins of Corsica. 'It's a bit . . . waspy, isn't it? You might be—'

'I'm fine, Mum,' he snaps. 'I'm all right.'

Every summer, since our entire world turned on its head, Charlie and I have spent a few weeks here with my parents. Mum is Corsican, and although she and Dad met in London and raised me there, it had been her long-held dream to return to the island one day. For ages, Dad had dug in his heels. Corsica was too hot, he complained. Too waspy, probably. He'd had numerous, sometimes shaky businesses over the years, and the city was embedded in his bones. But when it transpired that his accountant had been ripping him off for years (financially, my parents were scuppered), he'd finally come around to the idea.

Mum had inherited the rickety cottage that had been in her family pretty much forever. So to Corsica they came, having settled their debts, ready to enjoy a quiet life tending their garden and small apricot and clementine orchard up in the hills.

Charlie and I have loved having this beautiful island to come to. It's been our little piece of heaven – until now. Clearly, he wants to be left alone. But I plough on because

4

that's what any pissed-off seventeen-year-old wants, isn't it? Their mum banging on at them as if they're a little kid? 'You know that's Minnie's towel,' I remark.

'It's fine.'

I pause, trying to dredge up a thrilling alternative to sitting here. 'Want to come and get a cold drink with me?'

'Not right now.'

'You sure? Not a Coke or something?'

'No thanks.'

I look down, aware that I'm undoubtably annoying him just by being here, but at a loss as to what to do. 'It's really hot,' I say unnecessarily. 'D'you have a drink in your rucksack?'

No response.

'It really is very hot. You need to hydrate—'

'I'M FINE, OKAY?!'

I reel back, shocked by his outburst because he's never been a shouty boy, not really. He was always the one sitting quietly in class, working dutifully, the last one to put up his hand or draw attention to himself. *Works very hard, but it'd be nice if he'd speak up now and again*, his teachers would tell me.

'Come on, Charlie,' I say now. 'Don't be like this. We're in *Corsica* . . .'

'I know where we are, Mum.'

'Can't you at least pretend to be enjoying yourself?' I'm aware that I've swerved down the wrong track, and that it's not going to help. But still I barge on: 'Or we might as well be in Luton!'

He peers at me through narrowed eyes. Then, to signify that our exchange is over, he swivels away and jabs his nose back into his book.

I hope I've always been a kind and supportive mum.

I've been on hand to help with his homework (although he usually got on with it without fuss) and welcomed his friends round to guzzle enormous quantities of pizza and popcorn. In fact, considering Charlie's shyness, I was so relieved he had a small group of mates, they'd have been welcome every day of the week. Every weekday morning through the primary school years I went that extra mile to make exciting packed lunches, apart from that one time on the Cubs trip, when I forgot to send him off with anything at all. ('It's okay, Mum,' he'd said stoically. 'Someone gave me a few crisps.')

Since Charlie was seven it's just been the two of us, and whenever I worried if I was a good enough mum, I'd remind myself that I was doing my best and that my reserved little boy was very loved. Which meant I was doing a pretty decent job, didn't it?

But now I'm standing over him in public, barking at him to 'hydrate'. I'm the kind of mother who snaps, *We might as well be in Luton!*

What's happened to us? We've always been so close, the two of us. Other mums often said how lucky I was to have such a great little mate. And now I catch him visibly flinching when I approach. As if I might be about to make him turn out his pockets or shine a glaring light in his face.

Nearby, a group of extremely attractive teenagers (no parents bothering them!) are draped all over each other on a raggedy patchwork of bright towels. Some are snogging enthusiastically. Poor Charlie, I reflect. He should be like them, not trapped on holiday with his fifty-one-year-old mother. An elderly couple walks past us, hand in hand, and an English family with two little blonde girls stop to pick up shells to drop into a bucket. Everyone apart from us is having a perfectly lovely time.

I start to walk away from Charlie, realising with crushing dismay that our beloved island no longer thrills him. In fact he *would* rather be in Luton, because Luton is only eleven miles away from the Hertfordshire village where we live. Then he'd be close to his friends, apart from his best mate, Remy, who is currently enjoying a very different kind of holiday from ours.

I've probably only got away with so many magical summers here with Charlie because, these past few years, we've brought Remy too. My mother dotes on him and he's no trouble at all. In fact, he feels like family. However, this year he politely declined to come with us. Apparently he had 'other plans'.

I stop and glance back at my son, slumped miserably now with his fine dark hair flopping over his sharply angled face.

'Charlie?' I call out.

His head jerks up. 'Yeah?' He sounds less hostile, I think. Maybe he feels bad about being snappy and will try to be more pleasant from now on.

'D'you have any sunscreen on?' I ask.

A scowl. 'Can you stop going on?'

'I'm not going on, I only asked . . .' Now my maternal laser-gaze has landed on a distinctly pink upper arm. He's already burning in the late July sun. Striding back, I pull a plastic bottle from my raffia beach bag and hold it out for him. 'Here, you need a bit of this on.'

He shrinks away as if I've offered him a rotting fish. 'No, I'm fine.'

Fine for the burns unit, yes! 'Come on, Charlie. Just put some on—'

'Leave me alone!' he commands. But I can't, can I? I can't just smile and say, 'Okay, see you later.' Then, under my breath: '*Don't come running to me for calamine*

7

lotion!' I can't accept that at seventeen he's old enough to make his own decisions regarding UV protection.

I can't just leave it, and I know that's wrong.

So, I'm not a 'good mum', am I? I'm ridiculous, treating this almost fully fledged adult man like a little kid. The teenagers on the towels can see it. As they murmur between themselves and look over sympathetically, I can sense Charlie wishing he could dig a hole in the sand and crawl into it.

Maybe it's because of what happened, and the fact that we've been a tight little unit for a decade now; the two of us rock solid (*too* solid probably), trotting out to the cinema together long after his peers had found their parents disgusting and refused to have anything to do with them, beyond the necessities.

Charlie was never like that. He was a wonderful kid, so stoical and brave, even when he'd witnessed something he really should never have seen. And he'd been gamely up for adventure when we'd left our London home, closing the door on all the tension and sadness one final time.

'You'll love it out here,' my best friend Kim had said of the pretty Hertfordshire village where she'd settled with her husband and their twin daughters a few years before. 'It'll be a fresh start for you and brilliant for Charlie. We can't wait to have you close to us!'

I was still worried because he'd never found it easy to make friends. The ones he had in London were quiet, bookish types, like him. How would he manage, having to start all over again? But, happily, he liked the idea of moving to the country. He'd always loved being in nature and camping, all that outdoorsy stuff – especially sitting outside the tent and looking up at the stars at night.

8

We found a cosy red-brick cottage with an overgrown garden, and moved just after Charlie's eighth birthday. Kim had been right: it was good for him, for both of us, to start afresh. I tore into the garden, shaping it just the way we wanted it, with Charlie a willing helper, always at my side. Digging, planting, laying gravel paths; it was our joint project and we were immensely proud when it began to bloom beautifully.

It was wonderful being close to Kim too. While I've never shared her enthusiasm for cold-water swimming, I've been happy to provide a thermos of hot home-made soup and watch from the sidelines while she's plunged into our nearby lake. Meanwhile her twin girls, who are a little older than Charlie, regarded him as a delightful new play-mate. They knew he was into his books and science and astronomy, and they loved him for who he was.

To my delight, he also found a new best friend in Remy, who lived down the road, and after a few weeks he barely mentioned his old London friends at all. I made new friends too, with Remy's mother among them: Ellie, who seemed rather brusque at first but was kind and welcoming beneath the brittle exterior. Charlie's new life centred around school, Cubs and then Scouts. Secretly, he still played with his Lego long after most kids would have put it aside. Only Remy knew about that, and they'd build intricate space missiles together. But most of all, Charlie was drawn to a Victorian observatory perched on top of a hill, less than a mile from our house. They ran events for parents and children and we trotted along to them together, with Charlie enthusing about meteors and comets ('They're like a snowball of gas, shooting through space!') all the way home. Even after the other kids had stopped bringing a parent along, Charlie still liked me to go with him. He just enjoyed being with me, as I loved being with him. And he never seemed embarrassed about that.

However, he's not in the Young Stargazers anymore and recently there's been a marked shift in attitude. I catch his agitated looks and sense him wishing I'd vaporise into the atmosphere when all I've done is ask how school went that day.

I keep telling myself that this is fine and normal and *exactly* how things are supposed to go. Most kids start to go off their parents much younger, when puberty hits. Kim reckoned her girls suddenly found her appalling when they moved up to secondary school. 'Bella stormed out of the kitchen,' she told me once. 'All I was doing was unloading the dishwasher!' And Charlie's almost a man, for goodness' sake. Of course I'm repugnant to him.

I'm marching away from him now, aware of the fierce Corsican sun beating down on my head. Meanwhile my son's tender skin is slowly frying because of his stubbornness. I can't bear it. I can't let him do this to himself. So I swing round and, once again, I hurry back to him, simultaneously squirting a dollop of sunscreen onto my hand.

'What are you doing?' he exclaims.

'Let me put some on you.'

'No.'

'Just a little bit, please—'

'You've gone mad!'

'This is ridiculous,' I protest. 'It's like you want to burn to make some kind of point—'

'You're not putting it on me—'

'I am!' I lurch at him, and as I splat the lotion onto his upper arm he flies back, his shoulder slamming into the bin – 'Agggh! Fucking hell, Mum!' – sending the wasps spinning into a frenzy.

10

'Oh God, I'm sorry,' I start. But Charlie's focus is on his upper arm, which he is now clutching and staring at in alarm.

'See, you *are* burnt,' I start.

'No, Mum. I've been stung.'

'Have you? Let me see . . .'

'Get away from me!' he shouts.

'What's that lady doing to that boy?' a child's voice rings out. I look round to see the shell-collecting family all staring, horrified, *at the lady attacking the boy*.

'Come on, darling,' the woman says primly. 'It's nothing to do with us.' Off they all march, with the mum occasionally glancing back, looking concerned, as if she might be considering calling the police.

Above us an aeroplane trail cuts across the cloudless sky. The turquoise sea sparkles and the teenagers jump up from their towels and run, all laughing, into it. My son has been stung, and he's barking at me to *just get away* and there's nothing I can do to make it better. So I turn away, my heart slowly cracking as I remember all the times Charlie would charge joyfully into the sea, just like those beautiful kids have now.

Years ago, when he was still a little boy, the two of us loved to swim together. I'd swum competitively as a child and Charlie had taken to it easily too. Until that terrible day, the final straw with his father and me – after which he'd refused to ever go into the sea again.

At least he still enjoyed the beach. I was relieved about that. He'd poke about, collecting things, running over to me with an unusual shell or a piece of amber glass. 'A sea present for you,' he'd say, all pleased with himself.

Of course, he doesn't bring me sea presents now or even want to hang out with me. I'm fine with that. I'd be fine with anything if only Charlie wasn't making it so obvious that he wishes he hadn't come. And now, as a tear rolls down my cheek and I ram my tube of Factor 30 back into my bag, I think, at least I was right about *one* thing.

We might as well be in Luton.

CHAPTER TWO

JAMES

My daughter has 'packed' for our trip. By this, I mean she's dumped three enormous open suitcases in the hallway with mounds of stuff spewing out. They look as if they've been searched in haste by border force officials.

Bottles and tubs of mysterious stuff (one with its lid off, leaking some kind of goo) are scattered all over the wooden floor, along with various electrical appliances, presumably for styling hair but possibly for soldering or waffle making – who knows? Not to mention handbags, hats, jewellery strewn about like tinsel and tiny lacy scraps of things, plus clothes – *so* many clothes, scattered in multicoloured drifts. She must be planning several outfit changes per day. Was it really such a good idea for us to go away together?

Of course it is, I tell myself. Since her mother and I split up I've taken Esther on holiday plenty of times. Okay, so the last time – when she was seventeen – she lay by the pool, sunglasses clamped on, barely uttering a word all week apart from asking what the Wi-Fi password was. And the next year she made it clear that she wouldn't be repeating the experience. However, she's twenty now, and I came up with the idea as a way of helping to 'clear her head'.

I hadn't really expected her to say yes. 'A whole fortnight?' she'd exclaimed. 'With *you*?'

'Yeah,' I said.

'But what'll we do?'

'You can just relax and do whatever you like. I promise I won't drag you around museums or anything like that.'

Esther smirked then. She'd just broken up with her boyfriend because he'd slept with someone else, and it was good to see a hint of a smile again. Although I can't stand the guy I'd still been worried about her, barely eating, smoking loads, mooching around with her hair all tangled and purplish shadows under her eyes.

'D'you know what?' she'd said. 'That might be really fun!' As if it was something of a novelty, going away with your old dad, like digging out the snakes and ladders at Christmas.

I was happy to be a relic unearthed from a cupboard of dusty old junk because, actually, I had a secret plan. Hopefully, while we were away, I'd be able to gently persuade Esther that the 'renowned DJ' (i.e. he owns a few shit records) and supposedly 'recovering sex addict' (not much sign of recovery as far as I can make out) didn't deserve her, and that she was better off without him. I was also hoping she might consider different career options to the one she's fallen into; i.e. being an influencer and a bit of a social media star. It's all quite baffling and, although I don't disapprove of it exactly, I can't help thinking that taking a different direction might make her feel more fulfilled in the long run.

However, that wasn't my priority. My more immediate hope was she'd come back from Corsica happy to either enjoy being single or meet someone closer to her own age who wasn't a compulsively lying narcissistic fuckwit.

Unfortunately, my plan backfired. No sooner had I booked the holiday than Esther had moved back into Miles's east London flat with its black walls, pink velvet chaise longue and a taxidermied bat dangling from a string, ready to clonk you on the head in the hallway. Baroque, he calls it. Creepy, more like. I'd fibbed that it would be impossible to change the name on the booking and take someone else. In truth, I wasn't interested in going with anyone else and, miraculously, Esther said she'd still come.

So this is Miles's hallway her stuff is strewn all over. Her boyfriend of two years who *claims* he's forty-five, and okay, maybe I should be cool with the age gap but I do find it incredibly difficult. Especially as I suspect he's even older than he claims – as ancient as me, even! – although Esther shrugs off my concerns, saying, 'The industry he works in is incredibly ageist, Dad. You don't get it. No one cares how old vets are, do they?'

Well, yes, thankfully people don't require you to exude youthfulness in order to treat their pets. Anyway, at least Miles is out tonight, 'doing a gig'. So I haven't had to sit on my hands to stop myself from punching him.

'This is just about it,' Esther announces now, re-appearing barefoot from the bedroom laden with yet more clothes.

'You can't need all this,' I protest.

She fixes me with a look. 'Well, I do.'

'But what *is* all this stuff?'

'Just basics, Dad.'

'Basics? We'd need to charter a plane for this lot!' I pick up a clear plastic bottle from the floor and examine it. 'No need to take water. You can buy it there.'

'That's not *water*-water,' Esther scoffs.

'What is it then?'

'Micellar water. For cleansing,' she adds.

I look around, feeling weighed down by the sheer volume of stuff. 'What are those sachets?'

'Anti-ageing face masks.'

'You're twenty years old! What d'you need those for?'

'You wouldn't get it. You're a man . . .' She shakes her head despairingly.

Another object catches my eye. 'Come on, you're not seriously planning to bring that—'

'What?'

'The fur coat.'

'It's *faux* fur,' she announces with a snort. 'It's actually really light.'

'It can't be light. It's fur!'

'Well, it *is* . . .'

'It'll be like wearing a carpet. D'you know how hot Corsica is?'

'Stop being such an old man, will you?' She swivels her eyes towards the dangling bat. I can hear Miles's white rat gnawing away in its cage in the kitchen. Of course Miles has a rat. I'm not against them; of course I'm not. But if I'd been asked to guess the preferred pet of a self-professed nocturnal wild man . . . let's say I wouldn't have said a cockapoo.

'You'll get heat stroke if you wear that,' I warn her.

'So you can say, "I told you so" when I wind up in a Corsican hospital,' she says with a grin.

I try to keep down a smile. 'C'mon, you'll have to whittle this lot down. I'm only taking cabin baggage—'

'Yeah, 'cause you're a man—'

'I've booked a checked-in case for you. But just the one, okay?'

'We can check in more, can't we?'

'You can't take three suitcases!'

She sighs loudly, transmitting the silent message: *Mum would let me bring whatever I like.* So often, where my daughter's concerned, I find myself holding back from saying what I really want to say; not because I'm a complete pushover (I don't think), but because it seems like the only way to maintain some semblance of calm. So instead of reiterating that she can only bring one suitcase, I compromise and say, 'Okay then – *two*.'

The plan had been for her to stay over at mine tonight so we could head out to the airport in the morning together. But now she's announced that, as she and Miles won't be seeing each other for a whole fortnight, she wants to be here when he comes home tonight.

'Oh, come on,' I protest. 'It'll be a lot easier this way.'

'I want to see Miles, Dad. We want to spend this last night together.'

'"This last night"? You're only going away for two weeks, not to a Tibetan monastery for the rest of your life—'

'He'll be really upset if I'm not here tonight.' Like I'm remotely concerned about his tender feelings. 'And you don't need to pick me up in the morning,' she adds. 'I'll meet you at the airport instead'.

'It'll be much easier to go together.'

'No, Dad.'

I exhale heavily. 'You will be in plenty of time then, won't you?'

'Yeah, don't worry,' she says brightly.

'Okay, but remember we have to check in two hours early, so that's seven o'clock—'

'I know how planes work,' she retorts. 'I realise you don't just turn up when they're about to go, like a bus—'

'And no need to ask Miles to drive you. Just get an Uber . . .'

'No, no, he'll bring me. He really wants to see me off.' She catches my doubtful look. 'He *can* drive, y'know . . .' After a fashion, yes. 'He's really trying to be nice,' she adds with a pained look.

'Are you sure he'll be up for getting up that early?' *I've always had the impression he likes to sleep in until sundown, like a ghoul.*

'Of course he will,' she says firmly.

'Okay. But can I ask you one other thing?'

She lets out a theatrical sigh. 'What?'

'Can you pack something waterproof? Because it does rain there, torrential storms apparently—'

'Like an umbrella?' She blinks at me.

'Well, more like an anorak . . .'

'An anorak!' she guffaws, cringing.

'And another thing,' I add, trying unsuccessfully to trap in a laugh because she's maddening. I came home from work yesterday to find that she'd popped round for an impromptu visit. Which was lovely of course. It's always great to see her. But when I opened the fridge to grab the samosa I knew was there, she'd already scoffed it. And all that remained of the packet of treacle cookies I'm partial to was a scattering of crumbs on the worktop, and the cellophane wrapper lying near – but crucially not in – the bin. 'There's never anything to eat here, Dad,' she announced.

'We'll be doing some walking,' I remind her. 'Don't pull that face. It's a beautiful island and we're going to explore it on foot . . .'

'What, *all* of it?' she wails.

'. . . So don't just bring sandals, okay? You'll need proper shoes with supporting structure . . .'

'With supporting structure.' A solemn nod.

'Got that?'

'Yes, Dad.' She hugs me tightly, and I'm thinking now how much I need this holiday. I haven't been anywhere for, God – two years, I think it is? And after all the crap Esther's been through with Miles, she needs it too. So never mind the crazy fur coat and the big bottle of whatever that water stuff is. My daughter and I are going to Corsica together and it's going to be *great*.

CHAPTER THREE

JAMES

The toughest thing I've had to deal with in recent months wasn't telling Maria Kowalski that her cat had an inoperable brain tumour, or the O'Haras that it had been too late to save their Dalmatian who'd eaten poisoned meat in the park. Yes, those sorts of situations are terrible. They're the very worst aspect of running my small north London veterinary practice. But I'm trained for it, and even if I can't make everything right, I always try to do the best and kindest thing for both the pet and the owner.

But I can't do the best thing for Esther because there's nothing I can do to stop her from loving Miles Lattimer-Jones, serial shagger and heir to half of Somerset as far as I can make out.

'It's an illness, Dad,' she'd said, when his infidelity had come to light. 'He's promised to get treatment.'

Then: 'He made a mistake and he's sorry.' Like he'd come home with the wrong kind of plant milk. However, I have to accept that I have very little influence over how she lives her life these days. As for catching our flight tomorrow, I remind myself that she's a savvy young woman who's done incredibly well for herself, despite my strong reservations about the kind of life she was entering into.

'Chill, James. Relax!' my ex-wife Rhona is fond of barking at me. Or, somewhat unnecessarily: 'Take that broom handle out of your arse' – a favourite whenever I've said no thanks, I can't sit knocking back cocktails with her and her boyfriend when I have work the next day. 'He can't possibly have a drink on a school night,' she's retorted on many occasions, while laughing at my squareness. Neither would she if she was operating to remove a stone from a guinea pig's bladder at eight-thirty the next morning. Call me a party pooper but it wouldn't be ideal, to have shaky hands and alcoholic sweats in those circumstances. But I guess Rhona is right in that I probably over-worry and should learn to relax more.

So, yes, I should be able to trust Esther to turn up for our flight in plenty of time. After all, what other option is there? *Chill, James. Relax!* I tell myself as I arrive at the airport at 6.30 a.m. Apparently Miles is on best behaviour at the moment so of course he'll get her here on time.

By 7.05 a.m., too uptight to sit at a table, I'm standing at the coffee bar where we've arranged to meet. She's only five minutes late, which counts as nothing. As she'll be here any minute, I'm hanging off buying a coffee so I can get one for Esther at the same time. Miles too, if he comes in to see her off. I make a mental note to be friendly and not hostile towards him, so Esther and I don't start our holiday on a sour note.

Time ticks on. My body is craving caffeine so I buy an Americano and tell myself to calm down; *take that bloody broom handle out of your arse, James, she'll be here any minute*. The traffic's probably bad.

Here she is, hurrying towards me with her long red hair bundled up messily on top of her head. Hair that

21

seemed, mysteriously, to double in volume a few weeks ago. How did it do that, I wondered? When I mentioned it, Esther said something about 'a treatment' she'd had – 'and before you ask it was only fifty quid.' Why had she felt the need to tell me that? I couldn't remember any occasion when I'd asked her, as an adult, how much something had cost.

I reach for my suitcase, relief surging through me as the red-haired girl approaches, until I realise my mistake. (Somehow I seem to have packed my glasses in the case rather than having them to hand in my pocket.) It's not Esther after all. But not to worry. They're just running late, which I'd expected. That's why I'd built in an extra hour. But as the hour slides by and text after text – then call after call – go unanswered, catching our flight is the last thing I'm worried about.

I pace around, pulling my wheeled case and gripping my phone as I try to figure out what to do without panicking anyone, like her mother. I'm also trying not to imagine Miles's flashy red sportscar a mangled wreck at the roadside and other terrible scenes I can't even allow into my brain.

Surely, if there'd been a problem this morning, she'd have called me? Yes, we'd had a tetchy message exchange late last night, just after I'd gone to bed. But I thought that was just Esther being Esther, seeing how far she could push me. Surely she hadn't expected me to agree? *I'm going to sleep now*, I'd finally messaged at around 1 a.m. *You should too, okay?* And that had been that. No further messages received.

I wipe a slick of sweat from my brow with my hand. Something dark and heavy seems to have lodged itself in my gut. Why did I even ask her on this holiday? I was an idiot, I decide now, to believe it would all go smoothly without any drama. I realise, too, that Esther only agreed to come so as not to let me down. In amongst all the bravado and insistence that she knows everything – whereas I'm just some blundering fool who somehow managed to stumble through vet school – there's a good, kind heart.

My lovely, caring, chaotic Esther who I'm so proud of and love very much. I don't tell her that nearly enough. Too bloody worried about her wearing footwear with structural support and being on time for things. Fuck, when will I ever stop being so uptight?

Now I'm thinking I'll have to tell the smart young executive couple next door that I won't need them to look after Walter, my cat, after all. Because I absolutely don't want to go on holiday now. Not without Esther. I don't give a toss about wasted flights or the hotel or anything else.

But maybe she *is* just running late, and we can catch another flight or stay here overnight in a hotel and go tomorrow? I really don't care. All I want is to see her running towards me in that ridiculous fur – sorry, *faux* fur – coat, having defied me by bringing those three enormous cases. She can bring fifteen cases – plus hand luggage – as long as everything is all right.

CHAPTER FOUR

JAMES

'Dad?'

'Esther! My God, I've been so worried. Are you okay?'

'I'm fine.'

'Where are you?'

'At home.'

'At home? What're you doing there?'

'Calling you—'

'I said seven, remember? You promised you'd be here on time. It's gone nine and our flight leaves in, well, we've probably missed—'

'I'm not coming, Dad.'

'What?' Realising I'm clutching a cup half filled with cold coffee, I dump it on a sticky table.

'I'm not coming. I'm sorry. I mean, I'm sorry you were worried . . .'

My heart is racing. She's alive, and she sounds fine – unhurt, uninjured. Thank Christ for that. My eyes are moist, and I rub at them with my fingers. 'I've been so, so worried.' I lower myself onto a seat.

'I'm sorry,' she says, her voice cracking a little. 'But

after what you said last night, after that conversation we had . . .'

'About Miles not coming with us?'

'Yeah. We were, like, really upset . . .'

They were upset? For the past hour I've been panic-stricken.

'He'd have paid for his own flight,' she offers. 'It wouldn't have cost you anything.'

'It wasn't about money . . .'

'We just thought, y'know, it'd be a good opportunity for you and him to get to know each other properly . . .'

'I'm not going on holiday with Miles,' I snap.

'You wouldn't have been going *with* him. He'd have just *been there*,' she points out.

I exhale slowly, trying to keep it together. I'm not even angry; it's gone way beyond that. I'm just overwhelmed with relief. 'You could've called me two hours ago to tell me this,' I say levelly. 'I've messaged and called you so many times. D'you realise what it's been like, thinking you're lying dead in the road?'

'I'm sorry,' she murmurs. 'I just didn't know what to do.' A pause. 'What're you going to do?'

'I don't know,' I reply flatly. 'I doubt if I'll catch the flight now . . .' I slide my gaze towards the departures board. All around me people are strolling towards the gates, chivvying children along, giggling in big groups. Happy people all heading off on their holidays.

I see now that my flight has been delayed. If I hurry now I could still catch it. Her mother is always on at me to be spontaneous – to 'live a little!' as she puts it.

'I feel so bad about worrying you,' Esther says. 'But Miles really wanted me to stay with him, and I felt torn between him and you, and—'

'I've got to go now,' I cut in, grabbing at my case.

'What?'

'I'm going now. Bye, Est—'

'Dad!' she exclaims. 'Where are you going?'

'Corsica,' I reply.

CHAPTER FIVE

LAUREN

'It's probably because Remy's not here,' Mum suggests as we potter in the garden together. 'He just wants to be with his friends. That's natural at his age, isn't it? This pulling away from you thing, I mean?'

Of course it's Charlie we're talking about. He's still in a mood, currently reading in his room with the curtains firmly shut, lest a chink of Mediterranean sunshine should force its way in. After yesterday's wasp incident I'm giving him a wide berth, and being out here with Mum, tending her potted herbs in the dappled shade of the fig and eucalyptus trees, is making me feel a whole lot better.

'You're right,' I reply. 'That's what Kim says too.' My best friend has reminded me that her twin daughters, Bella and Scarlett, 'turned sour like milk left out overnight' at thirteen years old. So in fact I've had *bonus* years. 'I'm just sorry he's not being his usual sunny self,' I add.

'Don't worry.' Mum smiles kindly and wipes her soily hands on the front of her gardening apron. 'I'm just glad you're here. You know your dad's hardly full of sparkling conversation.' We chuckle and stroll towards the small clementine and apricot orchard where the trees are already laden with fruit. 'Maybe I should have left Charlie at home this time,' I suggest.

'D'you think he'd have been okay on his own?' Mum asks.

'I'm sure he would. And Kim could have dropped in every couple of days to keep an eye.'

'That's true,' she says as we sit side by side on the old wrought-iron bench.

'I know I'm ridiculous,' I add. 'He doesn't need anyone keeping an eye, does he? He's leaving home next year. You know he's set on doing physics or astronomy—'

'Yes, love. But you just care about him,' she says, ever supportive.

'Hmm. Too much, probably.'

'There's no such thing as caring too much,' Mum insists, and before I can protest that there is – it's not mothering but *smothering* – she adds, 'It's funny to think of Remy running around Paris!'

'Yes, isn't it? No wonder Charlie's feeling a bit put out.' She smiles wryly in recognition of the shift in their friendship. Only nine months older than Charlie, Remy seems to have catapulted into an entirely different life stage involving swapping his scruffy sweatshirts and jeans for designer attire and – the part I still can't get my head around – going to Paris *with a girl*.

An actual girl, in an actual hotel, without adult supervision! Apparently he'd never so much as booked a table at a restaurant before. In fact, until recently he was still scared of cooked carrot and our airing cupboard, which he'd scramble past in case anything should jump out. Now he's in charge of a hotel keycard with unfettered access to a minibar. I bet no one's nagging Remy to hydrate.

What's more, apparently the Paris trip has been paid

for with his earnings from writing a song for a well-known artist. To be accurate, he hadn't written it specifically *for* her, but had sent it to her management company and she'd loved it and recorded it. Remy is a singer-songwriter who's already supported a couple of successful acts. He's a lovely boy – charming and hardworking – and has been a regular addition at our dinner table over the years. But over the past few months his life has swerved off in an altogether more thrilling direction.

I can't help feeling sorry for Charlie being left behind. His only means of earning cash at the moment is his Saturday job at the dusty old newsagent's in our village, owned by Brenda with the hacking cough and flat-footed stomp. I know he wants to jack it in, but there are precious few part-time jobs where we live and, whenever he's on the brink, Brenda sends him home with a box of out-of-date Curly Wurlys and he stays on through guilt. Charlie's never had a girlfriend as far as I know (not that I expect him to tell me anything anymore). And now Remy has Freya, he doesn't seem to need Charlie very much at all. Maybe, if I were in his situation, I too would be huddled under a dog towel next to a bin.

Later, as Mum pops out to visit a friend, I head indoors to find Dad muttering away in his tiny study. He's at war with an ancient computer that's prone to overheating and which sporadically emits a smell of burning dust. I'm terrified the thing will blow up in his face. However, he's batted off my suggestions that perhaps it's time to invest in a new one.

'Nothing wrong with this one,' he huffs. I leave him jabbing at the keyboard, which appears to be matted with dog hair and jam, and find Minnie stretched out in the shade in the garden.

'Fancy a walk?' I ask her. Scrambling up, she pants in

delight as I fix on her lead. I wish my son was as happy to hang out with me.

'I'm taking Minnie up to the pool,' I call inside to Dad and Charlie in their respective caves. With no response from either, we head out.

As well as its beaches, Corsica is also famous for its natural mountain pools. There's one fairly close to Mum and Dad's place that Minnie loves. We all loved it once, as a shady picnic spot, but I can't imagine Charlie hanging out there with me anytime soon.

The light has turned golden by the time we've cut through the forest path and reached the pool, and Minnie wades straight into the clear water. Mum came up with her name as a joke as she's an enormous shaggy rug of a hound, already fully grown when my parents took her in here as a stray. As I watch her swimming in her stately fashion, any remaining traces of gloom ebb away. Never mind that this is probably the last time Charlie and I will spend a month here together. It'll be good for him to branch out and do his own thing – like Remy has.

'*We* still have fun, don't we, Minnie?' I call out to her. With no one else around, the only sound is birdsong in the surrounding woods. I love this island like nowhere else on earth. As well as being my home from home, it's also been a huge source of inspiration for my work. I create recipe content for magazines and corporate clients, and recently I've been commissioned to produce a regular newspaper column entitled 'A Corsican Kitchen'. Perching on a rock, I breathe in deeply. For now at least, the scents of wild thyme and rosemary have replaced the gusts of resentment from my son.

Minnie reaches the edge of the pool and lollops out. I get up from the rock, primed for her to bound over and spray me as she shakes herself off. But she just stands there, eerily still and looking dazed. 'Minnie?' I prompt her. 'Come here, girl!' I pat my thighs loudly.

Still she doesn't come. She seems to wobble a bit, as if disorientated. Then – suddenly – she collapses to the ground. 'Minnie!' I shriek. 'Min, what's wrong?'

Panic rattles through me as I run to her and crouch at her side. I try to hug her – gently, without moving her – and when she doesn't respond I cry into her soggy brown fur. I can't tell if she's breathing, or even if she's still alive. 'Minnie,' I urge her. 'Please, girl. Come on . . .' I no longer care that those idyllic summers with my son appear to be over. All I want is for Minnie to get up and reassure me that she just had a funny episode, and it'll turn out to be fine. But she's just lying there, inert.

I look around, desperately hoping to see a local out walking, or tourists on a hike. 'Hello?' I yell. 'Can anyone help me?' My French is pretty good but they're English words that tumble out of my mouth. 'Something's happened to my dog!' I cry out into the forest as a fresh bout of tears fills my eyes. 'Please, is anybody there?'

I feel sick now, and I'm shaking. How am I going to tell Mum, Dad and Charlie that Minnie died?

'Hey, I'll help!'

I look around, wondering at first if I imagined the voice. 'Hello?' I cry out.

'Hang on, just a sec . . .' A tall, lean man with short salt-and-pepper hair has appeared at a gap in the trees. He hurries towards us, bobs down at Minnie's side and moves his hands gently over her body.

'Is she alive? Please say she is—'

'She is, yes. What happened?' He looks up at me briefly.

'I . . . I don't know. She was swimming, she always swims here, nothing like this has ever happened before—'

'And she collapsed?' His gaze meets mine through his silver-rimmed glasses.

'Yes, soon as she came out of the water—'

'I'm a vet,' he cuts in. 'I'm going to try CPR, okay?'

What am I going to say? *No, I have a better idea*? I blink at him and nod, still stunned by his sudden appearance. 'Will it work?' I ask.

The man doesn't answer. He pulls off his specs and flings them aside, and now his mouth is already down on Minnie's nose.

CHAPTER SIX

LAUREN

I can hardly breathe as he blows into Minnie's nostril, then pushes gently against her side. *Breathe, push. Breathe, push.* Over and over he goes in a steady rhythm.

It feels as if time – as well as my heart – has stopped.

He could be lying of course, and not actually a vet; just some random weirdo who believes he can heal animals or wants to impress me or God knows what. But somehow I sense I can trust him. Even if he stops and says he's sorry, there's nothing else he can do – and Minnie dies after all – at least he'll have tried.

'D'you think you can save her?' I blurt out.

He looks round briefly. 'I'll do my best.'

Come on, girl, I will her. *Please, darling Minnie. Come on.*

The man stops. Minnie flinches. 'She moved!' I yelp. A hind leg twitches, then her head. Now her side is rising and falling – barely detectable but there's definitely movement – as she breathes in and out. 'Oh, my girl,' I exclaim. 'Is she going to be all right?' She makes some sneezy, spluttering sounds and lies still for a moment before getting up unsteadily.

'I hope so,' the man replies, 'but you'd better have her checked out properly. Is there someone locally you can take her to?'

I hug her as much as she'll allow and wipe at my wet face with my hands. 'Yes, I'll get her looked at. Thank you so much. She's my parents' dog. They adore her, we all do . . .'

'I'm sure you do. She's a lovely girl. And it's okay, honestly.' He looks relieved as he pushes a hand back through his neatly cropped hair. He has a lean, handsome face with a strong nose and clear blue eyes that radiate kindness. After picking up his specs from the dirty ground, he wipes them on the front of his grey T-shirt before putting them back on.

'What could've caused it, d'you think?' I ask.

'It could be so many things. She might have had a reaction to something she's eaten, or the heat, or an insect bite or something like that. Or it might be neurological—'

'Could it happen again?'

'If she gets a full check they'll be able to give you a better idea,' he says. With Minnie at my side, we start to follow the path through the forest that leads back towards the road.

'I'm Lauren,' I add.

'I'm James.'

'Hi, James.' I smile, still overcome by gratitude. 'I can't believe our luck, that you came along and knew exactly what to do. But then, I guess this is pretty normal for you . . .'

He grins broadly and those blue eyes glint in the dappled light. 'Not really. I mean, not in this kind of scenario.'

'Well, I'm very grateful,' I say, glancing down at Minnie. She is trotting along quite happily, as if a stranger rushes over to blow into her nostrils every day of the week.

The winding road is visible through the trees now. It clings to the mountainside, its hairpin bends and sheer drop to the side terrifying drivers who aren't used to this sort of terrain. As James asks about my connection to the island, I tell him how my Corsican mum persuaded my dad – a Londoner through and through – to move out here, and how his initial reluctance has turned into a grudging love of the place.

'Is this your first time here?' I ask.

'Yeah.' James nods. 'I only arrived yesterday.'

'Enjoying it so far?'

'Er, yes,' he says, a touch over-brightly. Perhaps he hasn't had time to acclimatise yet.

'We love it so much,' I tell him. 'Me and my son, I mean. At least, he used to. He doesn't seem so enamoured with it anymore.' I give James a wry look. 'Teenagers,' I add, going on to tell him about the bin, the wasps and the shrouding with one of Minnie's rank old towels. James laughs in a way that tells me he's familiar with the life stage. 'D'you have kids yourself?' I ask.

'Yes, just the one. A daughter, Esther. She's twenty.'

'Is she here with you?'

'Nope, it's just me,' he replies, sounding brisker now. Then after a pause: 'Esther was meant to come too but, uh . . .' He tails off. 'There was a last-minute change of plan.'

'Oh.' I'm not sure what else to say. 'I'm sure you'll enjoy yourself anyway,' I add, not wanting to pry any further as I'm picking up the tension in his expression now. I'm pretty sure he doesn't want a stranger quizzing him about what happened.

'Yeah, I'm planning to do some walking and cycling,' he explains. 'And maybe some kayaking and snorkelling, stuff like that. And canyoning, that sounds like fun—'

'Active!' I cut in.

James laughs. 'Ha. Yeah. Well, there's a lot to explore here, isn't there?'

'Oh yes, so much. I'm sure you won't be bored for a second.'

At the roadside now, he tells me his hired bicycle is a little further up the hill. 'Well, it's been lovely meeting you,' I say, clipping on Minnie's lead now. 'And thanks again. I can't tell you how grateful I am.'

'Honestly, I'm happy to have helped.' As if he'd given me directions to the post office.

I smile, wondering now – despite his obvious competence and the fact that he's just saved Minnie's life – if there's something a bit lost about James. He certainly seems determined to cram his holiday with activities. I just hope he'll allow himself time to simply enjoy the island and soak it all in; to get to know a little of the *real* Corsica, in all its thyme-scented wildness. But of course, he can spend his holiday however he likes. 'How long are you here for?' I ask.

'Two weeks,' he replies.

'Well, if you'd like me to show you around one day—'

'Oh, I wouldn't want to—'

'No, of course,' I say quickly. It's not James who's feeling a little lost, I realise now. It's me. Despite knowing the island so well, and having plenty of work to get on with while I'm here, I'm conscious of not quite knowing what to do with myself. Since Charlie's shunned me I've been trying not to follow him round like a sad dog, hoping for a biscuit. 'Of course, you want to do your own thing,' I add, 'with all your activities—'

'I just meant I wouldn't want to take up your time,' James cuts in, looking concerned that he might have offended me.

I almost laugh at this. 'Honestly, time is something I have plenty of right now.'

'Really?' His warm smile crinkles his handsome face and does something terribly attractive to those clear blue eyes. 'That'd be great then. Thank you. I'd like that very much.'

CHAPTER SEVEN

LAUREN

It turns out that James doesn't actually know what canyoning is. 'I saw something about it in the in-flight magazine on the way over,' he admits as I drive us along the coast road. 'Something about it being the ultimate thrill for adrenaline seekers.' He glances at me and laughs.

'And you thought you'd give it a whirl?'

'I thought I'd give anything a whirl at that point.' I know he's referring to the somewhat less than ideal situation he'd found himself in. He has already told me about his daughter calling to announce that she wouldn't be joining him on the holiday after all – when he was waiting for her, with panic rising, at the airport. And I thought Charlie had been a bit difficult lately! Our fight over sunscreen seems nothing compared to that. It seems pretty outrageous actually. Honestly, who'd do that to their parent?

Anyway, fortunately for me, James had decided to come on his own – because why not? As he explained, he'd arranged cover at work and the alternative option, to slope off back home and waste the holiday, was too depressing to contemplate. 'So,' as he put it, 'I kind of *fell* onto the plane.'

'As far as I know,' I tell him now, 'canyoning involves hurling yourself off cliffs and scrambling along riverbeds in a crash helmet with a bunch of strangers.' I catch his mouth flickering with amusement. 'Is that your kind of thing?'

He laughs, adjusting his specs and checking out the view. 'I'm not sure it is, to be honest.' What *is* his thing, I soon discover, is taking in the beauty of the island with an enthusiasm that's hugely refreshing after the waspy bin incident and Charlie's subsequent hibernation in his room.

Two days have passed since James saved Minnie's life. Yesterday Mum and I had her checked out by the local vet, to be told that there was nothing wrong that could be detected; no obvious heart problems or evidence of a seizure. ('Perhaps a touch of sunstroke' was the verdict.) Reassured, we brought Minnie home and I got on with making a creamy fennel and chestnut soup, to eat with some little pastries filled with tangy soft cheese from the market. They smelt so good, even Charlie emerged from his lair to snatch one. At least he'd seemed concerned about Minnie, and had wanted to know what the vet had said. It was just a pity it had taken a near-death experience for him to show a little of his old, sweet self; the boy who'd once greeted me on Mother's Day with a tray bearing perfectly toasted crumpets, a home-made fruit salad and a tiny vase of flowers from the garden.

'Makes me sick,' Kim had joked with just a trace of bitterness, having been 'served' incinerated toast.

Having carried out a bowl of soup and the pastries to my parents' garden, I photographed them set out on the wrought-iron table, then started work on the words to accompany them. The day flew by, busy and productive.

I wasn't even annoyed with Charlie anymore. As Kim has often reminded me: 'It was bound to happen one day. You're lucky he's adored you this long!'

So I went to bed feeling happier than I have in a long time, and when I woke up this morning I had that 'today is a good day!' feeling before I'd even figured out quite why that was. A warm breeze wafted through the window, carrying in the scent of lavender and thyme. I lay there, not quite sure why I was so excited at the prospect of seeing James again, but unable to deny that I was.

'I'm a recipe content creator,' I tell him now, when he asks what I do for a living. 'Sounds a bit pretentious, doesn't it?'

'Not at all,' he replies. 'Although I can't pretend to understand what it means.'

'I devise recipes, then test them, write them up and cook them for photography. And I usually shoot my own pictures too.'

'You do the whole lot?' he asks in surprise.

'Yeah. I suppose it is quite unusual to do the whole package.'

'How did that come about?' As we take the road inland that climbs high up into the mountains, I tell him how I'd landed a job as a secretary on a magazine at twenty-one – thirty years ago now. And when a vacancy had come up in the cookery department I'd moved over to that. 'Mum's a brilliant cook,' I add, 'and I grew up alongside her in the kitchen, always watching how she did things and wanting to help.'

'Sounds like that was a dream job,' James says.

'Oh, it was. And it was the golden era of magazines really. But then they started to sell less and less, and it became so easy to find recipes online, so those cookery departments that were so expensive to run began to disappear. Magazines started reusing old recipes and photos from the archives, changing the colours of the tablecloths, the plates and whatnot in Photoshop—'

'You're kidding!'

'Honestly, they really did.' I've surprised myself by telling him so much. I suppose it's a novelty, spending time with someone new. My friendships are all fairly long-established now.

'So what happened then?' James asks.

'I was made redundant and set up as a freelancer, working on my own.' It's not quite as simple as that, but I'm sure he doesn't need to hear all the details.

'That *is* impressive.'

'Not as impressive as saving a dog's life!' I cast him a quick look.

He shrugs self-deprecatingly, as if it was nothing. 'So, did you teach yourself photography? Or do a course?'

'I just picked it up along the way,' I say vaguely, really not wanting to go into all that now. Because the day is perfect: sunny and bright and showing off Corsica at its very best. He certainly doesn't need to know the whole story, I tell myself. He's a hardworking vet who just wants to have a fun time.

We stop at a mountain village where pale stone cottages huddle around the ancient church. There's a second-hand bookshop and an inviting coffee shop where we sit outside, and our chat turns to James's work. 'Are you a birthing calves kind of vet, or more dogs and cats?' I catch myself and sense myself reddening. 'Stupid question. I'm sorry. I always imagine there are just the two kinds.'

'Well, there are really,' James says. 'It comes down to whether you're country or urban, and my practice is close to where I live.' We've already established that we're both north Londoners although, unlike me, James has never moved out. 'So it's mainly dogs and cats,' he adds, 'with a few rabbits, ferrets and the odd gecko and tortoise thrown in to keep things interesting.'

'The only thing I know about tortoises is that they live to be a hundred years old. Is that even true?'

'Even older in some cases,' he says.

'Poor tortoises. Everyone's obsessed with their age.'

'It's kind of important,' James says, with an earnestness I can't help finding endearing, 'if you're thinking about taking one on. I mean, in terms of commitment . . .'

'Charlie wanted stick insects but it turned out that one of his friends' mothers just wanted to offload them, so I said no.'

'Probably wise,' he says with a smile. It strikes me again how attractive he is with those kind, intelligent blue eyes. I discover that being vet is literally all he ever wanted to do. 'Probably because I wasn't allowed a pet,' he explains. 'My aunt wasn't having it so of course I was obsessed with animals. You know how kids always want the very thing they're not allowed to have?'

I nod. 'You lived with your aunt?'

'My aunt and uncle, yes. So I started walking neighbours' dogs, doing some cat-sitting, that kind of thing.' As he doesn't elaborate further, I don't ask why he lived with his aunt and uncle and not his parents. However, I do learn that he's divorced, and that his daughter, Esther – who was supposed to be here now – does something to do with social media; again, he skims over the details and I'm trying not to fire too many questions, interrogating the poor man. 'You're so nosy, Mum,' Charlie's teased me over the years. I probably am, although I prefer to think of it as *being interested in people.*

As the glorious afternoon unfolds we drive further up into the hills, stopping for lunch in a shady café where crimson bougainvillea cascades from the terracotta-tiled roof. Later still, we stroll with ice creams as I take James to the spot where the spectacular valley opens up below us. In between our stops, we've chattered away in the car I've hired for my stay here, due to my parents' vehicle being 'a bit rustic', as Mum puts it, with a grimace: 'In a taking-your-life-in-your-hands kind of way,' I tell James. 'But Dad refuses to get a new one. He really is the stubbornest man on earth.'

'What's your dad into?' James asks.

'Shouting at his computer, railing against millennials . . .'

He laughs. 'And your mum?'

'She worked as a translator but her passion these days is the garden and orchard. She's created it from nothing really. It was wildly overgrown when they moved in.' I pause. 'What about yours?'

'They're long gone, sadly,' James says.

'I'm sorry,' I say, wishing I hadn't asked. I'd guess that he's around my age so of course there was a high probability that his parents wouldn't still be alive.

We drive back to the coast, falling back into easy chat about our jobs and lives back home. James's hotel has come into view now. This, too, could be described as rustic, but charmingly so with its faded green shutters and stone planters filled with lavender on the terrace.

'I've had a really lovely day,' James says. 'Thank you.'

'I've really enjoyed it too,' I say. In fact, showing him some of my favourite places has ranked as one of my happiest days here since, well, I can't remember. It's on the tip of my tongue to say, *Shall we do this again?* But this is his holiday, and maybe he's one of those people who prefers to do their own thing?

Frank, Charlie's dad, was always horrified at the

43

prospect of making friends on holiday. 'Oh my God it's that couple!' he'd hiss, virtually dragging me into a souvenir shop in order to avoid them. We'd cower behind a revolving stand of postcards until they were safely out of sight. Because heaven forbid we might meet some nice people!

'Erm, I was wondering,' James says as he unclips his seatbelt, 'if you'd like to meet up again sometime? If you're not too busy, I mean?'

'That'd be great,' I say with a note of surprise, as if the possibility hadn't crossed my mind.

His smile seems to light up his face. 'Maybe we could go for dinner? I mean, if there's somewhere you'd like to go?'

'There are lots of places,' I say inanely because of course there are; Corsica is famous for its food which, like my parents' car, is best described as rustic, but in a delightful – rather than life-endangering – way. I write about it for my column: the fragrant slow-cooked casseroles, the delicious charcuterie, cheeses and lemony cheesecakes that melt in the mouth. The island is dotted with citrus orchards and olive groves, the fat, glossy fruit showing up in hearty pasta and gnocchi dishes. As I wrote in my column yesterday, Corsica blends French and Italian influences and makes them its own.

'When are you free?' James asks.

I could say in two or three days' time, so I don't seem too eager or as if I have nothing going on. But actually, what I really want is to see this kind, interesting and undeniably handsome man again as soon as possible. 'How about tomorrow?' I say.

CHAPTER EIGHT

JAMES

What possessed me to come out with all that canyoning and snorkelling stuff? What kind of blokey bollocks was that? I suppose I didn't want Lauren thinking I was some sad loser who'd found himself unexpectedly alone on holiday and with no idea how to fill it.

Why it mattered what she thought of me, I have no idea.

I mean, she was just this strikingly beautiful woman with greenish eyes and light brown hair who seemed so friendly and positive, even after the awful scare at the pool. And as soon as Minnie seemed fine it struck me that it'd be nice to run into her again (in less dramatic circumstances, obviously). But what could I say?

Fraser, my longtime friend and the other vet at our practice, would have rattled out some line on the short walk back to the road: *Would you like to meet for coffee? Maybe you could tell me the best things to do around here.* Or: *D'you mind exchanging numbers? I'd really like to know how Minnie's doing in a day or two . . .* But I'm not Fraser, who's never settled with anyone long term but is rarely without a girlfriend, whereas I've been single for quite some time – three years – since Polly moved to Peru.

'Not that she was keen to get away from you, James,' my ex-wife, Rhona, teased me when she found out.

It wasn't that. Polly, a geologist, had gone there for work. But perhaps it had knocked my confidence a bit, so I was actually surprised, and delighted, when Lauren suggested meeting up again.

'Such a beautiful night tonight,' says the restaurant's owner as she tops up our wine, even though I get the impression it's not really a topping-up kind of place. I suspect she just wanted to come over and chat. Lauren has already told me that Camille is a longtime friend of her mother's, and that her parents have been coming to this beachside restaurant for years. The bare wooden tables are wobbly, the plates chipped and mismatched, and the place put together with a rickety selection of furniture. But I don't think I've ever sat in a lovelier restaurant in my life.

'It really is,' Lauren says, adding, 'This is James. He's on holiday from London.' She goes on to tell Camille how I 'saved Minnie's life'. (Unsure how to react to this, I find myself taking a rapt interest in the plants furling down from the raffia canopy.) Just when I think we're about to move on from the subject, Camille calls over her husband and the whole episode is described again, all in English – with Camille now claiming, gleefully, that at the sound of Lauren's screams I'd thrown down my bicycle and charged through the forest, scooping up Minnie and 'breathing life into her mouth'. Despite our protests, Camille insists that our wine is on the house, and that we must also have tiny glasses of deliciously syrupy liqueur from a dusty bottle.

The pinkish sky has darkened now, and it strikes me

how happy I am that Lauren doesn't seem to be in a hurry for the night to end. So after dinner we find ourselves strolling along the otherwise deserted beach.

I've already heard that she and her son, Charlie, were extremely close until he 'went off' recently, which has obviously hurt her a great deal. She asks more about my daughter, and why she decided at the last minute not to come here with me. So I tell her about Esther's insufferable boyfriend, and how she'd begged for him to come here with us, saying, 'It'll be a chance for you and Miles to get to know each other. I promise we won't go off and leave you on your own.'

'I said I wasn't going on holiday with him. She said, "You wouldn't be going *with* him. He'd just be *there*."' Lauren laughs loudly at that and, encouraged by her response, I go on to tell her about Willow Vale, the alternative secondary school Esther attended. 'The kids only went to lessons if they felt like it,' I explain. 'I mean, it was all optional. You can guess how that went,' I add.

'I think I can.' She smiles.

'There was quite a lot of dicking around.'

'Was that a subject they could take? French, geography, dicking around?'

'Advanced dicking around for the seriously committed.'

Lauren chuckles. 'Sounds like it wasn't quite your first choice. The school, I mean . . .'

'I was kind of steamrollered into it,' I admit, hoping that doesn't make me sound like a pushover. Because I want to make a good impression. It's a startling realisation because I can't remember the last time I felt this way; that making any kind of impression – at least, on a woman I'd just met – featured on my radar at all. In normal life I just get on with my job and see Esther, and my friends, all the usual stuff. I'm also fairly private normally. I mean,

I'm not a big sharer of information, especially when I've just met someone new.

But now I find myself telling Lauren all kinds of stuff; about how Rhona and I broke up fairly amicably nearly a decade ago, and how she's now with Luc, the enormous Belgian with whom she runs a cocktail bar. I explain that I like them both and we mainly rub along okay, although their insistence that I should 'live a little!' can jar slightly.

'We split up when Charlie was seven,' Lauren explains, when I ask about her son's dad. 'It hadn't been good for years but, y'know . . .' She shrugs. 'There was a final straw.' Another pause. 'There always is, isn't there?'

I nod. 'I guess there is.'

'But unlike you, we don't really have anything to do with each other. Frank lives in New York. He's a fashion photographer. Charlie talks to him now and again, and I think it's important that they keep that contact going. But I do wonder if he just does it out of obligation.'

'Charlie or his dad?'

'Um . . . both?' she says. 'Frank's kind of . . . his own person. It was pretty difficult with him but lots of good things came out of it,' she adds quickly, perhaps to signify that she doesn't want to delve into the details now. There's a lull then, which feels entirely natural. How often does this happen, that you meet someone and it seems fine to *not* fill all the spaces with chatter? In fact, it's better than fine. It's as if we're letting all this new information settle between us.

It's Lauren who suggests we go on to a bar before calling it a night. Yes! What a brilliant idea! 'You sure?' she asks. 'I don't want to keep you out too late.'

'No, no, it's fine. I'm not remotely tired. Are you?' *I don't think I've ever felt less tired in my life.*

'No, I'm not. Not at all.' There's a little flicker of something as our eyes meet, and her hand brushes against mine as we stroll along the dusty street. One side of the bar is open to the beach, lit with glowing lanterns, and we settle on a soft leather sofa on the decking. Lauren asks more about Esther, so I explain that she's pretty well known, at least in Gen Z circles; that following her appearance on a reality show set at her school, she became something of . . . 'An It-girl?' she suggests. 'Do people still say that, or does it age me horribly?'

'Don't ask me,' I say. 'It's a weird world she's in – that's all I know.'

'You must be proud of her, though?'

'Yes, of course I am,' I say truthfully. 'She's very spirited and bold in how she lives her life, and she's managed to make a really decent career out of something that so many others would love to do, but haven't managed.' I stop and sip my wine. 'But sometimes,' I add, 'I wish the TV thing hadn't happened.'

'Why?' Lauren asks, frowning.

'Because before that she'd been good at lots of things. Art, English and especially history. That was her favourite. She'd had a real rapport with Amanda, her history teacher. It was all first names at Willow Vale . . .' Lauren smiles at that. 'And instead of focusing on dates and battles and all that dry, boring stuff, she took the kids to ancient forts and archaeological digs. We'd done a bit of that too, when Esther was younger. She loved digging around and discovering things, like it was a treasure hunt. It really grabbed her imagination. But then the TV thing happened, and after that . . .' I catch myself and stop. *Have you forgotten how to talk to women in this kind of situation? You don't start going on about your daughter's history teacher and boring this lovely woman to death.*

I take a big swig of wine and check Lauren's expression. She is, gratifyingly, still alive. 'It's probably brought a lot of good stuff to her life too,' she offers. 'Opportunities, I mean.'

'You're right. It has. And she was desperate to be a part of it, when the TV production team came to the school to meet the teachers and pupils and decide who they wanted to be in it. I was just worried about her being manipulated or shown in a bad light. It felt like something that sounded fine – just a bit of fun – but could easily spin out of control.'

'I can imagine,' Lauren says, then adds, 'Actually, I can't imagine what all this has been like for you because Charlie's the last person who'd ever want to take part in something like that. He'd absolutely hate it, standing out, being noticed. These days he won't tolerate me taking a photo of him. Not even here on holiday . . .' She scrolls through her pictures to show me a glimpse of his ear, and a palm thrust forward, face obscured.

'Like a disgraced politician,' I remark.

'Exactly.'

We're laughing about the eccentricities of teenagers as we leave the bar when somehow she links her arm with mine. I don't mean 'somehow' in that I don't know how she did it; just that it felt so natural I didn't even register it happening. And now I have, and that small gesture has triggered an immense wave of happiness in me, and I know I'm smiling, probably looking like a ridiculous idiot.

Also, I'm a bit drunk. We both are, I think. We must be after a whole evening of chatting over drinks; a night that, no matter what happens next, I know I'll remember forever. We call a taxi and sit in the back together. Now everything seems shimmeringly clear on this beautiful starlit night. I'm conscious of the closeness of her, of the warmth of her bare arm against mine.

The breeze through the driver's open window catches her long light brown hair and blows it across her finely boned face. I try not to watch as she pushes it behind her ears. She is incredibly beautiful with those expressive greenish eyes, a long, elegant nose and a big, warm smile that does something funny to my heart. Okay, so she's not with Charlie's father but she probably has a boyfriend at home. Of course she does; she has it all going for her. But then . . . he's not here, is he, this mythical incredibly handsome and highly successful boyfriend I've just conjured up in my head? As we near my hotel – she'll take the taxi on to her parents' place – I try to figure out how to ask, 'So, are you single?' without it sounding weird.

Are you on your own? Go on – make it sound like you think she has a sad, empty life.

Do you have a boyfriend? How old am I? Fifteen? For God's sake, why am I even thinking like this? She's just being friendly, showing me around the island she knows so well. The trouble is, I'm just not used to this kind of scenario. I'm used to asking Mrs Etherington how long her ferret's been off his food, and whether the Andersons' elderly Labrador can still manage to jump onto the sofa. Lauren's showing me around, being a tour guide, because of what happened with Minnie. She's just being kind, I tell myself as the driver pulls up at my hotel.

Then I'm not thinking about Minnie or even Mrs Etherington's ferret because this beautiful woman is asking me, 'So, what are your plans for tomorrow?'

'No plans,' I tell her. 'I have absolutely no plans at all.'

Perhaps I was a bit too emphatic about my availability because both of us laugh. 'No canyoning booked?' She raises a brow.

'I haven't got around to that yet.' The look we exchange

seems to say, *Isn't this great, that we're both free?* Then we're hugging goodnight, and there's a kiss, brief but a proper kiss on the lips – to think I'd almost not got on that plane! *Sod it*, I'd thought. *I don't want to go now. I'm so not in the frame of mind to spend two weeks in Corsica on my own—*

'Night then, James,' Lauren says as I climb out of the cab.

'Night, Lauren. See you tomorrow.' I'm still a little dazed from the kiss, and a million tiny sparks seem to be shooting around my brain as I stride towards the hotel.

CHAPTER NINE

''Course I've heard of Esther Burton,' Charlie retorts. 'Where d'you think I've been, Mum?'

'I just didn't think you'd watched . . . what was it called again?'

'*Willow Vale*. I didn't.' A shrug. 'But everyone knows her.' Well, *I* didn't, but then I hardly recognise anyone on celebrity magazine covers these days. And I'm still amazed that she's featured on Charlie's radar at all. Apart from sci-fi movies with Remy, all he's ever seemed to watch over the years are science programmes and documentaries.

It's the first time since we arrived here that I've managed to have something resembling a proper chat with my son. I've wanted to find out if he's okay about Remy suddenly having a girlfriend and money and hardly being around for him anymore. But when I mentioned it, he just brushed me off. Well, of course he did. A seventeen-year-old boy hardly wants to admit that he has a best friend, let alone one that he misses.

Despite Charlie avoiding me a lot of the time, I've also started to feel a little guilty about spending so much time with James, away from my family. Normally I'm with them all of the time, apart from the odd trip to the beach or the market for ingredients for my food columns. And these past few days I definitely haven't been around so much.

Since our dinner at Camille's, James and I have hired scooters and zipped from village to village, loving the sense of freedom and stopping wherever we fancied. We've lingered over coffees in the afternoon sun, followed a dirt track to a secluded cove and even gone for a dip together. My parents aren't swimmers, and it's been a decade now that Charlie has refused point-blank to venture into the sea. So it was lovely – and something of a novelty – not to swim alone. Then yesterday, still on scooters, James and I headed to the ancient southern town of Bonifacio. Although I've been there numerous times, it was almost like seeing it for the very first time, perched dramatically on the cliffs with the caves – *les grottes* – underneath. We took a boat trip so James could see them up close. Seeing his thrilled reaction reminded me how special this island is, and how lucky I am that my parents live here.

There have also been little affectionate gestures: a brief hand-hold, an arm around the shoulders, a quick kiss goodbye. While I wouldn't say James is flirtatious exactly, he is attentive and I can sense a mutual attraction fizzling away just beneath the surface. However, there's also a feeling of taking this slowly, simply because there's no need to rush. He's a little shy, certainly, and I think we're both out of practice with this kind of thing. Anyway, I just want to enjoy it, whatever 'it' turns out to be, and not worry about where it's leading. It's a lovely thing in itself, uncomplicated and fun. Every time we meet I sense my heart swelling with happiness.

Of course Mum hasn't minded me not being around

so much. 'It's lovely that you've met someone nice,' she insisted. Meanwhile, Charlie seems to actively prefer me to not be constantly buzzing around him with my enraging bottles of sunscreen. And I doubt if Dad, whose computer is now emitting an ominous whirring noise like a malfunctioning fan heater, has even noticed my absences.

'So,' Charlie asks now, 'what's she like?'

'Who, Esther? I really don't know, love—'

'He must've mentioned her, surely?'

I try not to seem amused by his curiosity. 'Well, yes, of course he has.' I pour us glasses of home-made lemonade at the garden table and consider the best way to put it without sounding judgemental – although I'm already forming an opinion of Esther as being extremely self-centred and difficult.

I can't help it. To suddenly demand that her boyfriend came to Corsica too, and then throw what basically amounted to a gigantic adult tantrum when James said no; it seems outrageous to me. But then, I haven't actually met the girl, and I'm aware that my own quiet, bookish son might seem odd to people who don't know him.

'She sounds quite . . . strong-willed,' I explain, tentatively. 'Bit difficult maybe. Knows her own mind. She only told James she wouldn't be coming on holiday on the morning of their flight.'

'Wow.' Charlie frowns. 'That's weird.'

I nod. 'James was waiting at the airport for her, terrified out of his wits. Obviously he thought something awful had happened . . .'

'God, yeah. I can imagine.' He plucks a fresh lemon slice from his glass and nibbles on it. 'So, what else?'

'You mean, what else do I know about her? Nothing really—'

'Don't pretend you haven't googled her, Mum!'

'Why would I do that?' I laugh, feigning innocence.

'Because you just would,' he teases with a playful glint in his dark eyes. This flicker of humour seems like nothing short of a miracle. A small one, compared to James appearing from nowhere and saving Minnie's life, but a miracle all the same.

'I still don't quite get what she's all about,' I admit. 'That *Willow Vale* show was a few years ago, wasn't it? And it seemed like it was pretty niche . . .'

Charlie nods.

'. . . But I keep spotting the phrase "Very Esther Burton" being bandied about. I guess it means effortlessly stylish, a mixture of vintage and new. That seems to be her style . . .' I look at my son. 'Is that right?'

'See, you *have* been googling,' he announces with a note of glee.

'Okay,' I concede. 'I might have a little bit. And I get that she's an influencer . . .'

'D'you know what an influencer is?'

'Yes, of course I do, Charlie.' I smile. 'Where d'you think I've been?'

His mouth twitches with amusement. 'That's it, then. That's what she does.'

'Yes, but what's she actually famous for?'

'What d'you mean?' He looks genuinely confused.

'I mean, what does she do?'

'She's an influencer!'

'I know, but—'

'Mum, that's it,' he says with a shake of his head. 'That's her thing. People don't have to *do* anything anymore. I mean, they don't have to sing or act or do anything particularly amazing. They just have to . . . *be*.'

'Yes, I get that, but—'

'And people want to know all the details of their lives,'

he continues, in full flow now, 'like what their house is like, and what they eat and where they go on holiday. So they share all that and their follower numbers increase until they have a few hundred thousand. Then they're in the magazines . . .' Magazines? I didn't think anyone bought them anymore. And Charlie only ever reads *New Scientist* and *Astronomy Now!* What does he know about this kind of stuff? 'And they're asked to endorse things and do collabs and paid posts,' he adds.

Collabs? Paid posts? Has my social-media-shunning son been abducted and replaced by this replica with the same deep brown eyes and dark hair, outgrowing its cut, who seems to be surgically attached to a yellow T-shirt with a pineapple on the front? For years now, virtually all of Charlie's attentions have been funnelled into the properties of the stars and planets; the physics of the solar system. He has a proper telescope that he begged for at the age of thirteen, and forensic knowledge of astronomy courses offered in universities all over the UK. The fact that he is also aware of Esther Burton's social media presence is as amazing to me as Remy's Parisian hotel adventure. 'And it all kind of snowballs from there really,' he says with a shrug.

I sip my lemonade. 'Right.'

'So, what's her dad like?' Charlie asks with studied nonchalance. Clearly, he's trying to hide his curiosity about James.

'He's a really nice guy,' I say lightly. 'He's a vet—'

'Yeah, you said.' Amusement glints in his eyes. Have I been going on about James a bit too much?

'Are you okay with me showing him around, love?' Because of course, that's all I'm doing, showing him around the island.

''Course I am,' Charlie retorts. 'Why wouldn't I be?'

'I just wondered. Because if you weren't—'

'Mum, it's fine,' he says, draining the last of his lemonade. Then: 'D'you think you'll see him when we're back home?'

'Oh, I don't know.' As if the possibility hadn't even occurred to me. 'He's in London—'

'That's not far, though, is it?' he asks.

'And we're both busy!'

''Course you are. You're far too busy,' Charlie says with a smile – a proper smile that's rarer than a four-leaved clover these days. And it lifts my heart.

CHAPTER TEN

JAMES

Who knows what'll happen when we're thrown back into our normal lives? I keep telling myself to just 'live in the moment' as everyone seems to say these days. And that seems preferable to wondering if this lovely thing will end when I fly back home.

Instead, I'm trying not to think that far ahead. I'm just focusing on all these wonderful times I'm having with Lauren as we get to know each other, bit by bit.

What I don't know much about is her ex-husband – Charlie's dad. I just get the feeling the subject has a line drawn round it. And that's fine; it's absolutely her business. What I did find out pretty quickly is that Lauren drives along those terrifying mountain roads (hairpin bends, sheer drops) at quite a speed, chatting all the while with a casualness as if she were just popping out to Tesco.

I have also learnt that, before his retirement, her London-born dad was something of an entrepreneur: 'Selling things, basically. But quite often not the kind of things people needed or wanted,' she explained.

'Like what?' I asked, intrigued.

'Cheap deckchairs that collapsed as soon as people sat on them. Starter garden kits of runty little plants that withered and died . . .' She smiled with a barely detectable eye-roll.

Another thing about Lauren is that she loves Corsican wines as well as strong black coffee and, as her job would suggest, she is passionate about food. Oh, I know everyone is 'passionate about food' now, in that they rave about restaurants where you have to stand outside in the cold, queuing for a table, and buy obscure ingredients like 'liquid smoke' – whatever the heck that is.

Esther requested once that I 'get some in' for when she stays over, even though she *never* cooks. She'd just read about it somewhere, that it was the new 'it' ingredient, as she put it. Which meant she had to have it. She has also asked for artichokes, fresh beetroot (i.e. encrusted with soil rather than being preserved, conveniently, in a jar) and black garlic, which costs about ten times as much as normal garlic. Of course these items all withered in my vegetable rack, despite my reminders that they needed using up. 'Dad, can you stop going on about that garlic? You're obsessed!' She once claimed, unfeasibly, that she heard me shouting, 'Use up the black garlic!' in my sleep.

I drew the line at buying micro-herbs for her. Christ, when I was her age, in my student house in Hackney, we still considered pesto exotic and were slightly in awe of what we called the 'avocado pear'.

Anyway, I think it's more a case of Esther aspiring to be the kind of person who cooks with micro-herbs, as in reality she and Miles have pretty much all of their meals delivered. Despite the copious drugs he's consumed over the years, his diet leans towards the 'clean' and preferably raw, involving dehydrated algae and something fermented, displaying an evil-looking froth. Maybe he's trying to compensate for all the bad stuff he's done to himself – like donating to a tree-planting charity whenever he takes a short-haul flight. Anyway, the smoked water is sitting in my cupboard, its seal intact.

My ex-wife's partner Luc is also passionate about food in that he'll spend an entire afternoon tramping about on the banks of an urban canal, looking for edible weeds to pick – which baffles me as there's an excellent greengrocer in their street. What's different about Lauren is that she is actually *is* passionate about eating in an obvious and very physical way. Over the course of our dates (is that what they've been? I don't know what else to call them as 'meetings' doesn't seem right) I've seen her face light up when she's picked up a menu, even at places she's been to dozens of times before. She eats with enthusiasm, by which I don't mean she chomps down her dinner like a starved horse. Just that she clearly views food as a source of unbridled pleasure – and now I *am* making her sound like a horse.

She tears into locally baked bread, dipping it into dishes of golden olive oil and urging me to do likewise: 'Try it, James. The olive grove where this is from is just up the road. We can visit sometime!' She takes me to meet the farmer, another friend of her parents, and interprets as the weathered elderly man explains that the olives are picked by hand, and when a new batch of oil is about to be produced, early samples are tasted with a sense of ceremony, 'just like a wine tasting,' Lauren says. When the farmer's wife brings us slices of almondy cake, she uses a finger to mop up the crumbs from her plate.

There's no cry of, 'No, I shouldn't!' when Camille at the beachside restaurant offers us freshly made cheesecake flavoured with grappa and clementines. I have to say it's incredibly attractive. The cheesecake, yes, but also Lauren's enthusiasm for it. That's very attractive. In fact, everything about her is attractive.

I tell myself not to read too much into things because we're just having a lovely time together, and I should be happy with that.

*

'So, what's Esther's boyfriend like?' she says one afternoon as we dry ourselves off on the beach after another swim. She already knows I'm not one hundred per cent crazy about the guy. But not wanting to seem negative or like some horribly overprotective dad, I suppose I've kept my real feelings about him under wraps.

'Bit of a jerk really,' I say.

She gives me a quick look. The sky is a wash of vivid blue, the aroma of chargrilled lamb and rosemary drifting from Camille's restaurant. I start to tell Lauren about the age difference – 'She keeps saying age is just a number and that he's incredibly young *in his head*' – and, crucially, the fact that he's treated Esther extremely badly.

'You must be so worried,' Lauren says with a frown.

'I am, yes. I'm worried sick sometimes. But I also feel quite powerless to do anything.' I pause and look at her. 'I wish it hadn't happened that way. Esther not turning up at the airport, I mean. And I wish our relationship was better, and that we could talk to each other properly, as grown-ups, instead of her sighing and huffing as if she was still fifteen . . .' I pause. 'But then, if I hadn't come here by myself then I wouldn't have been walking through the woods, and heard you calling—' I break off, a little surprised by my admission. But it's true. In a way, I have Miles Lattimer-Jones to thank for meeting Lauren.

'I'm glad too,' she says. Sunshine catches her green eyes

as she smiles. 'I mean, I'm glad you were right there when we needed you.'

A pause settles, and I'm aware of my heart thumping as she moves closer, and we kiss. It's not so brief this time. It's a kiss that says: something is happening here. Something really special. I feel different, I realise; lighter to the point where I could describe myself as actually being carefree. *Live a little, James!* Well, I am now. I really am. And I don't think I have ever felt this way in my life.

The days stretch on, blue-skied and perfect like some kind of wonderful dream. The kind you wake up from feeling slightly crushed that it wasn't real. I'd thought Corsica would be nice but I hadn't expected *this*. I'd imagined I'd be staggering through some gorge with a bunch of strangers with crash helmets on, being chivvied along by a 'leader'. Not getting to know this smart, funny and beautiful woman and literally smiling and laughing the whole time, feeling as if I'm twenty years old and everything is thrillingly new, just waiting to be discovered.

I know I am falling in love with Lauren. It's an incredible and slightly terrifying feeling. Fuck it, I think. What can I do about it anyway? Of course I realise she has her life back home with Charlie, and her work, and I have my life too. And what if she doesn't feel the way I do? What if I've been misinterpreting things, reading too much into our affectionate looks, our hand-holds and those lingering kisses? And what if it makes things complicated back home?

I have my life set up pretty well there, I think. I work. I come home. I cook pasta or make an omelette – okay, sometimes, if I'm really knackered, it's beans on toast. I put the bin out and shove a wash on. There's always food in the fridge and clean clothes in my wardrobe. Walter, my elderly cat, roams in and out as he pleases and isn't overly affectionate. But it's good to know he's around, like a genial flatmate. I have the odd large glass of wine some nights as I flick through the TV channels or research something unusual that's come up at work.

I'm a functioning workaholic who hoovers regularly enough to keep Walter's hair at bay (although I've worked with animals for twenty-five years, it still astounds me how much fluff can come off one smallish animal). Somehow, it all chugs along without anything terrible happening. And for a long time I've assumed that this is the best life can be. That there are no disasters or heartache or anything like that. I haven't lived with anyone since Rhona and I split up nine years ago (my most recent girlfriend, Polly, had her own flat). Although my work days can be unpredictable, there's a lot of routine stuff: vaccinations, neutering, worming and annual check-ups. The life of a single fifty-two-year-old vet positively sizzles with glamour.

But now something has happened. Something I'd never envisaged in my wildest dreams.

The thing is, I decide, it doesn't matter whether or not it's a good idea to fall in love with someone.

You just do.

CHAPTER ELEVEN

LAUREN

I cry when he tells me that his parents were killed in a car accident on the motorway. I can't help it. 'James, I'm so sorry,' I say.

'It was a very long time ago,' he says, trying to make light of a life-changing event that saw him orphaned at thirteen, and from then on brought up by an aunt and uncle who, as he puts it, 'did as good a job as they could considering that they didn't have kids, had never wanted them, and didn't have a clue what to do with me really.' By that stage his two much older brothers had left home so it was just James in what sounds like a pretty loveless home. 'But something good came out of it,' he says. He has already told me about cat-sitting for neighbours, and walking their dogs, and how he was absolutely set on becoming a vet.

'What did your aunt and uncle think of that?' I ask.

'They said I didn't have the brains,' he replies.

'So you were determined to prove them wrong?'

'Yep.' He nods. 'That's exactly what I set out to do.'

'So if they'd said, "James, we know you could sail

65

through those veterinary exams with flying colours", then your life might've taken a completely different course?'

'Quite possibly, yeah!'

'Were they proud of you, though?'

'I think they were relieved to have me off their hands,' he says with a smile. Our stories have tumbled out as the end of his holiday approaches, and perhaps those tears I quickly wiped away were partly due to the fact that he's flying home tomorrow.

After lunch we stroll along the lane that eventually leads to my parents' house, tucked away at the end of an unmade track up in the hills. We know already that we want to see each other back home, and even though there have just been hand-holds and kisses, something's building here and – yes, I want to sleep with him. For years now I've thought I'm really not that bothered about sex, that I can take or leave it. I've even joked to Kim that I'd rather have a lovely glass of dessert wine and a nice pudding.

I couldn't be less interested in pudding when I let myself imagine being in bed with James. The thought of it makes my whole body tingle.

Stop this! I tell myself. I must banish all thoughts of ravishing the dishy vet because we've just arrived at my parents' house! Dad appears, looking distracted, shakes James's hand very firmly and says, 'D'you know anything about extension drives?'

'Er, I'm sorry, not really,' James replies. It's on the tip of my tongue to say, *He's a vet, not a computer expert*, but now Dad is making chitchat about the Corsican roads and the various gradients of every hill in the area. Then we're onto cars: 'I've got a problem with my motor,' Dad announces. 'Something to do with the carburettor, I think. Know anything about those?'

'I'm not sure I do.' James looks as if he really wishes

he could help, even though carburettors belong to a bygone age, like smoking in cars with all the windows shut, as Dad used to do before Mum forced him to quit.

Having clearly marked this visitor as a double fail – in car mechanics and computer maintenance – he mutters that he must get on, perhaps forgetting that *he saved the life of your dog, Dad!* And now something requires his urgent attention in his study. Mum, on the other hand, festoons James with freshly made orange juice and just-baked Florentines studded with pistachios and cherries, while Minnie seems delighted to see him again and rolls on her back for a belly rub.

Predictably, I have to go and fetch Charlie from his room. 'Could you come out and say hi to James?' I ask, standing in the doorway.

'Oh, I'm all right, Mum,' he says dismissively.

I look at him lying on the bed, engrossed in a book. 'C'mon, love. He'd like to meet you.'

He peers over at me. I don't want to haul him outside and make him feel uncomfortable. But it's only saying hello, for goodness' sake. James isn't going to bite his head off. I can't help feeling exasperated sometimes as shyness can easily come across as aloofness or rudeness. And how will Charlie cope when he's thrown into situations with all those new people at university next year? It's not all about learning and studying. There's the social side too and it terrifies me, frankly, to think of him hiding away in his room in university halls all on his own.

'I brought James over to meet my family,' I prompt him, and finally, with a fair amount of sighing – as if I've interrupted something terribly important – he mooches out after me, blinking in the afternoon sun.

In the garden James adopts just the right approach, chatting a little about how lovely the island is, and how lucky Charlie is to be able to spend so much time here. I sense my son thawing slightly as he finds himself agreeing. 'Yeah, it is pretty nice. Glad you're having a good holiday.'

See, Charlie? It's really not that difficult!

Making things even easier for everyone, Minnie trots back towards James to be fussed over again. 'She's a lovely girl,' James says.

'Yeah.' Charlie nods. 'Thanks for doing that thing. That thing at the pool when she collapsed . . .'

'I'm just glad she's fine,' James says. 'That's all that matters.'

Charlie musters a smile and endures a little more chit-chat before disappearing again. 'He seems like a great boy,' James says later when we take Minnie to the pool.

'Thanks.' I smile. 'Y'know, he's not brilliant with new people. But he likes you, I can tell.'

'I'm honoured then,' he says with a grin. We sit on a rock by the pool, exactly where we first met. This time, rather than wading in, Millie just potters around at the water's edge. She seems cautious after her little adventure almost two weeks ago now. Our time together, which felt as if it would stretch indefinitely, has whipped by in a flash. It's nearly over now. Perhaps that's why I want James to know all about me and my past, and why my situation with Charlie's dad is so very different to what sounds like an amicable set-up with Esther's mum.

After taking Minnie back home, James and I head out for one last dinner at Camille's restaurant at the beach. Although his flight home is at 11 a.m., it's as if there's an unspoken agreement not to mention it tonight. Meanwhile, this time Camille doesn't keep flitting over to top up our glasses. She just gives me a knowing smile and leaves us be. It's as if she *knows*.

After we've eaten, James asks what I've been shooting,

and I show him some pictures on my phone. I always take a few on my iPhone before switching to my camera for the 'proper' shots, to get a feel for how it's all looking. We've moved from the table now to the squishy old sofa under the raffia canopy, and are sipping one of Camille's mysterious liqueurs. Edging closer now, I show James my shots of linguine with wild mushrooms, goat's cheese and sage pastries, and gnocchi with slow-roasted tomatoes and thyme. All the while I'm aware of the closeness of him, next to me.

There are lamb cutlets with peppers and charred shallots, a tart with glossy green olives and a jug of home-made lemonade glinting in the sunshine in my parents' garden. 'It's all making me hungry again,' James remarks.

I smile, aware of the insistent rhythm of my heart. 'That's the idea!'

'They're all so natural,' he adds, studying a picture more closely. 'As if they haven't been set up or arranged, but everything just happened to be there.'

He's exactly right. That's what I love to do; to make things look as if they were *just there*. But even though I'm still scrolling through my food photos, I know we're not focusing on them anymore. They could be an old pair of pants lying in the gutter for all the attention we're giving them. Because something is happening. I can sense it, and James can too. We both know the mood is different tonight.

I place my phone on the table and look at him. He has tanned golden brown and his eyes seem even bluer than when he arrived, looking a little stressed and distracted back then, I realise now – and not just because, rather than enjoying a stroll through the forest, he'd found himself administering CPR to an elderly dog. He'd also just had that awful to-do with his daughter and had barely recovered from that. James seems so capable and together but I've discovered that he's also sensitive and worries perhaps a little too much. But then, I worry too. Even though Charlie is virtually a man, I fret about his future, and how he'll make new friends and a young adult life for himself. I wake in the night worrying about it and wonder, will I be like this when he's thirty? Or forty-five? I'm fairly confident that his dad has never lost a second's sleep over anything to do with our son. That doesn't seem right either. But surely there's a happy medium?

Corsica has been good for James. That's obvious now. He seems so much more relaxed, and looks even more handsome than when I first set eyes on him. I can imagine that many of his clients, coming in with their cats and dogs and guinea pigs, have a crush on him. The handsome vet with a heart-fluttering smile; I bet they're delighted when Rex's vaccination time rolls around.

'So . . .' I start.

'Yeah.' He nods.

'Home tomorrow.'

He exhales. 'Wish I was here for longer.'

'I do too,' I murmur, leaning into him. Gently, he touches my hair.

'I've had the best time,' he says.

'Me too.' I turn and see his eyes glinting in the flickering candlelight. It feels so right being together. And that's why I tell him everything, right from the beginning, when I first learnt to take photos.

It's a clear night tonight. The cloudless sky is filled with stars, the sea shimmering in the moonlight. Taking his hand in mine, I start to tell him how I fell into this job that I love so much. In a way, it was the result of a not entirely positive situation – like James being determined to prove that he could pass his veterinary exams. But also, like with him, something very good came out of it.

With his arm around my shoulders now, I tell him that

I'd never intended to take pictures for a living. Frank, Charlie's dad, had been the photographer in the family – and a successful one at that. Fashion was his thing: ad campaigns, which were the most lucrative, and glossy magazines, which were more about artistic control and prestige, getting his name out there in the right places.

'He was deluged with work,' I explain. 'It was his whole life really. We never took a holiday, not even after Charlie was born, because there were always jobs he couldn't turn down. So I started going away with my friend Kim and her family, and of course Charlie and I would also come here every summer . . .'

Already, I've swerved off track. But James's kind, attentive expression reassures me that it's okay to spill it all out. 'Whenever I was away,' I continue, 'and I suspect at other times too, Frank was seeing other people. Having affairs, I mean.' I catch myself. 'D'you really want me to tell you all this?'

'I do,' James says. 'But only if you want to, if you feel okay about it . . .'

I nod and sip my wine. 'I do feel okay about it.'

'So . . .' He pauses. 'Did you know all along? What was happening, I mean?'

'No, not until later. Until after we'd split up, I mean. Things came out then – gossip and comments. But what *was* obvious to me was that Frank's, um . . . *lifestyle* was affecting him and his ability to work.'

'Lifestyle?' James asks.

I nod. 'Drink and drugs, copious amounts, which isn't exactly unusual in that kind of world. But the trouble with fashion photography is that there are other people and an awful lot of money involved. And you're expected to show up on time and be in a fit state to . . . y'know.'

'To work?' he suggests.

'Exactly. And more and more, Frank wasn't. He'd have been out on a bender all night and then show up late for a job, looking knackered. Clients started getting pissed off. He got, I suppose . . .' I grimace '. . . a reputation. It's okay being wild and fun and a bit of a character – people love that. But when it tips over into chaos . . .' I pause and glance out to sea. 'Frank was getting fewer calls, less work. He had to give up his studio and his assistant. And, as his career seemed to be stalling, he started to hammer it even more.'

James exhales slowly. 'That must've been a tough time for you.'

'It was a bit of a blur,' I say truthfully. 'Charlie was only three or four at the worst of it, and I was trying to get some freelance work going. At the same time, Frank started taking on some still-life photography. You know – objects instead of people. Accessories, homewares – anything really. He was good at it and it kept the money coming in.'

'Did that seem strange? I mean, when he'd been so successful with his fashion photography?'

I consider this. I haven't talked about any of this since it all happened, and only my closest friends know. I never even told my parents – although I suspect they knew he was pretty chaotic – and thankfully Charlie was shielded from it because nothing ever happened at home. Frank was hardly around anyway. He wasn't exactly what you'd call a hands-on dad, although he'd always been great at the boisterous games and revving up Charlie to a peak of excitement, just when it was time to wind down for bed. As for Frank's grown-up games, these took place in private members' clubs with his fashion friends, where everyone would be elegantly off their faces as opposed to stumbling out of pubs with puke on their shoes.

I glance into the restaurant and realise we are the last customers here. Although she's too polite to say, I know Camille will be ready to close up and head home. So we hug her goodbye and take a taxi to James's hotel. I don't know what the stern-looking reception lady thinks, when she sees that James has brought a friend tonight. I half expect her to shout, 'Excuse me! Are you booked in here?' Or even chase after us and grapple me to the ground, shouting, 'Are you planning to sleep with this man? In *my* hotel?' We speed-walk past her, avoiding eye contact – probably looking as if we've stolen something – and I can't help laughing as we step into the old-fashioned cage lift.

It's going to happen, I tell myself. My God, it's really going to happen. I'm going up to his room and my heart is thumping so hard I'm sure the reception lady can hear it too.

CHAPTER TWELVE

LAUREN

On the second floor we make our way along the corridor, passing oil paintings of Corsican coastal views, their colours dulled with age. The hotel is traditional with bumpy stone walls, intricately tiled floors and none of that sleek keycard business. It's a regular key with a hefty metal fob the size of a letterbox cover. I don't know if it's a flurry of nerves, but there's some fumbling with it as James jabs it into the keyhole, jiggles it and finally succeeds in unlocking the door.

Once inside the room, he takes my hand. 'Come see the view,' he says, opening the louvered doors that lead onto a balcony. He makes tea, which I'm not sure either of us wants, but we drink it anyway, sitting side by side on spindly wooden chairs overlooking the sea. 'So,' he says, 'you were telling me about Frank?'

On the way here I thought we'd fall straight into bed. But now, even though James is flying home tomorrow, it feels as if we have all the time in the world. So why rush things? It's beautiful out here, the calm sea glinting beneath a crescent moon, and a million stars twinkling above us.

'The message he put out was that he wanted to scale things down while Charlie was little,' I start to explain. 'I'm sure that seemed a bit weird to some people. But he managed to make the switch quite smoothly, and whenever he was photographing cookware or watches or whatever it happened to be, there'd be no one else there. No make-up artist, no models – no one to witness his comedowns or ranging hangovers. And he insisted on working that way,' I add. 'He didn't want a client sending over a stylist or an art director or anyone else to oversee things. He didn't want anyone breathing down his neck, as he put it. If they wanted Frank to do the job, they had to let him get on with it by himself.'

'Did he do these shoots at home?' James asks.

'Yes, in our spare room, which he set up as a still-life studio. And I started helping him, watching and learning along the way.'

'Amazing! It really is,' James says, slowly shaking his head. 'I mean, you are. *You* are amazing.'

My heart seems to turn over. 'Oh, I don't know about that,' I say, all in a rush. Yes, I learnt all those skills, but at fifty-one I still don't know how to accept a compliment. Instead, I toss it back like an embarrassing hat.

'But you've achieved so much,' he insists.

'There's a lot more I'd like to do . . .'

'Like what?' He seems genuinely keen to know. It's entirely new, this meeting someone who appears to be interested in what I do.

'I'd actually really love to write a cookbook.' I'm surprised that I've even told him this. Not even my friends know; not because it's some dark secret. But it seems pointless to even mention it until there's some chance of it actually happening.

'What kind?' James asks.

'One about Corsican food,' I reply. 'Not just with local recipes but a real feeling of the island, the markets, the produce that grows here. I'd do the whole thing – the words and photos. I've got it all planned out in my head and I even know what the cover would look like . . .' I laugh. 'So, that's my dream. It's a bit niche, don't you think?'

'I think it sounds wonderful,' he says, with such sincerity I want to hug him.

'Well, thank you. That's good to hear!'

'I think you could do it,' James says simply. 'I really do.' And then, so softly and gently I almost feel as if I'm floating, he kisses me.

We sit in silence for a few minutes, just looking out to sea. A young couple are paddling around in the shallows together, laughing and splashing each other. 'Isn't the sea amazing here?' I remark.

'It's fantastic. I swam before breakfast this morning.'

'That's the best time! I often do it myself,' I say.

'Does Charlie ever swim with you?' James asks.

I shake my head. 'Not anymore. I mean no, not at all. Although he used to love it . . .'

He's frowning now. 'Did something happen?'

I exhale slowly, figuring that I don't want to tell him tonight. The last thing I want is to dampen the evening by going into it all. 'Yes, it did. But it was a long time ago.'

James seems to know not to press me for details. 'Maybe it's just a matter of time,' he suggests, 'and he will again one day?'

'Yes, maybe. We'll see.' It's been a *very* long time already, I reflect. But who knows what can happen when we least expect it?

I smile and lean over and kiss this man who's lifted my heart, and we get up from the balcony seat and go back into his room.

*

It's been three years since I've slept with anyone. Three years! I'd started to wonder if I'd remember what to do. After passing my driving test at nineteen I hadn't driven again until my mid-twenties and so I'd booked some refresher lessons. I knew I'd feel better if there was someone to guide me through the basics again.

Happily, refresher lessons aren't needed tonight. There is no embarrassment, no mounting the pavement or emergency stop required. There's no awkwardness at all. It feels thrillingly new, yet also warm and familiar as if we have always been together.

Afterwards James and I lie there in the rumpled bed for I don't know how long. The room is still and calm, and I can feel his steady heartbeat as he strokes my hair. Gradually, daylight starts to creep in through the fine white curtains, and I realise we must have slept a little on and off. We shower together and go down to breakfast where a different receptionist is on duty and gives us a wry look as we stride past.

'It's been quite a holiday,' James tells me after the waiter has brought us coffee and croissants.

'You've had a good time?'

He nods and beams at me. 'It's been the best.'

'Even though you didn't manage any canyoning?' I tease him.

'Yeah, amazingly.' Those kind blue eyes meet mine.

'There's always next time for that,' I add. 'If you're an adrenaline seeker after the ultimate thrill, I mean . . .'

'This has actually been the ultimate thrill,' he says with a smile. 'All of it, I mean. Not just last night.'

'But especially last night,' I suggest.

'Yes, especially last night.' James touches my hand, and I feel as if I could burst with happiness despite the fact that he's leaving soon, and our real lives are about to engulf us again.

'So, I was wondering,' I start, 'when I'm back home, maybe you'd like to meet up?' *He lives in London, he's very busy, we both are. I haven't even thought about it.*

'Of course I would!' James exclaims. 'Of course I want to see you. Did you think I wouldn't?'

'Well, y'know . . .' I know I am grinning ridiculously. As if to make it clear that both of us would *absolutely* like to see each other again, he leans forward and we kiss, briefly, on the lips. Then all too soon we've finished our breakfast, he's checking the time and we're hugging goodbye outside the hotel. 'Will your parents be worried?' he asks with a slight frown. 'And Charlie?'

'No, I messaged Mum last night.'

'Will they mind that you stayed here with me?'

'Of course not,' I say. 'I am a grown-up, you know.' He laughs, and there's another hug and a kiss goodbye, then he's off to pack up his things and I run to catch the rickety bus that snakes its way up to the mountain villages. I climb aboard, and as it chugs up the hill I look out at the valley and the glittering sea beyond. It's true; they won't mind one bit. Dad and Charlie will have barely noticed, and as for Mum, she'll be happy that I've met someone.

'I do wish you'd meet someone lovely,' she's said many times.

And now I have.

CHAPTER THIRTEEN

JAMES

It can turn out badly, when you try to recreate a wonderful holiday experience back at home. Bringing back Blue Curaçao from Tenerife was never going to be a good idea. Those Flaming Lamborghini cocktails, which my friends and I had tanked down in vast quantities in the bar, weren't the same back in our shared house in Hackney with the mouldy shower curtain and the mysterious puddle that always sat under the fridge, as if it had wet itself. Who wants a dyed-blue tongue on a wet Tuesday night when there's an essay to write?

A couple of years later, the first time Rhona and I had gone on holiday together, I'd been so taken with the weathered ochre-coloured houses on Symi that I'd come home and slapped similarly coloured paint all over my bedroom walls. 'Trying to evoke the romance of a Greek isle?' she'd said with a laugh when I'd finished. It looked like an old man's pub ceiling, nicotine-stained from a million cigarettes.

So I haven't felt sure how things will work out with me and Lauren, even though we've kept in touch while she's still been in Corsica. We've chatted via Messenger and even exchanged the occasional picture of stuff we've been up to in our respective lives.

She's sent me a photo of herself in her parents' garden, proudly holding a home-made clementine and almond cake, as if offering me a slice. She looked so sunny and beautiful, I could hardly believe this was the woman I'd be seeing again soon, when she was home. It feels like the best thing to have happened to me in years. However, I've struggled to come up with anything quite as photogenic to send back to Lauren. Obviously, she'd hardly be entranced by a picture of me about to tuck into a big bowl of penne with bought tomato sauce after a lengthy shift at the surgery.

Feeling mildly self-conscious, I took a selfie in my garden, relieved that Esther wasn't loitering on the sidelines, sniggering. (I can imagine that 'Dad taking selfies' would rank as even more mirth-making than 'Dad dancing', and that's something I try to avoid at all costs.) I sent it to Lauren, apologising that it wasn't as photogenic as her cake – by which I meant my rookie effort wasn't as photogenic as she was, surrounded by dazzling flowers in that Corsican garden.

No need to be bashful, she messaged back with a smiley emoji. *You look good to me!*

I'm just not used to this kind of flirty exchange. But I've found myself looking forward to her next message, and fallen into a habit of checking my phone in case I've missed one – something I've never done before now. Esther has teased me that I'm the only person she knows who 'puts their phone away' which, to be fair, I only do if Fraser, the other vet, is on call. Because otherwise, why would I need to keep looking at it? Now, though, it's always close to hand, having acquired a new significance in my life.

As a joke, I send Lauren a picture of my ailing lavender plant in a cracked pot at my back door, in contrast to her parents' herbaceous borders bursting with colour. I also send one of Walter, hoping it doesn't scream 'lonely cat man'. She messages, *I hope you're going to invite me over to meet him.*

'Of course I am!' I reply, poised to add: *He can't wait to see you.* No, don't put that, I tell myself. It could sound faintly pathetic because of course, it's not Walter who's counting the days, like a child anticipating Christmas, until Lauren comes home.

One Saturday evening, back home after a few drinks with Fraser and a couple of other old friends, I message: *So looking forward to seeing you again. I've really missed you.* Immediately I wonder if it was a bit much. When her reply comes – *Can't wait to see you too!* – I relax again. But it still feels a bit too good to be true.

A couple of days later Tony Lomax arrives with Bob, his mildly arthritic but otherwise perfectly healthy – if ancient – collie cross. Somewhere in his seventies, Tony has been bringing in Bob for over a decade and always, very sweetly, places a packet of shortbread on the reception desk for us all. By 'all' I mean Fraser and me plus our practice manager, receptionist and two veterinary nurses. We're a close-knit team of six, and we're very fond of Tony in his unravelling sweaters and threadbare cords. We're also aware that Casey, our practice manager, doesn't charge him for consultations, which is absolutely fine. ('Don't you worry about that, Mr Lomax. Lovely to see you. Take care!')

They're hardly classed as consultations anyway when Tony comes in and says, 'Do Bob's eyes look a bit milky to you, James?' They are a little, but no more than they were two weeks ago when he last brought Bob in. But I go through the motions of giving them another inspection anyway.

'Nothing to be concerned about there, Tony,' I tell him. 'Just a sign of his age, but his vision seems perfectly fine.'

How could we charge an elderly man for that? As Fraser once put it, 'Billing Tony would be like taxing his loneliness.' We know he's a worrier; that Bob's slightest ailment has him imagining the worst. I'm behaving like Tony now, I realise, deciding that the holiday was so lovely – actually perfect – that it can't be the same here in drizzly Britain with our jobs, our families and lives to navigate.

Maybe I'm trying to prepare myself for being disappointed when it fizzles out. Or maybe I'm just being realistic.

'He's just not quite right,' Tony says as he and Bob are about to leave.

'He's in great health for his age,' I try to reassure him. 'His heart and lungs are good. He's the perfect weight, he eats well and his coat's in lovely condition. I can't see anything to worry about right now.'

Tony looks down at him and frowns. 'But when he does go, what are the options?'

His question takes me by surprise. 'When he passes away, you mean?'

He nods, lips pressed together firmly. What's brought this on? 'Honestly,' I start, 'I don't think—'

'I've looked into those pet cremation places,' Tony cuts in. 'Two hundred quid, some of them charge. I can't afford that. What am I going to do?'

'Tony,' I say, 'if you'd like to talk over the options sometime, we can do that. You can chat to Casey or come in and talk to me. But honestly . . .' I glance down at

Bob; bright-eyed, *bristling* with health and currently sitting on my foot '. . . I really don't think you need to worry about that now.'

After they've gone, I feel bad for not sitting Tony down with a cup of tea and going through it all, patiently, with him. We're all well aware that it's often company he wants rather than going home to an empty flat. I know he lives alone and that, from what I've gathered from our chats, there's no family. No one he's ever mentioned, anyway. But the rest of the team have gone home, and after eleven hours of non-stop consultations I'm itching to lock up and do likewise.

Later, as I clear up after dinner, I wish I'd said something like, 'It's good to have a plan in the back of your mind. But instead of worrying, how about just enjoying Bob while he's fit and well?' I should have tried to help Tony focus on the positive. And something switches in me, and I think, why not just look forward to Lauren coming back, and see what happens? I'm out of practice, I guess; unused to this early stage when it still feels pretty fragile, like a houseplant you could easily over-water or under-water or place in too hot or too cold a room, as is evident by my plant-killing abilities. ('Thank God you're better with animals, Dad,' Esther announced as I disposed of the peace lily I'd bought, under her instruction, as apparently *every home needs living plants*.)

I've wondered, too, if I'm actually not that good at relationships either. After all, Rhona and I divorced and Polly, my last girlfriend, 'travelled six thousand miles to get away from you', as Rhona is fond of joking – accompanied by barking laughter from her boyfriend.

When Lauren comes back and we go for dinner it turns out she's had similar thoughts to me. Could it really be like it was in Corsica? How will we see each other with

83

me being in London and Lauren in her Hertfordshire village?

It's not that far, we agree, and she comes back to my house and stays the night, and of course it's just as wonderful as it was in Corsica. There's no Blue Curaçao feeling at all; no hint of old-man-pub nicotine ceilings.

It is actually perfect being with her again. I don't even get around to introducing her to Walter.

CHAPTER FOURTEEN

LAUREN

My life seems to have taken on a new vividness, as if the brightness setting of the world around me has been turned right up. Even when James and I are apart, I'm aware of a newfound sense of happiness; of feeling fully alive. Weekend after weekend we spend together, sometimes at his place in north London and sometimes at mine, with James getting to know Charlie a little, bit by bit.

We don't want to force that part. Okay, it's not as if he's a little kid. But taking things gently feels like the right thing to do, especially as we've never been in this kind of situation before. Me having a boyfriend, I mean. At least, one who spends time at our place, drinking coffee with me in the mornings, and having dinner with us, just being here.

'D'you like James?' I ask Charlie one evening in late September after I've just waved him off.

'Yeah. 'Course I do,' Charlie replies. I want to dig further; to ask: *What d'you think of him really?* I want to discuss him endlessly, the way you do when you're in love – because I am.

James says, 'I love you, Lauren,' one night at his place. We're in bed, just lying together in each other's arms, and I can feel the steady beat of his heart. Feeling as if I could burst with joy, I kiss him.

'I love you too.'

He takes my hands in his. 'Sometimes I can't believe this has happened.'

'No, me neither.'

'If I hadn't gone walking through the woods that day . . .'

'If Minnie hadn't had a turn!' We love to pick over it, to revel in how fate threw us together. It's all wonderful – and not just the drinks, the meals out, the cinema trips or any of that. Perhaps better still are the ordinary things like wandering around a flower market together, or waking up in my sun-filled bedroom to see James still asleep. When I lie there, studying his face, thinking how handsome he is, while hoping – tiny frisson of danger here – that he won't suddenly pop open an eye and catch me being a staring weirdo.

Then he wakes, and there's that first smile, warm like honey. It's felt incredibly easy to switch from being perennially single to being with James, and Charlie seems fine about it. At least, he's perfectly able to fend for himself when I'm in London, and as pleasant as can be expected when James is here with us. They're not exactly best buddies but James certainly makes an effort to draw some conversation from him. And, actually, Charlie is more amiable with me when James is around. From time to time I catch myself thinking, I'm so lucky to have all of this.

One evening Kim invites me and James over for dinner. She and Lorenzo, her husband, make quite a fuss of James and we stay late, drinking and laughing around their kitchen table. It feels so natural and not remotely awkward, as if James has always been part of things here. 'He's lovely!' Kim whispers, when James and Lorenzo are locked in conversation. 'He's *perfect* for you.'

I beam at her, unable to disagree. We all meet up again for a walk next day; two couples strolling along the country lanes on a beautiful autumn afternoon. We have a late Sunday lunch in our village pub. A couple of weeks later Kim and Lorenzo's daughters, who are home from university on a weekend visit, join us for dinner at my place.

I look around the table and my heart fills with happiness. That day on the beach, when Charlie had parked himself by the bin, I realised with a jolt how empty my life had become, now my son no longer wanted to hang out with me. Next year he'd be off to university and it'd be just me, I realised – in the beautiful cottage I'd redecorated from top to bottom for the two of us. And soon I'd be flicking a duster around his empty bedroom.

The very thought of it crushed me.

But I don't feel like that anymore. It's not that I *needed* to meet someone, to feel complete; more that I've let someone into my life wholeheartedly, for the first time since I met Frank. And that's opened me up to new possibilities – like pushing my work further and seeing where it takes me. I feel energised, brimming with ideas, and my photos seem to have taken on a new vibrancy.

'We love what you're doing,' one of my clients has told me. 'We'd like to give your column more space, and could you do a special, longer story for the food supplement we're planning?'

So work – and life – feel great right now and of course I'm madly in love. There's just *one* tiny thing that's starting to niggle. I haven't yet met James's daughter.

The more time goes on, the more it starts to bug me. I love this little bubble of ours, but Esther is a huge part

87

of his life and I start to wonder, is he keeping me stowed away in a little compartment, away from her? Has he even mentioned me to her?

'I told her about us right away, as soon as I came back from holiday,' he said, looking taken aback, when I first broached this. Then I started to think: *Yes, but have you told her that it's actually quite a big thing that's happening with us? Or have you played us down?*

I know I'm being ridiculous and horribly needy, and I hate myself for it. Maybe Esther's just feeling a bit weird about her dad having a girlfriend and spending so much time out here with me? She's twenty, though – not a child. Perhaps he's putting off us meeting because he's worried she'll be offish with me? Privately I can't help thinking she must be a bit of a nightmare, to mess up their holiday in the way she did. I'm apprehensive about meeting her but also burning up with curiosity. More than that, I want James to feel that it's *time* for us to meet. Which I know is crazy. He loves me, and I love him. So why does it matter so much?

I'm just not used to being in this situation, having never dated anyone with adult offspring before. Or any offspring, for that matter. It feels like uncharted territory and it's a bit scary. And of course I want, desperately, for her to like me.

One evening, over dinner in a little Turkish place at the end of his street, I blurt all this out. James is astounded that I've been having all these thoughts. 'Of course I want you to meet Esther,' he says firmly.

'I just wondered if you felt a bit funny about it,' I remark.

'But why?'

'Because, well . . . it hasn't happened yet.' I take a fortifying sip of wine. 'And you've spent lots of time with

Charlie.' *Yes, because Charlie lives with you, idiot,* I remind myself. *And Esther is a fully grown and independent woman.*

James places his cutlery on his plate. 'Yes, I know. And he's warming up a little bit with me, don't you think?'

'Yes, he is. You're good with him. You don't bulldoze him into having massive conversations . . .'

'Well, I like him a lot.' This might be a little strong, considering that their chats have been pretty brief and superficial, but it's warmed my heart to see James making a real effort to draw Charlie out of his shell without treating him like a child.

A lull settles between us. It's the first time I've noticed even a tiny hint of tension between us. Am I not as glamorous as Rhona, his ex-wife? I find myself wondering, ridiculously. Might Esther wonder why on earth her dad's seeing me?

I finish my mezze plate and wait for him to say something about Esther being so busy, having such a crazy social life that he can never pin her down. I've already decided that, if that's the case, I'll just leave it and accept that, for whatever reason, James wants to keep us, and his family life, strictly separate. But instead he looks at me and says, 'It's not that I don't want you to meet each other.'

'But are you worried about how it'll go?' I ask.

'No, of course not. I mean, it'll be fine. It's just . . .' His mouth twists. 'I've loved it being like this. Just us, I mean. Me and you.'

'Like it was in Corsica?' I suggest.

'Yes, I s'pose so.' He smiles now, crookedly, with a hint of embarrassment. I love his clear blue eyes, his slightly off-centre smile, the way he pulls on jeans, a T-shirt and a battered old pair of Converse with not the faintest idea of how attractive he is.

'James,' I start, 'if you don't want me to meet her—'

'Of course I do! Like I said, it's not that.'

Another small silence. My passive-aggressive tone wasn't intentional and now I wish I hadn't brought it up. 'You want it to be just us,' I suggest.

He shakes his head now. 'I know it's ridiculous. And you're right. We need to do it . . .'

I can't help laughing at that. 'That sounds ominous, like getting the roof fixed . . .'

He grins. 'No, I *want* you to meet her.'

'I mean,' I add, teasing him now, 'if you think she'd be horrified by me—'

'Of course she won't be horrified!' He pushes back his salt-and-pepper hair and adjusts his glasses. 'So, what d'you think we should do? Should we all go out to dinner or something?'

'We could do that.' I try to picture us all, with Charlie there too; I couldn't not invite him, I'd want him to be there. But would he want to come? And, if he agreed, how would he feel being forced to sit at a restaurant table with a stranger who's pretty famous and 'a fairly strong personality' as James has put it, I suspect diplomatically?

My stomach swirls with nerves at the thought of it. 'Maybe we should do something less, um . . .'

'Less "the big introduction" scenario?' he suggests.

I nod. 'Could Esther come round sometime when I'm at your place?'

'She could, yes.'

'That wouldn't be awkward, would it? Me being there?'

'I don't see why it would be,' he says unconvincingly.

We look at each other and chuckle at how complicated we're making this. 'We're not nervous about this at all, are we?' I remark as we leave the restaurant.

''Course not,' James agrees with a wry smile. 'We're

completely relaxed.' It strikes me again how easy it's been until now, getting to know each other layer by layer without any complications at all.

'James?' I start as he lets us into his house. 'How about you bring Esther out to my place one time?'

He looks at me. 'Sure, if you think that'd be best?'

'What I could do,' I continue, warming to the idea now, 'is make a few dishes I've been wanting to test for my column, and we'll have a casual Sunday lunch. I could invite Kim and Lorenzo too, and make it a nice, relaxed thing, rather than an "I'm dragging you out to the country to meet Lauren" kind of thing . . .'

'That sounds great,' he says, 'if you wouldn't mind doing that?'

'Of course I wouldn't mind. It's what I love doing.' I pause. 'D'you think she'd agree to come?'

'Yeah, definitely.' He nods. 'I can't see any problem with that.'

'I think it'd be fun, don't you?' Now I'm picturing a casual lunch of various tarts and salads, maybe a cake, so everyone can help themselves. I'm visualising the wine flowing and everyone having a lovely time, like normal families do.

'It'll be great,' James says firmly, kissing me in the hallway.

I smile, thrilled but a little scared at the prospect of hosting such an event. *Just a casual lunch*, I tell myself firmly. 'Let's do it then,' I say.

'Okay! So that's that sorted . . .'

I look at James, trying not to blurt out the question that's burning away in my brain, but unable to stop myself. 'D'you think she'll like me?'

He gives me an *are-you-mad?* kind of look. 'Who, Esther? She'll *love* you,' he says.

CHAPTER FIFTEEN

JAMES

My daughter looks up at me across my kitchen table a few days later. 'Do I *have* to come?'

'Well, no, but I'm asking you. I think it'd be a nice thing to do.'

'I might have things on,' she says airily.

'C'mon,' I chide her. 'You can spare one afternoon, surely.'

She sighs and squirts a second load of ketchup onto her plate. Despite what her Instagram might suggest – that everything she ingests is raw and sprinkled with seeds – she virtually falls upon anything crumb-coated when Miles isn't around, and requested chicken nuggets and oven chips when she came round tonight. 'Why d'you even want me there?' she asks.

'Because I've been seeing Lauren for quite a while now,' I start, 'and I'd like you to meet her. That's all.' She continues to shovel in nuggets as if stoking a furnace. 'D'you feel . . . all right about me seeing her?' I prompt her.

'Yeah, of course! Why wouldn't I? God, Dad, you don't have to clear things with *me* . . .' Bit of an over-reaction, I'm thinking. I only asked. Dinner finished, Esther traipses through to the living room where she flumps onto the sofa, as if the process of eating has exhausted her.

I settle at the other end of it, wondering whether it's worth going all out to persuade her to come to this lunch. I'm certainly not going to make her. I'm not going to beg or make a great scene about it. If she won't come, then fine. Bloody great. We'll probably cancel it because the whole point was for her and Lauren to meet.

No, no, we *won't* cancel, I decide, irritation building in me now. The world does not revolve around Esther who's currently lying there, allowing me approximately one foot of sofa while she jabs at her phone. It's actually not like her to be so arsey when she visits. Generally, we get along fine. In fact I often suspect she enjoys a bit of respite from Miles with his joyless food and that terrible art in his kitchen that reminds me of a burst wound.

Not tonight, though. Tonight she's in a stinker of a mood and I have no idea why.

Finally, she places her phone on the floor, still within arm's reach in case she needs to grab at it. 'I've been asked to write this thing,' she announces.

'What thing?'

'For the jewellery brand I'm working with, y'know?'

'Oh, really?' I say. 'What do they want?'

'Something for their website in my own words.'

'Right. Well, that's okay, isn't it?' I know she used to enjoy creative writing at school before the reality show took over her life.

'Not really, Dad. I've got to write an essay about how wearing their jewellery fits in with my ethos, and how it matters to me that it's all responsibly sourced and ethically produced,' she blurts out, looking quite distressed as if it'll require significant research and many hours of labour.

'What *is* your ethos?' I ask.

'I don't know!' She rests a hand over her eyes as if to shield herself from the awfulness of it all.

'Well . . . can you get one?' I ask vaguely.

'Get one? We're talking about a personal philosophy. Not a tattoo.'

Yes, I do know what an ethos is. 'I mean, can't you drum up something that sounds good?'

She splutters. 'You don't just drum one up, Dad! This is going to take a huge amount of work and I really don't have time for it.'

I exhale slowly, trying to remain patient. 'How long have they given you to write it?'

'Three weeks.'

'And how long does it have to be?'

'Two hundred words.'

'You mean two thousand,' I suggest.

'No, two hundred.'

'Two hundred words?' I exclaim. 'That's not much, Est. You could write that sitting on the loo—'

'Oh, thanks, Dad,' she barks. 'Thanks for belittling what I have to do.' After that, there's no point in discussing it, and she heads home soon afterwards leaving a waft of disgruntlement in her wake. I still find it hard to think of Miles's bat cave as her home.

The next day I discover that she reported our exchange about the 'essay' – I'm sorry, but it's not an essay if it's two hundred words long! – to her mum. 'You could have been a bit more supportive,' Rhona retorts when she calls that evening. 'She said you weren't sympathetic at all.'

'Sympathetic about having three weeks to bash out two hundred words?'

'You know what I mean.'

'I've written shopping lists that are longer—'

'Yes, but not everyone's like you, tossing off—'

'Poor choice of language,' Luc guffaws loudly in the background.

'*Dashing* off your final dissertation,' she clarifies, 'without even breaking a sweat.'

'I didn't have a final dissertation,' I remind her. 'I had exams.'

'Stop splitting hairs, James.'

This is how it is with Rhona and me, jibing at each other – mostly good-naturedly – in a way that we wouldn't with anyone else. We met at university where she gained her law degree. She'd known me when I'd been swotting for my finals. She'd witnessed me slugging coffee all night and working all hours until it felt like my eyeballs were going to roll out of my head. Aunt June had been right in that I probably wasn't academic enough to gain a degree in veterinary medicine; at least, it hadn't come naturally at all. And maybe I should have gone for that clerk's job at the tax office, which she'd ringed in Biro in the newspaper for me. If I hadn't been one hundred per cent determined to qualify, I'd never have managed to drag myself through five years of study.

As a law student, Rhona was the one who'd breezed through all those essays and exams, while still enjoying long lunches and languid swims at the uni pool. It was as if gaining a first-class degree had required no more effort than the cryptic crosswords, which she also excels at, solving a clue like 'Big dagger wallowing in trifle, perhaps' (4,7) in twenty seconds flat. I can't do those either.

Still, Rhona's remarks stick, and I do worry about Esther and why she has this tendency to blow up the smallest challenge into a drama. So I make a mental note to be *hugely* supportive next time she complains about her colossal workload. And when I mention the so-called 'essay' the next time she comes round – *only* to see how she's getting on with it, nothing controversial about that, right? – she yawns and says, 'Oh, I decided not to do it.'

'Did you?'

'Yeah.' She nods, gnawing contentedly on a slice of pizza.

'Is that okay then?' I venture. 'To just not do it?'

'Yeah. They said somebody could do it in my words if I preferred that.'

I look at her, genuinely confused. 'But how can someone else do it in your words?'

'We just had a quick chat on the phone,' she says with a trace of impatience. 'It was fine, Dad. Stop worrying.'

I guess she managed to cobble together an ethos then!

After dinner we settle on the sofa to watch a comedy show together. It's one I'd never watch on my own, but with Esther it's fun as we comment and chuckle together. As soon as it's finished I ask, with studied casualness, 'So, what about coming to Lauren's this Sunday?'

Her gaze swivels towards me. 'What's it for again?'

'It's not for anything. It's just lunch.'

'How long will we be there?'

'I'm not sure. It's just *lunch*,' I repeat, concerned that it's becoming a tic now, this chirping of, 'It's just lunch! It's just lunch!' Said ever-so-casually to detract from the fact that I'm planning to drag my daughter all the way out to the Hertfordshire countryside to introduce her to the most wonderful woman I have ever met.

Esther flicks back her hair, seeming to be mentally checking her diary.

'I'd just like you to meet her,' I add. 'Lauren's important to me. I like her a lot. I mean, I'm really—'

'Yeah, okay, Dad,' she barks, as if terrified that I'll divulge more than she can stomach. 'I'll come to lunch. I'll meet Lauren. Okay?'

PART TWO

Reality Bites

When recreating those delicious dishes from your holiday, you may need to tweak the recipe. Ingredients – and the way we live and eat – may be somewhat different back home

CHAPTER SIXTEEN

ESTHER

Esther couldn't believe her dad had gone to Corsica on his own. 'What's he going to do there for two weeks?' she'd asked her boyfriend as he'd flipped from show to show on TV. A cookery thing, with someone demonstrating how to create a wavy edge effect on a pie. Then something with tractors and a terrible daytime soap. Esther isn't fond of channel flipping – or the TV being on in the day. It feels depressing but then, this is Miles's flat they're living in. So she doesn't make the rules.

'Dunno babe,' he'd replied, eyes fixed on the screen. 'Are there ancient ruins to look at? Does he like that kind of thing?'

'Guess so.' In fact Esther knows her dad is interested in archaeology. When she was little he'd taken her to archaeological digs. It was a bit like going on treasure hunts – they'd found shards of pottery and ancient coins – and for a while it had been one of their favourite things to do together. But she didn't mention this because Miles wouldn't have been interested. He'd have just done that glazing-over thing.

Anyway, her dad hadn't been looking at ancient ruins in Corsica. He'd been far too busy for that. He'd met a woman – an *actual woman* – and fallen in love with her! Esther would have been no more shocked if he'd come home with a neck tattoo.

Her dad never dated anyone (apart from Polly, who'd seemed nice enough despite her terribly ugly sandals and had suddenly disappeared to South America). Generally, Esther had always assumed he was far too busy with his work. But not now. Now he's seeing this Lauren person and seems all sparky and happy and different, somehow. This change in him, when he's always been so solid and dependable, always there for her . . . well, it's unsettling to say the least. And now he wants Esther to not only *meet* his new love, but go to her house, somewhere way out in the countryside!

A lunch is being put on. Some big fancy lunch so they can be formally introduced. This is sending out warning signals about this Lauren person. Esther is trying not to judge the woman before she's even met her, but it's hard not to when she's being pressurised like this.

After all, they could have kept it simple and just had a quick coffee at her dad's place. No big deal; it could have all been over and done with in twenty minutes. But for some reason Lauren couldn't do that. Nope, it had to be a big showy-offy occasion, taking up half of Esther's weekend. She has only agreed (begrudgingly) to go because she loves her dad and it obviously means a lot to him, for her to be there.

Now Esther has learnt that Lauren has a teenage son. Apparently he's going to be at this lunch too. 'Of course he is,' her dad had said, tetchily, when she'd quizzed him on this. 'It's his house, Est. It's where he lives.'

'What's he like?' she asked.

'Really nice. Quite studious and a bit shy,' he told her.

Well, this was going to be a load of laughs. 'It's only lunch,' her dad keeps reminding her. If it's that insignificant then why are Lauren's best friend and her husband coming along too? A whole fucking gang! If her dad had said this at the start – that half the village would be coming along for a gawp – then she'd never have agreed to go.

Esther goes rigid with anxiety every time she thinks about it. What if she doesn't like Lauren? Or Lauren doesn't like her? How awkward is that going to be, when her dad's so obviously smitten? People think, because of the kind of industry Esther works in, that she's super-confident and never fazed by social events. They're wrong, though. She's fine in work situations because she's developed 'the tools' to deal with them, as Chrissie, her therapist, would put it. She's created coping mechanisms and a persona she can slip into: shiny, sparkly Esther. But 'being Esther Burton' won't work when she meets Lauren, not with her dad being there – because he knows her better than anyone else. It would feel ridiculous, being professional Esther in front of him. Trouble is, she's relied so heavily on this version of herself, which she pulls on like a costume, that she can't remember how to just be her normal self.

Meeting this Lauren person and the bookish son seems so fraught with potential disaster that, three days before the big event, Esther calls Chrissie and insists she fit her in.

Esther doesn't think she's a qualified psychotherapist exactly, but when she tried to check out her credentials and found basically nothing, her friend Lily, who'd recommended her (she's Miles's friend really) said it's not about framed certificates on the wall. Just as well because there

101

aren't any. They are sitting in what Chrissie calls her therapy suite, which is a glorified garden shed. She hands Esther a glass mug of chamomile tea. Esther would rather have a coffee, a big jolt of caffeine to sharpen her up.

'I can understand why this is alarming for you,' Chrissie says. 'The thought of all these new people is making you feel unsafe.'

Lily was right. Qualifications don't really matter. As she pours everything out in Chrissie's shed, Esther starts to feel a whole lot better.

Chrissie understands that she only agreed to go to support her dad, and because she's still harbouring a residue of guilt over not going to Corsica with him. 'But then, if you had gone, he wouldn't have met Lauren and be so happy now,' Chrissie offers.

That makes Esther feel better immediately. 'I'd never thought of it like that. So, d'you think I shouldn't go to this lunch?'

'What do you want to do,' Chrissie asks, 'in your heart?'

'I don't know.'

'How is the situation making you feel?'

She considers this. 'Kind of like . . . being tricked into something,' she explains.

Chrissie nods understandingly. She knows that Esther and her dad don't always see eye to eye; that he'd made a big fuss about how many suitcases she'd been planning to take to Corsica, and then went on about her coat, calling it 'a carpet'. (Charming!) Now Esther is explaining how this whole meeting Lauren scenario is reminding her of the time he'd made her walk part of the Southern Western Coastal Path, or whatever it's called, near St Ives in Cornwall, where the two of them had gone on holiday when Esther was fourteen. He'd bought her some terrible walking boots that weighed about a ton each, which Esther

102

had refused to wear – because it was like having bricks strapped to her feet.

'You're *not* doing the walk in flip-flops,' her dad had said, as if she was six years old.

'They're sandals, not flip-flops,' she'd corrected him. He knew absolutely nothing about fashion.

'Whatever they are, they have no supporting structure.' Who even talks like that? Her dad is obsessed with foot-wear offering 'support' to the foot and ankle as if she was one of those people who hikes up mountains with spiky sticks. So she'd worn her flip-flops – *sandals* – and after about half an hour she was in agony and crying and they'd had to turn back. But it wasn't her fault. It was a misleading description thing. Coastal Path? It wasn't a path, it was *boulders*.

'You're worried that he's misleading you about this lunch with Lauren?' Chrissie prompts her now.

'Yeah. I mean, Lauren's invited all her friends along—'

'Really?' Chrissie asks in surprise.

Esther nods, aware that she's exaggerating slightly. But what if she's not? Nothing would surprise her now.

'You mean, you're worried that you're going to feel paraded in public?'

'Exactly,' Esther says, aware of a twinge of guilt now. Her dad would never 'parade' her. He's the kindest man you could imagine and sometimes she thinks he's the only one who actually takes time to listen to her, whereas with her mum it's all, 'Oh, is that right, darling? Great! Lovely! Sorry, gotta dash!' It was her dad who'd realised she was good at history, that she had a keen interest in it. Amanda, who taught it, was one of the few decent teachers at her school. Her dad had encouraged her to work extra hard, to put her all into it and get good grades. Even though he hadn't been keen for her to go to Willow Vale – with its optional lessons – he'd listened while she'd begged and pleaded, and after weeks and weeks of this (God, he hadn't made it easy) he'd eventually said yes, okay, if she was absolutely sure it was the right place for her.

Her mum, of course, had said, 'Fine, darling!' right away. Which was great. But in a way, Esther had liked it that her dad had put her through all that, because it meant he really cared.

Then came the reality show set at her school and filmed over a whole term. Amazingly, she was chosen by the production team as one of the main pupils to be in it. God knows why because she was really ordinary then. Quite shy, even. She hadn't yet grown into herself. It goes without saying that her dad was *really, really* concerned about how it would affect 'her education' (because back then everything was about her education) and whether – although he didn't put it this way – they'd make her look like a twat.

'The thing about you, James,' her mum had argued, 'is that you automatically see all the dangers and the things that could go terribly wrong.'

They'd ground him down, she supposes now. Esther feels slightly ashamed of that now because, even though he was unsure about it, he was still supportive. He just kept saying, 'If there's anything you feel even slightly uncomfortable about, you must let me know.' Whereas her mum was all, 'Go for it! Make sure you stand out! Who knows where this is going to take you?'

Chrissie twiddles the cluster of thin metallic bangles around her tiny wrist. She's wearing a crinkly patterned top, flowing wide-legged trousers and leather sandals with gold embellishments – the kind Esther's dad would be appalled at for having no structural support. 'Is there a way that you can go to the lunch, but still feel in control?' she asks.

Esther thinks about this for a moment. 'Miles could come too. Then I'd feel less outnumbered . . .'

'That's a good idea,' Chrissie says, smiling.

Esther looks at her. She hadn't thought of that before now. But obviously, it's the ideal solution. 'Yeah. But Dad can't stand him. He's made no secret of that. I mean, he refused point-blank to let him come to Corsica with us—'

'He wouldn't be outwardly rude to him, though?' Chrissie cuts in.

'No, no, he'd never do that,' Esther says firmly.

'Well, it sounds like a good compromise. And hopefully your dad'll be fine about that.' Chrissie pats her hand. 'You're being brave, Esther. It takes courage to stand up for what you want, especially when someone has a big personality like that.'

Does her dad have a big personality? She wouldn't put it like that exactly. He just gets on with his life, doing difficult stuff she has no idea how he copes with – like removing a tumour from a hamster's ear.

Way back in July, when she'd called him to say she wouldn't be going to Corsica after all – not if Miles couldn't go too – he hadn't even yelled at her. She'd been braced for an angry outburst but, weirdly, he'd sounded relieved but also upset. 'Right. Okay,' he'd said distractedly. What about the hundreds of pounds he'd spent on her flight and hotel room? She'd almost wished he had yelled at her – then she'd have felt less terrible. But her dad's not a yeller. He's a reasoner, if that's a word.

'For God's sake, James, d'you have to be so *reasonable*?' she's heard her mum say more than once. So her kind, sensible, *reasonable* dad was probably just relieved she wasn't dead.

It's Miles who has the 'big personality', she reflects now. Miles who came home recently making a massive fuss because someone had had the cheek to come up to the DJ booth and ask him to play a request. 'Do I look like a fucking wedding DJ?' he'd barked, pouring himself a massive tumbler of red wine. 'Do I look like I've got *Dancing Queen?*'

Session over, Esther heads back to the flat deciding that this time – unlike with Corsica – she won't ask her dad whether Miles can come along too. He'll just jump into the car when her dad comes to pick her up.

That way there'll be no argument. All she needs to do now is get Miles to agree to come.

CHAPTER SEVENTEEN

ESTHER

Esther doesn't care that Miles is older than her. Age is just a number – and sometimes she thinks she's more mature than he is. The only time it feels a bit weird and uncomfortable is when he's with a bunch of similar-aged friends, and they're dancing.

That, she finds difficult. She's not saying they shouldn't be allowed to have fun, or that there should be a law against anyone dancing above the age of, say, thirty-two. But she'd rather not be forced to see them thrusting their hips and 'throwing shapes' in public. Right now, on a Saturday night in an overheated club, she has an urge to be somewhere else – in another building or even another continent to ensure that she won't have to see them with her own eyes.

The spectacle is reminding Esther of the less inhibited teachers at Willow Vale, her old school, all leaping up for a 'boogie' or 'bop' at the end-of-year party, as Amanda, her history teacher, used to call it. That's not good, is it, that the sight of her boyfriend flinging himself about on the floor reminds her of teachers dancing?

Esther liked Amanda a lot. Now she's a bit older she realises how clever she was, to bring the lives of people who'd lived hundreds – or even thousands – of years ago to life, and make it all so fascinating. She was a *brilliant* teacher. But if she'd wanted to dance, Esther wished she'd done it in private at home. She can picture it now, the shambolic blend of feet shuffling, Nineties arm waving and Dave (head of maths) throwing his head back and pointing up at the stained polystyrene ceiling tiles as he shouted, 'Acieeeed!'

While no one's done that tonight (although there's still time), Esther has spotted Andi slowly pirouetting while hugging himself. Then Kevin stumbled, clutching at his dodgy hip – or maybe it was an experimental dance move? As her stomach started to churn and she decided she couldn't watch anymore, Esther slunk away to the bar.

Now a couple of Miles's friends have tracked her down. 'What's wrong, Est?' Kevin shouts, spraying saliva in her face. 'Don't you like the music?'

'It's all right. I'm just a bit tired,' she replies, at which he laughs loudly.

'Tired? You young 'uns, you've no stamina. When I was your age I was off my tits every night, up until six then straight off to work, sweating like a bastard!'

With that alluring image now placed firmly in her head, Esther checks the time on her phone just as Miles arrives at her side. Soon he and his friends are yabbering away, coked to the eyeballs, shouting over each other and clearly thrilled at how fantastically clever and funny they all are.

'Don't be so boring, Esther,' Andi insists, belly protruding over skinny jeans, buttons straining on his shirt, threatening to pop. Before they set off tonight, Miles promised he wouldn't do any drugs. He's trying to straighten out and he's admitted it doesn't 'help' him. But within half an hour he was off to the loo with his mate – 'just to chum him', he'd said, as if he was worried about Kevin being lonely in there on his own. And now they're off again, gyrating en masse, unfortunately still within Esther's sightline.

The scene reminds her of Miles's pet rat. It's perfectly acceptable, having a single rodent pottering about quietly in his cage. Likewise, she'd be fine – well, fine-*ish* – with just one middle-aged person dancing. But she wouldn't want a dozen rats in the kitchen.

Esther heads for the loo, not to take drugs – she doesn't do them; she doesn't even drink much normally – but because she needs to get away from them all for a few minutes. A girl in a vest top and jeans, with a delicate heart-shaped face, catches her eye in the mirror above the basins. 'Hi,' she says with a smile.

'Hi.' Esther smiles back and smooths down her hair with her fingers. The extensions have filled it out really well. Of course she realises, in the great scheme of things, that when people are battling with war, poverty and all kinds of horrors, 'having thin hair' is hardly a life-ruining condition. And it actually wasn't *that* thin. But there'd been some mean comments about it online, that it looked straggly and lank. Izzy, supposedly an old friend, had got in touch to let her know about this dedicated platform for haters where people in the public eye are slagged off. 'You really shouldn't look at it,' she warned. 'Please don't. I'll just upset you.'

Well, it was *exactly* like having a big pulsating spot. The more you're warned to leave it, the more you're poking and digging at it until it's doubled in size, is throbbing angrily and simmering hot to the touch. That's what Esther did with the haters' site, and it was so awful seeing herself described as a 'vain, dumb bitch with shit hair' that she rushed off and got extensions, which took five hours, cost £750 and made her feel a bit sick – not just because of the cost but because they turned out to be real human hair, harvested from, well, she doesn't like to think where the hair had come from. The word 'harvested' still makes her feel a bit nauseous now.

'Some poor girl sold her hair,' her mum's boyfriend teased her, 'just to make yours thicker!'

The girl in the mirror takes a cherry red lipstick from her bag and applies it deftly. 'That colour really suits you,' Esther says.

'Thanks.' The girl smiles, and Esther senses that flicker of recognition in her dark brown eyes. It happens sometimes: 'It's Esther Burton, isn't it?' Or: 'You look just like Esther Burton!' At first, the year or so after the *Willow Vale* reality show, she found it mortifying and didn't know how to react. Smile and walk away quickly? Laugh and say, 'Yes, it is!' as if they'd got a question right in a quiz?

'Just be gracious, darling,' her mum had suggested, but Esther couldn't work out what that meant. For a while, whenever she went out at night, she wore a big hat with a floppy brim, tugged down low, and enormous sunglasses. However, she soon realised that the outfit screamed 'I'm famous!' and was drawing even more attention. So Esther gave up on that. And she doesn't think she's that famous really. At least, not beyond a certain age group, and a certain type of person. She's pretty *niche*.

But even so, what happened after the TV thing wasn't all good. Izzy, her best friend all through school, went all snidey and distant, and Esther heard her one time in the school library, saying, 'She's really changed. She thinks so much of herself now.'

That so wasn't fair. Esther was trying her best to keep things normal when all these offers were coming in – more

TV stuff, social media opportunities, magazine interviews and copious gifts pouring in from PRs and fashion brands. She was sent clothes, jewellery and more make-up and skincare than she could ever slather onto her own face. It felt a bit crazy, like she didn't deserve it, and she didn't know what to do with it all.

'Izzy's just jealous,' her mum had said. 'She wasn't even picked for the show and you were the star of it. She just can't handle that, sweetie.' But that hadn't made it any easier.

Her dad had listened and sympathised and suggested that maybe Izzy felt threatened because their friendship had changed (not that that excused her behaviour, he added). Esther knew what he was thinking: that she should never have taken part in that show. At least he hadn't said, 'I told you so.' Her dad's not like that. He doesn't care about being right; he just *cares*. He wants what's best for her. And what was happening at school was bullying, pure and simple. Esther was ostracised and gossiped about. Someone – she never found out who – painted ESTHER BURTON UGLY SLAG on the sports block.

Her dad was livid when he found out. 'I'm going to go in and talk to your teachers,' he'd announced.

'No, please don't!' she'd cried. 'It'll all die down and it's nothing really. I don't care.'

Of course she cared deeply, her face burning every time she glimpsed that cruel graffiti in the periphery of her vision. The school caretaker took a week to get around to painting over it. Although the bullying continued, Esther stopped telling her dad about it. Instead, she started hiding in the school loos, sitting there for hours, wiping away her tears with that horrible scratchy toilet paper they had at school. And she reassured her dad that everything was okay now.

Esther did still have friends she'd grown up with. But Gracie and Jess had gone to a normal secondary school, and at Willow Vale she had no one after the show had been aired and she'd emerged as its unintentional star. As Izzy's influence spread, more of the girls started avoiding her, gossiping in groups and falling silent whenever she approached. The boys were still nice, which fuelled the girls even more: 'She loves attention!' But Esther *didn't* love it. If anything, she'd always been envious of Izzy with her cosy family home, her mum baking mince pies at Christmas and wrapping a huge number of tiny thoughtful gifts every birthday, the number of parcels matching her age.

At birthdays and Christmas Esther's mum gives her money as she's too busy to choose things, she says – and she never knows what to buy her. Her dad's busy too. He's the busiest person she knows. But he always manages to find her some interesting books, some nice stationery, and fun things like a vintage record player in a portable case.

Miles made an effort too, at the start, with flowers, jewellery and adorable cards scrawled with loving messages. He was so thoughtful and really cared about her. That's why they got together – because after finding she had no friends left at Willow Vale, she really needed someone. And Miles was different. Older for one thing. More mature. He'd seen and done it all with his music career. He *understood*.

'You're Esther Burton,' the girl says now in the club loo.

'Yeah.' Esther smiles. 'Are you having a good night? What's your name?'

Her dad had suggested flipping the attention to the other person, if she didn't know how to react. 'Maybe

ask their name, how they're doing, that kind of thing?'
he'd said. Of course, Esther thought; he's used to dealing
with the public all day long.

'Anya,' the girl says. 'It's brilliant here, isn't it?'

'Yeah.' Esther tries to sound enthusiastic. 'Your lipstick's
lovely. You really suit red. I can't wear it at all . . .'

'Oh, I bet you could,' Anya says kindly. They have a bit
of a chitchat, admiring each other's jewellery and exchanging
tips on vintage shops. Esther feels better as they say goodbye
and head off back into the crowd. Anya's reminded her
that people can be lovely, and if she's feeling a bit out of
sorts tonight it's not really Miles's fault. He's just having
a night out with his friends, so of course he wants to kick
back, have some fun and do a few lines. He's worked *so*
hard lately. He deserves it.

'Hey, gorgeous.' He's back at her side now, planting a
noisy kiss on her cheek. 'You having fun?'

'Actually,' Esther says, 'I'm a bit tired. And I've got
that thing with Dad tomorrow . . .'

'What thing?' He frowns.

'*You* remember. I've got to go meet his new girlfriend?'
He looks blank. 'The one he met in Corsica, remember?'

'Oh, yeah, the holiday romance!' He laughs unkindly.
'Where does she live again?'

'Out in the country. Essex or Bedfordshire, something
like that—'

'You're going for the whole day?' Although he grew
up in the wilds of Somerset, Miles always looks a bit
unsettled whenever the country comes up in conversation.
He once said he 'didn't see the point of it'.

'Just for lunch. Remember I told you she's a cookery
writer kind of thing?'

'Oh, yeah.' His tone tells Esther that he has no idea
what she's talking about.

'So I'm going to head home,' she adds. 'You stay if you like.'

He seems to weigh up the options then says, 'Nah, babe, I'll come home too.'

They say their goodbyes, and she manages to dodge a hug and kiss from Kevin, who now has cheesy white stuff in the corners of his mouth. On the way out she spots Anya with her friends, all laughing and looking like they're having a great time being together. It's all girls, no boys at all. The bolt of envy that hits her is like a kick in the gut. Esther can't remember the last time she went out with the girls, because she doesn't have 'the girls' anymore. Gracie and Jess are away at university in Durham and St Andrews, living their lives, making new friends, studying economics and medicine – proper clever stuff. On the rare occasions when they all get together, the conversation is peppered with words like *semester*, *essay*, *dissertation*, and it all sounds pretty thrilling, running around with piles of books, being with all those super-brainy people.

Esther didn't apply for university even though Amanda, her history teacher, had urged her to: 'You're made for it, Esther. Honestly, you'd love the whole experience.' However, she was already earning money and in demand; people were paying her to endorse things on social media. Her main income at the moment is through a paid partnership with Bethani jewellery. Nothing wrong with that, Esther reminds herself. The world needs doctors and economists but it also needs beautiful earrings, right?

Spotting her, Anya waves and Esther waves back. 'Who's that?' Miles asks.

'Just a nice girl I was chatting to in the loos.'

He chuckles. 'You girls, always chatting in the loos.'

Esther smiles and takes his hand, and on the way home in the cab she snuggles close to him in the back seat. Maybe she's a little bit drunk. (She did neck a few vodkas to anaesthetise herself from seeing Miles and his friends all jumping about on the dance floor together.) But now she's thinking they've been through a lot already, the two of them. They broke up, they worked it out and now they're fine again. She's glad they're together and making plans for their future. But something in the shorter term is more concerning to her right now.

'Miles?' she starts.

'Uh-huh?'

'Would you come to Lauren's with me tomorrow?'

'What?' he exclaims, as if she'd asked him to go to Tibet.

'Would you come with me and Dad? Please?'

They've stopped at traffic lights. Miles glances out at a group of cheerful studenty types all carrying guitar cases, then frowns at her. 'You don't want me there, babe.'

'I do!'

'What for?'

'Because you're my boyfriend. Why else?'

'That's not a reason, Est . . .'

'For a bit of moral support then.'

'Why d'you need moral support? You're an adult. It's not as if you're about to get a new *stepmother* . . .'

'I know that,' she says tetchily, realising now that she absolutely needs to persuade him to come. Lauren is obviously a big deal to her dad; since he came back from Corsica, all tanned and smiley and seemingly having forgiven Esther for not going with him, there's been a kind of lightness about him that she's never seen before. He just seems happier in himself. And she's pleased for him; of course she is. But she is also aware of this simmering pressure to like Lauren instantly, and she knows she'll feel better if Miles is right there at her side.

115

However, there's more to it than that. She also wants him to do something for *her*, for once – to show he cares, like he did at the start, two years ago when she was just eighteen years old and he adored her. It's a kind of test, she supposes. Will he do this tiny thing for her? Will he venture out to the terrifying countryside for one afternoon?

'Please come,' she says.

He sighs. 'It's not really my kind of thing, babe.'

'What isn't? Meeting people? Eating food?'

'Don't be silly.' He shakes his head irritably.

'It's not far, Miles. I mean, it's not the North Pole—'

'Where is it then?'

'I told you. Kent or Surrey, somewhere like that . . .'

He winces, sucking in air through his teeth as if she's suggested a fun trip to a stinking landfill site. 'Tomorrow?' he asks.

'Yeah.'

'I've kind of got stuff on.'

'Like what?'

His mouth twists. 'I was going to do some cleaning—'

'Cleaning? Miles, you never clean! What were you planning to do exactly?' This is true. His cleaning lady, Petra, comes in once a week, gliding through the flat with incredible efficiency. Although she's lovely, Esther never knows what to do with herself while she's there. Sit around while she mops and hoovers and flicks her feather duster over Salvador, the taxidermied bat? Offer to help or hang around chatting, getting in the way? It's easier all round to go to a café and hide there, dawdling over coffee after coffee until it's safe to go home.

'I thought I'd do something about the tile grout,' he mutters.

'What?' Esther splutters.

'In the bathroom, between the tiles where the black bits are . . .'

'You're *not* planning to spend Sunday scrubbing the tile grout,' Esther retorts.

'I might!' he says defensively.

She pouts. 'You never do anything for me.'

'That's *so* not fair!'

'It *is* fair,' she snaps, aware of how childish she sounds. As they fall into a grim silence Esther wonders what the driver's making of this – if he hears couples rowing all the time or if he's even listening. 'I've just spent three hours in that club with your friends,' she adds.

'Didn't you like it?' He looks hurt, as if he personally owns the place.

'It was all right.' *A load of middle-aged sweaty dancing and Kevin with his cheesy mouth? Yeah, I loved it.*

'I thought it was great.' His nostrils flare. 'Sorry you've had a shit night . . .'

'It wasn't shit. I just—'

'Oh, babe,' he cuts in, slipping an arm around her narrow shoulders. 'We'll do what you want next time.'

'Next time we go out, you mean?'

'Yeah.'

She checks his expression. 'Okay. So come to Lauren's tomorrow . . .'

'Ugh, God, do I have to?' he groans.

'Yes, you do,' she says firmly. He sighs and takes hold of her hand as they pass a row of crumbly shops, their signs faded and peeling. The streets are quieter now, and fine rain has started to fall.

'What's she like?' he asks.

'I don't know. I hardly know anything about her. But we'll find out, won't we?'

He grins. 'Is she hot?'

'Miles!'

He's laughing now, and she senses her shoulders relaxing

as she thinks, *At least he's agreed to come. He might be an idiot sometimes but I do love him.* 'How long will we have to be there?' he asks.

She splutters. 'How old are you?'

'I'm only asking . . .'

'Not long, I don't think. It's just lunch, Miles. No big deal at all.'

CHAPTER EIGHTEEN

JAMES

'We can't be doing with other vets,' Mariana Gomez announced on Friday, to explain why, despite having moved to deepest Croydon, she still treks across London to our practice with her anxious greyhound. 'He goes for anyone else,' she added. 'He's snarling and snapping before we've set foot in the door – but not here, James. Not with your amazingly calm vibes.'

I'm not sure I'm emitting calm vibes now as we drive out to Lauren's in Hertfordshire. For one thing, I hadn't banked on Miles joining us today. 'Hope you don't mind,' he announced with a tooth-baring grin, 'me gate-crashing the big event?'

'Not at all,' I lied as he clambered, uninvited, into the passenger seat. *It's not a big event. It's just lunch!*

'Wonder how everyone's going to get along?' he muses now with a trace of glee. Having ambushed me successfully, he's obviously feeling terribly pleased with himself.

'Fine, I'm sure,' I reply, focusing hard on the road ahead.

'So, where are we going again?'

I tell him the name of the village.

'Never heard of it!'

As if I might have made it up. 'It's a nice place,' I say blandly, glimpsing Esther in the rear-view mirror, hunched like a little kid in the back seat.

'So, how're things in vet world?' Miles enquires, as if he's remotely interested.

'Oh, fine. Pretty good, very busy . . .'

'Lots of sick animals?' Is he taking the piss or is it just my default reaction? The mere sight of him in his skinny jeans and flimsy shirts clinging to his narrow, sunken torso gets my hackles up. *My daughter is in love with this man and I am powerless to do anything about it.*

'Just the usual,' I reply.

'D'you ever get attacked? Like, scratched or bitten?'

Is he planning to carry on like this for the whole journey? Should I start firing banal questions at him about his 'job'? *So, Miles, how exactly do you place a record on the turntable – or is 'decks' the correct term? How, precisely, do you 'work the crowd'?*

'Not often,' I say, 'but it can be an occupational hazard . . .'

'I admire you, man,' he announces. 'I could never do an ordinary job like you, tied into the nine-to-five, same thing week in, week out. Fuck, man. It'd do my head in.'

Maybe you should try it sometime. But then you don't have to, do you? Apparently his elderly parents still reside at the family seat in Somerset, where there are fifteen bedrooms, a lake and a village of workers' houses in the grounds. I know this not because of anything Esther has told me (Miles seems to want to keep his aristocratic ancestry under wraps) but through extensive googling. 'They're just ordinary people,' I've heard him insist – but ordinary people don't have stable blocks. I'd guess that

120

a private income allows him to DJ once a fortnight and call it 'work'.

But I don't say any of that. I just tell him that I enjoy my job, wishing he'd plug in his earphones as Esther has, rather than pretending he wants to talk to me. Of course, ideally he wouldn't be here at all. I'm not an unfriendly person, and occasionally Esther has introduced me to a boy who I didn't think was exactly *ideal* for her – a bit attitudey, verging on rude. But it was fine, I could accept that, because that was the difference – the word 'boy'.

I know for a fact that Miles lies about his age. That was easy to find out. I realise it's sounding as if I spend *all* my spare time googling him, but I knew he'd been in a band as a youngster and they'd enjoyed a single hit (way back in the mists of time, almost pre-CDs! I mean, almost *pre-electricity*, when record players were wound up with a handle). Within minutes I'd found lead vocalist Miles Lattimer-Jones in a YouTube clip from 1989. He was wearing a red leather bomber jacket, a lightning bolt earring and his hair was bleached yellow, long at the back and spiked into meringue-like peaks on top – the most mulletty of Eighties mullets. Crucially he was an adult at this point.

You say you're forty-five, Miles? More like fifty-two!

Thankfully he has now produced earphones from the pocket of his skintight black jeans and stuffed them in. I'm fine with the insistent tss-tss leaking out, if it means no more conversation.

We just need to get this first meeting over and done with, I decide now. Lauren was right: it's just a necessary thing to do if we're going to be together. And I want very much for us to be together. For the first time in living memory, work doesn't feel like the sole driving force of my life. I find myself looking forward to seeing Lauren to the point where even those difficult days fly by if we're meeting that evening. Even those aspects of work that used to get to me, like belligerent owners behaving unreasonably because we haven't been able to see them at a moment's notice, without an appointment; all that seems to slide off me now.

Before I met Lauren I definitely worried and stressed more. I'd feel bad that we couldn't see absolutely everyone who called in. Fraser is equally committed but somehow, he's more able to keep work in its place. The difference is, he's always had a pretty intense personal life, with dramatic break-ups, reconciliations and God knows what demanding his attention. Whereas for many years pretty much all of my attention – family aside – has been funnelled into the practice.

Nowadays, those evenings when I'm at home alone, which could often seem dreary before, are okay too – not only because there's our next date to look forward to. Life just seems *lighter*. The feeling of being with Lauren stays with me even when we're not together.

This is going to be *fine*, I reassure myself as I turn off the motorway. At least Esther agreed to come, and I'm sure Lauren will make her feel welcome and put everyone at ease. And of course Kim and Lorenzo will be there too – 'to defuse things', as Lauren put it – so it should all be very jolly and fun.

'Are you nervous?' I asked her when we spoke last night.

'A bit,' she admitted. 'Are you?'

'Fucking terrified,' I joked, and she laughed.

'What's the worst thing that can happen?' she asked.

'Um . . . that it's all a bit stilted?'

'Well, that doesn't really matter, does it?'

''Course it doesn't,' I said firmly.

'D'you think Esther and Charlie will get on?'

'Honestly, I have no idea,' I said truthfully. 'It'd be great if they did. But it's not really about them, is it?'

'No, it's not,' she agreed. 'It's about me and you.'

'Exactly . . .'

'And, James?' she added. 'They're our kids, remember. They're lovely people. It's going to be *fine*.'

CHAPTER NINETEEN

LAUREN

'It's going to be fine,' I told James last night, and now I actually believe it will be. Kim and Lorenzo have arrived early to help get things ready, and the mood is jovial as we set the table, whip up salad dressings and check the various dishes in the oven. Even Charlie seems reasonably happy today. Since Corsica, I figured he'd actually been missing Remy more than he'd let on. They'd been exceptionally close, and now Remy's life is all about going on city breaks with Freya and playing gigs all over the country. These days, their lives couldn't be more different.

I'm relieved to see Charlie and Lorenzo bantering happily, although they've always got along exceptionally well. Lorenzo reckons Charlie's brain is 'the size of a bus' and calls him Patrick Moore, who's the only astronomer most non-experts have heard of. However, I'm not sure how Charlie feels about meeting Esther. My guess is that he'd rather this wasn't happening at all.

'I hope they'll get along,' I murmur to Kim as she polishes wine glasses with a tea towel.

''Course they will,' she insists, adding, 'You look gorgeous, by the way.'

I glance down at my simple emerald green dress and suede trainers. 'You think?'

'Totally.'

'Not too dressy?'

'Absolutely not.'

'Or too casual? Or too *green*?'

'Stop it,' she says, laughing now. Charlie appears at the back door, having ventured out on this crisp October day to gather late-blooming flowers for the table. I hadn't even asked him. He just thought it'd be nice – or maybe it was a distraction activity to take his mind off the anxious waiting? Better to be out in the garden *doing* something than hovering about, right? My heart swells with love for him as he arranges them messily in a stripy jug. I manage not to interfere as he places it on the table because actually, the tumbly mixture looks beautiful and – oh, here they are!

As James's car doors open I realise they've brought an extra person. *This* is a surprise. A warning text might've been nice, just to be polite. But it's fine. Of course it is. The more the merrier I decide, as I quickly rearrange my expression to that of the unflappable hostess and greet my guests.

*

'So lovely to meet you. Wow, Esther, you're so like your dad . . . Can I take your jackets? This is Kim . . . Lorenzo . . . and Charlie, my son . . . nice to meet you, Miles . . .' I'm aware I'm babbling as I hug each person in turn and thank James effusively for the wine and flowers as if he'd brought me a Tiffany ring. Nervous? Of course I'm not nervous . . .

'Hope it was okay to bring him along,' James murmurs with a grimace as we step away from the group. 'I didn't know he was coming. He just *appeared* . . .'

'Like a genie?' I suggest with a smile.

'He just jumped into the car!'

'Why are you talking through your teeth like that?'

'I mean, I could hardly push him out—'

'On the motorway? I think you were wise not to . . .'

'No, I mean before we set off—'

'James, it's *fine*,' I hiss. 'Honestly. What difference does it make?' I'm a little taken aback to see how much this is bothering him. He didn't seem this tense, even when he was blowing up my parents' dog's nose. Was it really such a good idea of mine to push him into doing this today?

Assisted by Kim, I fetch everyone drinks. Lorenzo – thank God for easy-going Lorenzo – is already chatting in his usual jocular way to Esther and Miles: 'So you've been dragged out to the sticks . . . Look at all this food; I think Lauren's been preparing for a famine . . .'

Charlie is hovering on the periphery and Esther is smiling rather stiffly. I'm determined to push any preconceived ideas I have about her firmly out of my head. So, she's been difficult in the past, leaving her father in a state of blind panic at the airport. But never mind that. The whole point of today is to get to know each other a little.

'It's lovely to meet you at last,' I tell her as I hand her a glass of wine.

'You too,' she says. She's astoundingly beautiful, not in a modelly way exactly; her face is more interesting than that. She has striking hazel eyes, a smattering of freckles across her upturned nose and wavy reddish hair tumbling all the way down her back. She seems a little distant, although perfectly at ease. Charlie, I notice, is still hanging back.

'I love your dress,' I offer. She's wearing a floral shift

126

in navy and violet with a light blue cardi thrown over, plus flat tan boots and delicate jewellery; the kind of casual, quirkily put together look that just works, and that I could never emulate.

'Thanks. It's just an old thing from a market . . .' There's some chatter about where Esther lives, and where she grew up, and then Kim skilfully draws Charlie into the conversation, far more effectively than I ever could, as he'd just resist my attempts. Soon he's joining in. He's trying, anyway. He's standing there with a beer (he doesn't drink much) being polite. And James is good with him. I realise this sounds as if I regard Charlie as a child who can't handle adult company. He can, of course. But having realised how very reticent he is, James seems to have settled at just the right level with him; friendly and coaxing him out of himself, without being overbearing.

Miles is standing a little way back, clutching a glass of red wine and gazing around my kitchen in an arched way, with what seems like a hint of bemusement. But maybe he's just feeling out on a limb among these strangers. While I know James isn't crazy about him, and that he's been shitty to Esther in the past (and, actually, I'm not one hundred per cent sure about this guy myself), I want him to feel relaxed in my home. So I pour myself a glass of wine and breeze over to him.

He seems pleased when I ask what he does for a living. 'I'm in the music business,' he says.

'Oh, what d'you do?' I ask, unprepared for the floodgates that open; it's all gigs, sets, clubs I've never heard of (of course I haven't; it feels like two hundred years since I last went clubbing) and how you 'get a feel for the mood of the night. You don't play crowd-pleasers,' he asserts. 'You're taking your audience on a musical journey . . .'

I'm really having to focus to maintain an expression of

rapt interest. His receding dark hair is quite possibly dyed, his face not unhandsome but definitely lived-in. He's wearing a leather thong with a tiny silver cross at his open-necked shirt, and I've spotted what looks like a very old, smudged tattoo of a snake wound around a naked woman on the back of his left hand. I'd rather be chatting to Esther, trying to get to know her, but there's no chance while he's in full flow. On and on he drones, barely pausing apart from to snatch a leaf from the salad bowl as Kim carries it past him. Of course I don't mind. It's only a bit of rocket. But it seemed a bit entitled, grabbing at it like that.

I catch James's eye and we exchange a look. We can do this now, condensing an entire conversation into just one glance. I'd forgotten it was even possible to communicate in this way. I used to try with Frank, giving him a look across a crowded room to say, *Take it easy, you might think you're hilarious and charming but you're hammered already, being a pain in the arse.* But he'd be too off his face to notice.

Now Miles is describing a night he used to do at some club near King's Cross. Clearly, I should have heard of it. 'But I had to stop,' he explains. 'Couldn't do it anymore.' He shudders visibly.

'Why?' Kim asks, joining us now.

'People would come up to me with requests.' I try to look suitably appalled, as if he'd said, *People would come up and slap me.*

'Isn't that allowed?' Kim asks, deadpan. 'Requests, I mean?'

'It's not weddings I do,' Miles retorts, then asks half-heartedly what I do for a living, as if my answer couldn't possibly be of interest to him.

'You make recipes?' he clarifies.

'That's basically it, yes. D'you cook at all?'

'No, we have things delivered from a great place, every-thing calorie-counted and perfectly balanced nutritionally...'

'You mean all the time?' I ask.

'Yeah, it makes it so easy,' Esther pipes up, arriving at his side and beaming up at him. I want to ask, *But don't you have treats? Don't you crave a big slice of pie sometimes?* But now, with an air of obligation, Miles has moved on to ask Kim what she does.

'I'm a maths teacher,' she tells him.

'*Riiiiiight*,' he drawls, glancing at the window as if considering throwing himself through it.

Still, the mood seems to be easing as everyone helps to carry things to the table. Everyone except Miles, that is. He just stands there sipping his red wine, observing all the activity going on around him as if watching a play. Obviously a former pop star is far too important to slice bread, fetch cutlery or carry a stack of plates. As we all take our seats, he virtually barges Kim out of the way with his skinny hip as he bags the place next to Esther. God, this guy is rude. Sitting next to Charlie, I catch him watching Miles across the table as if fascinated to see what he'll do next.

'Your house is lovely,' Esther offers, perhaps in an attempt to compensate for her boyfriend's behaviour.

'Oh, thank you,' I say in surprise.

'And your garden,' she adds. 'You're so lucky to have one.' I'm wondering now if, like Charlie, she is actually a little shy beneath the poised exterior.

'I love it,' I tell her. 'Charlie and I made it from scratch when we moved here.'

'I'd love to be able to grow things,' Esther adds.

'It's really not difficult,' I say.

She smirks. 'Tell that to my dad. He managed to murder a cactus—'

'Not deliberately,' James protests, in mock outrage.

'How's that even possible?' Esther asks, and she and Miles whisper and giggle about something (her dad's plant-killing tendencies perhaps?). She's just young, I remind myself. She's been thrown into a new situation and perhaps isn't quite as confident as she seems.

Perhaps she even feels odd about her dad seeing me – even though James has insisted that 'she's fine, of course she is. She has her own life. She's not really interested in anything I'm doing . . .' Even that struck me as a little odd. Cold, actually. Wasn't she pleased that he'd met someone and was happy? I've gathered that James is an extremely caring dad who'd do anything for her. The way he talks about all the stuff they've done together – the camping trips, the archaeological digs they went on when she was little – has made me love him even more. Charlie's dad barely did anything with him. One year he'd even gone missing for his birthday party. Charlie had tried to be brave when I'd explained that his dad had had a sudden 'work meeting' to go to – although God knows where Frank had really been.

The talk has turned to Esther's work which, admittedly, I still haven't quite managed to get my head around. While I know it's social-media-focused, I'm not sure how it *works*. 'We've been having a look at your Instagram, Esther,' admits Kim.

'Oh, have you?' she asks, looking pleased.

'Yes, it's all so gorgeous and dramatic . . .'

'I s'pose it's all right . . .' Esther says with a self-deprecating laugh. 'And it's gone a bit that way – a bit darker – since I moved in with Miles.' She casts him a fond glance. 'It's all antiques and deep, rich colours, isn't it, Miles? That's your taste, really.'

He nods, drains his glass and grabs at the bottle of

red wine. I'm not the booze police; I don't care how much he drinks. But I do notice that he pours himself a giant glass, like a teenager might in case they're not offered any more. A 'get it in while you can' approach.

'So, d'you advertise things?' Kim asks Esther. 'I hope you don't mind me sounding so dumb. It's just, I don't do social media at all. I don't want the kids seeing me on it – my pupils, I mean. So it's a world I know nothing about.'

'A lot of it's collabs,' she explains. 'Collaborations, I mean. Or paid partnerships with brands I'm working with. So they're kind of like of ads but less blatant than that. More of an endorsement . . .'

'Who are you working with?' I ask.

'Quite a few at the moment. Some clothing brands, fashion and accessories. My main one – the one I'm most excited about – is a jewellery brand called Bethani . . . D'you know it?'

'Erm, no, I don't think so . . .'

'This is one of their pieces.' Esther indicates the pendant – a spiral of gold encrusted with tiny gems – at her neck.

'That's gorgeous,' I enthuse.

'It's really special,' she adds, seemingly in her flow now. 'Every gemstone has a powerful effect on the wearer and balances the chakras.' She leans forward, offering me and Kim a closer look.

'Lovely!' we both coo.

'Like this tourmaline evokes calmness and wellbeing, and the moonstone creates feminine energies . . .' I catch Charlie watching Esther across the table as if transfixed by a particularly riveting scene in a film. 'And the amazing thing is,' she continues, 'every piece is personally blessed in a ceremony by a Balinese priest, in *actual* Bali, so it brings joy and good fortune and makes wishes come true.'

I'm trying to banish all traces of scepticism from my face. By now Kim, Esther and I have created a little sub-group while the guys – apart from Miles, who remains almost silent – have fallen into a chat about TV, with Lorenzo mentioning a documentary he knows Charlie will have seen, and soon they're discussing it in immense detail. Finally my son seems to have relaxed. This morning I was trying to convince myself that it didn't matter, that 'everyone meeting' was just a step James and I had to take, and if it didn't work out, then what was the problem? But of course, it'll be so much easier if everyone gets along.

There's a flurry of offers to help from James, Kim and Lorenzo as I start to clear away plates and the remains of the tarts, salads, colds meats and cheeses, all the different breads and olives and picky bits. Now it's dessert, and there are murmurs of appreciation as I bring over a clementine cake, a jug of cream, a cheesecake and plate of home-made Florentines. When that's all over I wonder if Esther is a little tipsy as she announces, loudly, 'I'd love to get a place like this, Miles. With a beautiful garden . . .'

'We will, babe,' he says quickly. 'We will.'

'But you don't like the countryside,' she reminds him with a frown. 'You always say you can't see the point of it, that the people there are so dull and narrow-minded . . .' *Charming!*

'We can do whatever you want,' he announces, cheeks florid now.

'D'you mean it?' she asks.

'Of course, my angel.'

'I'd love a pretty little cottage in the country,' she gushes, resting her head momentarily on his shoulder. His arm wraps around her, pulling her close. *Please don't start snogging here*, I will them. It feels weird enough for them to be discussing their future plans in front of all of us. But then, she's also been saying kind things about my home, so maybe she's trying her best. I'm certainly trying hard to like her. Even when she sits there, seemingly oblivious to the rest of us as Miles starts to nibble her ear and at one point *darts his tongue into it*, like a chameleon catching a fly – well, I'm reminding myself that they're young (at least, she is). And this is what young, loved-up people do.

James and I exchange another look that seems to say: *What can we do?* We can't prise them apart or throw cold water on them. We just have to get through this, being all jolly and polite until it's over. Then we'll never have to do this first-time-meeting thing ever again.

'We won't be in my poky little place forever,' Miles announces, cutting through my thoughts.

'Miles grew up in the country,' Esther offers.

'Would you really want to move back to it?' I ask. *Considering that we're all narrow-minded dullards?*

'Yeah, sure,' he says loudly, squeezing Esther's hand. 'When we have a baby—'

'Miles!' Esther splutters.

'A baby?' This comes from James, who's turned chalk pale and is staring at them, fork held in mid-air. All the chatter has stopped dead.

'He's just being silly, Dad,' Esther mutters.

'Are you?' James asks him, still looking stunned.

''Course I am,' Miles sniggers. 'Relax, James. Christ, you looked fucking scared there . . .'

James seems to exhale slowly before getting up from the table. For a moment, I wonder if he's going to march round, grab Miles by the shirt front and drag him out to the garden. Of course he's horrified by the thought of his daughter being impregnated by *anyone*, and especially this leaf-snatching, ear-tonguing 'DJ' who's at least double her age and is already ploughing into a second bottle of red. But James is also a thoughtful, considerate man who performs delicate operations on small animals. So of course he doesn't attack Miles.

He just walks out of the room, with all of us staring after him. Hearing the front door open, I throw Kim and Lorenzo a look of alarm and scoot out after him.

CHAPTER TWENTY

'James,' I start, 'what're you doing out here? Please come back in.'

'I just need a minute,' he mutters, pacing around and exhaling forcefully. I look at him, wondering what possessed me now to suggest this lunch. We should have just carried on in our own, wonderful little world, and never attempted to thrust our two very different families together.

A terrible thought strikes me: perhaps we're not meant for each other after all.

No, no, I tell myself. Don't over-react. This has happened because of Miles, who's nothing to *do* with James. It's not even Esther's fault really.

'It's going to seem weird, us standing out here in the cold,' I remark.

James grimaces. 'Sorry. I just had to get out of there for a minute before I said something I regretted.'

I rub at my goose-bumpy upper arms. It's a chilly late October afternoon, and there's a scattering of golden leaves on the lawn. 'I can see why you're upset,' I offer, touching his arm. But they're not actually having a baby, are they? He's just trying to wind you up. Can't you see that?'

He nods, throwing a quick glance towards my house. 'I guess so. But she's only twenty, and if they're even *thinking* of—'

'He's just an idiot,' I cut in. 'Can't you talk to her about this later?'

He pushes back his hair distractedly. 'I can't, can I? She's an adult. She can make her own decisions. It's nothing to do with me . . .'

I take hold of his hand and squeeze it. 'Maybe she'll get sick of him and meet someone her own age.'

'That's what I'm praying for,' he mutters.

I'm at a loss as to what else to suggest. It makes my worries about Charlie being shy and never having had a girlfriend seem pretty trivial in comparison. I like to think I'm broad-minded, but how would I feel if *he* fell for somebody *my* age?

'There's not an awful lot else you can do right now,' I add.

James smiles wryly. 'I could get him into the surgery and neuter him.'

I splutter. 'He's an adult man, not a dachshund—'

'A very, very *old* adult man . . .'

I give his arm a gentle tug. 'C'mon, let's go back in.'

'I'm sorry,' he mutters.

'It's not your fault.'

'I should've said he couldn't come—'

'Sounds like you didn't have an awful lot of choice,' I suggest as we head back inside and through to the kitchen where Esther, Miles and Charlie seem to have found themselves sitting together at the table. Kim and Lorenzo have launched themselves into a whirl of activity at the sink, washing up (even though I have a dishwasher), drying dishes and putting things away. Cupboards are opening and closing, the sink tap is gushing and the coffee percolator is sputtering away.

As I reach for mugs on the shelf I catch Esther asking, 'So, what're you into, Charlie?'

'Uh, science mainly,' he replies, sounding surprised that she's taking an interest. 'Astronomy. Stuff like that.'

'I'm into that too,' she says.

'Are you?'

'Yeah. I read about it all the time.'

'Oh!'

'I'm Taurus,' she adds. 'What sign are you?'

Is she teasing him or is it a genuine mistake? I really must *try* to like her, I remind myself, and give her the benefit of the doubt.

'Erm, I meant astronomy, not astrology,' Charlie says apologetically, as if he made the mistake.

'Oh, sorry,' Esther says with a throaty laugh. 'I always get them mixed up. So it's about the Milky Way and the galaxy, all that?'

'He works in a newsagent's,' Lorenzo calls out with a grin. 'Spends his Saturdays selling chocolate, don't you, Charlie?'

'Most of it out of date,' he says, smiling now.

Esther seems intrigued by Charlie, but I'm still not sure if her interest is genuine. 'Can I ask you something, Charlie?' she starts.

'Sure,' he replies.

'Where does the moon go in the daytime? I've always wondered that . . .'

'Me too,' Miles announces, face set in rapt attention.

I try to focus on getting all the coffee things together as Charlie starts to explain how it all works. But I'm still wondering if this is all perfectly innocent, and they're just being friendly, or it's some kind of cruel joke: *Get the boffy kid to explain how the universe works while we pretend to be interested, haha!* James, Lorenzo and Kim are all chatting between themselves now. Maybe I'm being overprotective; a ridiculous mother prowling on the periphery, when her son is perfectly capable of handling himself.

'You know such a lot,' Miles announces, pulling up his chair to be closer to him. 'You've got, like, an *encyclopaedic* brain.'

'I don't really.' Charlie reddens and shrugs.

'Oh, you *doooo*,' Miles crows, definitely piss-taking now. 'So, what else d'you do when you're not mapping the stars?'

'Um, I like reading and stuff,' he murmurs, fiddling with an unused fork on the table.

'Would you like a coffee, Miles?' I chip in.

'No thanks, I'm fine with wine.'

'Esther? Charlie?'

'No thanks,' they say in unison, unaware that I'm trying – ineffectually – to break up their little clique. In fact, short of producing a board game and demanding that everyone plays, I'm at a loss as to what to do.

'D'you ever miss London?' Esther is asking Charlie now. We've already mentioned that we lived there until he was eight.

'No,' he replies. 'Not really.'

'Not much to do out here, though, is there?' Miles remarks. 'D'you just sit in your room with your books? Is that *it*?'

I shoot a look over at James, urging him – perhaps unreasonably – to step in and do something, to stop his daughter's idiot boyfriend from grilling my son. But he's still locked in conversation with Kim and Lorenzo. They all liked each other instantly, right from when they first met.

'A lot of the time, I s'pose,' Charlie says quietly.

'No wonder he's a genius!' Miles exclaims.

'He probably went to a much better school than mine,' Esther offers.

'Don't put yourself down, babe.' Miles pats her leg.

'I'm not, I'm just saying—'

'It's not the be-all and end-all, is it?' he adds. 'Books, science, passing exams . . .'

'No, it's not,' Charlie mutters, looking distinctly unsettled now. Or maybe that's just me, projecting my discomfort onto him?

His dad always said I was too protective, due to his shyness. 'You can't keep him swaddled forever,' Frank announced, which stung because I didn't do that. Drama club, swimming, judo and music lessons; I took him to everything going in the hope that, once I'd left the building, he'd make friends.

'Spending all day with your head in a book isn't for everyone,' Miles reiterates now, to no one in particular.

'He didn't say it was,' I remark, aware of Charlie's fierce glare, just for standing up for him. 'He just said—'

'Mum!' he barks, eyes wide.

'Erm, anyone like more cake?' I call out, feeling helpless.

No one wants cake and Charlie certainly doesn't want me wading in, protecting him like he's a little kid. Even so, I cut the remains of the sponge into thin slices and do the rounds with it again like a demented waitress. 'I think it's best to let people find their own way in life,' Miles slurs sanctimoniously.

'Me too,' Esther agrees with a nod.

139

'Like, Esther went to a school where everyone could please themselves and only learnt stuff when they wanted to . . .' Miles's lips are wine-stained, his voice slurred. 'Is your school like that?' he asks my son.

'Can we leave this please, Miles?' I chirp, my heart thumping.

'Um, it's just a regular school,' Charlie replies.

'What I mean,' Miles continues, in full flow now, 'is that not everyone wants to spend their young life swotting when they should be out having fun—'

'I think we've already established that,' I blurt out, aware that James, Kim and Lorenzo have turned, startled, to face us.

'It's not the only route to a happy and fulfilled life,' Miles barges on, looking at Kim now. 'Sorry, I'm sure you're a *very* good maths teacher . . .'

'I *am* actually,' she mutters, dumping her coffee cup on the worktop and reaching for her unfinished wine.

'I didn't sit any GCSEs,' Miles gloats.

'Maybe they weren't invented then,' James mutters.

'I heard that, Dad,' Esther snaps.

'My point is,' Miles goes on, 'I didn't sit any exams, not a single one, even though I could've passed them all – because I followed my passion. If I *had* gone down the expected, traditional route, then I'd have become a teacher or a vet or . . .' His gaze skims past me. 'What d'you do again, Roberto?'

'*Lorenzo*,' I correct him.

'I'm a youth project coordinator,' Lorenzo replies steadily. 'I work with young people in inner-city areas.'

'Well, anyway,' Miles blusters, 'I'd have missed out on all those amazing opportunities—'

'Like being on Saturday morning kids' TV in 1989?' James cuts in.

140

'Dad!' Esther exclaims. 'What're you on about?'

Miles's florid face breaks into a grin. 'I do believe you've been googling me, James!'

'I just happened to see it,' James mutters.

'What did you find?' Miles asks, crooking a brow.

'Just you being interviewed,' James replies quickly, clearly wishing he hadn't brought this up.

'So, what was I like?' Miles enquires, feigning innocence.

'Miles, can we drop this please?' I say in an over-bright voice. 'It's not really important, is it?'

'You had blond hair,' James says. 'Spiky on top, long at the back. A mullet, I s'pose you'd call it . . .'

'Dad!' Esther exclaims. 'Why are you *humiliating* Miles?'

'I'm not,' James protests.

'He's not,' I bark, before I can stop myself.

'Oh my God,' Kim mutters, shielding her eyes with a hand. Charlie, looking mortified, is studying his beer glass intensely.

'Anyone like more coffee?' I trill, wondering now what possessed me to do this thing; to have this stupid lunch, throwing everyone together and expecting it to go swimmingly.

What a terrible, terrible mistake.

Miles is peering, squiffily, at James. 'Maybe I should be flattered that you've taken such an interest in my past . . .'

'I'm not getting into this,' James replies, looking thunderous. A rogue thought hits me: *Please, James, get these people out of my house.* I love my cosy cottage that was a wreck when we moved in, and took years of painstaking work to make it the home it is now. It's a place of love and warmth and safety. And now a washed-up DJ is strutting about, jeering at James while everyone watches, stunned, and Esther jumps up from her seat.

'Is this why you brought Miles here?' she barks at her father. 'To make fun of him in front of everyone?'

'They don't bother me, babe,' her boyfriend announces, grabbing at the table edge for support.

'I didn't bring him,' James insists. 'He just jumped in the car—'

'You never liked him, did you?' she announces, hazel eyes brimming with tears as she turns to me. 'Sorry, Lauren. It's been lovely meeting you but we're going now. Miles,' she commands, 'call us a taxi to the station.' She grabs her jacket from the hook at the door and pulls it on.

Charlie looks at me open-mouthed. I exhale and shrug. What can I say?

'Don't be ridiculous,' James says firmly.

No, it's fine, let them go . . .

'Miles,' I start, 'it's Sunday. There are hardly any trains from—'

'We'll wait for one, then,' he announces, glaring round at all of us. There's a moment of confusion as he pulls his phone from his pocket, pushes back his thinning, suspiciously dark hair and looks at me. 'Um, so where are we again?'

CHAPTER TWENTY-ONE

JAMES

It didn't help that I managed to dissuade Miles from calling a taxi, herded everyone into my car and drove us all back to London instead.

What a jolly drive that was, in grim near-silence, a cloud of disdain filling the car that wouldn't dissipate, even when I turned on the radio and opened a window to let in a blast of chilly October air. Just two sentences were spoken during the entire journey, both by Esther: 'Can you turn the radio down?' and 'I'm cold.' Miles just sat there, smug and mute with earphones in, having bagged the passenger seat again.

As a young child, I'd been obsessed with ejector seats. In films and cartoons, people (usually baddies) were propelled out of vehicles with pleasing regularity. James Bond, Batman, Scooby-Doo, all my favourites back then; you wouldn't have long to wait before some troublesome individual would be pinged into oblivion via the jab of a button. But my car doesn't have a button. At least, not one that does that. And Miles isn't a cartoon baddie but my daughter's boyfriend who's *planning to get her pregnant*, for crying out loud.

Of even more immediate concern was the fact that I'd wrecked Lauren's lunch. Not single-handedly, obviously – Miles had kicked things off, and Esther had behaved pretty badly – but I should've known better than to react in that way. There'd I'd been this morning, driving out to Hertfordshire with a heart full of hope, even with Miles tapping irritably on the dashboard, thinking we could somehow have a perfectly nice time like normal people.

I'd really hoped that Esther would show her best side, and that she and Lauren would get along. Not to be best buddies – that had seemed like too much to wish for – but to be relaxed with each other and find some common ground. After all, they're both creative and drawn to beautiful things – Esther with her social media, Lauren with her photography.

I can't see that ever happening now and, for the first time since we met, I wonder how it's going to pan out with Lauren and me. Whatever must she think of my daughter now? Esther didn't use to be like that, I want to tell her: causing a scene and demanding to go home. Before her TV fame – and certainly before Miles – she was a lovely, smart and sunny girl who people had always been drawn to. Outgoing and chatty, she'd never been one to shy away in a corner. Yet she'd also been inclusive with others, and never unkind. I'd have honestly said she didn't have a mean bone in her body.

And now I'm not so sure.

Had she really wanted to know where the moon went during the day? Or had she been quizzing Charlie for her own amusement? As I really couldn't tell, it had seemed more sensible to chat away to Kim and Lorenzo rather than wading in. And then, when I had stuck my oar in, about Miles being on Saturday morning kids' TV; well, that had been the end of it.

'I'm so sorry,' I'd muttered to Lauren as we'd left.

'It's fine, it's fine,' she'd muttered quickly, virtually shooing us out. She looked stressed and upset and had closed the front door before we'd even pulled away.

What a shitshow. We should never have forced everyone to meet, I decide now, back home alone on this gloomy Sunday evening, having dropped off Esther and Miles in near-silence. We should have kept our family lives firmly locked away in two separate boxes and never flung them together like that.

At least we tried. We had to at least once; Lauren was right about that. I try to occupy myself by attempting to compose various messages to her, deleting them, then switching to taking the cafetière to pieces and thoroughly cleaning each component.

It won't screw back together properly. How is it possible that I'm capable of removing a trapped chicken bone from a Dobermann's large intestine, yet I can't fit the steel disc and little screw-on bit back onto the plunger? Am I an idiot? Yes, according to my daughter. I can't even keep a cactus alive. In irritation I dump the cafetière pieces into the sink and try again to compose messages to Lauren, veering from serious and apologetic to attempting to make light and even a joke out of it. But nothing feels right and, again, I delete them.

No word from her so far.

Really sorry about today, I fire off quickly.

Still nothing.

Of course that wasn't enough. Things can come across abruptly in messages and that was definitely abrupt.

I type: *I shouldn't have said that thing to Miles. He was being a prick but I shouldn't have reacted. It's all my fault.* Did that have a hint of martyrdom about it? Too late, I've sent it now. That's the thing with messages; you can't grab them back. The whole messaging thing, in the way Lauren and I do it, is new to me anyway, although I have to say I soon got the hang of it; of being affectionate and telling her how much I'd loved our weekend together, how much I was missing her, all that. My ex, Polly, and I rarely texted, and whenever she did, her style was somewhat to the point: *Film tonight? Odeon 7.30.* And that would be that. There were none of the 'x's that Lauren and I scatter liberally on our messages to each other.

Or rather, we did.

Sod it, I'm just going to call her. We need to talk this out. But it just rings out and now, at 10.27 p.m., I'm figuring that Kim and Lorenzo, who were still at Lauren's when we left (looking shocked and appalled, obviously) are probably still there now. They'll be hanging out, finishing the wine and picking at French cheeses in Lauren's homely kitchen amidst the jugs of garden flowers, the mismatched china, the old kitchen chairs gleaned from charity shops: that lovely relaxed vibe she's created, like Camille's beachside restaurant in Corsica.

As I pour myself a large glass of wine, I picture them agreeing what a messed-up family we are; that Esther is spoiled and Miles is a nightmare. And Lauren will wonder what on earth she was thinking, getting involved with me.

It was just one of those holiday things, she'll decide. Pity it didn't translate into real life.

Feeling simultaneously furious with *and* sorry for myself, I down my wine quickly in a few big gulps. Then, instead of pouring another – which I want very much – I force myself upstairs to bed. Because, even if I fucked things up today, I *am* a good vet. And I'm neutering Annie Lancaster's ferret at 8.30 a.m.

CHAPTER TWENTY-TWO

LAUREN

Charlie sits up with Kim, Lorenzo and me late into the night. It's good to see him hanging out with us, more relaxed now than he was at lunch. While he agrees that Miles 'seemed a bit weird', that's all he seems to want to say on the subject.

'What did you think of Esther?' Lorenzo asks.

'She's all right,' Charlie replies noncommittally.

'Did you mind her grilling you about where the moon goes and all that?'

'She wasn't *grilling* me,' he says with a shrug. 'She only asked.' Later, when he's mooched off to his room, the three of us carry on tucking into the cheeses and yet more wine, around the table where mulletgate happened.

'I can't understand what she sees in him,' Kim marvels, meaning Esther and Miles of course.

'Neither can I,' I say. 'But there must be something, mustn't there? I mean, she's in love with the guy. You can see that . . .'

'James must hate it,' she adds. 'Their situation, I mean.'

She turns to Lorenzo. 'How would you feel if one of our girls had a boyfriend like that?'

'D'you even need to ask?' He looks aghast.

'Anyway,' I add, 'so much for our relaxed, getting-to-know-each-other lunch. What an idiot I am.'

'Why d'you say that?' Lorenzo exclaims, frowning.

'It wasn't your fault,' Kim insists.

'But it was my idea to do it.' I rub at my face and check my phone to see messages there.

'James?' Kim asks, and I nod. 'Are you going to reply?'

'I will tomorrow,' I say, realising there's a missed call too. My phone's on silent and it's too late to call back now.

'Don't let this spoil things between you,' she says firmly, squeezing my arm. 'He's lovely. And you're so happy. It'd be awful if it wasn't the same after this.'

'It just feels a bit weird now,' I murmur.

'It was just unfortunate,' Lorenzo offers, 'that Miles came at all, and then was such a dickhead and James rose to it. Put it out of your mind.'

'I'll try,' I say. Put like that, it doesn't seem like such a big deal; that someone who hadn't even been invited had ended up sabotaging the thing. 'James was already upset about Miles going on about babies,' Kim remarks.

'Yeah.' Lorenzo cuts off a sliver of Brie. 'I can't blame him, to be honest . . .'

'Maybe things'll be better with Esther next time you meet,' Kim offers. 'When her boyfriend's not around.'

'Yeah, maybe,' I say, feeling marginally better now, and grateful that my friends weren't in a hurry to leave tonight. 'Y'know, I didn't expect me and Esther – or Charlie and Esther – to become instant friends,' I add. 'I mean, I didn't imagine they'd be skipping off down the garden together.'

Kim smiles. 'They might surprise you.'

'I very much doubt it,' I say, realising that we've avoided discussing what we really thought about Esther today. I suspect Kim and Lorenzo haven't wanted to voice their true feelings, and I've just wanted to push mine away.

What do I think really? I didn't warm to her especially. Although I suspect I'm oversensitive, I'm pretty sure she was teasing Charlie, albeit gently – and there was no need to leap up and demand to leave. *But she's James's daughter*, I remind myself, after Kim and Lorenzo have gone home. I so wanted to like her – and for her to like me – because she's part of who he is. A huge part, obviously. We can't have an awkward scenario every time our paths cross.

I go to bed, trying to figure out how to reply to James's messages, settling on a short: *Don't worry, we'll talk soon*. Obviously that signals the opposite: *DO worry! Worry an awful lot for bringing that prat to my house!* But it's all I can come up with right now.

There's no message from him when I wake up. Instead of obsessively checking my phone, I throw myself into testing the recipes I'd lined up for today. I bake batches of herby crackers and courgette patties and whip up a creamy cheese dip, and photograph them in a casual set-up on the kitchen table with milky sunshine streaming in. I carry on working away, keeping busy, deciding that I won't let one fuck-up of a lunch spoil things between James and me. I know he'll have been busy at work but we often message or call when he manages to grab a quick break. Today there's been nothing. I'm hoping that he's not the one feeling weird about us.

I don't want him to feel bad. It's not his fault that I'd spent hours getting everything ready, only to have our lunch wrecked by some jerk with dyed brown hair who reckons he's forty-five (and the rest!). And I'm reconciled to the fact that seeing a man who has a family of his own is bound to throw up a few challenges. I want to be with James. I love him and that's that. The last person I dated – three years ago now – was a man I'd got chatting to on the train. He was on his way to visit his mother and we'd fallen into conversation as our train had pulled out from St Pancras.

George was attractive and pleasant and around my age, and when he'd asked if I'd like to meet up for a drink I'd thought, why not? While it soon became clear that we didn't have masses in common, I'd been feeling a bit lonely and tried to convince myself that we were having fun over the course of a handful of dates. He did ramble on rather a lot about his DIY projects, and wasn't remotely curious about my job. But then, my work is pretty niche, I told myself. Why would he be interested in recipes?

Then one time in bed together, he'd literally just rolled off me – charming! – when he started to tell me that some idiot electrician had put the wrong kind of fuse in his oven. 'I think that's why it won't work,' he explained. 'I've tried everything else I can think of.' I realised he must have been thinking about his oven – 'I wonder if it's the fuse?' – the whole time we were having sex.

While I can't claim to be able to read James's mind, I'm hazarding a guess that domestic appliances are never on his mind whenever we're together – in bed or anywhere else.

So what does it matter that our little gathering didn't work out as we'd hoped? Oven-fuse-George didn't have children, an ex-wife or seemingly any baggage at all. I know where I'd rather be, and maybe it's just going to take a little time for me and Esther to get to know each other.

Even if we don't, it's really all about James and me. So I fire off another message: *Hey, I know you're probably feeling a bit crap and I wanted to say please don't. It wasn't your fault. And it doesn't matter. We can talk about it but everything's okay as long as you are. I love you xx.*

A minute later he messages back: *I love you too. So glad you're okay. Will call soon as I've finished work xx.*

I smile, then reply: *Okay, call me then. And remember we're old. We are ancient people! We have families and lives and sometimes things are going to get a little bit complicated.*

CHAPTER TWENTY-THREE

JAMES

Our messages and calls have reassured me that Lauren and I are fine after that car crash of a Sunday afternoon. Bloody Miles. I *must* stop fixating on him. As Lauren suggested, I need to step back and let his thing with Esther burn itself out. 'It's bound to,' she said. 'She's a smart young woman. She'll see what an idiot he is and meet someone her own age eventually.'

I can only hope she's right. Meanwhile, I'm feeling a whole lot better on this chilly Tuesday morning as I vaccinate a Dutch rabbit named Guinness, administer an injection of apomorphine to a spaniel who'd gnawed his way into a drum of cocoa powder and devoured its contents, and see Tony Lomax again with his ageing collie, Bob. The sensitive matter of what to do when Bob passes away still seems to be a major concern.

'The thing is,' Tony says, 'those pet cremation places say it's just *your* dog they cremate on its own. And you get the ashes to keep. But how d'you know? I mean, who's to say it's just your dog in that little pot? It's not like you can go there and make sure they do it properly, can you?'

'Tony, we deal with these people quite a lot. They're reputable and very respectful,' I try to reassure him. 'We can help and advise you when—'

'And I live in a flat,' he cuts in, 'with a shared garden. I can't go burying Bob out there. The neighbours wouldn't like it.'

'Bob's as healthy as a dog of half his age,' I tell him.

'I've got to face facts and be prepared,' Tony insists.

'Yes, I know that. But I promise you won't be left on your own to deal with this when it happens. You can ring me anytime or just pop in.'

In fact, today Tony showed up without an appointment (we always manage to squeeze him in) saying Bob was squinting, and could I check his eyes again? 'There's nothing wrong with his vision as far as I can tell,' I explained, having examined him.

'He's just not quite himself.'

As is often the case, I suspect Tony just wanted a chat, some company and reassurance. I give him a worming tablet for Bob, just so he feels something's been done. We have a few Tony Lomax types who are here far more often than necessary – but *the* Tony Lomax is our most regular, and however we try to help, it never feels like quite enough.

I try to push all that out of my mind as, after a quick chat with Lauren (we're now able to laugh about mullet-gate) I cycle the couple of miles, mainly through residential streets, to a basement cocktail bar named Foraged. It's a cosy and intimate little place, all bare brickwork and arched roofs, with dim lighting and candles flickering in the booths. But I'm not here for cocktails. Foraged is co-owned by Rhona, my ex-wife, and her longtime boyfriend, Luc, and I'm here to talk about Esther.

Apparently – even though my daughter and I haven't

153

been in touch directly – I totally overstepped the mark on Sunday at Lauren's. So Rhona suggested I drop by for a chat.

'What are you drinking, James?' booms Luc across the room.

'Nothing for me thanks, Luc.'

'Oh, come on. We've got a couple of new ones for you to try.' He has biceps like grapefruits and can't seem to be able to communicate without SHOUTING. I was hoping Rhona and I would be able to chat on our own, tucked away in a corner, but it looks like there's no chance of that.

'Honestly,' I reply. 'I'm only here for—'

'How about a London Mule?' he bellows. 'Not too sweet, a hint of rhubarb I found growing over by Wormwood Scrubs. Or a Piston Slinger? That's lime, bitters, foraged sloes . . .'

'I'm on my bike, Luc,' I remind him.

'Just leave it here,' Rhona commands. 'Get a cab home. Live a little!' Laughing, she catches Luc's eye, and I get the subtext: *He's so uptight. Can you imagine what it was like being married to this guy?*

In fact, it's not that I'm being particularly virtuous. But I know it's going to be a tricky conversation and that I need to keep a grip on my faculties.

'Honestly, James,' Rhona starts when Luc has had the goodwill to leave us alone. 'I can't believe you ridiculed Miles's haircut when he was a teenager. D'you remember what *your* hair was like in 1989?'

'That's not the point, is it?'

'It's the year we met,' she reminds me. 'Remember you had a fluffy quiff you'd dyed blond yourself and it looked like a little yellow pom-pom?'

'You must be thinking of someone else.'

'No, I have the pictures,' she says with a sly grin. 'Remember when that flatmate of yours – the one who used to eat spaghetti with Marmite – tried to dye it brown for you and it went *carrot*?'

'This is great,' I remark, 'getting together to do a full inventory of my terrible hairstyles. But is that why you asked me to come over?'

She chuckles and smooths back her sleek dark bob. Rhona was stylish, even back in the decade that style forgot. Jeans and a crisp white shirt were her uniform back then, with hair worn in a boyish crop until fairly recently. Now Luc has reappeared and places a Bloody Mary, Rhona's preferred tipple, in front of her. 'Thank you, darling.' It has some kind of woody herb sticking out of it, which he lights with an oversized match. They like this here, the decorating of drinks with sprigs of things that they then set fire to.

'I just wanted to know why you felt you had to attack Miles like that,' she explains.

'I didn't *attack* him. I might've wanted to but—'

'That's the way Esther sees it,' Rhona cuts in.

'So why hasn't she talked to me about it instead of filing her grievance through you?'

'We were just talking,' Rhona says defensively. 'It happened to come up.' She picks up her drink and sucks hard on the straw.

'You don't like him either,' I remind her. Of course we've discussed Miles numerous times. I thought we were allies in this.

'You know I'm not crazy about him,' she says, 'but they seem to have worked through their difficulties—'

'Their difficulties? You mean him shagging someone else?'

'—And I have to admire them for that,' Rhona

continues, giving me a stern look. 'Don't you think that's admirable? And they are quite sweet together . . .'

'What does that mean? That he can't sit near her without twiddling with her hair?'

'That's *not* what I mean,' she snaps.

'Or that he got some friend to make her that leotard thing covered in Quality Street wrappers—'

'It wasn't a leotard, it was a basque . . .'

'. . . which was obviously highly flammable, yet he sat her in front of a load of church candles to take her photo in it—'

'The thing is,' Rhona cuts in sharply, 'he's her partner and we have to accept and respect that, like it or not.' Luc reappears and places a highball glass containing a curious pastel pink liquid in front of me.

'Non-alcoholic,' he booms, as if to make a point. *For the guy who needs to live a little!*

'Thanks, Luc,' I say as he plonks his gigantic frame in the booth with us, next to me.

'Luc foraged the meadowsweet for that,' Rhona says, jabbing a manicured nail towards my drink.

'Really?' I ask, keen to get back to the matter in hand, so I can go home, call Esther and try to smooth things over with her. I no longer care who was in the wrong. I just want to get along with my daughter.

'Yeah, there's a bit of marshland by the River Lea where it grows like crazy,' Luc enthuses. 'I could have filled a juggernaut with the stuff. Isn't that amazing, in a city like London, that places like that exist?'

'It really is,' I reply. It's not that I dislike Luc. It's just that everything about him is so *big*: the booming voice, the muscular arms straining at the sleeves of his T-shirt and the hair that sits in a silvery swoosh like a giant metallic meringue. Mercifully, one of their young bartenders has arrived, busying away behind the bar, and is now waving over to Luc, wanting his opinion on some new concoction. He jumps up and bounces over.

After another fortifying swig of her drink, Rhona leans towards me across the table. 'Look, James, it's not just the mullet thing she's concerned about.'

'Oh. What else then?'

Her mouth twists. 'She's really happy for you, meeting Lauren, but she's worried you've jumped headfirst into it.'

'What?'

She pulls a pained expression. 'I'm just saying what she thinks.'

'But . . .' I'm struggling to digest this. 'I don't know what that means. We're just seeing each other. I'm not jumping into anything. I'm just having a nice time.' It's more than that. Way more. But I'm not even going to start to try and explain it.

'She says you seem different,' Rhona adds.

'In what way?' I ask, genuinely baffled.

'Well, more reactive for a start.'

'More *reactive*?'

'Yeah, like on Sunday, when you went for Miles—'

'Bloody hell, I didn't attack him. I didn't *go for* him. I just objected when he started ranting on that "not everybody needs to be academic, Charlie. Not everyone has to be huddled over their books . . ."'

'Well, they don't,' Rhona says firmly. 'That is actually true—'

'So you're on his side now?'

'I'm just saying not everyone's cut out to swot their way through five years of vet school . . .'

'You swotted too!' I remind her.

'I didn't work nearly as hard as you, though.' How

crazy is this, that we're playing a 'who was the swottiest' game when we have a combined age of 104? And the only reason she didn't have to slog away as hard as me is that she's so darned smart, she breezed through it.

After graduating, Rhona teamed up with a friend, managed to find a backer and opened a tapas-style café that became a great success. They sold it at a vast profit, which enabled her to open Foraged with Luc. She is a powerhouse and has done very well for herself. I admire her for it, and mostly we get along fine. But at times like this it strikes me how she's carved out the part of the fun, spontaneous, free-spirited one for herself – swigger of Bloody Marys on a Monday night, the one who was adamant about letting Esther choose her own school without any real discussion at all. Whereas I seem to have been cast as the 'sensible' parent, the worrier about stuff like exams and prospects – a role that's as appealing as being the arse end of a pantomime horse.

'Not everyone's like you, James,' Rhona reiterates. 'Not everyone has their career path mapped out at thirteen and wants to spend their days jet-blasting a Jack Russell's anal glad.'

I stare at her. 'You don't jet-blast a dog's anal gland. I'm not Dyno-Rod. You gently squeeze it.'

As Rhona shudders, I pick up the pink drink and sip it. Despite its pastel hue that might suggest a flavour similar to strawberry ice cream, its taste is subtle – like a glass of stale water that's been sitting on the bedside table for a week. Miraculously, the instant Rhona's glass is emptied Luc reappears with another Bloody Mary for her. 'How's it going, guys?' he shouts, looming over us.

'Great,' I reply.

He clamps a meaty hand on my shoulder. 'You worry too much about Esther and Miles. It'll all turn out fine.'

Of course Luc, never having had kids of his own, knows all about the gut-wrenching worry they can trigger.

'Yeah, I'm sure it will,' I mutter. *I know this is your bar, Luc, but please go away.*

He bobs down to crouch beside me, in the way that a teacher might when addressing a primary school child. 'The thing is, she's a great girl.'

'Yes, of course she is,' I say tightly.

'She's amazing, so talented,' he adds, which is starting to rile me – not because I'm averse to anyone bigging up my daughter but because he's implying that I don't 'get' my own child. Okay, so I *wasn't* delighted when Esther was set on going to Willow Vale: a 'democratic school', as they say in the marketing brochure, 'because everyone has a voice', and where pretty much everything – even turning up – is optional.

'So, when they do go to lessons, they're really moti-vated,' Rhona explained, totally sold on the idea. But what about all the times they didn't go? What would they be doing then? 'Playing!' she announced. 'What's more important than play, James?'

'Fine,' I said; of course it was important. I wasn't going to disagree with that. But I still couldn't get my head around the idea of the kids doing whatever they liked all day long, because I know I'd have arsed around with my mates, climbing trees, listening to music, having the odd sly beer and a smoke and showing up for a lesson some-thing like once a fortnight. That's just human nature, surely? The only reason I finally applied myself was because I knew I'd need good grades to get into vet school.

So here we are again, with totally different views (what does she mean, that Esther and Miles are *quite sweet together*?) and no way, really, of compromising. I get up and pull on my jacket. 'Well, I'd better head back,' I start.

'I don't want you to feel got at,' Rhona says, frowning now.

'I don't. It's fine—'

'How are things with Lauren?' she asks.

What, the woman I've 'jumped in headfirst with'?

'Things are great,' I say tightly.

'So you're having a nice time, the two of you?' she asks, clearly fishing for details.

'I am. Yeah.'

'Good for you.' She chuckles indulgently. 'There we all were, worried about you having a completely crappy time in Corsica all on your own . . .'

'Well, I was okay,' I say, blandly, keen to leave now.

'Seems like it,' Luc offers with a barking laugh.

Now Rhona turns serious. 'Look, James, I know Miles can be a pain in the arse. But Esther loves him.' As if it's as simple as that. But then, I suppose it is – because our daughter is a grown woman now. We can't choose who she loves. As it seems we can no longer influence her in any way, perhaps Rhona actually handles things better than I do. She's realistic, I suppose. And maybe she's right and I *do* worry about Esther too much. I mean, if Esther chooses to have a baby with Miles, then I guess I'll have to accept that too.

This is why my working life is so much easier and less heartbreaking than my family life. Because no matter how stressful or absolutely tragic a working day can be – having to put an animal to sleep, and consoling the devastated owner – at least with veterinary work, you have some kind of control over how things turn out. Not always, admittedly. But you do your best. You make a diagnosis, and you know from your training what treatments are possible and advisable. You weigh up any risks, and estimate the costs, recovery time and long-term effect on the animal, and you discuss all of this with the owner.

Effective communication is a big part of what we do. (Believe it or not, at work I am known as a good communicator.) At work I generally know the best course of action to take. And if I'm unable to make things better or save an animal, then at least I know I've tried every option, and that nothing else could be done.

With young adult offspring there's no taking the best course of action. It's more that you try to persuade and cajole them; you might even nag or beg them, and end up making a show of yourself at your girlfriend's special lunch. But ultimately, your powers are limited and mostly you have to just step away and watch helplessly from the sidelines. And what's all this about Esther being concerned about me and Lauren? It can't really be that – about me jumping in too fast. It must be bothering her somehow, that I'm seeing someone. I can't for the life of me figure out why.

Rhona reaches for her Bloody Mary. 'Sure you don't want to stay for a proper drink?'

'I'm okay, honestly,' I say.

'Well, great to see you, man.' Luc slaps a shovel-sized hand against my back. 'You look a bit tired, though. You've been working too hard, not making enough time for this new girlfriend of yours . . .' He waggles a brow and they both laugh.

'You should take some time off,' Rhona advises. 'Do some fun stuff . . .' She turns to Luc. 'Weren't you complaining that no one will ever go foraging with you?'

'Yeah, we could go together, James,' Luc enthuses. 'There are so many incredible places around here.'

'Sounds great,' I reply, making my escape before I accidentally admit that I'd rather eat my own hair.

CHAPTER TWENTY-FOUR

LAUREN

I'm aware that things have happened pretty fast with James and me. Although we don't see each other every day – it's still mainly weekends – I went on holiday as a single woman and came home madly in love.

But actually, with Frank, it was faster. Of course we had happy times together. Full of life and mad ideas, he was my first love. We met at a party thrown by the magazine I was working on and I was bowled over when he came over to chat. From that night we were fully ensconced in each other's lives. I moved in with him after just a few months and we grew together, side by side, through our mid-to-late twenties. By the time we'd hit our thirties we very much wanted a baby. It took a while, but when I'd just turned thirty-three our beautiful Charlie was born.

However, pretty much the whole time there was also an awful lot of drama. Not just the major stuff, like when we took Charlie to a festival and Frank went off on his own, 'just for a wander'. This 'wander' lasted for twenty-four hours and had me frantically checking the medical tents and reporting him missing to the police. He'd bowled up finally, obviously wrecked and wearing a mohair jumper I'd never seen before that looked like it had been run over by a tractor. He then crawled into our tent and slept for an entire day. For Charlie's sake, I had to pretend that everything was okay.

For Charlie's sake. I could have applied that phrase to so much that went on during those years. It was as if our marriage was a shabby house requiring superficial fixes – that special paint that miraculously covers damp patches – to get it ready for viewing. There was the time, at Kim's fortieth, when he'd arrived late for her party, already smashed, and insisted on pounding the venue's piano very badly until, having taken a poorly aimed swing at Lorenzo, he was packed off home. They were among the big ones but there were numerous mini-dramas too; forgotten photography equipment left in various locations, emergency dashes to collect cameras, tripods and lights from all over London and beyond.

For those first few weeks with James I couldn't quite put my finger on what was so different about being with him. How absolutely unlike my marriage it felt, and how light it made me feel – rather than weighed down with worry. Of course the difference is, there's no pretending or glossing over things. I'm not performing a perpetual cover-up job. The fact that Esther and her boyfriend caused a bit of a scene at my house is all forgotten now and, as I've told James several times, that wasn't his fault.

He is unfailingly thoughtful and kind, and when he says he's going to do something, he simply does it. James is reliable. It's a much underrated trait. I've had all the fireworks and drama and it's immensely comforting to be with someone who arrives at my place when he said he would on a Friday night; who just does things, without fuss, like booking restaurant tables, cinema tickets and saving my parents' dog's life.

James is a genuinely lovely man who works hard and clearly loves his daughter and tries to do the right thing.

Secretly, I might have fantasised about Charlie and Esther hanging out together on subsequent visits, becoming friends and drifting away to watch a movie together. But this isn't about them. It's about me and James, and we are fine; in fact, *better* than fine as our lives intertwine. We meet each other's friends and he takes me into the surgery to meet everyone there. Although I don't want to get in anyone's way, Mikhail, one of the veterinary nurses, lets me 'help' (I'm not sure I'm much help really) by holding a chinchilla as he bandages its paw.

Over the past few months we've crossed paths with pretty much all of my friends in the village. I know they've all been curious to meet James. There have been ripples of excitement about 'Lauren's new man'; the handsome vet I met on the first day of his holiday. 'Did the Corsican passport control guys tip you off that he'd arrived?' a neighbour teased.

One crisp November evening he meets a bunch of my friends from our magazine days. We drink too much in a Stoke Newington pub and everyone makes a huge fuss of him, firing questions about his work as a vet, which he doesn't seem to mind.

'They're a bit of a force of nature en masse,' I remark later, in bed.

'They're great. How brilliant that you're still all so close.'

'Yeah, I'm very lucky,' I say, thinking, in *all* ways I am. I'm so lucky that things turned out this way.

Kim says I'm 'glowing' and any residue from that awkward lunch has long gone. I haven't seen Esther since then, and James and I haven't talked about getting us all together again.

Once, I feel, was quite enough.

So it's a bit of a shock when I'm enjoying a lazy Sunday morning at James's, sipping coffee while curled up on his sofa – and the door opens suddenly and Esther breezes right in. 'Oh, Lauren! Hi!' As if she's amazed to find me here. She's all smiles but her eyes are flinty.

'Hi, Esther.' I jump up and we hug stiffly. 'How are you? How're things?'

'Oh, great, great!' she enthuses.

We stand and look at each other for a second. 'Still working with the jewellery people?' I ask.

'Yeah.' She nods. 'Yeah. It's going great . . .'

'That's great!' How many times are we going to say 'great'?

'Hey, Est. I'll be down in a sec,' James calls out from upstairs. He's been having a shower. Thankfully he won't bound down naked.

'Okay, Dad,' she calls back sweetly.

I'm feeling a little panicky now, dressed as I am in James's towelling dressing gown with nothing on underneath. Of course the belt won't untie itself and the thing won't flap open. It's just that same vulnerability you experience when you're wearing a lightweight skirt in high winds. Something about Esther's presence induces a fear in me that I'm going to be exposed and look ridiculous.

Will it *always* be this awkward between us? The vibe she's emitting suggests that I shouldn't be wearing a dressing gown at all at 11.30 a.m. – and especially not her father's. By this hour, her brittle smile says, I should be fully, respectably attired. If I excuse myself by saying, 'I'm just going to get dressed', will that highlight how very undressed I am? Fortunately James appears – wearing jeans and a sweater – which gives me the opportunity to squeak, 'S'cuse me a sec,' and beetle off.

Bloody hell, what's wrong with me? I'm usually so relaxed here and love nothing better than flopping around on a weekend morning with coffee, if not in his dressing gown, then in one of his soft, roomy T-shirts and my knickers.

I could've been worse, I tell myself as I pull on my jeans and top in his bedroom, and take a deep breath before rejoining them downstairs. By now Esther and her dad are chatting away. Or rather, Esther is talking – a *lot* – and James is sitting next to her on the sofa, listening. Apparently, things with the jewellery people haven't actually been 'great' at all recently. 'They say they want one thing, then they want another,' she tells him. 'I don't know *what* they want, Dad . . .'

'Well, are they giving you any kind of suggestions or direction?' James asks.

She shrugs, looking quite anguished now. 'They're saying my pictures are too dingy.'

'Too dingy?' he repeats.

'Yeah.' She nods glumly. 'They're not sunny enough, they reckon. Not in the spirit of lightness and joy that they want to evoke . . .' She sighs heavily and shakes her head. 'What does that even *mean*?'

Erm, that they should be less dingy? 'What d'you think, Lauren?' James asks, turning to me.

'Oh, I'm not sure,' I reply quickly, catching Esther's startled look which seems to say: *Why are you asking her?* In fact I could offer suggestions, having checked out her Instagram again recently. Although she still looked beautiful – it would be impossible for her not to – her recent pictures tended towards the arty and dark; all low lighting and shadows and, I have to agree, not an awful lot of sunniness. But saying anything would feel way out of line.

'It's just, with Lauren being a photographer,' James adds, 'I just thought—'

'Yeah, but don't you photograph food?' Esther cuts in with a frown.

'Yes, I do at the moment,' I reply. 'But I've done all sorts over the years.'

'Oh.' She seems to consider this. 'What d'you think then?' Almost reluctantly she shows me her Instagram feed. (Naturally, I pretend I'm not intimately familiar with it.) Here's Esther draped on a cerise chaise longue, black wall behind her, dimly lit from the glow of a tarnished antique lamp. Now she's sprawled languidly across a dark green satin throw, then curled up on a deep blue velvet cushion in a tiny cave-like room, or possibly a cupboard; and now perched on the kitchen table, looking pale and depressed with a huge abstract painting behind her – blood red splattered on brown, as if someone had an accident on it. Finally, she's lying on a grey shag pile rug with her mouth slightly open and skin deathly pale as if, well . . . dead.

While there's jewellery in these pictures, it's certainly not shown off to its best effect. And there are no smiles, no 'lightness'; just moody stares into the middle distance. I can imagine that these photos aren't quite in the spirit of the Balinese jewellery brand, from the way she's described it.

'So,' Esther says, 'what d'you think?'

I bite my lip. 'I think, uhhhh . . . they're very evocative,' I reply.

'You like them?' She fixes me with a gaze.

'I do, yes.' I pause. 'They're so, um, moody and intense . . .'

'Yeah, and I thought they were fine with that.' Her mouth twists into a frown. 'But it turns out they're not happy at all.'

Conscious of treading carefully, I try to figure out the best way to proceed. 'They obviously liked what you were doing in the first place. Otherwise they wouldn't have approached you . . .' I pause. 'Is that how it works? They loved your Instagram and got in touch, asking you to work with them?'

'Yeah, exactly.' She nods. 'That's before I moved in with Miles. I was just doing pictures at home – at Mum and Luc's – messing about in the house and garden . . .'

'What were they like?' I ask. 'I mean, what kind of style were they?'

She shrugs. 'Just natural. Spontaneous, I s'pose. I was just having fun and didn't put much thought into them. They weren't set up and staged like the ones Miles does . . .'

'You were just being yourself,' James remarks and she nods again.

'Guess so. Yeah.'

'So, why not go back to those kinds of pictures?' he suggests. *Before Miles started doing them for you*, is what he means. *Before that jerk took over.*

She gives me a look that suggests her father has no idea about such matters. An eye-roll, almost. 'But that's my environment now, Dad,' she says with exaggerated patience. 'It's where I live. There's not much I can do about that.'

Well, you could leave him, is what I'm thinking. *On top of lying about his age and cheating on you, he's now imposing his own aesthetic on your social media . . .* 'Could you show me some of Bethani's advertising,' I ask, 'so I can see what they do?'

'Er, yeah. Sure.' Looking pleased that I've remembered the brand name, she brings up images of glowy-skinned women in vests and faded denim shorts. They're strolling on beaches, or relaxing at the poolside, or wandering through meadows ablaze with wildflowers. The vibe is natural and carefree. While I wouldn't dare to make assumptions, I'd guess that black walls, splattered artworks and playing dead on a frankly grubby-looking rug don't quite fit.

'It's all very sunny and outdoorsy, isn't it?' I remark.

'Yeah,' Esther says with a sigh.

I'm surprised, and even a little flattered, that's she's actually engaging with me a little over this. After all, it's her dad she's popped round to see today. 'This might seem like a mad suggestion,' I say, feeling emboldened now, 'but how about we try doing a few pictures out there?' I nod towards the window.

Esther stares at me. 'You mean, *you* take some pictures of me?'

'Well, yes. If you'd like me to . . .'

'In Dad's garden?'

'Er, yes. There are plenty of things we could try out there—'

'I think it's raining.' She frowns and prods at her phone. 'I'll just check.'

James splutters. 'You're checking the weather?'

'*Yes*, Dad . . .'

'Why not just look out the window?' he asks, catching my eye with a grin.

'This is more accurate,' she murmurs distractedly, then, seemingly reassured about the climactic conditions, she jumps up from the sofa. 'Okay then. Let's go.'

'It's not raining?' I ask, straight-faced, as I follow her into the hallway.

'Nope.' She picks up the bag she'd dumped on the floor, pulls out a tangled necklace and unknots it with a sigh of impatience before slipping it on. There's a quick sweep of the hair with her hands – it tumbles in glossy russet waves all down her back – and a slight adjustment of her moss green skinny-rib top, worn with softly faded jeans today, and we're off.

CHAPTER TWENTY-FIVE

LAUREN

It's a typically narrow, rectangular London garden, bordered on three sides by tall fences. James has admitted that it verges on neglect, and I know he attacks it with gusto whenever it's edging towards being out of control. Today the air is fresh and clean after a heavy shower. The shrubs are gleaming, the yellow and purple winter pansies peeking out from terracotta pots.

'Your garden puts mine to shame,' James admitted, the first time I came here. But actually his little patch of greenery is quite beautiful with its gnarly apple tree, several rickety wooden birdhouses attached to the fences, and an ancient moss-covered stone birdbath on a stand on the lawn. Using my phone, I rattle off a few shots just to get a feel for the space, and for the light at this time of day.

'So,' Esther says, looking a little unsure of herself now, 'what shall I do?'

I look at her and smile, wondering again if she's quite as self-assured as she seems. I still can't understand why this stunning and obviously smart young woman is with a man like Miles who, age issue aside, has treated her so shabbily. 'Just be yourself,' I suggest. 'Do whatever feels natural for you. We can take our time with this . . .'

She moves slightly as I start to shoot. She's just standing there in a simple top and her old jeans with the delicate gold necklace twinkling against her honeyed skin. Cool sunlight crosses her face. The effect is quite beautiful and something starts to happen. Now I see what Esther Burton is all about.

She's not like a model. I met plenty of those when Frank was still doing fashion photography. And while those models all looked very different, they shared a kind of other-worldliness with their angular faces, the bones almost visible beneath smooth, taut skin. Their long, gaunt frames were often the result of picking at sandwich fillings and avoiding the bread. Before the days of all kinds of body shapes being represented, extreme skinniness was the beauty standard, the desired aesthetic. The world of fashion was populated by skinny girls of five foot ten who seemed to survive on black coffee and cigarettes.

Esther is nothing like that. For one thing she's tiny compared to your average model; no more than five foot four, I'd guess. But there's also a realness about her with the freckles, the upturned nose and not-quite-perfect teeth. While I'm pretty sure her hair has been filled out with extensions, she hardly wears any make-up and her natural beauty shines through. The word 'luminous' is overused – but that's what Esther is. She is *wonderful* in front of a lens. It feels as if it would be impossible to take a bad picture of her.

I take dozens of shots in her dad's terraced garden; against the dark wooden fence with the birdhouses and the brick wall of the house. I do more of her perched on the back step, sipping from an enamel mug of tea, and sitting cross-legged on a faded corduroy cushion on the lawn. The light is soft and milky, the setting perfect for the casual feel of our pictures. But we could be in the middle of a municipal tip, surrounded by old cookers and mattresses and somehow the whole thing would still look quite lovely.

This is what those jewellery people want, I realise now. Not the black walls, the bat-on-a-string and the challenging splattered art in her boyfriend's flat. They want Esther being her lovely, natural self.

'They're really nice,' she says with a note of surprise as we head indoors to look through the shots together.

'I'm so glad you like them.'

She musters a smile, almost reluctantly. 'You're a good photographer!'

I can't help smiling at that. 'Thank you. I really enjoyed doing them.'

I watch as she looks through them again, seeming to lower her guard with me now. I catch James's eye and he grins. 'Honestly,' she adds, 'you're wasted on all that food stuff . . .'

I happen to enjoy that food stuff . . . 'Thanks.' I chuckle and catch James's eye again, knowing that we're both thinking the same: that perhaps we won't have to keep the rest of our lives so separate after all.

*

The next day Esther calls me. A young person – an influencer – actually calling *me*! 'They love them,' she says, still with a note of surprise in her voice.

'I'm so glad,' I say.

'Thank you so much,' Esther adds. 'I think you might've saved things with them . . .'

'Honestly, it was nothing,' I say truthfully. Normally

I'd far prefer to shoot a goat's cheese and olive tart, or a plate of pistachio cookies, to an actual human. People are too tricky, I've always reckoned – remembering Frank complaining about models 'having histrionics' on shoots. They'd complain about being too hot, too cold, or the sun being 'too bright' on an overcast day.

But Esther was a joy to photograph. And when she asks if we can do more pictures sometime – 'At your place, maybe? Would that be okay?' – my heart seems to swell. 'I'll pay you of course,' she adds quickly.

'Absolutely no way,' I say firmly.

'Oh.' She sounds crushed. 'Don't you have the time?'

'No, I mean I don't you want to pay me, Esther. This is fun for me – something completely different from my usual thing. I loved photographing you and I'd love to do some more.'

And it's not just about taking pictures, I reflect as we arrange a date. It's about being accepted by Esther and getting to know her a little bit more, and already I'm looking forward to our next shoot.

CHAPTER TWENTY-SIX

ESTHER

Esther's therapist told her to try and appreciate the good things in her life, rather than dwelling on the bad. 'Write a gratitude journal,' Chrissie suggested. She meant that, at the end of every day, Esther should list three things she was grateful for that day.

Her dad once saw her curled on his sofa with her journal, wondering what to write. 'Oh, d'you still keep a diary?' he asked in surprise. Years back, when Esther was about nine or ten, she'd started one in a burst of enthusiasm. She'd record thrilling events like 'Kasey stuck her chewing gum on my furry pencil case' and 'Jake Matthews did a massive poo in the school loo. Mr Bloom had to chop it up with wire so it would flush away.' Her interest had waned before January was out and the other eleven months had remained blank.

'It's not a diary,' she'd told her dad. 'It's a gratitude journal.'

'What's that?' he'd asked. She couldn't believe he hadn't heard of the term. 'Is it to do with all that mindfulness stuff?'

'Why d'you have to say that?' she'd asked, prickling with annoyance.

'Say what?' He looked confused.

'"All that mindfulness stuff". It's just *mindfulness*, Dad. That's what it is. Why d'you have to be so cynical?' She felt guilty then because he isn't cynical at all. He's the very opposite, whatever that is. Straightforward, she supposes. He just says what he means, with no attempts at manipulation or twisting the truth (unlike her boyfriend, for instance).

Her dad just doesn't get the whole spirituality thing. He probably thinks it's just a load of woo-woo that the gemstones used in Bethani jewellery can evoke different qualities and have been blessed by a priest. But that's hardly unusual for a man of fifty-one, fifty-two or whatever he is. Esther reckons her dad's generation aren't in touch with their inner landscapes, the way young people are. They've been too busy burning coal, pumping out disgusting fumes from factories and wrecking the planet (not that Esther holds her father *completely* responsible for that) to think deeply about spiritual matters. Her dad just goes to work and treats all those animals, comes home, does the stuff he has to do, goes to bed, gets up; repeat, repeat, repeat, like a machine. Oh, he sees his friends for drinks occasionally – and of course now he has Lauren.

These days Esther has plenty to be grateful for. She has written in her gratitude journal that her latest Instagram posts have been her most popular ones ever. The Bethani people were delighted, so it looks like their relationship is good again. 'We loved all those fresh, natural pictures in the garden,' they enthused. 'They were so much more *you*, Esther. And so much more on brand than the black walls and those challenging abstract paintings.'

176

Esther has Lauren to thank for that. But still, she can't help feeling uneasy about what's going on with her dad. For as long as she can remember he's been the one who's had her back, who's been involved in the day-to-day workings of her life. Far more than her mum has anyway. She's always been more wrapped up in her bar, and Luc, and her own social life than anything Esther's had going on.

Of course she's an adult now and no longer needs looking after. But still, she likes to know her dad's *there*. To Esther, he's like the life jacket they always go on about when you're about to take off on a flight. While you hope you'll never need it, it's good to know it's stashed away for use in an emergency.

He's had girlfriends before, of course. Well, actually just the one that Esther can remember. She was happy for him, as she'd started to worry that he'd be on his own forever, and would end up alone at eighty-five, spooning in tinned soup from a bowl on a tray in front of the TV. (Esther and Miles eat off trays in front of the TV, but that's different.)

The other reason she was happy with the situation was that Polly didn't *change* him. The whole time he was seeing her, he was basically the same person he'd always been. He was still Esther's dad. He still had plenty of time for her and hadn't acquired that madly besotted look he has now. She's figured that he can't have been truly in love with Polly, because when she ran off to South America he seemed perfectly fine. Esther, whose relationships had so far been all about drama and scenes, couldn't understand it at all.

'Aren't you upset?' she'd asked him at the time.

'No,' he'd replied, looking surprised. 'It's an amazing opportunity for her.'

'But what about you?'

'I'm fine, Est. Of course I am.'

'Didn't you try to stop her going?'

He'd actually laughed at that. 'How could I have stopped her?'

'I don't know, but—'

'Should I have confiscated her passport? Honestly, I'm happy for her. It's *fine*.'

Esther can't imagine he'd be 'fine' if Lauren went off to South America. He'd probably throw in his job and follow her out there, if his recent behaviour is anything to go by. Her solid, dependable dad is most definitely madly in love with Lauren, and it worries Esther. Scares her, even.

Of course he's still her dad. Nothing will ever alter that. But can she still count on him to put her first, as she's always been able to? Sometimes, after all the craziness with the reality show, he was the only thing in her life she could depend on, no matter what.

It's not that she begrudges him his happiness. God, no. He's a wonderful man – the best one she knows – and he deserves to find love. It's just that sometimes, with Miles, Esther has a niggling fear that the plane she is on is about to plummet from the sky. And she worries that her life jacket might not be there when she needs it.

*

It's a cool and misty November afternoon when Esther arrives at Lauren's cottage in the pretty Hertfordshire village. This time, there's no Miles. Her dad isn't even here. There'll be no talk of mullets or whether academia is important or any awkward scenes today. Esther has come alone by train and is ready to do the shoot that she and Lauren arranged together. As Lauren picked her up from the station, and they chatted politely on the short drive, Esther decided she really must banish any negative feelings from her head.

After all, her dad is happy and that's what matters.

It was Lauren's idea to do a wintry shoot here in her garden. Esther is taken aback to see that she has strung fairy lights all across the twiggy trees, threading them through the branches like twinkling blossom. She doesn't remember them being there last time and wonders now if she's done this specially, to make it look all sparkly and lovely for her. The plan is to shoot in the late afternoon light and into the dusk. 'I thought it'd look great with the fairy lights,' Lauren explains. Esther agrees, and she's keen to get on with doing the pictures.

She's brought a bag filled with Bethani necklaces, earrings and bracelets – the whole caboodle. In Lauren's kitchen she tips everything out onto the table they'd all gathered around for that terrible lunch. Miles hadn't behaved well, she'd decided later. What was he thinking, going on about having a baby with her? Esther has no intention of getting pregnant right now – or in the fore-seeable future. He'd probably just felt out of his depth and he'd definitely drunk too much. Esther has decided it's best not to mention the lunch today; to pretend it never happened.

'What kind of shots are you thinking of?' Lauren asks now, handing her a mug of tea.

'Just like you did before,' Esther replies, swinging round as Charlie arrives home from school.

'Hey, Esther!' He looks surprised to see her and dumps his bag at his feet.

'Hi, Charlie,' Esther says. 'How's it going?'

'Good,' he says, shrugging off his jacket. He's a good-looking boy, Esther decides, having not really noticed that first time she met him – whenever Miles is around he tends to demand all of her attention. Charlie's eyes are a chestnutty brown, his hair wavy and dark and falling into his face, a little unkempt. With that typical teenage boy's leanness, he could probably guzzle pie and chips every mealtime and never gain an ounce. He gives his mum a quick hug, which strikes Esther as sweet, although the vibe he gives off suggests he's just being nice because they have company.

'Good day, love?' Lauren asks.

'Yeah, all right.' He grabs a banana, peels it swiftly and chomps down half of it in one bite.

'Got your exams coming up?' Esther asks. What a typical thing to say to a teenager, she thinks, then remembers that she only turned twenty in February.

'Yeah, prelims in January,' he replies.

'Which subjects are you doing?'

'Maths, physics and chemistry.'

'Oh my God. That's so difficult. Think you'll do all right?' Esther has never encountered anyone quite like Charlie before. None of the boys at Willow Vale were as obviously academic as he is, and now she's curious to know what he's all about.

'Hope so,' he says with a shrug. 'But yeah, it *is* hard.'

'Bet you'll do fine,' she says, which is silly really as she doesn't know him at all. She guesses he'll put in the work, though. Not like her, even though Esther's teachers had reckoned she could have done really well, if she'd pulled her finger out.

'Did you do A levels?' Charlie asks, having devoured the banana and set about eating another one.

'Yeah. I mean, I showed up,' she says with a small laugh. 'I did history, which I loved, and English and art. But I didn't work nearly hard enough.'

'But you've done really well,' Charlie says, with such earnestness she could hug him.

'It's been a lot of luck really,' Esther says truthfully. 'I've kind fallen into anything I've ever done. I mean, there's never been a grand plan.'

'Nothing wrong with that, is there?' Charlie starts to pick over the jewellery that's still scattered all over the table.

'No.' She smiles. 'There's nothing wrong with it. But my two best friends are away at university. Gracie's at Durham and Jess is at St Andrews . . .'

'D'you still see them?' Lauren asks.

'Not much,' Esther replies quickly. She wishes now that she hadn't started this conversation because it's difficult for her, constantly seeing what Gracie and Jess are up to, hundreds of miles away from her. Their lives don't include her anymore. They're far too busy making tons of fantastically clever new friends. She's heard about the flat parties, the sprawling picnics with wine and proper wicker hampers, and the boozy dinner parties where everyone dresses up in their poshest clothes. 'Frocks', they call them. Her friends wear frocks! And they go on big group holidays with their uni friends because someone always knows someone whose family own a ramshackle house in Provence, and they all lie around getting gently pissed on French rosé in the afternoon sun.

They don't go to terrible clubs where middle-aged people dance badly with sweat flying off them.

'Not everybody has to go to university,' Charlie remarks now.

'As Miles pointed out,' Esther says with a trace of a smile. She catches his eye – he smiles too – and she decides she likes this shy boy who seems to be into the solar system in the way that 'normal' boys of his age tend to

181

be into gaming, football or just hanging out, being a pain in the arse, basically. 'Sorry about that,' she adds, reddening. 'About Miles, I mean.'

'Nothing to be sorry for,' Charlie says with a shrug. Although Lauren is busying about with a camera at the worktop, Esther can tell she's listening in.

'You want to go to uni, though?' she asks.

'Yeah, I do,' Charlie says.

'What'll you study?'

'Astrophysics, hopefully.'

'Not astrology?' She raises a brow.

'I'm considering that too,' he says, chuckling at her joke, looking the most relaxed she's seen him so far.

'Good to keep your options open,' she says, almost wishing they could hang out and chat for longer as she and Lauren head into the garden to do the shoot.

*

It's bizarre, Esther thinks when they're done, how a little connection seems to have sparked up between her and Charlie today. They gravitate towards each other again as Lauren makes hot chocolate, and the two of them wander around the wintry garden together, sipping from mugs and chatting about this and that. He's a sweet boy, Esther decides as Lauren serves up bowls of mushroomy pasta. Later, as Lauren drives her to the train station, she can't resist finding out a bit more about him. 'Does Charlie have many friends in the village?' she asks.

'Yes, of course,' Lauren says. A hint of defensiveness there, unless Esther is mistaken. Although they'd got along fine while doing the shoot, she is aware of a slight formality emitting from Lauren now. Of course she's been fantasti-cally helpful, doing *two* shoots with her now and basically rescuing her relationship with Bethani. But does Lauren actually like her, Esther wonders? She can't read her at all and wonders how things will pan out if her dad keeps on seeing her, and they move in together, and maybe he'll even move out here to the country and she'll hardly ever see him and – oh God, that would feel weird, if he actually *married* her! Would Lauren and Charlie become his primary family and she'd just be some weird little offshoot?

Curiously, Esther doesn't feel uneasy about the possibility of her mum marrying Luc one day. Her mum had been friends with him for a couple of years before they'd got together; she hadn't met him on holiday like some teenager on their first trip to Magaluf. The thought of her dad having a 'holiday romance' still makes Esther feel a little queasy. To think how worried she'd been about him in Corsica on his own – and he'd probably barely given her a second's thought!

She realises Lauren is glancing at her as if expecting a response. 'I was just saying,' she reiterates, 'Charlie's closest friend was a boy called Remy . . . I mean *is*. I shouldn't use the past tense. But he's not around so much anymore . . .'

'Is he at university?' Esther asks, embarrassed at being caught not listening.

'No, he's a musician – a singer-songwriter – so he's away touring a lot, plus he has a serious girlfriend so Charlie's been a bit left behind.' Lauren glances at her and smiles. 'I probably shouldn't have told you all that.'

'Oh, I won't say anything,' Esther says quickly, thinking how similar that sounds to her situation with Gracie and Jess. Perhaps that's why Charlie lingers on in her mind over the next few days, and why she experiences a little fillip of pleasure when she sees he's followed her on Instagram. Over the next week or so he makes the odd comment on her posts. Nothing amazing; just the odd 'nice picture!' – stuff like that. It makes her smile. She's not quite sure why. Maybe because she senses he's not entirely comfortable with social media but is making an effort to be nice?

He seems like a decent boy, Esther thinks; studious, thoughtful and kind. And while not all of the boys at Willow Vale were arseholes with no respect for girls, Esther would say that, actually, *most* of them were.

And Charlie is most definitely not like that.

CHAPTER TWENTY-SEVEN

JAMES

I wouldn't say I had a terrible life before I met Lauren. I had Esther, a full-on job that I cared deeply about, and good people to work with. I was content, I suppose. Okay, I'd be at a *bit* of a loose end on the weekends sometimes when friends were busy and I'd find myself going for a run or a swim just to fill up the time. Or I'd research work stuff or even go into the practice to tackle non-essential jobs while we were closed. It did occur to me that I was in danger of turning into Lonely Cat Man. But what could I do about that? I wasn't going to try any dating apps. That wasn't me at all. And I wasn't expecting to meet someone in the 'normal' way because, in the circles I moved in, that just never happened.

So that was that, I supposed. It was just me, an elderly cat named Walter and a daughter I'd see once a week, if I was lucky. And back in July, when I stepped on that plane bound for Corsica, I hadn't imagined anything changing.

However, my life *has* changed in ways I'd never imagined. It's so much fuller now, with weekends spent here at my place, or at Lauren's, where we hang out together and go for walks and pub lunches. I feel her hand in mine as we follow the path that snakes alongside the river, and we catch up on what we've been up to since we last saw each other.

She tells me about the dishes she's cooked, that her column has been shortlisted for an award, and we celebrate with a wintry picnic of home-made bread, cheese, brownies and mini bottles of champagne. She says she loves hearing about the goings-on at work; about how, while she was busily writing up recipes last night, I was operating on a Labrador to remove a small pebble from its gastrointestinal tract. More thrillingly still, earlier in the day a flustered woman had brought in a tortoise with an injured leg. 'Her son had trodden on him. He hadn't seen him on the lawn,' I explained.

'Oh no! What can you do?' she asked.

'I'm figuring out how to make a splint for him,' I explained.

She smiled at that. 'A splint for an injured tortoise. You make it sound as if it's a slightly challenging DIY job in the home.' And she kissed me on the lips. 'How I love you, James.'

'I love you too,' I said. And I do love her – very much. I'm in awe of her talent and energy and love of life. She radiates sunshine even on a bitterly cold November day. More and more I treasure the time we spend together because, as the weeks go by, it becomes trickier to see each other.

Admittedly, this is due to me rather than Lauren. Being freelance, she is pretty much in charge of her own life. However, as December arrives – and with no real explanation – Esther seems to want to spend more time at my place. She and Miles are still together – unfortunately.

But one Friday afternoon, when I'd been planning to head out to Lauren's after work, she calls and asks if we can have an evening together, just me and her and a takeaway, maybe watching a movie on TV. I'm about to say, 'Another time, Est. I'm going to Lauren's tonight.'

But something snags at me and I hear myself saying, 'Yes of course we can.' And I call Lauren to explain how weird and unusual it is, for Esther to want to spend a Friday night with me, and perhaps something's wrong and she needs to talk.

'Oh, okay then,' Lauren says with a tinge of disappointment.

'I'm sorry. Shall I come over tomorrow?'

'Maybe it's not worth it this weekend?' she asks.

'Why not? We could still have most of Saturday and Sunday—'

'But what if something *is* wrong?' she cuts in. 'Shouldn't you be around for her, just in case?'

I consider this and decide she's probably right. But it leaves a hollow feeling deep in my gut, and when Esther arrives, all chatter and uncharacteristic cheeriness, I keep wondering when the big announcement's coming, and she'll spill out whatever bad thing has been happening in her life.

No announcement comes. As we sit up late chatting and watching TV, I try to banish a niggle of resentment that actually, Esther could have easily come over in the week instead, and I could have been at Lauren's tonight as planned.

I won't let that happen again, I decide. I'll put Lauren first and, bar a disaster, stick to what we've arranged. But our plan to meet up during the week falls apart when we're overloaded with a spate of emergency appointments at work, and Fraser and I decide we'll both have to put in some late shifts to keep on top of everything. And the following Friday evening I have just arrived home when Esther calls, asking to come over and stay at mine again.

I don't resent this. She's my daughter after all. But I can't quite see why Miles having flu means that she needs to decamp to my place for a couple of nights. 'It's disgusting, sleeping with someone who's sweating and snorting all night,' she announces, which is more than I needed to know really.

Again, Lauren and I don't see each other. I suggested she came to my place instead – but she was too busy, she said. She's explained that newspaper and magazine work is hectic in the run-up to Christmas with editors wanting her columns in early, all done and dusted before the holidays. Plus, she's creating content for a bakery chain and a series of Easter recipes for a print magazine. Hot cross buns and simnel cakes in mid-December! It's normal for her to work so far ahead, I've discovered. So, yes, we are busy people who also happen to live a ninety-minute journey apart. But we are still very much together and we speak most days, or message. Or at least, we try to message most days.

Actually, when I think about it, we're not in touch nearly as much as we were at the start. But that doesn't mean anything, does it? When we do speak, we agree that we must see each other as much as possible over Christmas, because on the big day itself we'll be with our own families. Lauren will spend it with Charlie, of course, plus Kim, Lorenzo and their twin daughters, as is their custom. I'll spend it at Rhona and Luc's, with Esther – although I gather there's a bit of drama going on because Miles wants Esther to stay home with him this year. And Esther has been trying to persuade Miles to be with us for Christmas, which Rhona is fine about. ('We can't ban our daughter's boyfriend, James! Not very festive, is it?') It's pretty exhausting and I'm actually a little envious of Lauren's relatively simple set-up.

'It wasn't like this in Corsica, was it?' she remarks when we speak one evening. I *think* she's smiling, that she means it wryly and isn't becoming tired of our cancelled dates.

'No, but that wasn't our real lives,' I remind her.

'Oh. Is real life different then?' A small silence falls.

'You know what I mean. We had nothing else to think about then . . .'

'Yeah, you're right.' Her tone softens. 'I kind of liked our Corsica life, though,' she adds. 'Didn't you?'

'Of course I did. It was wonderful,' I say truthfully.

'Can we get that back again, James? D'you think it's possible?' She sounds hesitant.

''Course we can,' I say firmly. 'It's just life and Christmas coming up. All that stuff. Things'll be normal again soon, I promise.'

I mean that, and I believe it. And I hope she believes it too.

CHAPTER TWENTY-EIGHT

ESTHER

Next time her dad's going to Lauren's, Esther asks if she can come too. She sees him hesitate, as if he's thinking, *I was hoping we'd have some time alone this weekend.* Esther really can read him that well. But then, Charlie's usually around when he's there, isn't he? So why shouldn't she be there too? 'I could just do with getting out of town for the day,' Esther adds. 'I'll get a late train home.'

Of course he says that's fine because he's concerned about her relationship with Miles. She only has to hint that things aren't one hundred per cent okay and her dad will pretty much do what she wants.

In fact, Esther has stacked up a whole bunch of reasons why she wants to go to Lauren's this weekend. Firstly, Miles has been caning it with his friends lately, crashing in at all hours, waking her up with his stinky breath and clammy hands all over her. She's not keen on clubbing with him after the last time, and he accuses her of being boring for not wanting to go out. In fact, Esther does want to go out – to nice restaurants, the movies or even a proper grown-up party. She does *not* want his mate

Kevin roaring at her over the music, spraying spit and never wiping that gunk from the corners of his mouth. It makes her want to vomit. Nor does she want Miles staggering in at 4.30 a.m. and peeing into her T-shirt drawer, thinking it's the loo, as happened earlier this week.

It's pretty grim, frankly. She hasn't admitted this to anyone – not even to Chrissie. She can't bear to admit that she loves someone who behaves like this. But, while Miles is in this phase, she needs to get away from him once in a while.

The other reason she wants to go is that it's still worrying her, how her dad seems so besotted. It's all Lauren-this, Lauren-that. Esther has literally never seen him like this in her life, and feels she should step in a bit. Not as a chaperone, that would be ridiculous – but to dilute things a little. And to remind him that he has other people in his life.

Is this selfish of her, Esther wonders? Probably – a bit. For a while she was scared she was 'losing' him to this woman he just happened to meet on holiday. Esther doesn't feel like that now. She's tested him several times, by suddenly 'needing' to spend time at his place. And he's always cancelled his plans with his girlfriend and put her first. However, in tagging along this weekend she hopes to stop things from getting too intense. Esther would hate to see her dad getting hurt, or the relationship affecting his work and the rest of his life – i.e. his *family life*.

And now, as they arrive at Lauren's on a crisp and sparkly December morning, Esther realises there's another reason why she wanted to come today.

To hang out with Charlie again.

*

191

'Hey!' she says when he comes out of his room. They have a quick, slightly awkward hug, and she asks again how his exam prep's going, and of course he plays down how hard he's working. She still doesn't know much about him, although she did ask her dad about Charlie's dad, and he said he's a fashion photographer, that he lives in New York, that he was a bit wild in his time but he's probably straightened up now.

Of course Esther googled him. She doesn't know why Charlie's dad is so interesting to her; he just *is*. There was lots of his work online from years back, but nothing recent that she could find, and not much about the man himself. It doesn't feel right to ask Charlie about him today. It might be a sensitive topic and she wouldn't want to pry.

Lauren and her dad have been drinking coffee in the garden, wrapped up in winter sweaters and scarves, and now Lauren has appeared in the kitchen. 'The light's lovely out there, Esther,' she says. 'Fancy doing some more pictures?'

'Are you sure?' Esther asks, as if the possibility hadn't occurred to her.

'Yes, of course!' As they head outside and start to shoot, Esther finds herself wishing again that there'd been boys like Charlie at Willow Vale, who'd wanted to pass their exams, go to university and study astrophysics.

'How did it go?' he asks when the shoot is over.

'Really good,' Esther replies. 'Want to see the pictures?' Maybe it's silly to ask, as he's into stars and planets and all that – not photos for Instagram. But he nods and seems keen, so they sit and scroll through them.

'They're great,' he says. 'Amazing.'

Esther smiles. 'Your mum does a good job, y'know.'

He looks over as James and Lauren stroll into the kitchen. 'You're actually quite a good photographer, Mum!' he teases.

'Oh, thank you, Charlie,' Lauren says, grinning. He's right, though. The pictures are beautiful with the soft, wintry light and twiggy trees silhouetted against a pale sky. Lauren really is talented.

Esther doesn't go home as planned that night. When Charlie's friend Remy comes round with Freya, his girlfriend, Charlie invites her to have a few beers with them and they all sit up chatting in Charlie's room.

It's cosy up there, and kind of magical with the skylight in the sloping ceiling, and the telescope. She has a few drinks and finds herself telling them about Gracie and Jess, her best friends who she misses so much. How, last time she'd called Jess, she'd said, 'Sorry, Est. Got to go, we're having a party on the beach. Speak soon, yeah?'

A beach party with her super-brainy university friends. That had sounded fun. Esther had googled St Andrews beach, and as she'd gazed at the wide stretch of golden sand, tears had dropped down her cheeks. Miles had thought she was mad, getting upset over something like that. But her tears had kept falling as if a tap had been turned on. Why hadn't she gone to college? Why had she gone straight from living with her mum and Luc to her boyfriend's place with its creepy bat, without sharing flats like her best friends were doing?

She doesn't tell Charlie, Remy and Freya that part.

Lauren says of course it's fine for Esther to stay over in the spare room, and when she wakes she's surprised to hear birds tweeting instead of Miles snoring, then saying in his gruff morning voice, 'Make some coffee, would you, babe?'

For a moment she actually wishes this was *her* bed she was lying in, out here in the countryside. Being here feels so good. But of course she has to go home, and she's aware of a heaviness pressing down on her chest as her dad drives them back to London on Sunday evening. She's had a lovely time hanging out with Charlie, just chatting about everyday stuff. It's felt totally unpressurised. She enjoyed meeting Remy and Freya but she actually prefers just being with Charlie really.

Esther could never have imagined being friends with a seventeen-year-old boy. But she already feels that Charlie *is* her friend. He listens to her. He's smart and interesting and never talks over her the way Miles does. She's never met anyone quite like him. For some reason, Esther decides not to mention any of this to Miles. It isn't that he'd be jealous or even bothered; it's just, she wants to keep something for herself. Not that it matters, because he's not really interested. Even when she shows him the new pictures Lauren took of her, he seems distracted.

'Yeah, nice,' he says quickly, as if he has other, more urgent matters on his mind. Like attacking the grubby tile grout? *Very* occasionally Esther finds herself wondering what it'd be like to have a boyfriend closer to her own age. There's been a couple but no one that serious, and no one ever mentioned grout.

She curls up on their bed and goes through the pictures on her own, choosing the best ones. Shoots are so fun and easy now, compared to when Miles took charge of them, getting her to lie on the rug like a corpse and curl up in a little ball in the walk-in cupboard where he keeps a busted old keyboard and some African drums. 'Let's make it edgy,' he used to say. 'If those jewellery people want boring, happy-smiley stuff, tell them to fuck off.'

He was only trying to help; she realises that. But Esther likes working with Bethani. They're such nice girls in the London office, and they take her for lovely lunches at a place right on the river, and they're basically Esther's main income these days.

She didn't want to tell them to fuck off. Also, she

doesn't want Miles telling her what to do, getting involved in her work when he knows nothing about it. And it occurred to her recently that that's Miles's default reaction to pretty much any irritating situation she might happen to mention, like back in the summer, when she'd been packing for Corsica and told him, 'Dad'll go mad when he sees how much stuff I'm bringing.'

Miles: 'Tell him to fuck off.'

Me: 'Miles, that's my dad!'

Miles: 'So?'

He hardly speaks to his own dad, who owns half of the West Country and reckons he's an artisanal cider producer when he's actually an army guy, a colonel or something, if they still exist. Or a brigadier? Is that a thing, the Brigadier of Somerset?

So no, Esther wasn't going to tell her dad to fuck off – or the Bethani girls, for that matter. They've loved her pictures since Lauren started doing them. And she suspects that might bother Miles a little bit because later, he grudgingly has a quick look through yesterday's shoot.

'Anyone can be a photographer with a phone,' he remarks, stifling a yawn.

'Lauren has proper cameras too,' she tells him. 'She's professional, Miles. She does shoots for newspapers, magazines, websites – all this incredible food photography. It's just, with a phone there's that spontaneity—'

'Ooh, spontaneity!' he teases.

She glares at him, telling herself not to rise to it. In fact, he too has a proper, very expensive camera, which he's used once – to take a picture of his own reflection in a tarnished mirror. He has a problem with instruction manuals, he says. He can't learn things that way. 'Do a photography course then,' Esther suggested, but he said he didn't have the time.

'You don't need to feel threatened because Lauren's been helping me,' Esther tries to reassure him. Her therapist said that, when someone is behaving in a way you don't like, it's best to try to understand 'the why'.

'Why should I feel threatened, babe?' he asks, looking baffled.

'I'm saying, you shouldn't—'

'I don't feel threatened by *anyone*,' Miles retorts.

CHAPTER TWENTY-NINE

CHARLIE

'Everyone thinks they're a photographer now,' Charlie's dad announces, his reddened face looming on the tiny screen. 'They've got their phones and filters and that's it, they reckon. That's all there is to it. They're a bloody photographer!'

He laughs bitterly and Charlie waits patiently for him to stop, to ask how *he's* doing, to try and find out what's going on in *his* life. Charlie would actually love to bore the tits off his dad by telling him about the intricate workings of Brenda's newsagent's. He'd like to send him into a comatose state by describing how she likes the magazines to be arranged slightly overlapping each other, and the sweet display topped up at all times with no unsightly spaces.

As they FaceTime tonight, Charlie can see flat grey sky behind his father, and a section of graffitied wall. He's up on the roof of his building, probably having a smoke. Frank lives in an apartment in a converted garment factory in Brooklyn with his girlfriend, Patty. They've been together for two or three years but Charlie has never met her, apart from to say hello on screen. He hasn't seen his dad in years either, at least not in real life. He's never been out to New York to see him. He's asked him, and Charlie would love to see it – but not with him. He's fully aware of what his dad's like. He remembers what happened in Mexico. How he'd made out that Charlie's mum had over-reacted that day on the beach, when every single person they'd met had warned them not to swim there.

Still, he's his father, and his mum has always said they should keep a connection going. 'But why?' Charlie has asked her more than once.

'Because he's your dad. And you might regret it if you don't.'

'Why might I regret it?'

'Well, there might be a time when you really wish you could talk to him—'

'But he's not interested in me.'

'He is, Charlie,' she insisted. 'You're his son. He loves you. He just doesn't know how to show it.' So they still FaceTime now and again, and it goes like this: his dad talks about all the great stuff he's doing, not just photography now but film; he's always shooting something and talking to 'people' about 'projects'. What a wanker, Charlie can't help thinking when he's in full flow.

Sometimes, when his dad's ranting on, he tunes out and amuses himself by imagining Frank being a contestant on a TV quiz show, specialist subject 'Your Son'. It would go like this:

Quizmaster: Okay, we'll start with an easy one. Which subjects is Charlie doing for A level?

Dad: Um, English? Art? How many do they do?

QM: Three generally but never mind. What does he hope to study at university?

Dad: Uhhh . . . I'll have to pass on that one . . .

QM: And what would he like to pursue as a career?

Dad: How would I know? He never tells me anything . . .

Now Frank is complaining that everything's become 'too easy' these days, whatever that means. As far as Charlie's concerned, life isn't easy at all. There are all kinds of things he'd like to talk to his mum about; he just isn't sure how. 'Like these influencers,' his dad is ranting on, 'given tons of free stuff and holidays all over the world. A few shots with their phones and that's that. Quids in!'

'Don't you think that's a good thing?' Charlie asks.

Frank blinks in surprise. 'What d'you mean?'

'That photography's become so accessible,' he ventures. 'People can try it for fun and express themselves that way without having to buy loads of equipment. It's kind of . . .' Charlie searches for the right word '. . . democratic.'

'Oh, is that what you call it?' his dad asks dryly. Of course Frank doesn't think that's a good thing. He thinks he's not getting work because influencers are 'stealing' all the jobs – when he's actually an unreliable drunk.

'Anyway, how's your mum?' he asks as an afterthought.

'She's fine.'

'That's good.' Charlie doesn't mention that she's been seeing James for months and she seems so happy; happier than he's ever seen her. He wouldn't be interested anyway. He probably *would* like to hear about Esther, with her being pretty famous, and it would give him an excuse to start banging on about influencers again. But Charlie doesn't mention her either.

He doesn't tell him that he and Esther have started hanging out whenever she comes here with her dad, or sometimes on her own, when his mum's doing a new set of pictures of her. He doesn't share with his father that she's not at all what he'd imagined, before he met her. Or even when he first met her, when she'd showed up with her boyfriend for that awful lunch. His first impressions were all wrong, Charlie realises now. Esther is actually a very sweet person.

One time, when she was over, Remy and Freya came round. *That* was a surprise. Charlie hadn't seen or heard from Remy in weeks. He'd almost given up on him. In fact, as Charlie had been feeling a bit weird about Remy – kind of abandoned by him – it was a good thing that Esther had been there too. And Freya of course. It had been more relaxed that way, and they'd all had a few drinks and a laugh as if everything was normal. But next morning Esther had curled up on the sofa next to Charlie and said, 'So, were you and Remy really close?'

Were, she'd said. She'd picked up that things weren't the same anymore. How perceptive, Charlie thought.

'Yeah, we used to hang out a lot,' he said quickly. He was aware of Esther looking at him, almost reading his thoughts. She's so smart, he thought then. He can't understand why she's with that idiot Miles.

'And now he's seeing Freya,' she added lightly.

'Yeah. I'm really happy for him. She's good for him. They're good together.' A little silence fell, which didn't feel awkward at all. But Charlie was aware of her gaze, the way it burrowed into his brain and read all those scrappy little thoughts he'd been trying to keep stashed away.

His mum and James had gone out for a walk with Kim and Lorenzo, so it was just the two of them in the house. Esther squeezed his hand. 'Look, the sun's just come out. Don't s'pose you'd do some pictures for me, would you?'

'What, of *you*?' His mum had already done some yesterday.

'Yeah. C'mon, I bet you've got a good eye, just like your mum. It'll be fun.'

So that's what they did. Not that Charlie tells his father any of this – that they hung out in the garden and he took pictures of Esther sitting on the old stone wall in the cool December sunshine. He doesn't tell him that she looked so beautiful in those pictures, with her dazzling smile and her long red hair blowing around her delicate face. He doesn't tell his dad that, the night before, as darkness fell and Remy and Freya had gone home, he and Esther had sat in his room looking at the night sky through his telescope.

'This is amazing,' she exclaimed. 'I've never seen the stars as bright as this. We hardly see them at all in London.'

'There's too much light pollution there,' he said. 'Even out here there's quite a bit of it.'

'So where isn't there any? I mean, where's the best place to see stars?'

'There are a few places,' Charlie replied. 'There's a Scottish island that's meant to be the best, though. The best in Britain, I mean.'

'Have you been there?' she asked.

'No, but I will.'

She smiled then, and hugged him. 'I know you will,' she said. She slept in their little spare room that night, having borrowed one of his oversized T-shirts to wear. Charlie liked it, that she was near. Not in *that* way. In a friend way, he meant. Because Remy used to stay over, or Charlie would stay at his, and he knows things move on and change, and he really is happy that Remy's doing so well with his music, which is brilliant, and he's happy that Remy's with Freya now, because Charlie's life is moving on too.

He has a new friend. They joke and message constantly. They send each other funny little films and chat about all kinds of stuff.

Esther posted the pictures Charlie took of her and the jewellery people loved them. He doesn't tell his dad this, because Frank reckons photography should be difficult, and involve a proper camera, tripod, lights, all that, to be any good. Like it must require *equipment*. All this time he's been chattering on about a film he's making, about how he's trying to raise the finance and it's going to be gritty and real, he says. It's going to be amazing.

'So, what've you been up to?' Frank asks finally.

'Nothing much,' Charlie says.

'Looking forward to Christmas?' As if he's nine years old.

'Yeah, I s'pose so . . .'

'Doing much?'

'Just the usual,' he replies.

'Aw.' Frank sniggers. 'You're spending too much time huddling over your books, son. Live a little!'

CHAPTER THIRTY

LAUREN

It's not that I mind Esther coming with James for week-ends at my place. Of course I don't. I'm flattered that she obviously enjoys being here, and I'm surprised – and delighted – that she and Charlie seem to get along so well. But at the same time I'd love it just to be us two, me and James, for a couple of days – like it was in Corsica. Yes, my parents were there, and Charlie too, but James and I could just disappear into the hills, or down to the beach, for great swathes of time and no one minded or even seemed to notice.

Those two weeks were heavenly and it hasn't felt quite the same recently, with James staying in London unexpect-edly a couple of times, when Esther needed time with him. I've tried not to be resentful, and to remind myself that our kids always come first – even when he admitted that, actually, Esther had seemed completely fine. 'Which is good of course,' he'd added. 'I mean, it's not that I *wanted* anything to be wrong . . .'

I knew what he meant, though. Why had she wanted to see him so urgently, just when he'd been about to drive out to spend time with me? A tiny part of me wonders if he's being manipulated, and that Esther isn't terribly keen on him being with me at all. Sure, we do great pictures together and she's perfectly polite and pleasant company. But there's a tiny hint of something else going on, I'm sure of it. And I can't quite put my finger on what it is.

And now Christmas is hurtling towards us and it feels even more important to figure out how we're going to spend some time together. Which sparks an idea for a gift . . .

I'm horribly out of practice when it comes to gift-buying for men. At least, a man I'm dating. Way before we'd split up, Frank had decided it was 'silly' to spend money on each other, meaning it was far too much effort to hoof around the shops (online shopping hadn't existed then). And faulty-oven-fuse George and I hadn't reached the gift-giving stage. I want to give James something thoughtful, that he'll really enjoy. But what would a fifty-two-year-old vet – who's not terribly interested in 'stuff' – possibly want?

Clothes? A *sweater*? Surely we're not at the stage where knitwear is the default option. Aftershave, then? I know James well enough to know he doesn't wear it.

He's actually very hard to buy for in that he just isn't interested in fancy things. I don't mean he's completely unsophisticated; just that being given a posh pen, or some kind of gadget, would probably baffle him. His leather wallet is old and battered, but I know he's fond of it as Esther saved up her pocket money to buy it for him about ten years ago. We're certainly not at a sock- or dressing-gown-buying stage, and he doesn't wear pyjamas – at least, not when he's with me.

What he does keep saying, jokingly – although I suspect there's a grain of truth in it – is that he'd love to propel us back to Corsica, 'away from all of this'. Away from endless family shenanigans and a relentless workload, he means. As I've gathered that he only has a short break over Christmas, that's not really on the cards right now. But a little probing reveals that his practice closes for four days over New Year, and when I suggests he 'keeps it free' he says, happily, that he'd planned to do just that.

'What d'you have in mind?' he asks.

'A little surprise,' I reply. Then, secretly, I pore over accommodation for a little jaunt, just the two of us, far away from it all. As it's New Year there isn't heaps available – but there's enough. I gaze at cosy hotels in pretty Dorset villages, wooden lodges with hot tubs in the depths of the New Forest and even a luxury tree house in Wales. Then I remember how fondly he's talked about all those Cornish holidays with Esther when she was younger; how Esther had insisted on walking a section of the South West Coast Path in flip-flops. I can't help smiling at that, and admire his dogged optimism that it was going to turn out all right. We only do our best, after all. We don't set off intending for our kids to have bleeding feet.

There'll be none of that, if I can find us a little New Year retreat. I scroll on, checking out clifftop hotels, sleek harbourside apartments and even a restored fishing boat on a creek. As I stop and sip my coffee, a phrase leaps out from the screen at me: off-grid. Or, more specifically:

An utterly secluded, off-grid haven

With stunning coastal views, our fully restored 18th-century cottage offers the ultimate romantic retreat. In our attic room, formerly an artist's studio, the glass wall offers stunning views of the night sky (no light pollution here!).

There's no Wi-Fi or phone signal. You can't even plug anything in. But you'll never be bored for a moment at Saltspray Cottage. Heated by wood-burning stoves – and with solar panels providing our electricity – it sits in 70 acres of our own woodland, where a winding path takes you down to our own private beach. Perfect for nature lovers and adventurers yearning to truly get away from it all.

I allow myself a few moments to gaze at the cottage, and check out photos of the nearby coastline with its secluded silvery coves. And I picture James and me, strolling along that winding coastal path – with not a bleeding foot between us – then returning to the cottage to cuddle up in front of that wood-burning stove . . .

This, I decide, will be my present to James on our first Christmas together. My heartbeat quickens as I click 'book'.

CHAPTER THIRTY-ONE

ESTHER

When she tells her parents that Miles has been on better behaviour, Esther is aware that it makes him sound like a child. But he *is* better now. He's being super, super nice – even complimentary, which he never really was before, unless she asked him, 'D'you like this outfit?' And he'd look a bit bored and say, 'Yeah-great-babe!' And Esther knew she could've been wearing a blanket dragged out of a skip for all he was really taking anything in. Now it's all, 'Is that new, sweetie? Really suits you!' and 'You're the most beautiful creature, Esther Burton.' Which is nice, of course. She's grateful for it, and tries to remember to write it in her gratitude journal.

He's started cooking too – actual meals, served up at around the time normal people eat. Before his transformation to Ideal Boyfriend, it was all those calorie-counted meals consisting of some shredded vegetables, tempeh and sauerkraut, those fermented foods that are meant to be so good for the gut. 'I'm twenty,' Esther has grumbled under her breath many times. 'I don't have to think about my gut.' Whereas Miles does, a lot – or rather his 'tummy'.

(She always feels a tiny bit sick whenever she hears a grown man saying tummy.)

When she thinks about it now, a vast proportion of their relationship has involved having to listen to him ranting on and on, about his DJing or his acid reflux. But not anymore. Now he's buying fresh fish, parcelling it lovingly in foil and baking it in the oven. It's still super healthy – served with salads with surprising things in them like fresh herbs and mango. (How did Miles even know where to buy mangoes?) Then he'll spend about sixteen hours detailing precisely how he made it, which is more information than Esther probably needs in relation to salad assembly, especially in winter when, actually, some chips would be nice – but he likes to keep his weight down. Hers too, she suspects. 'How are things with the scales these days?' he'll ask her occasionally.

'They're working fine, thanks,' she's retorted, refusing to share the fluctuations of her weight. Anyway, at least they're finished with those tedious boxed meals from the subscription plan.

One of Miles's salads is so pretty with its scattering of pomegranate seeds and fresh mint, she suggests he takes a picture of her with it, in the kitchen with daylight streaming in, the way Lauren does. In natural light, that is – rather than in the gloomy cupboard or lying on the smelly grey rug. She posts the picture on Instagram, captioning it: *Look at this salad my boyfriend made, all twinkly jewel colours just like my new Bethani pendant.* And they love that one.

'You're really in the flow,' says the woman who handles their marketing. 'We've loved what you've been doing in that cottagey garden in the countryside. The quality of the pictures is *amazing* . . .'

'Thanks,' Esther says. She hasn't mentioned that she

now has a professional photographer on the job. Anyway, they're not all by Lauren, she reminds herself, in justification. Charlie has taken some too and sometimes, like today, she'll still ask Miles to rattle off a pic or two. It's a real mixture these days. It's more about capturing a *moment*, Esther reminds herself. And really, anyone with a phone and a half-decent eye can do that.

'I shouldn't say this,' the Bethani woman adds, 'because we can never tell. But I'm pretty sure we'll want to keep this relationship going with you for the long term.'

Esther wants that too – not just with the jewellery people but with Miles. Never mind the age difference that her dad seems so hung up about, or the fact that he's let her down in the past. He's a new Miles now: lovely, caring and thoughtful.

'How did I almost screw this up?' he asks over dinner one night, in her favourite Moroccan restaurant down the road from his flat. Tears are shining in his eyes, and Esther squeezes his hand across the table.

'We don't have to go over that anymore,' she tells him.

'I've been a jerk. I really don't deserve you, Est . . .'

She's feeling especially happy tonight, because more brands have been getting in touch to talk about working with her. Esther has now signed with a prestigious agency who'll manage this stuff for her. A few weeks ago, everything was falling apart and now it feels as if the Balinese priest is shining good fortune down onto her.

'Miles, we've all done stuff we're not proud of,' she says firmly.

'You're such an amazing person,' he gushes. 'Thank you, babe.'

She leans forward to kiss him. 'The main thing now is to learn from it all and move on from the past. Because the future is what really matters.'

Maybe all this therapy has been worth it, because it could have been Chrissie saying that.

*

They even go away for a weekend, to an apartment in Bath, for a pre-Christmas treat. Miles has often said he 'doesn't see the point of other cities' (apart from London, he means) and Esther knows he's a bit funny about 'The North', as he puts it. Although he mainly grew up in the country, his parents also had a beautiful townhouse in Chiswick with its own boat mooring on the river. So he considers himself a Londoner really. He seems to think that anywhere north of Brent Cross is all football violence, terrible food and constant rain. He was amazed when Esther told him about all the holidays her dad used to take her on, when she was younger – not just to Majorca and France but places in England too, like Cornwall, the Lake District and Yorkshire.

'Yorkshire?' he gasped. 'What did you do there?'

She told him all about the creepy ghost walk in Whitby, and the donkey rides and ice creams on Scarborough beach. Then there was that time they'd stayed on a farm, some-where in the Yorkshire Dales, she thinks, where the farmer had let her bottle-feed a lamb and collect eggs in the hay barn every morning – all those brilliant memories with her dad. But Miles had stopped listening by that point.

'I said I bottle-fed a lamb!' she snapped.

'What? Sorry, babe. I *was* listening, honestly . . .'

There's none of that tuning out as they check into the beautiful holiday apartment. Okay, so Bath's not in the north. But still, in the two years they've been together, this is the first time Miles has booked a trip. (All the other times, Esther's done it.) And the city is so pretty and clean, awash with posh shops and dinky cafés, that Miles doesn't even seem to mind that it's not London.

They have fantastic pub lunches and browse in book-shops, where he hangs about at the door, looking a bit bored, but at least he's letting Esther choose things to do instead of taking control the whole time, which is how he always used to be.

Later they wallow together in a bubbling rooftop spa pool. 'This is so lovely,' she tells him, gazing up at the darkening sky.

'Glad you're having fun, darling,' Miles says.

'It's the best weekend I've had since . . . well, I can't remember.' She feels as if she could literally burst with happiness.

'We should do it more often then!'

'Can we?' Esther doesn't know why she does this; asks him for permission. 'I mean, I'd love to,' she says quickly.

He goes a bit quiet and slips his arm around her shoulders. All around them, young couples are canoodling in the water. The spa is clearly a date destination, despite the 'no displays of intimacy' signs that are dotted about. 'I want to make it up to you,' Miles adds. 'Seriously, after everything I've done.' Shockingly, his eyes fill with tears. What's with all the emotion these days? Esther used to wonder if he ever cried; if his body was even capable of making tears. Now he seems to be permanently welling up.

'Oh, Miles, it's okay,' she says, kissing him on the mouth.

'I've messed up in the past,' he says, 'but I really am trying to be a better person . . .'

'I know you are,' she says gently. 'You're seeing Raoul. It seems to be helping a lot.' Like her, Miles has a thera-pist, only his is focused on his apparent sex addiction,

211

what triggers it and the steps he can take to deal with what Miles describes as 'intrusive thoughts'.

'Miles?' she says later over dinner. 'I was just wondering, have you ever thought about keeping a gratitude journal?'

'God, no.' He laughs and shakes his head. 'It's not really my thing, Est.'

She shrugs. 'I've found it quite helpful.'

'What? You keep one?' Her dad knows, and yet her boyfriend didn't, is the thought that springs to mind.

'Yes I do.'

'What for?'

'You know what they are, don't you?'

''Course I do. Yeah.'

'Well . . .' She pauses and picks up the last teeny little starter; a nest of crispy filo pastry with a sliver of salmon inside. 'I just think it's a good thing to do.'

'All that "live, laugh, love" stuff?' he teases. 'You're a walking wall decal, darling.'

'No need to take the piss.'

His hand covers hers on the table. 'I'm only kidding. I think it's great, if it works for you . . .'

She nods. 'It does actually. Like, at the beginning, when I started it, I could hardly think of anything to put in it. It made me focus and think, well, *some* things in my life are good . . .'

'So what kind of stuff did you write back then?'

Esther smiles at the memory. 'When I was really scraping around for things, I once wrote, "I have clean knickers."'

'Always a good thing!' Miles smirks.

'But I don't put that now.'

''Cause your knickers are dirty?' A raised brow and a naughty grin.

'No, because my life's so much better and I have bigger things to write about now,' she explains.

'Okay, so what's the last thing you wrote?'

Esther pauses for effect. 'Bethani have asked me to speak at their big spring launch!'

'Really? Wow!' Miles is beaming now, seeming genuinely impressed. Esther realises she has never seen him looking that way before. 'Well done,' he adds. 'I'm so proud of you. What will you have to do?'

'Talk about the brand, what it means to me, how we work together . . .'

'They'll pay you for that?'

She stares at him across the table. 'Of course they will. They're paying me a lot, Miles. A *huge* amount to be their ambassador—'

'I'm so happy for you, sweetie.'

'But money's not the main thing,' she adds quickly. 'I mean, it's not what makes me happy, Miles. Not at all. This does – being away together . . .' She sips the delicious white wine. 'We're getting along and I can see a real future for us—'

'Oh, honey,' he says, welling up again. 'I love you so much.'

'I love you too. And that's what I mean about the journal – that there are much bigger things to be thankful for now. Like being here and having these amazing experiences together. Just being with you.'

As Miles leans over and kisses her, Esther's heart seems to fly. 'Well, I reckon I'm the luckiest man in the world,' he says, smiling broadly, 'so maybe I should start a gratitude journal too.'

CHAPTER THIRTY-TWO

ESTHER

Only, it turns out Miles wasn't quite telling the truth that night in Bath. Because a few days later, on Christmas Eve, Esther is getting ready to meet her mum, dad and Luc for dinner at a restaurant. It's a last-minute thing. Her mum insisted on them all getting together seeing as Esther won't be joining them for Christmas Day after all. Miles begged her to stay home with him, 'So it's just the two of us. What could be better than that?' Finally, she had agreed.

It would just be too awkward, she realised, for her boyfriend and dad to spend Christmas Day together. It's like they can't be in the same room without there being a weird atmosphere. And she can kind of understand it, from Miles's point of view. Yes, he'd been drunk that day at Lauren's house – but now she and Miles are madly in love again, she can see that her dad was out of order too.

Imagine ridiculing him about his mullet in front of everyone. She's seen photos of her dad in the Eighties with his silly bleached quiff and red mohair sweater and pixie boots! What did he think *he* looked like? Anyway, her mum has booked a table at this amazing new place that everyone's desperate to go to. She knows the owners. That's how she managed to get a table. Esther can't understand how a table can be miraculously 'found' at a restaurant that's fully booked, but never mind. Apparently the place is all about 'nose to tail' eating, 'meaning none of the animal goes to waste,' her mum enthused, which isn't *quite* Esther's thing. It's not that she's vegetarian. But surely certain animal parts, like ears and bum holes, weren't designed to be eaten? Still, Esther is going along to keep everyone happy. She wouldn't dare to upset her mum's plans.

She's all ready, about to head out, when she checks the weather on her phone and realises it's raining. So her sandals won't do. At least, not in the presence of her dad, enforcer of 'appropriate footwear' and obsessive over things being one hundred per cent waterproof. Is this something that happens with age, this fixation with dressing according to the climate? When Esther turns, say, forty, will she be constantly on at Miles for not wearing a rainproof coat? She glances at her phone again – so much easier than checking the weather out of the window – and decides, okay, boots then. Which means a whole rethink of her outfit.

Having changed, she's now cutting it fine time-wise as she burrows under Miles's antique king-sized bed, knocking aside socks, headphones, various chargers and a matted hairbrush in search of her flat tan boots. She *thinks* they're here somewhere. She pulls out a pair of Miles's jeans, tugged off with the pants still left in them. It's a habit of his, the peeling off of clothes in one layer because separating them out would be far too much effort. For some bizarre reason, Esther has become the one who does all the laundry around here, as if operating the washing machine is beneath him. For a split second her brain shoots her back to being sixteen years old, before the reality show was filmed at her school. Back then, she used to enjoy picturing herself at the age she is now. At twenty, she'd imagined, her life would be filled with history lectures and fabulous flat-shares and friendships she'd have forever.

Nope, Esther. You WON'T be floating around a beautiful university town with your history books. You'll be peeling the festering pants out of your boyfriend's jeans!

Lying flat on her stomach now, in order to search even further under the bed, she pushes aside her zebra-print suitcase and notices a shoebox sitting there. Maybe it's some shoes she's forgotten about? Would they do instead of boots? She's sent loads of free stuff from PRs and fashion brands in the hope that she'll do posts about them. It's a perk, and Esther realises how lucky she is; she's written about that in her gratitude journal too. But sometimes, to her shame, these freebies end up being kicked under the bed and lie there, forgotten.

She pulls out the box, straightens up and picks the bits of under-bed fluff off herself. When she takes off the lid she discovers it's not shoes in there after all. It's a book – a hard-backed notebook – and on the front, in gold type, it says, *My Gratitude Journal.*

She places it on the bed and stares at it. It's not her gratitude journal. Hers has a pale grey cover with tiny white clouds over it, and this one has blue diagonal stripes. It must belong to Miles. Or maybe, she's thinking now, he's bought her a new one for when her current one's all filled up?

It seems weird, though, and something shifts uneasily, deep inside her stomach. She has a feeling she should put it back in its box, shove it under the bed and think nothing more about it. It's wrong to pry, but she can't help herself.

Esther is having *intrusive thoughts*. They're saying, *Just a little peek won't hurt. Just a tiny look, then you can put it back and never look at it again.*

Perched on the edge of the bed, Esther holds the journal on her lap and flips it open. Similar to hers, each page is divided into halves horizontally, and at the top of each section there's a space to write the date. Her gaze lands upon Miles's spidery writing. She can see now that he was definitely lying when they were in Bath, pretending he thought gratitude journals were a bit lame – because the first date she spots is 29 July of this year. All this time, he's been keeping one too. Why didn't he say?

Esther thinks back to the end of July and what was going on then. She's pretty sure that's when she was supposed to have been in Corsica with her dad. It seems that on that date – the first entry in the journal – Miles had plenty to be grateful for because he wrote:

> *Beautiful sunny day.*
> *Esther home with me and not in Corsica.*
> *So grateful for my love.*

Oh, that *is* lovely. Her heart seems to squeeze, and she feels guilty now about reading it. As she skims the pages she realises Miles hasn't filled in his journal every day, and that sometimes days – or even weeks – passed without him writing anything at all. Then there was a flurry of activity when he must have felt inspired to do it for a few days on the trot.

Esther sits there, poring over his words, vaguely aware of the sound of Dylan the rat trundling along on his exercise wheel in the kitchen – poor little thing, never getting anywhere. She's engrossed in what Miles has been grateful for; lots about his weight, and his 'tummy' feeling better. Sweet things that jump out at her, like:

Coffee this morning with E.
Mellow music, the two of us hanging out.
Funny squishy-looking clouds.

Esther smiles at that. She'd never realised Miles notices clouds.

Great gig, got paid at last.

Well, that's a bit less cerebral but everyone needs money to live.

New shoes fitted fine, pleased with them.

Good for you, she thinks with a smile; that's one first world worry sorted. Just one more page, she tells herself. Then she'll put it back in its box and—

Found choc ice at back of freezer.
Night went well, another great set tonight.

Then – she has to reread it in case she's having some kind of bizarre hallucination:

Tabitha's tits.

PART THREE

Mishaps in the Kitchen

If your crème pâtissière splits, don't panic. A quick blitz with a hand-held blender and everything will merge together beautifully

CHAPTER THIRTY-THREE

LAUREN

I know I'm lucky. I keep telling myself that, even though a bit of distance seems to have crept in between me and James lately. It's just practical stuff; I realise that. Our lives are busy, especially at this time of year. Once Christmas is over we'll have our Cornish break, and then everything will be just as it was between us. My heart seems to lift every time I think about it.

As usual, I'm hosting Christmas Day. There'll be Charlie, Kim, Lorenzo and their daughters, who are home from university and are like cousins to Charlie. Although Kim and I have been friends since primary school, we've grown even closer since Charlie and I moved out to the village where they'd settled a few years before. They've become our family really; the one we've made.

I always do the big festive roast, which I love: all the planning and making things a little different every year, trying new tweaks with stuffing or roasted parsnips, all that. Kim and Lorenzo bring cheeses, chocolates and copious amounts of booze, and it's always wonderful.

Christmas Eve is pretty special too, when we all get

together in our local pub in the village. There's the same line-up as Christmas Day, plus Remy's parents, Ellie and Brian, and a few other local friends. It's a fun, rowdy night with live music, a huge, twinkling real tree and much jollity. We adults have settled at one big table, and the younger ones – including Charlie, Remy and Freya – are all clustered around another. Remy seems so much more confident than Charlie now. With his gigs and performances, he's much in demand – whereas Charlie is mainly in demand by Brenda, who's always on at him to do extra shifts at the newsagent's. But maybe his friendship with Esther has given him a new spring in his step. That last weekend she was here they'd spent the whole time hanging out together. I'd heard laughter coming from his room and was amazed they'd got on so well.

'Such a shame James couldn't make it tonight,' Ellie announces now, pink-cheeked, a couple of drinks down already.

'Oh, it couldn't be helped,' I say, keen to gloss over it. 'You know what it's like at this time of year.'

'What happened?' She frowns, over-egging it now as if it's some massive deal. (Ellie is always eager for gossip.) And it isn't really. It's just that James had planned to come along to our Christmas Eve pub night, stay over with me and then head to Rhona's for Christmas Day in the morning. I think he was hanging on to a shred of hope that Esther would change her mind and be there at her mother's too.

I was perfectly happy with his plans as, that way, we'd have a *little* bit of Christmas together. In preparation I'd printed out the details for Saltspray Cottage, with photos of the house nestled deep in the woods, and the views from the glass-walled loft. Four whole days off-grid! What could be better? I'd slipped the sheets of paper into an envelope and couldn't wait to hand it to him when we woke up together on Christmas morning.

Only, he hasn't been able to come here tonight. At the last minute Rhona had managed to get a booking at some hugely in-demand place that's apparently full until Easter. And his presence would be required.

'She's pulled strings to get a table,' James explained, sounding sheepish.

She's pulled your strings, I thought bitterly, hating that I was reacting this way. Of course his family came first. 'It's fine,' I said resignedly.

'I'm sorry. There was nothing I could do.'

'Of course there wasn't,' I said, more snappily than I'd intended.

As a stony silence settled between us, I found myself wondering: is this what it's going to be like? Feeling as if I'm way down his priority list, with plans cancelled at a moment's notice? Yes, it probably is, I decided. This is what happens when you fall in love with someone at our age. Like it or not, other people are going to be part of it too. *Grow up*, I told myself firmly. Wouldn't I put Charlie first too?

'I really wanted to see you tonight,' James added.

'Well, never mind.'

'I'll call you tomorrow.'

'Oh, you'll be busy,' I said, with a new brusqueness that had bubbled up from somewhere – I'd no idea where.

'We can chat, can't we?' He sounded taken aback and a little hurt.

'Yeah, see how you go,' I said, wanting to get off the phone before I said something I regretted. And actually, as I set off with Charlie for the pub, I did regret being snarky like that. But it was done now. And it occurred to me that this was the first Christmas since Frank and I

223

broke up that there'd been anything like a complication. A tiny one, yes, but it was there all the same. And now Ellie seems to have latched on to the fact that something is up.

'So, what's James doing tonight?' she asks now, pink lipstick smudged.

'He's seeing his family,' I explain. 'His ex-wife's organised dinner for them all tonight.'

'His ex-wife?' She blinks at me. 'He's spending Christmas Eve with her?' Ellie and her family live in one of the biggest – and prettiest – houses in the village. While she has her own events company, and her husband Brian is something terribly high up in management consultancy, I have never envied their life. Instead of sitting at our table, Brian has gravitated to a cluster of middle-aged men at the bar; commuter guys, barely glimpsed in the village, who seem to prefer the company of men.

'Well, it's a family thing,' I clarify. 'James gets along fine with his ex and her partner, so he's happy to—'

'But you *will* see him tomorrow?' Ellie cuts in. Across the table, Kim gives me a quick glance.

'Erm, no,' I reply. 'He'll be with them then too.'

'With his ex-wife?' she gasps.

'Um, yes.'

She gives me a look that clearly says, *Rather you than me with this complicated set-up.* At the bar, Brian and his friends are guffawing loudly with the barman.

Kim leans towards us. 'It's pretty normal for people to spend Christmas with their families, Ellie,' she points out.

'His ex-wife is family?' she squawks. 'Poor Lauren!'

'There's no "poor Lauren" about it,' I say with a forced laugh, as I try to shake off my irritation. 'I'm going to have a houseful. These guys are coming, *and* their girls . . .' I indicate Kim and Lorenzo at our table, and

224

their daughters who are ensconced in the younger group. 'And me and James have only been together a few months,' I add. 'We're not at the Christmas-together stage yet.'

I down my wine, grateful when Lorenzo brings me another. I shouldn't let Ellie stir me up, I decide, glancing over at the younger contingent's table and seeing them all laughing and talking over each other, just like old times. And it's true that I wouldn't expect James to be with me tomorrow – but still, I can't shrug off the disappointment that he's not here tonight.

I check the time, murmur that I'm off to the ladies' and slip away from our table. But instead, I step out of the pub, realising that, after our chilly exchange earlier, I really need to talk to James.

Need. The word snags at my brain. 'Needing' to hear someone's voice is an entirely new thing for me, and I'm not sure I like it. All these years, when it's just been Charlie and me, I've worked hard to make sure that the ground feels solid beneath our feet. And now it seems a little shaky.

'Hey, darling.' James answers immediately, sounding surprised – but happy – to hear from me.

'You're not at the restaurant already, are you?' I ask.

'No. I've just set off. Just walking to the tube—'

'Oh, that's good,' I say, realising now that those couple of wines have already rushed to my head.

'Everything all right?' he asks lightly.

'Yeah, yeah, I'm good. Everyone's here. Drinks are flowing. You know . . .'

'Wish I could be there too,' James says.

'Me too.'

He clears his throat. 'I was going to bring you your Christmas present tonight.'

'It doesn't matter,' I say quickly. 'I mean, we'll have plenty of time at New Year—'

'Let's hope so,' he says, which triggers a rush of anxiety in me. The Cornish cottage is booked and there's no cancelling it now.

'You *are* free those days, aren't you?' I ask. 'The ones we talked about, I mean?' *Or has Rhona organised things for then too?*

'Yes, of course I am,' James says firmly.

'It's just, our plans seem a bit doomed at the moment, don't they?'

'Well, there's been a lot going on . . .'

'Let's hope nothing gets in the way of New Year,' I add, before I can stop myself. 'I mean, it can't, James. Nothing can get in the way.'

'What d'you mean?' he asks.

'I mean,' I say, knowing now that I can't keep my plans under wraps any longer, 'we're going away together. Me and you. And if there was some kind of drama . . . I mean, some sort of situation where your presence was needed . . . well, they wouldn't be able to get at you.' That didn't come out quite right; my implication that his ex-wife and daughter are forever trying to 'get at' him.

'I don't understand,' he says. 'What d'you mean?'

'James, I've booked us a trip. And now I'm thinking, was it a mad idea? Because if it is, and you hate the thought of it, and it was stupid of me to do this without checking with you, well, I'll just – I don't know – write it off, I suppose . . .'

'Lauren, please. You won't be writing anything off. But what is it?'

'It's, um, a cottage in Cornwall that's completely off-grid,' I explain. 'I mean, there's no phone signal or Wi-Fi or even mains power . . .' I tail off. 'Of course, you know what off-grid means.'

He's chuckling now. 'Erm, yes. I do.'

'I think you'd call that womansplaining,' I add, smiling.

'Who knew it existed?' he asks, teasing me.

'Oh, it probably was a bit impetuous of me to book it without telling you. But it's my present to you,' I add. 'I just thought we really need time on our own . . .'

'Where no one can get at us?' I detect the smile in his voice, and my heart seems to turn over.

'You know what I mean.'

'I do. Of course I do.'

The pause that follows feels anything but awkward. 'So, I wasn't mad to book it?' I ask tentatively.

'Not at all,' James says. 'I love the idea of being cut off from everything with you . . .' He seems to hesitate, and now my heart plummets in anticipation of the 'but'. Every time the pub's front door opens, a ripple of chatter and laughter drifts out. I should get back in there and let James go to his dinner. 'Will Charlie be okay?' he asks.

I open my mouth to speak. So that's what's worrying him? Whether Charlie can cope on his own? 'James, he's nearly eighteen,' I remind him. 'After being cooped up over Christmas and forced to play board games with us all, he'll be delighted to get rid of me.'

'Great. So . . . how will we get there?'

'I'll drive.'

'And when do we go?' His voice is tinged with excitement now.

'The 30th. We'll be there for four nights. Are you sure you're okay with this, being cut off from the world?'

'Am I okay?' he exclaims now. 'Of course I am. I can't think of anything better, just being with you.'

'D'you think it'll be like Corsica?' I ask, unable to keep down a smile.

He chuckles. 'Well, I can't imagine there'll be any dog-related emergency this time, so . . .'

'Oh, James, this is just what we need, isn't it? Some time together, just the two of us?'

'It's absolutely what we need,' he says. 'Thank you. It was so thoughtful – an absolutely genius idea for people like us . . .'

'People with lives and baggage,' I say, laughing now.

'Exactly,' James says. 'And I can't wait.'

CHAPTER THIRTY-FOUR

ESTHER

'Esther! It's Esther Burton!'

She clatters up the tube station steps, ignoring the male voice behind her. She's late of course, after reading that thing; that gratitude journal of Miles's. She couldn't just run straight out and be normal. For ages she sat there rereading what he'd written, imagining all kinds of scenarios – all involving a naked woman called Tabitha.

Tabitha's tits. What did that mean? That he'd admired them from a distance? That he'd interacted with them? Feeling sick to her stomach, Esther had rummaged through Miles's stuff for evidence of what he'd been up to. At least, as much as she could manage. He's a hoarder. He doesn't call it that, of course; he says he's a *curator*. All those (unread) ancient leather-bound books, the dusty antiques and quirky ornaments ('objets', he calls them, pronounced the French way) tell the story of his life, he reckons. 'It's not clutter,' Miles says. 'It's *a living museum of me.*'

'Tosser,' Esther mutters under her breath. What about the pants he'd thrown in the direction of the linen basket, and which are lying behind it all furred with dust? Are they part of the Miles Museum too?

With her heart racing, Esther had perched on the edge of the bed, still clutching that damn journal. *Take a breath*, Chrissie would advise, *before jumping to conclusions*. Had she misread it? Miles's writing is awful, all jagged and scrawly, the letters lurching forward as if tumbling drunkenly on top of each other, whereas Esther's is exceptionally neat. They taught them something at least, at Willow Vale. But no, that was definitely what he'd written. Maybe they weren't *real* breasts, attached to an actual woman he'd either slept with or wanted to sleep with, but just some fantasy thing swirling around his murky brain? Or he'd been watching porn (she's caught him doing that before) and Tabitha was a girl he particularly liked?

While that hadn't made Esther feel hugely reassured, she was aware that time was rattling on and she really should have set off by now. Her mum can be flaky about lots of things but she hates anyone being late. 'D'you think your time is more valuable than other people's?' she once retorted. But Esther had to try and put her mind at rest. Only then could she go out and put on a smiley, festive face for her family.

So she'd sat for ages googling Tabitha's tits. Of course it was just load of porn links that came up. None of it reassured her, and she still had a niggling feeling that Miles's scribblings were probably connected to someone he knew in real life. Esther's eyes were scratchy, her head thudding dully when she checked the time again. With a jolt she realised they'd all be at the restaurant already, rolling their eyes and complaining about her tardiness. So she quickly stashed the journal back in its box, shoved it back under the bed and rushed out.

'Esther! Esther! Hey, don't run away!' It's a bunch of boys who are shouting and laughing some way behind her as she reaches street level. She marches along with her head down against the light, steady rain, pretending they're not there. 'Hey, Esther! Come and talk to us!' The boys are closer now. 'Can we get a picture with you?'

She remembers her dad suggesting that, if she's stuck for what to say to people, she could switch the focus to them and be nice and chatty, asking questions in order to deflect the attention. But she can't do that tonight. She doesn't have it in her to stop and be nice when they're being jerks and she's late – *so* late – already. Luc is probably gnawing a pig's rectum by now.

'Stuck-up bitch!' one of the boys shouts.

'Leave her alone,' says another, laughing as if it's just banter. Esther hates that word. It seems to be used by men as an excuse for being arseholes. *It was only a bit of banter! Lighten up!* She's heard that plenty of times.

'Give us a photo!' the first one yells again. Something snaps in Esther and she spins around and almost laughs at the gaggle of boys who can only be around seventeen – Charlie's age, although he'd never behave like this; she's certain of that.

'Do your mums know you're out?' she snaps.

'What the fuck?' the skinny one exclaims.

'Just leave me alone, would you?'

'We were shouting at you,' he clarifies, looking put out.

'Well, I don't like being shouted at.'

'Can we just have a photo?' asks the heavily built one with a pink baby face and a fuzz of blond hair.

'Sorry, not now.' Why is she even apologising?

'Aw, come on.' Babyface steps forward and jabs at her wrist. 'Just one picture, darlin' . . .' His arm flops around her shoulders.

'Stop it!' Instinctively, she shrinks away.

'Just one picture,' he repeats. 'Tom, take it, quick—'

'Leave her alone—'

'Just fuck off,' she yells, pulling away and catching the skinny one looking mortified.

'Fuck you,' Babyface shouts as Esther hurries away, aware of more abuse being hurled at the back of her head and wondering why not one single person in the vicinity has said anything. To all these people heading out to celebrate Christmas Eve, seeing a girl being hassled means nothing.

'Ugly bitch!'

Esther is running now, trying not to cry because they're not worth her tears, they're just idiot boys who probably can't even get served. They'll have fake IDs and this is a fun part of their night, to humiliate a girl out on her own. She's lost now, looking for a stupid restaurant where her mum and Luc will make her try something disgusting like a jellied hoof.

She swerves round a corner, having shaken off the boys as she checks Google Maps. Where *is* this place? Why couldn't they just have had a nice dinner at home like normal people? Who even goes out on Christmas Eve? Everyone knows the staff are all desperate to go home and service is shit.

Esther tries to focus hard on the blue dot on the map, wondering what Tabitha of Tabitha's tits is doing now. Could it be a band? she's wondering now. Does it have a kind of ironic post-feminist edge to it? Unlikely, she decides. She's picturing this mythical woman sitting in a chic bar, with a cocktail, when she spots the restaurant across the street. Too cool to display an actual sign, it just has just a tiny menu under glass beside the door. Esther hurries in, her hair all straggly and faux fur jacket soggy from the rain, and sees her mum, dad and Luc sitting at the far end of the restaurant.

She inhales deeply and wipes away her tears with her fingers.

'Hey, sweetie, we were getting worried!' Her mum waves and her dad jumps up in greeting, his face breaking into a big, relieved smile. There are hugs all round.

'You're soaking, love,' her dad says. 'Here, take that coat off . . .'

She shrugs off the great wet rug and a waiter whisks it away. 'You're really late,' her mum announces. 'You could've texted.'

'I know. I'm sorry,' Esther mumbles, pushing her damp hair out of her face.

'What happened?'

'I just lost track of time,' she says feebly.

'Right. 'Course you did. And your mascara's run, darling. Maybe go to the loo and sort yourself out?'

'She's fine, Rhona,' her dad says sharply. Sensing an atmosphere building, Esther forces a smile.

'I'll do it in a minute, Mum.' Her mother is wearing a glamorous black dress in a clingy jersey fabric and her hair's all piled up, artfully undone; she's obviously just been to the hairdresser. No straggly wet tresses or smudged make-up for her. Esther catches a man glancing at her mother from another table. She doesn't even notice if anyone's spotted her and she couldn't care less.

'Anyway, you're here now,' Luc says, with forced jollity.

'It's *fine*, Est,' her dad says quickly. 'Just sit down and relax and we'll get you a drink.'

'Thanks, Dad.' Esther smiles briskly. Still shaken up by Miles's journal and those boys jostling her, she busies herself by delving into her voluminous shoulder bag for everyone's Christmas presents. They're just little things

233

she's bought, but carefully chosen: fragrance from Liberty for her mum (she loves expensive scents) and a beautiful penknife with a hand-carved wooden handle for Luc, which she thought would be handy for his foraging. For her dad, who's the hardest to buy for – because he always says he doesn't 'need' anything – she's put together a bundle of beautifully illustrated books about animal behaviour from an antiquarian bookshop on Charing Cross Road.

'Oh,' she mutters, starting to sweat now. 'They're not here.'

'What's not here?' her mum asks.

'Your . . . your Christmas presents . . .' Her eyes are filling up again. Damn these uncontrollable tear ducts, humiliating her like this. Esther rummages some more but there's just her purse, keys, some loose make-up, scrunched-up tissues and that particular kind of bag grit that immediately embeds itself under your fingernails. 'I forgot them,' she announces. 'I must've left them sitting on the bed. I'm really sorry—'

'Oh, it doesn't matter,' her mum says. Esther can tell by her face that it does really.

'I'm so stupid,' she murmurs.

'No, you're not,' her dad exclaims. 'You've had a lot on your mind, Est. We can do presents another time.' He's already given Esther her gifts to open tomorrow, and her mum has transferred money into her account.

Esther tries to blink away tears. It's the sight of her dad's concerned face that's doing it. Concern not just over the fact that she's upset about the presents, but that she's living with a man he really doesn't like, and doesn't trust to treat her well.

He's right, of course. He has an instinct, her dad – about people. Esther knows she should probably listen to him

234

more. But what twenty-year-old really wants to listen to their dad?

She grabs a menu, focusing hard on the tiny lettering. Liver sausage and beetroot; ox tongue, duck blood pudding (she almost retches just reading it) and, as suspected, hoof. Chicken parfait with – ugh – something called cockscomb. Her mum must have spotted it at the same time because she's asking, 'I wonder what cockscomb is?'

A passing waiter stops at their table. 'It's the fleshy red part on a male foul's head.'

'Like a cockerel?' Rhona asks.

'Yes, or a turkey,' the waiter replies brightly.

'Festive,' her dad mutters as he glides away.

Is it even edible, though? Esther supposes it must be, unless the aim of this place is to challenge you to consume terrible things. Why not garnish it with some goat's toenail clippings and pony's teeth? The menu stops short of bum holes and penises but only just. Esther stares at it, knowing she'll have to choose something. It has also occurred to her how unfair it is, that the human body can produce tears but lack the ability to suck them back in, no matter how hard you blink or try to think calming thoughts.

'There's plenty of plant-based stuff, Esther,' her mum remarks tartly.

'I'm not vegetarian,' Esther reminds her.

'People *think* you are, darling . . .' Already tipsy, her mother is clearly up for a quarrel tonight.

'What're you talking about?' Esther glares at her, so not in the mood for smart remarks – even though it's true. On her social media she has aligned herself to a plant-focused lifestyle, simply because brands like Bethani like it. *It's in tune with our values*, they've told her, and fair enough; her followers don't expect to see her cramming a kebab into her face.

'Can we just leave it please?' her dad says brightly.

'Yeah, we're here to have a nice time, aren't we?' Luc remarks.

Really? Esther thinks bitterly. *I thought we were here to be horrible to me?* The restaurant is bustling, filled with happy people all having a great time – apart from them, the dysfunctional family forced together by her mother who doesn't seem to care about anything apart from managing to get a booking in one of London's most talked-about restaurants. A ring of tension seems to have been drawn around them. Even the waiters appear to be giving them a wide berth.

Esther catches her dad's stoical look. It's a look that seems to say, *Hey, it's all right, Est. Your mum's just a bit pissed. Don't rise to her.*

Finally, a server drifts over to take their orders.

'That one please.' Esther jabs at the menu.

'Chicken parfait and cockscomb,' he confirms with a nod.

'Are you really having that?' her mum exclaims.

'Yes? Why not?' She glares at her across the table.

'D'you know what that is? Did you hear what the guy said?'

'Yes, it's fine, I really fancy eating the frilly thing off a cock's head, okay?' Esther announces. Her mum, dad, Luc and even the waiter are all staring at her. She realises too late that she was shouting, and now her eyes are all wet again, threatening to overflow.

'Esther,' her dad says, frowning in concern. 'What is it, love? Please tell us . . .' As tears spill down her cheeks he looks round at the waiter. 'Could you give us a few minutes, please?'

'Yes, sure,' the young man says, and quickly scuttles away.

236

Her mum is staring at her and Luc is repositioning things on the table unnecessarily. 'What's going on tonight?' her dad asks gently. 'You don't seem yourself at all . . .'

'Is it the menu?' her mum asks, frowning. 'Because you don't have to make a point by ordering the weirdest thing on it. No one's forcing you to eat a cockscomb—'

'I know that, Mum—'

'If you want something plain, I'm sure they'd do it for you. Shall we ask?' her mother trills, looking around for a waiter.

'It's not about the food, is it, Est?' Luc cuts in. This man, who can spot a tangly ragwort, or whatever the stuff is that he yanks up from riverbanks, is more perceptive than her own mother.

'Some boys were hassling me on the way here,' Esther says, staring down at her hands.

'What?' her dad barks.

'Just boys. Three of them. Grabbing me, wanting a photo . . .' A sob bursts out and her dad leans towards her and grabs for her hand.

'Dad, it's fine. Please don't make a fuss,' Esther hisses at him.

'Did they hurt you?' her mum asks.

'No.' Esther shakes her head. 'They didn't do anything really.'

'They just shouted at you?'

'Yes, Mum.' Esther nods.

'Well, I hope you gave as good as you got, darling,' she says.

'What did they say?' her dad wants to know.

'Nothing really.' The waiter is heading back towards them, and Esther quickly rescans the menu, deciding now to have the snout terrine. She doesn't care what it is as long as it doesn't snort at her.

'Well, that's good, honey,' her mum says, arranging her expression into a beaming smile as she looks around at all of them. 'C'mon, darling, it's Christmas Eve. Let's all try and cheer up, shall we? D'you know people would *kill* to get a table here?'

CHAPTER THIRTY-FIVE

JAMES

Maybe I focused on all the wrong things as a dad. Things like Esther eating a proper dinner after school – with a vegetable component – and doing her homework (even though it was optional) and going to the dentist every six months. I knew Rhona was more relaxed about that stuff, and I probably came across as a bit regimented. Maybe I was overcompensating for us splitting up, trying to make everything seem 'normal' with Esther hopping back and forth between our homes, although she always seemed okay about it. I mean, as far as she'd ever let on. Yes, she'd been upset at the time of the break-up, but she'd seemed to adjust quickly without too much emotional fallout.

It had been Rhona's decision to split up. It came out later that she'd been seeing someone else; not Luc but a man who'd been a regular customer at her tapas bar and had become a friend and then, well, a lover, obviously. 'It's just a physical thing,' she'd explained at the time. Great, I thought furiously. As long as there are no emotions involved. Just tons of illicit shagging while I was at work!

Yes, I was angry and hurt and felt like a colossal fool for not spotting the signs. I'd loved Rhona. We'd been together since we were nineteen years old.

But actually, once the dust had settled, I came around to thinking that perhaps she'd been right. Not to have an affair, obviously – but in that we weren't right together anymore. We'd grown up in different directions, and the gap between us had only widened over the years. 'Why won't you take a risk, James?' she'd cry in frustration when she'd wanted to blow our savings by investing in her friend's crazy venture. At least, I thought it was crazy. But, hey, maybe the world needed an all-year-round Easter shop. ('Why not?' Rhona had retorted. 'There are Christmas shops, and who doesn't love chocolate?') That was Rhona all over: the loud, vivacious entrepreneur. And me, squeezer of Jack Russells' anal glands, apparently.

Although there's a *bit* more to it than that. Before we closed the practice for Christmas I'd come up with several prototypes for the tortoise's leg splint. I'd been looking forward to telling Esther about them tonight over dinner, before it all kicked off, as she's always enjoyed hearing about the less everyday aspects of my work. ('Tell me again about the guinea pig's ear tumour, Dad!')

Of course we hadn't got around to tortoises' leg splints. We'd just battled through the meal as best we could. Not that I felt like eating after hearing that those arsehole boys had hassled Esther in the street. And Rhona just brushed it off, her main concern being that it was dampening our festive night out! I admire Rhona, and think she's brilliant in so many ways. But sometimes – like tonight – she frustrates the hell out of me.

So, yes, I do wonder if I've got it wrong over the years because, surely, if I'd been a better dad, then we could have sat there and talked honestly, and comforted Esther

– instead of making her feel worse. As it was, Rhona was pissed off because we weren't 'being jolly' and Luc kept enthusing loudly, 'This food's great! I can see why there's been such a fuss about it . . .' Meanwhile Esther had cried, then continued to fight back more tears, while I'd gone quiet. (I know it drives Rhona mad when I do that.) Is anything more depressing than a family all herded together and each person hating it in their own particular way?

We parted company, having sent Esther back to Miles's in an Uber. (She'd batted off my suggestion to stay at mine instead.) I told the others I was going to walk for a bit, 'just to get some air. Then I'll call a cab.'

But I was lying. I felt so bad about Esther that I craved strong alcohol and now I've found myself swerving into a bar. Not a cool bar like Forage, with a young bearded guy snipping up rosemary sprigs, but a loud, brash party place filled with huge groups all shouting and exchanging gifts. At a rough estimate fifty per cent are wearing some kind of festive headgear: Santa hats, reindeer antlers, tinsel deely-boppers. Crammed against the bar, I ask for a large gin and tonic and gulp it down.

I order a second one and replay the parts of the evening when I really should have stepped in – like when Rhona was picking on Esther about her phoney plant-based persona. (Shouldn't we have been trying to cheer her up rather than getting at her?) Why, I'm wondering now, as I make headway on that second drink, did I go tonight anyway?

The plan had been for me to head out to Lauren's and spend Christmas Eve with her. The pub gathering had sounded fun, and I'd been looking forward to it. Then Rhona had booked the restaurant and of course I'd jumped to bloody attention as I always do.

I finish my drink, wishing Lauren was here. Because

when I'm with Lauren I just feel good, so lucky and happy to have met this wonderful woman when, back in July, it had looked like my holiday was going to be a washout. And it strikes me now that this kind of life isn't normal – this planning a holiday with your daughter and her just not coming, and being unable to enjoy a nice family meal on Christmas Eve without Esther crying and Rhona insisting that everyone 'cheers up' and tries a bit of the thing she ordered, the vile-looking lump made out of duck blood, whatever the fuck that was.

Feeling pretty pissed now, I make for the exit. I've done it all wrong, I decide as a man in a velour elf suit bounces in through the door, blowing a whistle. I should have been stricter and laid down the law – about the things that really mattered. Never mind Esther eating vegetables and having her teeth checked twice a year without fail. There'd have been no going to Willow Vale, no taking part in a reality TV show. As I step out into the cold night air, I try to imagine how I might have pulled that off; what references I might have drawn on in order to form my 'firm but fair' dad persona.

My own father had been kind and smiley, my over-riding memories involving him being mainly on his hands and knees on the carpet, playing Lego with me. Living with my aunt and uncle was very different. My uncle was far too distant to have been anything like a father figure. He hadn't had kids; apparently they'd never wanted them. He seemed to spend most of his time at the bowls club or hiding away in his shed.

Is it too late now to try and be a better dad? I think of Lauren and Charlie, just the two of them all these years. I know he can be a bit hard to reach, and Lauren worries about how he'll handle adult life when he leaves home. But he's a decent boy, he works hard, he has that newsagent's job but he also swots like mad, up till all hours, huddled over his science books. A rush of drunken guilt hits me as I catch myself comparing Esther to Charlie; so disloyal of me. Was Rhona right when she said I hadn't been supportive enough over that two-hundred-word essay she'd been asked to write by the jewellery people? My phone rings and I swipe it from my pocket, primed for another drama.

'Hey, sorry to call so late,' Lauren says. My heart lifts instantly.

'That's okay. It's not late. I mean, I'm still out. Is everything okay?'

'Yeah, I'm just back from the pub,' she says. 'Lovely night. Really fun. But I missed you.'

'I missed you too,' I say truthfully.

'I just wanted to tell you that,' Lauren says, and I know she's smiling. 'So, where are you right now?'

'Erm, I've just come out of a bar,' I say.

'You sound merry,' she remarks with a chuckle.

'You mean pissed?'

'Just a bit tipsy,' she says. 'I am too.'

'So it was fun, then, the pub?'

'It was,' she says. 'Quite a crowd there, but you know what was the best part?'

'What?' I ask.

'Seeing Charlie with Kim and Lorenzo's girls. Remy too, and his girlfriend, all on a table together – the young ones' table.' She pauses. 'You know what Charlie's like . . .'

'Yes, I do.'

'I couldn't remember the last time I'd seen him truly happy like that, having a laugh with his mates.'

'That's great,' I say, thinking of Esther, who never seems to mention those old friends of hers anymore –

Gracie and Jess who used to come over all the time – or to laugh for that matter. When did I last see my daughter laughing?

Two young women totter past me in sequinned dresses. I note their bare arms and legs and realise that, if I was their dad, I'd have suggested tights and a cardigan at the very least or, better still, a warm coat. 'It's December!' I want to shout after them. What's the point of checking the weather on your phone (rather than looking out of the window) if you're not going to dress appropriately for it? What's with this dogged desire to avoid being warm, dry and comfortable?

'So, was your night fun?' Lauren asks now.

'It was okay.'

'Oh. That sounds ominous.'

'You don't want to hear it all now. I'll tell you about it when I see you . . .'

'Okay,' she says. 'And you went on to a bar?'

'Yeah.' I weigh up whether to omit the fact that I was in there alone, necking gin, which I don't even drink normally. But it all comes out; about those boys hassling Esther and how bad I'd felt, that I hadn't been there for her, and couldn't make things better.

'James, you really care about her,' Lauren insists. 'You do your best but sometimes things happen that are out of your control. I mean, you can't be everywhere, no matter how much you'd like to be. So you mustn't blame yourself.' How did I find this wise and caring woman? 'I'm sorry your night's been a washout,' she adds.

'Oh, that's all right. It was just important to Rhona for us all to get together . . .'

'I think it's great that you and Rhona still get along,' she continues. 'I mean, tons of couples don't. You should give yourself credit for that . . .'

244

'You think so?' I don't mention how annoyed I'd been with her tonight.

'Of course I do,' she says with a note of surprise. 'I know you don't agree on everything but you're still a team, aren't you? I haven't spoken to Frank in years. And I don't think I ever want to.'

'I am so glad we're going away together,' I blurt out, 'just the two of us.'

'Me too. I can't wait.' A pause. 'Where are you now?'

'Just about to head home. Someone's just walked past wearing a Christmas tree,' I add. 'A kind of conical thing, suspended from her neck and covered in fairy lights.'

She laughs. 'Oh, I wish I was there with you. But I'd better get some sleep. I'm up at the crack of dawn tomorrow . . .'

'Feeding the masses,' I say. 'Well, have a brilliant day.'

'You too. I really hope it's okay, James.' I smile at that. It will be okay, I decide, even though it feels like my family is falling to pieces and Esther won't be there. It occurs to me that I *could* change my plans, and go to Lauren's for Christmas Day after all – but after not being able to join her on Christmas Eve I don't want to mess her around anymore. I mean, I can't just invite myself at the last minute. Anyway, it'll be fine at Rhona and Luc's, because it always is. It's become our custom. And once we've got through it, and I've downed several of Luc's experimental cocktails and nearly taken my eye out with a sprig of burning sage – well, there's Cornwall to look forward to. Me and Lauren off-grid.

And that's why, as we say goodnight, I feel so happy – albeit pretty drunk too. How is it possible that someone can lift you like this? Two hours ago I was sitting with my crying daughter and my ex-wife nagging me to try something made out of duck blood.

And now I feel like the luckiest man on earth.

CHAPTER THIRTY-SIX

ESTHER

Esther didn't write in her gratitude journal last night. After Tabitha's tits, being hassled by those boys and her mum implying that she was making a drama of it, it didn't feel as if Christmas Eve had thrown up much to be grateful for. To make matters worse, in the middle of the night she'd woken with nausea rising in her like a gigantic wave. She'd bolted to the loo and only just made it in time. After puking everything up – the meal that had probably cost £80 a head – Esther had crawled back into bed and lay there feeling cold and empty, and not just because of the food poisoning or whatever it was.

Miles still wasn't home. Esther knew he'd been meeting friends but she hadn't expected him to be this late. She was shivery, with a sour taste in her mouth. What *was* her boyfriend doing at 3.30 a.m. on what was now Christmas Day? Helping Santa on his journey around the rooftops of London? Esther wanted him home, taking care of her, keeping her warm. She could deal with the Tabitha stuff another time, when she was feeling better.

Unable to sleep, Esther pulled on her dressing gown, dug out her journal and wrote:

> *I have a family who love me.*
> *I wasn't dragged into an alleyway by those boys.*
> *Threw up but at least I made it to the loo in time!*

So there were things to be grateful for after all. And now, just as she's *really* starting to panic, Esther hears the front door crash open. Here's Miles – or rather, a huge silver helium balloon, as that's what bounced into the bedroom first. 'Surprise, baby!' he cries out. As it floats up to the ceiling he totters over and folds her in his arms, all boozy breath and kisses on her face and in her hair. 'I love you, darling,' he breathes. 'And I brought a balloon home for you!'

'Thanks,' she says curtly.

'Are you happy?'

After copious vomiting and worrying herself senseless over him? She's delirious with joy. 'Not massively,' she admits. 'Where've you been?'

'Oh, the night just went on a bit,' he says, implying that his friends made him stay out this late, perhaps by tying him to a chair and forcing alcohol down his throat. He pulls a cartoonish sad face. 'Sorry, babe. I didn't mean to worry you. But you were out with Mumsie and Dadsie, weren't you? How was it?'

'Fine,' Esther snaps. She doesn't have the energy to tell him about those horrible boys and her grim night at the restaurant. Instead, she lets him burble on about the club he's been to, who was there and how he'd really *really* just wanted to come home to her.

Gradually, she starts to relax and decides she'll forgive

him. Tabitha's tits was probably just some silly fantasy, she decides now. Or a mindless doodle. Yes, that was probably it. It was a doodle, but in words instead of a picture. Whatever it was, she *won't* let it spoil Christmas. It's comforting, just lying there with him on top of the bed, listening rather than having to be 'on form' as her mum always demands whenever they're out together. Like she must always be her shiniest best. She's never allowed to be a bit dull or tarnished.

'We're going to have such a special day tomorrow,' Miles announces, pulling her closer to his chest. 'Just you and me. Our first Christmas together!'

He's right because last year, Esther had buckled under pressure and gone to her mum and Luc's, leaving Miles here all alone – because despite all the money they've thrown at him over the years, he doesn't get on with his family. The thing is, Esther has realised, you can grow up in an enormous house with a west wing, a lake and an actual butler, and it doesn't mean anything at all.

*

On Christmas morning Miles wakes Esther with coffee in bed and the instruction to lie in while he takes care of everything. She blinks at him, wondering if there's a catch. But then, he *has* been trying lately. She decides to just enjoy their Christmas, which he says he's completely taken care of.

To kick off, there's something called a 'breakfast salad'. While Esther's family has their lovely buttery scrambled egg and that special festive smoked salmon her mum orders from a farm in Scotland, she and Miles crunch through their joyless shredded vegetables and seeds. She's poised for presents, even though they've agreed not to bother as, apparently, they don't need a special day to show their love for each other. But Esther didn't think they meant it. She has bought Miles a present, but decides not to mention it for now.

Next comes champagne, which whooshes straight to her head because she's not a day drinker. It's funny that Miles is so careful about avoiding E numbers and saturated fats when he doesn't have much problem ingesting copious chemicals and booze. 'I haven't eaten anything with a crumb coating since 1993,' he once told her, proudly, when they walked past a fried chicken shop.

'Not even after a big night?' Esther asked. But no; his method of dealing with a hangover is to hurl vitamins at it.

The day passes in a blur of them snacking (healthily), drinking champagne and repeatedly going back to bed, with Miles insisting, 'Isn't this great, not having to be answerable to anyone? No board games, no massive roast, no paper crowns or shit cracker jokes?'

They watch a movie he's chosen, which bores her rigid. Esther tries not to miss the board games and shit cracker jokes.

By now she is desperate to give Miles his present, so she hands him the tissue-wrapped parcel and watches him unwrap the slim gold bracelet she had engraved for him – *real* gold, from a tiny boutique.

'I love it, babe,' he enthuses. Then, with a grimace: 'We said no presents, didn't we? Weren't we just going to have a nice day?'

'I just saw it and thought you'd like it,' she says, fibbing, 'It wasn't much.'

'It's lovely. Thanks.' He examines it some more and tosses it onto the coffee table as if it had tumbled out of a cracker.

Dinner comes next. While Esther's family tucks into their vast Christmas roast and all the trimmings, she and Miles have special festive boxed meals from a new subscription plan, which he reckons is *way* better than their previous one, to eat from the sofa. Her mum would never allow anyone to eat from their lap in front of the TV on Christmas Day – or any day for that matter. 'I'd rather be dead,' Esther has heard her say. Today she'll have the huge oval table decorated with silver ribbons, flickering church candles, foraged fir cones and greenery. Esther and Miles are eating from those awful trays with padded undersides that he'd bought, saying they'd be 'handy', perhaps forgetting that they're not ninety-seven years old.

All at once Esther feels choked up. She's picturing Luc carving the turkey and her mum and dad delving into the various dishes, topping up glasses and tucking in. As her mum and Luc run a bar, they know how to make an event of it. There'll be carrots and parsnips with thyme, perfect devils on horseback and all the sauces: cranberry, proper gravy and even bread sauce that no one's that keen on but you still want to be there. It's a funny set-up, Esther supposes, with her parents being divorced and still spending Christmas together. But they've always done it and it's always been fine. Her mum gets on at her dad a bit, but he takes it well and she doesn't mean it. She's still fond of him really.

Esther looks down at her meal in a box. All the Christmassy things are there, but in miniature: tiny stuffing balls, gravel-sized roast potatoes and a single slice of turkey that's almost transparent, it's that thin. There's a teeny carrot, and a single sprout, and the whole thing has been liberally scattered with seeds. 'D'you think they needed to do that?' she asks. It seems unnecessary at Christmas.

'It ups the nutritional content,' Miles says, mouth full. 'Seeds are little powerhouses of energy.'

That's weird because the words are barely out of his mouth and he's fast asleep, head flopped back on the sofa, mouth open, snoring. Esther lifts the granddad tray from his lap and gently prises the disposable wooden cutlery from his hands, thinking about her family again with their roast dinner, the chocolate Brazils, raucous board games and a huge tin of Quality Street. Even though they can all be annoying, her heart aches for them. She wants to be with them, with her dad nailing the Trivial Pursuit science questions, her mum the art and literature ones, her the history ones and Luc not getting very many right at all.

To the accompaniment of Miles's throaty snores she scrolls through her contacts on her phone, wondering what Gracie and Jess are doing right now. Whatever it is, she bets no one's snoring in their vicinity at quite this volume. He can do this, Miles. It's one of his talents: the ability to go from fully awake to fast asleep in a second, as if a switch has been flicked.

Esther mooches through to the kitchen and pings off happy Christmas messages to everyone she can think of, just to get a response, to feel less alone. She calls her mum, who sounds tipsy and gets a bit emotional about her not being there: 'I just want to hug you, Esther. Are you all right, honey? What did Miles get you?'

'We decided not to do presents, Mum.'

'Oh, that's sad, darling. Christmas should be big and excessive, don't you think?'

'Yeah, I guess so,' Esther murmurs.

'I once said to Luc, "Let's not honour Valentine's Day," but I didn't mean it.' She laughs. 'It was a test. I'd've killed him if he'd believed me. Anyway, sweetheart, here's your dad . . .'

251

Esther clears her throat. 'We've had a lovely day,' she hears herself telling him. 'It's been great. Laid-back. Y'know, quiet . . .' Who wants a 'quiet' Christmas at twenty years old? Not that she's implying it's been dull, God no. They've eaten stuffing balls off padded trays and she's watched her boyfriend's tonsils rattling as he snored.

Of course she doesn't tell Dad any of that. 'We've really missed you,' he tells her, 'but I'm glad you've had a good day.'

From time to time people have said, 'You shouldn't just be an influencer. You could be an actress. You were amazing on that reality show!' Esther has always shrugged it off because great actors are incredibly skilled, and what has she ever done really? On the *Willow Vale* show she was just being herself.

She was picked for it because she was confident and looked fairly striking, she supposes, with her long red hair. (Esther would never say she's beautiful.) But she's a terrible actress, and of course her dad knows her day hasn't really been wonderful. 'What's that noise?' he asks now.

'Just something outside,' she fibs. It's actually Miles snoring.

'A motorbike?'

'I think so, yeah.'

'So, um . . . what're you doing tomorrow?' her dad wants to know.

'I'm not sure yet.' *Perhaps more off-tray eating and tonsil watching?*

'Fancy doing something nice?' he suggests, with a hopeful note to his voice. 'I don't mean all day or anything. Not if you have plans. But maybe we could have a walk through the park or something?'

A few years ago, around the time of the wrongly named coastal path and flip-flop controversy, she'd have thought,

Ugh, a walk? and felt the lifeblood draining out of her. But not now.

'I'd love that, Dad.' Right now she can't think of anything better.

'We could get coffee and cake somewhere?' he suggests.

Her dad knows she loves cake. Miles would no more consume his own leg hair than allow sweet carbohydrates past his lips. 'Will anywhere be open?' she asks.

'There's bound to be somewhere,' her dad replies. 'How about I come over around eleven?'

'Perfect,' she says, her spirits lifted, even though her champagne hangover is already kicking in, and she's ravenous. What she'd give for something crumb-coated right now. But that's okay because now there's her dad and coffee and cake to look forward to tomorrow.

Tomorrow will be a better day.

Only, it doesn't turn out the way Esther expects because much later, long after she and Miles have gone to bed, she is woken by mutterings in the living room.

It's not a big flat. So even though she's still in bed – and Miles was there too, his side is still warm – she can hear him quite clearly.

'Stop calling, Daze,' he hisses. 'I've told you we'll talk when I can.'

Esther sits bolt upright. Her heart is banging so hard it feels like it could burst out of her chest.

'I know it's difficult,' Miles goes on. 'No, of course I don't feel like that. It's just the way it has to be . . . Daze, would you listen to me?'

Daze? She's guessing that must be a Daisy? But it was Tabitha in his journal . . . She slips out of bed, unable to decipher his mumblings now as she reaches for the shoebox from under it. Maybe he's written more stuff in his journal that'll help her to understand what's going on.

Off comes the lid. The journal's still there but there's something else too: a tiny parcel wrapped in red paper with a gold bow and a gift tag. A proper wrapped gift for someone! *For me, maybe?* Esther thinks. But then, why didn't he give it to her?

To darling D, love M, reads the tag. His handwriting. Not her gift.

Esther exhales slowly, thinking about her life before Miles, when she still saw her friends and they all went out dancing together, like that nice girl Anya she was chatting to in the club; then her life *after* Miles, when her friends started to fall away and of course they knew, because everyone knew what an almighty jerk he was.

With tears stinging her eyes, Esther picks up the tiny parcel and strides through to the living room, thinking, he did wrap it prettily, she'll give him that.

CHAPTER THIRTY-SEVEN

JAMES

When your kid's still little, climbing all over you and dangling off you, you assume it'll always be that way. Okay, maybe not when they're thirty-seven years old – but you think they'll always be *there*. That there'll be endless time to talk about the silly things you talk about with them, all the teasing about their inappropriate footwear, their adoration of anything crumb-coated, their mockery of your musical tastes.

Then, seemingly overnight, all that cosy familiarity disappears. I miss those days with a force that shocks me sometimes – even those pain-in-the-arse days like Esther crying because she'd insisted on walking the South West Coast Path in flip-flops.

'I told you to wear walking boots! What did I say, Est?'

'You said it was a pavement.'

'I didn't say pavement, I said path . . .'

'You did!'

'When did I say it, Est? When did I say, let's go for a gentle stroll along the South West Coast Pavement?'

There'll be none of that today, though. On this crisp

and sunny Boxing Day we're just going to hang out, like we used to. I'm smiling, I realise, as I emerge from the tube station and stride along the unusually quiet street. A walk with a stop-off for coffee and cake with my daughter. It's so rare for Esther and I to go out together these days, just the two of us. Yesterday was fun with Rhona and Luc, but I did miss her, and I missed Lauren too, although we managed to chat a couple of times during the day.

You're a lucky man, I tell myself. In a couple of days Lauren and I will be heading down to Cornwall and that's going to be wonderful. Sometimes I can hardly believe the way my life's turned out. I no longer feel like that permanently knackered, workaholic middle-aged man. I have more energy, I sleep soundly at night, and I wake up feeling shimmeringly *alive*. And yesterday, when Rhona happened to mention one of Esther's favourite childhood Christmas presents – 'the Lego go-kart, d'you remember, James?' – it gave me an idea for a work conundrum I've been wrestling with.

So yes, life is good. So good that I find myself swerving into a shop, not much more than a corner shop stocked with basic foods, a few shrivelled carrots and sprouting potatoes and a couple of buckets of flowers.

Are carnations horribly naff? I've always been led to believe so but, back in the summer, I noticed that Lauren grew and picked them to display in her kitchen. So I choose a bunch of pale pink ones and leave the shop.

Don't even mention Miles today, I tell myself. The last thing Esther wants is me lecturing her and, anyway, it has zero effect. Is anything surer to make your young adult offspring want to do something than a parent telling them not to?

I've turned into Esther's road now. It's a smart street of

Georgian townhouses divided into flats. They are all beautifully kept, with black wrought-iron railings, and the shops around here sell things like French-style macarons in pastel colours and speciality coffee (ground to order) from around the world. I look down at the small bunch of pink carnations as I approach Miles's door. The prospect of doing something so simple as walking around with my daughter in the wintry sunshine triggers a rush of happiness in me. We still get on pretty well, and I'm grateful for that. Maybe I haven't been a rubbish dad after all.

I inhale, press the buzzer and wait. Miles's ground-floor flat opens right onto the street. I press it again and wait some more. No one comes. After a couple of minutes I pull out my phone, that default activity when a person doesn't know what to do with themselves. I buzz the door yet again – still no answer – and wonder whether to message Esther to say I'm outside, and has she remembered we're going out?

I flinch at the sound of shouting inside. That was Esther, I'm sure of it. More shouting follows and I can hear crying now. Alarmed, I jab the buzzer several times in succession, and am just about to call her number when the door flies open. 'Dad!' Esther says.

'Est, what's wrong?'

Her hair is unkempt, her face blotchy, her eyes pink and bloodshot. 'We've just, it's—' she starts, swinging round as Miles appears behind her.

'What are *you* doing here?' he barks.

'I'm here to see Esther,' I snap. 'Est, are you coming—'

'We're a bit busy right now,' Miles announces, glaring at me. He drops his gaze to the bunch of pink carnations and lets out a withering snort, as if I've brought her a cabbage. Then he turns away and marches off to the living room.

257

'Dad, I'm so sorry,' Esther starts as I hug her. 'I forgot we were going out for cake . . .'

'Hey,' I murmur. 'Never mind that. Whatever's wrong? What's happened, Est?'

'Sorry, Dad,' she says again, crying so hard into my sweater now, I just hold her there and drop the pink carnations at my feet.

CHAPTER THIRTY-EIGHT

ESTHER

Miles had bought her a ring. An actual *ring* for this Daisy something – Esther doesn't know her surname. It's been going on for a while, he admitted. Just someone he got to know 'out and about'. What did *that* mean? 'I just kept running into her,' he said, as if he'd had no control over his actions and his pants had just fallen off. He also implied that it was Esther's fault for not wanting to come out so much anymore. But usually she wasn't even invited because he was working, 'doing a set'. And he always said he didn't want her standing around being bored. 'I need to keep my mind on the job rather than worrying about you,' he'd insisted.

How Esther hates him, this pathetic man who truly believes he's a top DJ and an 'artist'. So many things he's ruined. That first lunch out at Lauren's. Their Christmas, frankly. 'So you weren't responsible?' she yelled at him. 'Is that what you're saying?'

'Just that things got out of control . . .'

'No, *you're* out of control,' she shot back. 'Or you pretend you are with your sex addiction, rather than just wanting to shag people. That's what you do, isn't it? You medicalise it, you make it a condition that you have no power over . . .'

'I do have problems,' he shouted back. 'You know I've been getting help.'

On and on it went, the two of them yelling at each other in Miles's kitchen under the watchful gaze of Dylan the rat. 'You didn't even get me a Christmas present,' Esther cried.

'I gave you a helium balloon!'

'What am I? Five?'

'You're acting like it . . .' Miles closed his eyes momentarily and placed a hand over them, as if this scene had exhausted him completely. Perhaps he needed seeds, those little powerhouses of energy he was so fond of?

'So who's Tabitha?' Esther demanded.

'What?' He stared at her.

'Tabitha from your journal, Miles. Who are Tabitha's tits?'

'Well, um . . .' He stepped back, away from her. 'Well, um . . . Tabitha's, of course. Who d'you think—'

'Are you sleeping with her too?'

'That was nothing,' he said quickly. 'That was just a—'

'Just a what?' She caught Dylan staring at them through the bars of his cage, probably thinking how weird they are, these humans.

'Just a . . . a . . .' He raked back his dyed hair and looked down at the floor. 'Just a thing,' he said. 'That's all it was with her. A *thing*.'

*

Despite the brightness of the morning they hadn't yet opened their bedroom curtains. Too busy fighting, obvi-

260

ously. And now, at just gone 11 a.m. her dad is here, listening as Esther spills it all out as they sit side by side on the bed. There's no centre light in the room; just an assortment of antique lamps stuffed in various corners that she's not about to go around switching on. So they sit in the gloom, with her dad's arm around her shoulders while she cries and cries. Miles is hiding away in the kitchen.

Clothes and shoes are piled up in a corner and champagne glasses from Christmas morning are still sitting on a bedside table. Everything looks slightly grubby, like the aftermath of a party.

'Jesus, Est,' her dad says finally. 'I'm so sorry, love. I can't believe this has happened again.' Miles cheating, he means. He knew all about the last time because Esther couldn't stop herself from spilling it out.

'It's a bit of a mess, isn't it?' She rubs at her sore eyes.

'Let's get you out of here.'

She turns and blinks at him. 'What, now?'

'Yes,' he says firmly. 'I hate what this is doing to you. What *he's* doing. You need to end it right now, okay?'

She bites at a nail, about to say no, it's fine, they'll sort it. She never does what her dad tells her to do.

Wear boots, Esther.

No, I'm wearing flip-flops!

You can't take that fur coat, it'll be like wearing a rug.

It's fine, it's really light!

However, today she decides to listen to what he's saying. For what feels like an age, she lets him talk and doesn't interrupt at all. They sit there together with the small bunch of pink carnations that he'd dropped on the floor now lying next to her on the bed.

'Thanks, Dad,' Esther murmurs finally.

'What for, love?'

261

She looks at him and manages a wobbly smile. 'For not saying I told you so.'

'Oh, Est.' He shakes his head. 'I'm not going to do that, am I?'

'No, I know you're not. I'm just . . .' She tails off and exhales forcefully. 'I'll need to get some things together, okay? Will you wait for me?'

'Of course I'll wait. I'll wait as long as it takes, Est. Where d'you think I'm going?'

She grimaces. 'How're we going to do this?'

'Just get your basics together. We'll get a cab over to mine. We can come back for the rest another time—'

'No, I want to take my stuff, Dad.'

'What, *all* of it?'

'There's not much,' she insists, jumping up. She knows he's remembering the three suitcases she'd packed for Corsica, but there's no way she's leaving without her precious things.

'I just think we should get going,' her dad starts. 'Before I punch him—'

'Don't do that! It won't help—'

'No, I know it won't. But c'mon, Est. Let's get your stuff.'

'Can you reach those down for me?' She indicates the cases stashed on top of the double wardrobe. 'There's another one under the bed. Can you get that too?'

He presses a thumb and forefinger over the top of his nose before doing as she asks. Esther starts to pull out stuff from various drawers and flings it all into the cases. She darts out to the bathroom and hurries back into the bedroom with armful of pots and bottles, all those mysterious potions that, seemingly, she can't live without. 'What's he doing anyway?' her dad asks, meaning Miles.

'Keeping out of the way. I think he's a bit scared of you, Dad.'

He splutters. 'So he should be.'

'You can actually be quite fierce.' Surprisingly, Esther finds herself smiling as she squashes several sweaters into a case. 'Could you go through that pile,' she adds, indicating the mound on the floor, 'and see if my red shoes are there?'

'Esther, we need to go.'

'They're my favourites.'

'You can get another pair—'

'They're last season!'

'So?' He genuinely doesn't understand.

'They don't *do* them anymore, Dad . . .'

Exhaling, he crouches down and starts to rake through the mountain of clothes, shoes and God knows what else is lying there on the floor. 'Could you put a light on?' he asks. 'I can hardly see . . .'

'Just a minute,' she says, rolling up more sweaters into tight sausages in order to fit them into the case.

'I can't see any red – whoa!' He yanks back his hand.

'What is it?' She stares at him.

'Is your rat in here? Something just bit me.'

'My God, Dad . . .' Throwing him a *have-you-gone-mad?* look she strides over and starts raking through the pile.

The bedroom door opens and Miles stands there, glaring. 'What's going on?'

'Esther's packing,' her father replies.

'What were you shouting about?'

'Dad says something bit him!' Esther announces.

'Is your rat out?' he asks.

Miles gawps at them. 'No?'

'Erm . . . Dad?' Esther picks up a sandal by its strap. 'I think it was just the Velcro bit on this. It must've got caught on your sleeve or something—'

'Oh.' Her father reddens.

Miles smirks. 'The sandal bit you?'

Her dad straightens up and turns to face him. 'Just keep out of our way.'

'It *is* my flat,' Miles reminds him. For a second Esther thinks her dad really is going to punch him. She sees him visibly wrestling his emotions under control.

Her dad turns to her. 'I'm calling a cab now, okay? Can you make sure you've got everything?'

She nods mutely, avoiding Miles's gaze.

'So, you really are leaving me?' he says with a trace of disbelief.

'Yes, Miles.'

He blinks slowly, this pathetic excuse for a man who somehow stole Esther's heart and two years of her precious young life. That's how it seems to her now, because it wasn't done by honest means. He was such a charmer; the washed-up pop star turned DJ. He flattered her into loving him and made her feel so special. 'My precious angel,' he called her; no one had ever said anything like that to her before. 'You've saved my life, baby. I'll be yours forever.' She hates him for it, and is fizzling with rage now as she and her dad zip up the cases. Miles makes a grand show of stepping aside to let them pass.

'C'mon, Esther,' her dad says, opening the door and stepping out into the crisp, bright, Boxing Day afternoon. She follows him out, filled with relief.

'You're a *vet*,' Miles scoffs loudly from the doorway, 'and you don't know the difference between a rat and a Velcro sandal?' Her dad glares at him, so obviously wanting to punch his smug face but, instead, he turns away and walks with Esther, side by side, to where the cab is waiting.

As they settle in the back, to Esther's surprise she

realises she's smiling. 'Dad,' she starts, 'that was kind of funny, y'know. The sandal thing, I mean.'

'It's a mistake anyone could've made,' he says in mock defensiveness.

Something in her chest seems to lift, as if all the tensions are leaving her body and floating away. It's over with Miles. Thank God for that. 'So, you'll stay with me for a while?' her dad prompts her.

'Yes, Dad,' Esther replies. 'I'll stay with you.'

CHAPTER THIRTY-NINE

I'd hoped to see James during these inbetweeny days before we go away. However, after all the drama yesterday he's been busy taking care of Esther, being on hand if she's wanted to talk. 'Not that she has really,' he says, when I call.

'How's she doing?' I ask.

'Hard to tell. She seemed glad to be getting out of Miles's place yesterday, and we had a nice evening with a takeaway, just chatting about this and that. She didn't really want to go over it anymore, and I guess that's understandable.'

'The main thing is, you're there for her,' I suggest. 'And she knows that.'

'It's all I can do really.' He pauses. 'Kids, eh?' I catch the wry smile in James's voice and wonder why I'm feeling so unsettled. Of course he has to be there for his daughter after all the crap she's gone through with Miles. If Charlie needed me for anything I can't imagine not being there for him.

However, something seems to have shifted in me. I'd

266

so looked forward to James coming out here for the pub night on Christmas Eve, and that hadn't happened – also perfectly fine. But what about the other times he'd cancelled with barely any notice? Does he expect me to *never* mind when our plans are thrown up in the air? *Don't I matter?* I've found myself wondering from time to time. Meanwhile, contact between us has been sparse and brief and I've started to feel, well . . . needy is the only way I can describe it. And – perversely – I've found myself pushing him away in order *not* to feel needy, and more like my usual independent self.

As I lie in bed at night, rogue thoughts start to snag at my brain: Does he really want to come on our little off-grid adventure? Or would he rather stay at home with Esther, and doesn't know how to break it to me? Perhaps the trip feels like an *obligation*. He doesn't want to let me down, but nor does he want to abandon Esther when she needs him. He's caught in the middle, I decide, irrationally – between Esther and me.

I call him one afternoon when I'm out on a walk, trying to shake off a growing sense of unease. 'James,' I start, 'can I ask you something?'

'Sure. What is it?'

'Are you sure you're okay about coming away? I mean, if it's tricky at all—'

'It'll be fine,' he says quickly. A small pause hangs.

'I know how I'd feel,' I add, 'if Charlie had just gone through a break-up . . .'

'But he hasn't been in a situation like that.'

'No, I know, James,' I say, frowning. 'I'm just saying . . .'

'I'm sorry. It's just been a bit of a time lately.'

'Please do say if you don't want to come.'

'I do. I do want to come, more than anything!'

'Could Esther stay with her mum while you're away?'

'Maybe. I'll see. We'll sort it.' We end the call curtly, with him sounding distracted. I try to shake off a prickle of annoyance, and remind myself that I'm an adult and I've had plenty of practice in fending for myself. But even so, it occurs to me now that we haven't talked about our Christmases – or anything really over the past few days.

If we had, I might have told James that Charlie had FaceTimed his dad on Christmas Day, as he always does. Up until that point he'd seemed perfectly fine and happy, enjoying hanging out with Kim, Lorenzo and the girls, all of us together. However, after the call it was as if a shutter had come down. I'd tried to broach it, asking, 'Did that go okay?'

'Yeah, it was fine,' he'd replied, snappily.

I knew there was no point in probing any further, so I'd let it go. And now James is saying, 'Esther can call me in Cornwall if she needs me.'

'James, she can't,' I remind him. 'There's no Wi-Fi, no phone signal. There's not even a landline—'

'No landline?' he repeats.

'No, it's off-grid remember?'

Another pause hovers. 'It'll be fine,' James says, unconvincingly.

'Will it, though? What if there's some drama while you're away?'

'There won't be any drama.'

How can you say that? I want to ask him. *There's always drama where your daughter's concerned.* 'But what if there is?' I ask, wishing now that I hadn't started us on this track.

'We can't just not go away, can we?' James says. 'We have to think of ourselves too.'

'Yes, but we could cancel it this time, and go away in spring, or—'

'I don't want to do that. It'll be fine. I promise. Everything's going to be okay.'

However, a snag of unease still hangs in the air after we've finished the call; that sense of our own lives – or rather, *his* life – coming between us. I try to believe it'll turn out okay, just as I did that day in Corsica when James blew into Minnie's nose. I had to trust what he said back then. I needed to believe him. But today, for the first time since that day, I don't feel too sure about us at all.

CHAPTER FORTY

ESTHER

'Of course you can go to work, Dad,' Esther had insisted last night. 'You don't need to stay here and look after me.'

'But what about me going away with Lauren?' he'd asked.

'That's fine too. Of course it is . . .'

'Could you go and stay with Mum?'

'I'm fine here at yours. Please stop going on.'

He'd still looked doubtful, or perhaps a little guilty at the prospect of leaving Esther alone. Since they'd arrived at his place after the dramatic move out of Miles's, he'd been hovering around her, giving her 'that' look. That 'I want to help but I don't know how' kind of expression that drives her mad sometimes. Esther didn't *want* her dad hovering around her, constantly checking if she was okay. She wanted some time and space to think.

Now he's gone off to work for a full, busy day before he goes away with Lauren in a couple of days' time. Esther has got up bright and early, filled with purpose for the day ahead. These days in between Christmas and New Year can feel listless and empty but there's tons she can do. She has emails to reply to, she could bank up a load of Instagram reels and start work on the talk Bethani have asked her to prepare for their big event in a few weeks' time. She's due a meeting with them next week and wants to show that she's given it lots of thought; that she's committed to the brand. She could also go out for a brisk walk to shake off the cobwebs, and her mum's been in touch, asking if she fancies a quick lunch at some point during the week. She was apologetic that she can't be around for Esther much just now, as they're getting the bar all ready for New Year's Eve. It's a huge night for them. There have been some issues with the menu and staff, the new chef off sick and the trainee not yet up to scratch, blah-blah. (Esther had stopped listening by that point.) She could also settle herself properly into her room here. It definitely has a spare-roomish feel about it these days, and she needs to make it more homely now she's living here.

I'm living with my dad, Esther reflects gloomily. The reality hits her that her relationship is over and she's been so caught up with Miles, and Miles's world, that she has literally forgotten how to function all by herself.

There's the space issue too. Miles's flat is in an amazing location but it's actually pretty tiny, and her dad's house is, well, a *house*. And today it feels too big, too quiet and empty as even Walter, her dad's cat, is out.

Esther thinks about writing in her gratitude journal that at least she won't have to suffer any more of those awful nights out, with Miles and his friends dancing wildly. Pretty soon, those terrible images that were burned onto her retinas will start to fade.

That girl in the club pops into her mind; Anya with the cherry red lipstick, laughing with her friends – all girls on a night out together. Esther thinks about Gracie and Jess.

271

They used to be such a little gang, the three of them. There were sleepovers with movies, face masks and glittery nail polish and even a chocolate fountain once, at Gracie's house. Even when Esther went to a different secondary school they'd still meet up to go shopping on Saturdays, idling for hours over a Frappuccino and trying on clothes. Esther misses them so much it triggers an ache, low in her gut. She misses them more than Miles, she realises now.

Her girlfriends. That's who she wants. She considers sending them a message, wondering what to say without seeming needy or obviously feeling left out. *Hey, did you have a good Christmas?* She's about to ping off identical texts, but what if they're together and compare? How would *that* look? Kind of pathetic, she reckons. And maybe they'd feel sorry for her?

Esther doesn't want her friends getting in touch out of pity. She'd rather be on her own than that. Anyway, they probably haven't messaged over the holidays because they're under pressure to have family time. Both Gracie and Jess are super close to their parents. It's probably just that, Esther decides.

She opens her laptop and tries to make a start on her Bethani talk. She has decided to focus on the fact that the brand is about a *feeling*, and a way of being and relating to the world. But it sounds so silly and pretentious when, just a mile away from where she's sitting now, her dad is probably medicating a diabetic guinea pig or something.

A proper job. That's what she needs; not this faffing around being paid by brands for doing what amounts to very little. Yes, it's lucrative. Esther can make a good living from it. But the thought of floating around, being never quite busy enough in this empty house, fills her with dread.

She paces around, relieved when Walter sidles in, so

grateful is she for the company of another living creature. But as she approaches him he shoots out of the room. It's hard not to take it personally.

Esther checks her phone, scrolling idly until she spots Gracie's Instagram story. It's like a kick to her stomach.

They're together right now, Gracie and Jess. At least, it looks like right now because the sky is bright blue in the photo as it is through her dad's living-room window. But instead of being stuck in their parents' houses they're out in a park, flying a kite! On closer inspection Esther identifies it as Ally Pally. *New Christmas kite!* Gracie has captioned it. *We managed to fly it!*

Esther stares at it for a very long time. Her two oldest friends, out flying a kite together. How very wholesome and cute! Their inbetweeny days aren't empty like hers. They're out having fun, and her mum will be busy at the bar and her dad's busy too, working through a stack of appointments before he and Lauren go away together. Everyone is doing their thing, Esther realises with a sharp pang. And she's sitting in her dad's house, her life a mess.

She realises with a start that it's nearly lunchtime and she's achieved precisely nothing so far today. Miles will be perched on a stool in his kitchen, tucking into a raw power bowl. How she hated those meals, and how glad she is that she'll never again have to listen to him going on about his acid reflux and burping for effect, complaining about 'bloat'. She can put *that* in her gratitude journal. But it fails to cheer her up because she finds herself staring at Gracie, Jess and the kite again, and without warning a tear plops down her cheek.

She needs to get out of there. That's what's wrong – being cooped up inside with even Walter shunning her. She throws on her jacket and heads out with no plan of where to go. Sod him, she thinks. Sod Miles and his stupid delivered meals – black beans and brown rice, barley and red cabbage and seeds sprinkled over, so many seeds; she must have ingested millions of the fuckers like some starved parrot. Sod Miles and his meal plans, dictating what she ate as well as everything else. 'I hate you,' Esther mutters out loud, marching faster, past the chain coffee shops and a sportswear shop and a pub.

A pub! That's what she'll do. She'll go in and have a large glass of wine, all by herself, like the breezy independent woman she now plans to be. *Day drinking! Why not?* she thinks rebelliously. That'll set her up for the afternoon.

The pub is almost empty apart from two very drunk old men in shabby coats at the bar, and it feels bleaker than it looked from the outside. She sits in a corner and knocks her wine back so quickly it rushes straight to her head. Too late, she realises she's drunk it on an empty stomach. Lunch is what's needed. Something to straighten her out because now she's thinking about the kite-flying again and is starting to well up.

Esther leaves the pub, blinking in the bright wintry sunshine and marches onwards, past a greengrocer's, an estate agent's and a couple of charity shops. At a scruffy-looking newsagent's she swerves in and buys a packet of cigarettes and a lighter. Esther hardly ever smokes these days. Occasionally, if she's out, she might 'borrow' one – but as she never buys her own she doesn't even think of herself as a smoker anymore.

Today, though, she has a whole packet of twenty all to herself. She can smoke as much as she wants now she's no longer with Miles. (Despite his enthusiastic drug use, he abhors the smell of cigarettes.) Her dad won't be thrilled if she starts smoking in her bedroom at his place. But she'll open the window and she doubts if he'll make a big thing of it, considering what she's been through lately.

The shops have petered out now. Esther stomps onwards, smoking and going over and over things in her head. By the time she looks up she realises she's arrived at a run-down retail park. She's never been here before. She didn't even know it existed. There's a pet superstore, an industrial bakery and a cheap clothing place. But she's not interested in any of those. The wine and hunger have combined to make Esther quite light-headed, and at the sight of a fried chicken place at the other end of the retail park her heart starts to quicken.

Fried. Chicken.

The devil's food, as far as Miles is concerned. It made Esther squirm, the way he'd say disparaging things about overweight people eating what he called 'brown food from cartons' in the street. 'Look at them!' he'd scoff, too loudly. 'Is it any wonder they look like that?' Well, his beloved delivered meals also came in cartons, but that was different of course. Getting closer now, Esther is actually salivating for fried brown food, in a crunchy coating, eaten from a carton – or, better still, a bucket. God, yes!

Minutes later she's perched on the edge of a low wall, plunging her hand into the bucket and ramming fried chicken pieces into her face. The fact that Miles would view this as completely disgusting makes every fatty, salty mouthful even more delicious. Okay, it's not healthy, but aren't we all meant to strive for balance these days? It might look like she's just gorging on battered chicken. But what she's actually doing is *offsetting* all those shredded vegetables and beansprouts she's endured over the past two years.

It's a yin-yang thing. Like a Bethani necklace, this fried chicken is balancing her chakras.

But actually, by the time she's halfway down the bucket,

the euphoria has begun to wear off, and Esther feels a bit queasy. She stops and rubs her greasy fingers on the front of her jeans, thinking, *My first day at Dad's and I've been to the pub on my own and smoked and eaten this horrible food.* And she thinks of her dad coming round yesterday, bringing her that little bunch of pink carnations that Miles has probably thrown in the bin. How safe and cared-for her dad makes her feel, in his soft grey sweater and old faded jeans. He and Miles are pretty much the same age; she knows Miles's real age, she's checked his passport. But whereas one of those men is only concerned with hoovering up coke and sleeping with random women – 'It was just a thing!' – the other is always there when he's needed, and never puts himself first.

The chicken has gone now. She's been picking on it without realising and all that's left are a few cold chips, which she polishes off quickly. Then she pulls out her cigarettes from her shoulder bag and lights one.

God, it feels good. She savours each inhalation, aware of it rushing to her lungs and her head, baffled now as to why she let a ravaged old has-been control her so much. All that stuff about wanting to direct her pictures for Bethani, getting her to lie on the rug like a corpse. Fury bubbles up in her now. She grinds out the cigarette in the chicken bucket and lights up another immediately, as if to *really* annoy him – although he's not here to witness it unfortunately.

But someone's watching, Esther realises now. At least, someone is standing there in the doorway of the pet superstore; a tall, athletic-looking man in black jeans and a leather jacket. At first she assumes he's looking at his phone, then she realises with a jolt that it looks like he's photographing her.

Apart from a few people wandering in and out of the pet superstore and the chicken place, the retail park is pretty quiet. Esther has only noticed this man because he seems to be entirely focused on her. Standing up now, she takes another draw on her cigarette and starts to walk over to him. She's not sure why she feels so emboldened. Maybe it's because of those boys who followed her out of the tube station – or maybe it's Miles, and she's not prepared to take any crap from anyone again.

''Scuse me?' she calls out sharply.

He lowers his phone and slides it into a jacket pocket.

'What were you doing there?' Esther asks.

'Nothing,' he replies with a shrug.

'Yes you were. You were photographing me, weren't you?'

'No I wasn't,' he protests.

'You were! You were taking pictures of me!' Filled with rage now, Esther is utterly unafraid. 'Let me see. Give me your phone . . . hey!'

For a split second, as he sprints away, Esther considers tearing after him. But she knows there's no way she'd be able to catch him and that, even if she did, she wouldn't be able to wrangle his phone off him.

Bleakly, feeling helpless now, she watches him pelt around the corner and out of sight.

CHAPTER FORTY-ONE

CHARLIE

Right now Remy is in Liverpool to play a gig. He drove there, which seems as unfeasible to Charlie as his best friend flying a Boeing 757. But Remy passed his test a few months ago and even bought his own car.

He's sent Charlie pictures of the snacks in the hotel minibar. Charlie is enjoying flicking through them because it means they still have a kind of connection. It might be a bit tenuous these days, but it's still there. Charlie doesn't like feeling needy, and thought he'd perfected the art of not needing *anyone*, since it dawned on him that his dad really is a useless arse. His mum's different in that he's tried to push her away, to show that he doesn't need her either – like in Corsica when he hid under the dog towel and got stung by a wasp. But, somewhat infuriatingly, she won't give up on him or leave him alone. Is it any wonder he feels smothered sometimes?

So, yes, the issue of needing people is tricky for Charlie, and he's aware of the little flurries of gratitude he experiences whenever Remy deigns to get in touch.

The minibar snacks are, admittedly, impressive. We're not talking Cheesy Doritos here, which they used to munch in gigantic quantities while watching movies together until their mouths were furred up with orange dust. Instead there are lime and chilli pistachios and a packet of what look like Wotsits but cost about ten times as much and the packet is tiny. Remy's hand is in the photo for scale. There are also olives in a silvery pouch (Charlie doesn't think Remy's ever eaten an olive) and a bar of dark chocolate encrusted with sea salt.

Gonna eat that chocolate? Charlie messages.

It's like £12!

Go on, treat yourself.

Rather have Dairy Milk!

They bat messages back and forth until Charlie hears Brenda's flat-footed stomp approaching. He's at the news-agent's and is meant to be working. Here she comes, marching through from the back room where there's a cracked sink, a bucket to catch roof drips and the Terrible Toilet, partitioned off only by a curtain made out of some kind of tapestry material. (When he started working here, Charlie took a picture of it and told Remy it was part of the Bayeux Tapestry.) By means of sheer willpower and denying himself fluids, Charlie has managed to never use the loo here. It's a wonder he's not entirely desiccated, like the coconut his mum keeps in a jar on the kitchen shelf.

As Brenda tidies the sweet display unnecessarily, Charlie stuffs his phone into his jeans pocket and tries to appear fully occupied with important tasks. His boss doesn't like him 'looking idle', as she puts it. It can be stressful, appearing busy when there's literally nothing to do. Charlie cracks his knuckles and neatens the small selection of magazines on the counter; all those weekly publications he's spent so much time looking at over the past two years, they have coloured his view of what adult life is actually like.

Mum's new hubby kept her locked under the sink!

Vengeful ex smashed up my tot's Wendy house!

Hubby left me on our wedding night – and bedded Auntie Sue!

All these hubbies and exes 'bedding' people they shouldn't – it's a particular kind of language that's seeped its way into Charlie's brain. Sometimes late at night, when he's been studying under the glow of his ancient Anglepoise lamp, he's found himself wondered how he might possibly fit into that adult world. It seems fraught with danger and potential heartbreak.

'. . . So I called the council and reported that awful pothole on Dawson Road,' Brenda is telling him as she adjusts the packets of Chocolate Buttons. 'Nearly broke my back axle, it did. I said to them, "You'll be getting the bill for that . . ."'

'Uh-huh,' Charlie says. As he doesn't drive, potholes aren't really of any concern to him. If he encounters one, he can simply walk around it. That's one benefit of not being able to drive, he supposes.

Brenda tweaks the Turkish Delights, which no one has bought since something like 1993. '. . . So with that loft insulation I was telling you about, there's dry rot in the joists. I'll have to get that sorted before they can even think about measuring up . . .'

'Mmm-hmm,' Charlie murmurs, trying to appear fascinated by the update.

'Daniel says it should be easy enough . . .'

'Right.' Daniel is Brenda's weird nephew, a goth in his forties, ghostly pale as he floats around the village in a long black flowing coat.

'. . . He'll start at the eaves, that's the best way. He says you just roll it out and stuff it into the crevices . . .'

Is this really his life? Charlie reflects. While Remy lounges in a hotel room, snacking on lime-flavoured nuts and enjoying one of those showers that blasts you from all angles, he has to endure all this talk of potholes and dry rot. It's making him feel itchy and weird, like he shouldn't be here, like he's in the *wrong environment* for a boy of seventeen years old. He has an urge to run out of the shop and never come back. But then, what would he do for money?

Brenda coughs loudly into a tissue and stuffs it up her sleeve. She is wearing a stained brown sweatshirt, tight jeans and collapsed-looking flat black boots. Her hair is gingery brown – dyed, Charlie thinks – and a couple of wiry hairs have sprouted out of her chin. He has no idea how old she is, and he and his mum have agreed that she's one of those people who doesn't actually have an age. And Brenda is certainly not good on other people's ages. Or at least, on Charlie's age as – despite him working here since he was fifteen – she must regard him as a much older person (of, say, eighty), judging by the way she goes on. Charlie keeps nodding and uh-huh-ing, wondering what she'd do if he were to suddenly leap onto the counter, rip up the weekly magazines with their 'cheating hubbies' and shout that he doesn't give a fuck about loft insulation.

No, not rip them up. That'd be bad because occasionally Mrs Arden, his chemistry teacher who he's quite fond of, comes in to buy a bunch of them to take to her mother in her care home.

Brenda continues to fiddle with the only *slightly* out-of-date Hula Hoops and Maltesers and stands back to observe the display, as if in readiness for a royal inspection. She coughs again, pulls the tissue from her sleeve and presses it to her mouth. Again, Charlie thinks about Remy in Liverpool and wishes he could have travelled up there to the gig tonight. He could have gone by train. Thanks to Brenda, he has the money. But Remy never asks him to gigs anymore, and Charlie would feel awkward suggesting it, in case he seemed like a hanger-on. He's seen him play in London of course, but that was ages ago.

Now Brenda is wittering on about her goth nephew, and how he 'can't close a cupboard door' whenever he visits and 'plays that terrible music, it's always coming out of his phone . . .'

'What kind of music?' Charlie asks, not that he cares really. But as it's potentially more interesting than potholes, he's grabbed on to it like a life belt.

'That goth stuff. I don't know.' She shrugs. 'Something Jesus and Mary. My Chemical Toilet . . .'

Charlie suppresses a smile as he makes a mental note to relay this conversation to Remy when he gets the chance. He does this, storing up titbits for him like a squirrel hiding nuts for later. Not much goes on around here but that's got to be worth sharing. Finally – finally! – Brenda says she's nipping home to 'see to the dogs', which means that Charlie will be left by himself for an hour or so.

He glances at the news on his phone, then picks up one of the tabloid papers, the ones Brenda orders for the regular customers; fewer and fewer these days because everyone reads their news online. He starts flipping through it just to pass the time in the absence of customers. A celebrity split, a politician 'caught with his pants down'; it's not that different to the magazines really. He keeps on leafing through, even though Brenda doesn't like him reading the papers or magazines 'because then they feel sullied'. As if he's not a perfectly civilised seventeen-year-old boy but a farm animal.

One of the older men from the village comes in to buy cigarettes and Polo mints. Once he's gone, Charlie continues flipping through the paper, vaguely registering the fashion page and celebs. He never reads celeb stuff. It doesn't interest him. He can never understand why people choose to 'introduce' their new baby through the pages of *OK!* and *Hello!* magazine. And who on earth is interested that that couple from *Love Island* have broken up?

So Charlie doesn't know what makes him stop at that page of the paper, the celeb page. It's just an interview with a singer who's launched her own drinks range ('Pure clear spirit with a hint of citrus'), a 'love rat' actor and then a series of pictures like the frames in a comic, only these are photographs.

There are six in all, showing different views of the same person. In the first one her long red hair is all around her face and you can't really see it properly. But in the next couple you can. She's sitting on a low concrete wall, and it looks like she's eating something with her hands from a huge carton on her lap. In another she's gnawing on something – maybe chicken? – then she's smoking a cigarette. In the final picture she's standing up, looking angry, and as if she's shouting.

The caption reads: *Cluckin' mad! Esther Burton looks like she has a bone to pick as she scoffs a whole BUCKET of chicken by herself, and enjoys a smoke afterwards!*

Charlie's heart seems to thud as he blinks at it. Esther, Instagram star and ambassador for that jewellery brand, and now his friend . . . eating from a bucket?

. . . didn't seem to care who spotted her, it goes on. *Wonder what the influencer's fans will make of this?*

Charlie pictures Esther the last time he saw her, so chatty and fun to be with. And he remembers the first time he met her, at his place, before her boyfriend started on at her dad. How she'd asked him, *So, Charlie, where does the moon go during the day?*

She hadn't been taking the piss. She'd genuinely wanted to know. And now some vile person had taken pictures of her and sold them and made money out of her. Fury rises up in Charlie as he imagines how she'll feel if and when she sees this.

Of course she'll see it. She probably has already.

So what if she had some fried chicken? he thinks furiously. What business is it of anyone's what she does? He checks the time on his phone, figuring that Brenda will have walked the dogs by now and is probably heading back to the shop. He grabs all six copies of that particular paper, slips through the back room past the cracked sink and the tapestry curtain and out to the yard where the wheelie bins are.

He doesn't go for the recycling bin because then Brenda might see. Instead, he squashes the newspapers into the black bin, the one for general household rubbish. He presses them down as far as they'll go, then he rearranges the bulging bin bags to cover them completely before shutting the lid.

CHAPTER FORTY-TWO

JAMES

'It's not that bad,' I tell her. 'Honestly, Est. It'll be fine . . .'

'Dad, they're everywhere,' she cries. 'It *is* that bad. It's about as bad as it could possibly be!'

'Don't say that. It'll be forgotten in a day or two and anyway, you weren't doing anything wrong. You were only eating chicken.'

'Fried chicken, Dad. Out of a bucket!'

She slumps, head in hands, at my kitchen table. I rest a hand on her shoulder, wishing I had some kind of manual so I'd know how to help her through this. It was so much easier when she was little and had grazed her knee or got a splinter in her finger. I can't fix things with a plaster or my trusty tweezers now. So, what can I do? Nothing, it seems, because the unflattering pictures are out there in the world. I'm actually shocked that they've caused such a stir.

'You weren't breaking the law,' I point out, tipping Esther's cold, half-eaten spaghetti into the bin.

'That's not the point,' she says with exaggerated patience, as if addressing a child. 'It'll still damage me. It's all about perception and how I come across . . .'

'But . . . you come across really well, don't you?' I suggest. 'All those pictures you've done with Lauren . . . didn't you say everyone loves them?'

'Something like this cancels all that out. Like, you make one tiny mistake—'

'Does it really, though?' I ask. 'Does it actually work like that?'

'Yes!' she says, head jerking up, eyes flashing.

'I still can't understand why it's such a huge thing.'

'Yes, because you're a vet, Dad,' she declares. 'No one cares what *you* do.'

'Erm, I think they do actually,' I say, trying to lighten the mood.

'I don't mean what you do with their *pets*,' she says quickly. 'I mean, outside of work, in your private life.'

We fall silent as I start to wash up. It's not that I'm being unsympathetic. I feel sorry for her, of course I do. But it strikes me that drama follows Esther like a cloud, and although she didn't mean to belittle what I do, it still stings a bit. Plus, other people have worries and problems and bad days too, if only she'd realise it. Tony Lomax came in today, not even pretending that Bob needed attention but just for a chat as he was 'passing by', he said. He had a cup of tea with us and admitted that he'd had a scare the other night. Someone had tried to break into his flat. Bob had started barking in the night, and when Tony had gone through to the living room he'd spotted a man at the window, trying to force it open. Clearly, an elderly collie cross trying to defend his territory wasn't going to deter him.

'Call yourself a guard dog?' Tony said, with mock seriousness. Bob had just gazed up at him and wagged his tail.

Then, after Tony's visit, I euthanised a beloved nineteen-year-old Persian cat. Her owner – an elderly woman in a smart trouser suit – was brave and stoical with her mouth trembling as she gave him one final kiss. 'You've been my best friend, Milo,' she murmured. 'I'm going to miss you.' Although I've been doing this job for twenty-six years, it still gets me sometimes. And today, spotting this, Casey made us tea and we sat in the tiny staffroom and had some of Tony's shortbread. Stuff it, we decided. The next client could wait ten minutes. The world wouldn't end.

And now, even though Esther's claiming that her life *has* ended – or her professional life that's so image-dependent, at least – all I want is to sit on the sofa and watch some rubbish on TV.

You'll soon be in Cornwall, I remind myself. *Off-grid*. I try to shrug off my worry that a bit of distance has crept between Lauren and me lately, because of course that's normal. It's been Christmas after all. We've been busy. Our lives are full.

'All the more reason to be going away together,' Casey remarked this afternoon with a smile. 'Honestly, James, it's a wonder you manage to see Lauren at all, the way Esther keeps you on toast. You've got to put yourself first sometimes!' She meant it kindly so I didn't mind. In her early thirties, Casey is a single mother of three, and is pulled in all kinds of directions. I'm sure she's way stricter as a parent than I've ever been – but it's a bit late to do things differently now.

'My career's completely over,' Esther announces now.

'Oh, come on, love,' I say. 'What can you do about it? I mean, how can you make things better?'

She throws out her arms. 'I don't know!'

'Could you talk to someone? Get advice, I mean?'

'There's no one really,' she says, sounding hopeless.

'What about the agency?' I know she's signed up with people who are supposed to manage her creative partnerships. So I'm not completely in the dark.

'It's not really their thing,' she says dismissively.

I lean against the fridge, dislodging the clay fridge magnet she made me a very long time ago, in less fraught times, of Walter curled up in his basket. 'Aren't they supposed to be guiding your career?' I ask.

'Yes, but they don't deal with that kind of thing.'

'You mean, the difficult things and not just the easy, money-making things?' It comes out sounding more judgemental than I meant. But surely these people – who, I gather, take a hefty whack of her earnings – are there to help?

'You just don't get it,' she mutters.

'What about seeing a friend, then?' I ask, filling the kettle to make tea. 'That'd cheer you up. How about meeting up with Gracie and Jess? They must be home for Christmas, surely?'

'I'm not sure,' she says quickly, looking down.

I frown at her, realising that there must have been some kind of shift in their friendship because, before they went off to uni, they always hung out on weekends, even though Esther had gone to a different school. I hand her a mug of tea, at a loss now as to how I can help her. 'I'll make an appointment to see Chrissie,' she murmurs, referring to her therapist.

'Right.' I blow across my mug. 'D'you think she'll be able to help?'

'I don't know. It's hardly her area . . .'

'What *is* her area then?' I ask before I can stop myself. Esther has mentioned that she's 'not exactly a conventional therapist' and I must admit, I have doubts about her credentials.

'She's a good listener,' Esther says firmly.

'Well, yes, but that seems like entry-level stuff,' I remark. 'It's like saying a dentist is good with teeth.'

She glares at me and now I realise I should have kept my mouth shut. 'Well, yes,' she retorts. 'But isn't that exactly what you want?'

CHAPTER FORTY-THREE

ESTHER

Esther has always enjoyed being at her dad's. She feels cared for here, with his squashy old sofa and bowls of spaghetti and a great mound of freshly grated parmesan to sprinkle on. And garlic bread! It's funny that he still gets it in for her as if she's a little kid. So yes, he does his best. But he's also incredibly annoying as, whenever anything goes wrong in her life, he's right there suggesting possible solutions.

Maybe it's because of his work. After all, if someone brings in an Alsatian with a fractured leg he can hardly shrug and say, 'Sorry, I don't know what to do.' He's solutions-focused. That's his job. But Esther isn't his job; she's his daughter – a fully grown woman capable of leading her own life.

Of course she can't ask the agency for help over these terrible pictures. That's not what they're for, to minimise damage over stuff like this. It's already being called 'bucket-gate' – she's seen that all over – and 'chickengate' too. That's not their area at all.

And now, on this bleary late December morning, Esther

stretches out in her pyjamas on her dad's sofa, elongating her body in the way Walter does. As he pads into the room she calls him to jump up and sit with her. But he slinks away under the armchair instead.

With a sigh, Esther reaches for her phone. As she checks her emails she notices one from the agency expressing 'regret that we feel we have no alternative but to cease working with you'.

She stares at it, willing the words to rearrange themselves before her eyes. Everything she's done, to reach a point where they'd represent her! The expensive facials and hair extensions; the lengths she went to in order to find a photographer who could translate her vision. Okay, it wasn't *that* hard to find Lauren, as she happens to be dating her dad – but still! Esther has forged a creative relationship with her, and the pictures have been amazing; everyone's said so.

She sits bolt upright and shivers in her PJs. She wears brushed cotton pyjamas now because Miles isn't here to complain. Esther had started to feel happier about being single; about being able to do whatever she likes without being judged. But she isn't happy now, because there's another email, she realises, which the agency has forwarded to her.

Esther's heart seems to clang as she reads it. Maybe it actually did, because nervous old Walter darts out from under the armchair and shoots out of the room.

Dear Esther, the email reads.

In light of recent media coverage we have made the difficult decision to end our relationship with you with immediate effect.

Wishing you the best for the future.

Love and light,

The Bethani team

CHAPTER FORTY-FOUR

LAUREN

Last time I packed a suitcase was for Corsica. Then it was all cotton vests, T-shirts and denim shorts: easy clothes for the hot Mediterranean sun. This time it's jeans and thick, cosy sweaters, including the beautiful Fair Isle one Kim knitted me for Christmas; the loveliest one I've ever owned.

This is where my life's at now, I reflect with a smile as I place it in my suitcase. I can truly appreciate great knitting. Remembering the sweaters Mum knitted for me when I was little, I wish I'd been more appreciative instead of cringing at the chunky necklines, the buttons on a shoulder, the fact that they didn't have labels inside like my friends' jumpers from Chelsea Girl and C&A.

I also pack sturdy walking boots because I know about James and his 'ample structural support', and I'm looking forward to producing them from my suitcase with a triumphant 'Ta-daaah!' Because there'll be plenty of walking in Cornwall. But I'm sure we'll be doing lots of other things too.

My heart quickens at the thought of our three days together, cut off from everything. 'Charlie?' I call out.

292

'Yeah?' He appears in my bedroom doorway looking a little bleary. With his prelims coming up he's been grafting away late into the night. We might not have had the easiest time together over the past year, and I've found it tough, being pushed away by him. But he does work hard, and we still have a bond of sorts. At least, I hope we do.

'How's it going, love?' I ask.

'All right?' He phrases it as a question.

I pause, not wanting to patronise him. 'Are you sure you're okay with me going away?' I place my toiletry bag in the case.

''Course I am.' He raises a smile. 'What if I said no? Would you start unpacking?'

I smile. 'I'm only asking. You do know we won't be contactable, don't you? Are you all right about that?'

He pulls an *are-you-mad?* expression and shoves his hands into his pockets. 'How d'you think I'm going to manage when I leave home?'

'Oh, I know, love. But Kim's going to cook for you, she'll message you when dinner's nearly ready—'

'I can cook!' he exclaims, laughing now.

This is true. He can knock together pasta dishes and roast a chicken – not that he'll be doing that, I'm sure. And it's not food I'm worried about really. It's about him being here alone.

Remy still lives at home, in theory – just down the road – but he's often away, and when he's home I gather he's wrapped up with Freya. However, as Charlie wanders off, I reassure myself that of course it's okay to leave him here by himself. James messages to say, *Can't wait for our trip.* I gather there's been some kind of drama with pictures of Esther being splashed about in the media; unflattering shots of her eating chicken or something like that. I'm thinking, James really needs this break. His work is full on, and now that Esther's living with him, I imagine that his home life is pretty intense too.

I wish I could help, but what can I do? So many times, I've had to hold back from saying anything about Esther, and the way she treats him – which isn't always respectful, in my view. But then, James is probably fully aware of that, and the last thing I want to do is criticise his parenting. He does a great job, I think. I just wish Esther was a bit more thoughtful sometimes. After all, he has a life too.

It's gone 10 p.m. by the time I've finished packing. James will catch the train out here first thing tomorrow morning, and I'll meet him at the station. Then we'll be off, away from everything. I should get an early night but, too excited to sleep, I sit up at the kitchen table planning some columns and ideas for recipes over the winter months. I know some people keep gratitude journals so they can remind themselves of all the things they have to be thankful for. I don't need to write that stuff down because I *know* I'm lucky. I have a wonderful son and a lovely home. I'm going away tomorrow with a caring man who I love, and who loves me. I have a job that fulfils and even thrills me sometimes, which I stumbled into purely by accident.

I was already shooting all kinds of objects for Frank, and it didn't bother me that clients assumed he'd done the pictures. It wasn't a modesty thing, and I certainly didn't feel martyrish about it. I just wanted to do the shoots so his clients would have their pictures on time, and Frank would be paid, and not gain a reputation for being unreliable. Then everyone would be happy.

That felt like my main purpose in life back then: *to keep everyone happy*. I'd been around enough shoots to see how things were set up – not just with Frank, but on food shoots back in my magazine days. I'd seen how to light a shot, and while I still had tons to learn technically, I picked it all up on the job, experimenting with lenses and lights and gradually getting better over time. I'd shoot anything from luxury goods like precious jewellery and handbags, right down the scale to jelly sweets and haem-orrhoid ointment. I didn't mind what it was because a thing is just a thing, basically.

In some ways I enjoyed doing the less glamorous shoots the most. It's harder to make a tube of bum ointment look appealing than a Prada bag, and I rose to the challenge.

Then one day a courier turned up with a box of French cheeses, a couple of them Corsican, and I went to town on that one, finding fresh herbs and table linens to make it look as appealing as possible. I even scoured charity shops for ceramics like the ones Mum and Dad have, and re-arranged our kitchen so the table could be set up in a shaft of sunlight.

The client loved them and a whole new food thing started: baked goods, fresh produce and confectionery, for cookery websites, magazines and product lines. It was huge fun. The work started pouring in. By then I'd fallen in love with taking pictures and even stopped telling Frank when 'he' was booked for these shoots. All the bookings had been coming through me anyway. Most clients thought I was his assistant.

Then one time a client showed up at our house and it was me shooting. I was literally in the middle of the job. We'd become friends by then, and the client said she'd suspected it was me doing the pictures all along. From then on I worked as me, Lauren Summer, focusing on food shoots and gradually creating recipes myself, styling the pictures and putting together the whole package.

I fell into this world, and back in July I fell into this lovely thing with James. Of course there'll be challenges but now, I'm sure we can handle anything that's thrown at us.

I get up and check the fridge to make sure Charlie has all the basics he'll need while I'm away, even though he'll be round at Kim's for some of the time and is perfectly capable of venturing to the shop. I've figured out the route to the holiday cottage, because the owner warned me that it's not the easiest to find. I've packed blankets because I have a yearning to sit outside at night and look up at the stars. There's no light pollution there. There's literally nothing for miles around, and my heart lifts at the thought of being alone with James, away from everything.

Frank didn't do holidays as a rule. Charlie and I would always go to Corsica for summer breaks on our own. It was always a bone of contention because I'd felt strongly that family breaks were important; time for the three of us to be together, away from work and everything else. Then, out of the blue – ten years ago – Frank announced that he wanted a family trip to Mexico. A friend of his had a villa we could stay in for free. But I think there was more to it than that. My work had started to take off. I was busy and in demand. Yes, I knew he'd had affairs but I'd never had the courage to leave him. Now I was successful and could take care of Charlie and me.

I wasn't scared of leaving Frank anymore. But perhaps, I thought, this holiday would be a turning point and we'd come back stronger. He was making an effort, I decided, and that meant a lot back then. He was Charlie's father, after all. And perhaps he was turning over a new leaf.

I felt stronger by then, and my confidence had grown. And, while I no longer needed Frank, the difference was that it was my choice now. And I'd chosen to give us one final chance.

CHAPTER FORTY-FIVE

LAUREN

A decade ago and Charlie is seven years old. He's a wonderful little boy, so sunny and full of fun. He loves the beach. I taught him to swim last year and he's already one of the best in his year at school.

He loves the water. And he loves staying with 'Corsica Gran and Granddad', as he calls them. Frank's parents are a lot older than mine and apparently not terribly interested in children. My dad can be cantankerous – he's always been that way – but he softens with Charlie, and he adores him, as does my mum. Charlie's bond with them has always been special.

On those Corsican beaches my little boy picks up fragments of smooth sea glass and shells, and says they're 'sea presents' for me. I guess we're exceptionally close, and I feel very lucky. I'd have liked more children, but it just didn't happen. As things aren't great with his father and me, I've convinced myself that it's probably for the best.

Anyway, Charlie is a wonderful kid and I couldn't wish for more, really. He is enough.

His dad has never come to Corsica with us. 'Too busy

with work,' he's always said. But this particular summer, we've been invited to stay at Frank's friend's villa in Mexico. He shows us photos. It has a stunning garden with jewel-bright hammocks strung between the trees, and is a short walk from the beach. I'm keen, and Charlie's keen, so off we go.

When I think about it now, this is the only other time Charlie has had a bit of a strop on a beach. A whole decade before the shrouding with Minnie's stinky towel, he's quite mad at me.

This time, in Mexico, it's not about sunscreen. At seven years old Charlie tolerates being slathered from head to foot in Factor 30. No, the issue today is about swimming in the sea.

We've come to a beach that's well known as the most beautiful for miles around. It's also notorious for rip tides. We know, from what locals have told us, that it's not safe to swim here – ever. I'd hazard a guess that it's doubly unsafe when you've been drinking beers and wine all day, as Frank has.

'It's fine, Lauren. I'm just going for a little dip!'

At that point he's keeping himself pretty much topped up throughout the day, and I've almost stopped noticing the squiffy eyes and blurring of the edges. It's just Frank being Frank. However, a week into our holiday I've started to wonder if I can put up with him for much longer. I'm not sure this is what I want for myself, or for Charlie. Being married to a drinker is at best pretty dull (all those repetitive rants) and at worst, stressful and frustrating – and deeply lonely too. And I have started to think about a future for myself that doesn't include Frank.

I'm just sick of making excuses and covering up for him. I'm also very used to drunk Frank, and often barely register it anymore. But that blistering-hot afternoon on a Mexican beach, it strikes me how very pissed he is.

'Frank, please don't swim,' I say.

'I'm a good swimmer!' he insists. 'You always think you're the best but I'm really strong, I'm like a fucking *dolphin* in the ocean . . .' That's not true and we both know it. But he's already torn off his T-shirt and shorts and is standing there in his trunks, ready to run in.

'You said we couldn't swim, Mum.' Charlie turns to me indignantly. As if I were boss of his dad and could control him in any way.

'That's right, love. It's not safe,' I tell him.

'Why isn't it safe?' He's outraged at the injustice of it as his dad jogs across the flat golden sand towards the sea.

'Because of the rip tides,' I explain, taking hold of Charlie's hand. 'There are really strong currents and they can drag you under.'

'I'd be all right,' he says.

'No, love – it's so dangerous. Remember what those people at the restaurant were saying? You could easily drown here . . .'

'Why's Daddy gone in then?' he asks.

Because Daddy is a fucking idiot. 'He's just being a bit reckless,' I reply.

'Mummy, let me go in!' He tugs his hand loose and starts to run after his dad.

'Charlie, no!' I cry out.

He ignores me, or maybe he's so focused on plunging into the water that he doesn't hear me. I yell again, my feet hitting the hard, damp sand as I race after him.

Frank is already in the water, waving and shouting and – this part I can't believe, I'm *incensed* – urging us both to go in and join him. 'It's lovely! You don't know what you're missing, you two!'

I catch up with Charlie and grab at him but he wriggles free like an eel. 'He'll be fine. I'll keep an eye on him,' Frank shouts as our son sploshes in to join him.

'He *won't* be fine! Frank, come out!' I'm terrified now. The vast, unblemished beach is almost deserted, apart from a small group of naked sunbathers in the far distance, who'd amused Charlie greatly when we'd first spotted them. 'Mummy, that man's going to burn his willy!'

'He'll fry his sausage,' Frank had agreed, and we'd all laughed. But I'm not laughing now as our son starts swimming out to sea.

'Come back, Charlie!' I roar. Then: 'Frank! Bring him out. This is scaring me . . .' I wade into the sea in my T-shirt and shorts. 'Charlie!' I bellow, 'if you don't get out of that sea right now we're going back to the villa and you're going straight to bed!'

'Lighten up!' Frank yells. 'We're on holiday in case you hadn't noticed. We're having fun. Remember that?'

'There are rip tides,' I call out, tears springing into my eyes, mixing with the salty spray. But the two of them are too far out to hear me and I watch them, telling myself that surely I can trust Frank to keep Charlie safe. After all, it's what the guidebooks recommend, isn't it? Let your child go swimming off one of Mexico's most dangerous beaches, with a drunk man?

First Frank disappears, then Charlie. A wave has crashed over them, huge and powerful. They both reappear briefly as flailing shapes, then go under again, out of sight. I'm probably screaming. I don't know. What I do know is that, although I'm a strong swimmer, there's no chance of getting out there to both of them. So I focus on Charlie, who reappears again – just a flash of his terrified face, then a skinny arm waving. I plough out through the pounding waves and somehow I manage to grab at his

301

arm, pull him tight to my body and swim with him back to the shore.

He's clinging to me with great sobs as we collapse together on the sand. 'What happened, Mummy?'

'It's okay, love. It's okay.' I'm gasping for breath, flooded with relief that he's here with me.

'Where's Daddy? What's happened to Dad?'

I don't know and I can't bear to look. But I had to choose Charlie; there was nothing else I could do. He's just a child – my baby. I hold him tight to my chest, his heart thumping hard against me, the hot sun bearing down upon us.

It's one of the naked sunbathers who has a surfboard and paddles out to rescue Frank. He brings him back to shore, spluttering, obviously in shock. 'You are so fucking lucky, mate,' I hear the guy yelling with an Australian twang. 'Idiot. What the hell were you thinking, going out there?'

I try to thank him but he shakes his head as if I am an idiot too. 'Letting your little boy swim here,' he says with disdain. He glares at the three of us, pushes his matted wet blond hair from his tanned face and marches off, back to his friends, still cursing us.

'Idiots . . . could've drowned. What kind of parents are they?'

It seems inconceivable that, so little time before, it had been all jollity and sausage jokes.

Next day a hungover and fragile Frank insists that I'd 'over-reacted', that they'd been perfectly safe and look what I've done now. Charlie is terrified of the sea! 'You've ruined it for him,' Frank declares. 'He loved the ocean and now he hates it and it's all your fault. You do realise he'll never swim again?'

*

Frank was right, and I haven't pushed it, even though I'd have loved Charlie to swim with me in Corsica over subsequent summers. Of course now he'd be appalled by the idea of us swimming together anyway. How embarrassing, being in the sea with your mum! Far better to cover yourself in a towel and be stung by wasps . . .

I get up at seven and stuff a swimsuit into my suitcase. Yes, it'll be freezing in Cornwall at this time of year. But Kim's always raving about the joys of cold-water swimming and, who knows, maybe I'll try it? Anything feels possible on this trip.

An hour or so later I remind Charlie yet again that, unless he can find a carrier pigeon, I'll be uncontactable while I'm away. 'Mum, I know. You've said, a *lot* of times now . . .' He's smiling, propped up in bed. Maybe he's delighted at the prospect of having me out of his hair for a few days.

I leave him be and pace around the house, running through a mental list of what I've packed, in case I've forgotten anything. After all, there are no shops near the cottage. I check the time, figuring that James will be setting off soon. I'm aware of a flurry of butterflies as I pick up my phone, poised to suggest that he brings swimming shorts too in case we're crazy enough to jump into the freezing sea. But just as I start the message, my phone rings. It's James.

Five months, we've been together. It's not terribly long, but long enough for me to have let down all those barriers and allow someone new into my life. Someone I love and trust and thought I might have a future with.

It's also been long enough for me to know, instantly, that James isn't calling with good news. There's a catch in his voice, like something stretched taut, as he says, 'Lauren, I don't know how to tell you this. I'm so, so sorry. But I can't come to Cornwall with you.'

PART FOUR

Just Desserts

When you think the meal is over, there's always room for a little sweet surprise

CHAPTER FORTY-SIX

LAUREN

'Are we nearly there yet?'

A long time ago, when Charlie was around five, we were driving to the south coast for the day, just the two of us.

Frank was right. Charlie used to adore the sea, tearing off his T-shirt and shorts before I'd even spread out a towel to set up our base for the day. And of course I'd have charged in after him, sometimes before I'd had time to strip off to my swimsuit myself. But I loved Charlie's exuberance and determination that no one was going to stop him plunging in.

'Are we nearly there yet?' It was just the two of us that day as Frank had been 'too tired' to come with us. Hungover, more like. And actually I was glad because hungover Frank was like a grumpy bear, unable to settle and prone to growling at us. I looked over at Charlie as I drove and laughed. He knew he was driving me mad with the repeated question, and to get him to stop we struck a deal. He knew I'd buy him an ice cream at the little kiosk on the beach. But if he managed not to ask me again for the rest of the journey, he could have a *double* cone – two flavours. And a Flake stuck in it.

'So, Mum,' Charlie says now, glancing at me from the passenger seat, 'are we talking double cone and Flake when we get there?'

I smile. 'You're too old for bribery now, darling.'

'Aw,' he teases.

Of course, seventeen-year-old Charlie is very different from his five-year-old self, and instead of the persistent questions and chatter he settles into silence, plugging in his earphones eventually. And that's fine. I'm happy to just drive. Well, not happy exactly. I was upset and furious and decided there and then that it was over.

Sod it, I thought. I've had enough of being let down by a man.

So, yes, I've cried a lot, then berated myself for being so stupid as to invest so much into this thing with James; to believe that we really had a future together.

We tried our best and it seemed like we had something wonderful. But real life got in the way.

At least James hadn't left me waiting and waiting, in the way that Esther had sent him into a panic at the airport. At least there was that. He'd called an hour or so before we were due to set off. But there was an awful lot of other stuff when we spoke. I learnt that Esther was devastated about the fallout from the chicken pictures, which it turned out that Charlie had known about – but had he told me? Of course not. He never tells me anything.

'I just don't feel I can go away right now,' James said. A pause followed and I wondered if he was leaving space for me to try and persuade him otherwise.

'You're obviously worried,' I said. 'You have to do what feels right.' I meant it, too. So much of raising a human seems to be about instinct, and doing 'what feels right' even if we end up getting it totally wrong.

'It's crazy, I know,' he admitted, 'the way it's blown up. It was only a bit of fried food . . .'

'I know. But to her it's a huge thing.' I amazed myself, how calm and understanding I was being, when actually I wanted to yell, *But what about us?*

Apparently we didn't matter at all. At least, I didn't. All the planning and excitement over our break – and we were only talking three days away together.

Well, stuff that, I decided.

James sighed loudly. 'It's not just that. Miles has given an interview to some rubbishy gossip site, saying she'd never behaved like that when they were together and maybe she's going through some kind of breakdown . . .'

'D'you think she is?' I asked.

'I think she's just very, very down. She's holed up in bed, reading stuff about herself over and over. It's like she's stuck in some terrible cycle—'

'I'm sorry,' I said, meaning it. 'Would it be okay for me to send her a message?'

'She'd like that, I'm sure. She said Charlie's been really sweet and supportive.'

'That's nice,' I said in surprise. All this communication that's been going on between them, without me realising.

He cleared his throat. 'Y'know, if we were going somewhere closer, or where I could be in contact with her, it'd feel okay—'

'Don't worry about it,' I said, just wanting to end the conversation now.

I was done with it, I really was. I looked down at my open case on my bed, all ready to go with Kim's hand-knitted sweater sitting at the top, and at the box on the floor, filled with provisions for our getaway.

Ingredients to rustle up a warming curry. Cheeses all carefully packed in a cool box. Bread I'd baked especially, plus fresh pasta and a basil sauce I'd made, decanted into a tub. I'd assured James that I wanted to take care of the food – because that's what I love and it's fun for me. But I'd also found a little pub a short drive away from the cottage and booked us a table there. An ancient pub clinging to the coastline with amazing seafood, the reviews said. That would be an extra surprise.

I'd also packed wine and, like an idiot, some lingerie I'd bought specially. Nothing outrageously sexy, just simple black lace.

Well, sod all that, I think now, although of course I've still brought everything with me – lingerie excepted. This is not a black lace sort of weekend. It's now a big, sensible knickers kind of trip. Another last-minute addition to our packing is a rucksack crammed with Charlie's textbooks, and his telescope is packed in the boot. Maybe that's what swung it for him; a complete absence of light pollution in the wilds of Cornwall. All those glittering stars.

After a couple of hours on the road he tugs out his earphones. 'Mum?' he starts.

'No, we're not nearly there yet,' I say with a smile.

He grins too, then turns serious. 'Are you angry with James?'

I bite my lip. 'No, I'm not angry, love.'

'You are a bit,' he suggests. 'I can tell.'

I wonder how to respond to this. He's an adult now, I remind myself; I don't have to gloss over things or pretend everything's okay, like I did with his dad. 'Okay, I'm absolutely furious,' I blurt out, meaning it as a joke – but without warning tears fall out of my eyes.

'Mum, don't cry!' Charlie exclaims, looking at me in alarm.

'I'm okay.' I try to blink them away and focus hard on the road ahead.

'You're obviously not, are you?'

'I am,' I say firmly, clearing my throat. 'Honestly. And I do understand why he hasn't come . . .'

'Really?' Charlie asks. It strikes me that it's a long time since we've had a proper conversation like this. In fact, I can't remember the last time. Maybe something good has come out of this after all. 'Couldn't Esther have stayed at her mum's?' he adds, studying me as I drive.

'Hey, I thought you were pleased to be coming with me,' I tease him.

'I am. I'm really pleased.' In fact, after his attitude in Corsica this summer I'd expected a curt 'No thanks' when I asked him. In preparation I'd considered asking Kim, but her girls are still home for the holidays and I didn't want her to have to wrestle over whether to leave them for New Year's Eve. I'd suspected that whichever decision she'd come to would have made her feel bad.

I'd also – briefly – considered coming on my own. I could work on a cookbook proposal, I'd figured. Give it some time and headspace at last. That way, I could turn my disappointment into something positive. But how would that have felt, being so isolated for three days? I was worried I'd brood and go over and over the whole James scenario, working myself into a stew about it.

The whole point had been to give me and James some space so we could just be together, like we were in Corsica. I wanted it to be like our blissful two weeks when we'd started to share our life stories, and I drove us around the winding mountain roads that had freaked him out so much. One time, when we'd parked up at a village square, he'd laughed and said, 'I need a sedative.'

Now I'm picturing those meals at Camille's beachside

311

restaurant with the wine and the glorious sunsets. And our first night together, at his hotel, with the clanking cage lift, the disapproving front-desk lady and the breeze gently wafting the gauzy curtain at the balcony door.

I was wrong, I realise now. It could never be like that again and maybe I was mad to even try.

'Yes, she could've gone to her mum's,' I say, glancing at Charlie, 'but James felt he had to be there. And you know,' I add, 'if you were in the kind of situation Esther's in, then maybe I'd have ducked out of a trip too.'

'It's not very likely though, is it?' Charlie smiles wryly. 'That I'd be papped eating food out of a bucket?'

I smile too. 'D'you even like fried chicken?'

'Yeah, sometimes. Me and Remy used to get it.'

'What, a bucket of chicken?' I ask in surprise.

'Occasionally, yeah. If we were in London . . .'

'I never knew that.' I cast him a quick glance.

'You don't know everything about me, Mum,' he says, and the playful glint in his eye tells me that perhaps things are changing again between Charlie and me. He's growing up for sure. He'll leave school in a few months' time and his life will open up thrillingly. I remind myself how lucky I am to be spending three days off-grid with my boy. He's planning to do lots of studying. We'll coexist quite happily, I think.

As for James and me, I've had enough drama over the years, the way things were with Frank. And although I do care – and sympathise over the chicken thing – I don't think it's for me. As I once said to James, life is complicated. Too complicated, I realise now.

As the miles go by any last residues of annoyance ebb away. I don't even blame him for what's happened. None of it is his fault. But I do hope that Charlie doesn't notice me blinking away more tears as I decide that it simply wasn't meant to be.

CHAPTER FORTY-SEVEN

Of course Charlie was going to say yes to going away with his mum. It sounded amazing, being completely off-grid. He'd always liked camping with her and, better still, when he went with the Cubs, waking up with that feeling of being outside and hearing the birds. Sitting around campfires, cooking sausages on sticks and spotting the odd bat or even an owl. They hadn't even gone very far from home but it had felt like a world away from their village.

However, this place really *is* a world away. 'Will you be okay without Wi-Fi?' his mum had asked apprehensively as they'd driven down, as if she'd said, *Will you be okay without food?* But Charlie isn't constantly on his phone or online, and he can study perfectly well with his textbooks for a few days. He doesn't really bother with social media, apart from keeping up with what Esther's doing. Remy had badgered him into having an Instagram account, saying he could follow astronomers and all the famous observatories, the planetariums and all that. But he rarely bothers with that. What Charlie loves is his books.

As soon as they arrived yesterday they'd lit the wood-burning stove and had dinner, and then Charlie had gone off to study in the little cabin in the garden. That's where he wanted to sleep, he'd decided. There was a comfy sofa bed and a skylight and it was magical. He didn't mind that there was too much cloud cover for any star spotting. You can't have everything, he'd told himself.

He'd said goodnight to his mum and hadn't expected to see her until morning. She probably needed a bit of space, he'd decided, closing his books for the night. But he could see the light was still on in the living room so he'd headed back to the house. She was drinking wine and gave him a beer and somehow the hours went by with them chatting about this and that. He couldn't remember the last time they'd hung out like this. She told him about a cookbook proposal she was putting together, with the plan to send it to an agent and try and get it published.

'You should definitely do it,' he'd said.

'You think? I do wonder if anyone'd be interested. I mean, I'm not a celebrity chef or anything—'

'Don't have that attitude,' he'd told her. 'You can do anything you want, Mum.'

She smiled. 'Thank you, love.'

'What for?' he asked, genuinely not knowing.

'For saying that. For believing in me.'

He'd shrugged and sipped his beer from the bottle, amazed that she hadn't even known that – that he'd always believed in her. There was never any doubt about that.

*

She bobs like a seal, just her head visible in the glittering sea. Only it's not a seal. It's his crazy mother who tore off her clothes down to her black swimsuit and plunged

314

right in. 'This is brilliant!' she yells. 'Honestly, Charlie. It's amazing!'

'I believe you,' he calls back, grateful that she isn't nagging him to join her. She'd tried to coax him gently a few times when he was younger, after Mexico. But he'd literally start shaking the instant a wave lapped at his toes. He couldn't bear the feel of it against his skin. So she'd let it go and, even though he was a good swimmer once, he's never been in the sea again.

She's out of the water now, simultaneously pink and blue with cold and pulling a huge towel around herself. 'Kim was right!' she announces with a smile. 'I always wondered what she was going on about. But it's an incredible feeling—'

'C'mon, Mum, let's get you warm and dry,' Charlie says, as if he's the parent. They hurry along the narrow path that leads steeply to the cottage. While she's showering – thankfully there's plenty of hot water – he lights the wood burner and fixes lunch.

They fall into this pattern, with him disappearing off to the cabin to study for the early part of the evening and then joining her in the cottage later. The days are spinning too fast, Charlie realises. He loves it here.

Then, miraculously, on their last night the sky clears and he calls her upstairs to the glass-walled room to look through the telescope. 'Oh, Charlie. This amazing,' she announces. 'I've never seen anything like this. The stars are incredible . . .'

'It is pretty special.' He is glowing with pride as if he'd put them there.

'I thought we had clear skies back at home. But it's nothing like this, is it?'

He shakes his head. 'This is one of the best places in Britain for stargazing,' he tells her.

'Really? Where else is good?'

'The very best place is meant to be a little island off Scotland,' he replies.

'Well, I'm sorry I didn't take us there,' she says, laughing.

'Mum, this is great.' He smiles. 'Thanks. I mean, I'm sorry James didn't come but—' He breaks off, not wanting to upset her by going into it now. They've hardly mentioned him while they've been here, and he assumes it's over.

'It's fine, Charlie,' his mum says as they head downstairs to sit by the fire. The walls are rough whitewashed stone, the floor stone-flagged and scattered with bright stripy rugs. There's a shelf crammed with books, and several lamps glow invitingly. Solar panels, bottled gas and the wood-burning stove ensure that they have everything they need.

'Isn't it amazing to live so simply?' Charlie remarks.

His mum nods. 'It actually reminds me a little bit of Gran and Granddad's place, you know? It just has the essentials and it's all the cosier for that.'

'Yeah, it is a bit like theirs.' There's a lull then. As the fire crackles he can sense her building up to asking him something.

Here it comes. 'Charlie,' she starts, 'why were you so fed up in Corsica last summer?'

'Oh, I dunno,' he mutters.

'Was it because Remy didn't come with us?'

'No, it wasn't that,' he says quickly. 'I . . .' He pauses because he's not quite sure how to explain it. 'I just . . . needed a bit of space, Mum.' He shakes his head. 'I'm sorry.'

'You don't need to be sorry,' she says. 'You've nothing to apologise for. D'you remember I was trying to actually put sunscreen on you, as if you were a little kid? I'm the one who should be sorry . . .'

'Yeah, maybe.' He laughs awkwardly. 'The thing is, Mum, I was trying to work things out.'

He can sense her trying to figure out what he might mean. She does her best not to pry but she can't help herself from trying to read the inside of his head. It drives him mad sometimes.

'We've always done loads together, haven't we?' he starts. 'Camping, building the garden, going to Young Stargazers and all that . . .'

'Yeah,' she says, sounding cautious as if she's wondering where this is going. 'I thought you wanted me there,' she adds. 'At Young Stargazers, I mean.'

'Well, I sort of did . . .' He looks at her and smiles. 'I also didn't like to think of you sitting at home, being miserable, on your own.'

She stares at him. 'I was fine, Charlie. I wasn't miserable at all back then. What were you so worried about?'

'Just after all the stuff with Dad,' he replies.

She gets up and hugs him, and to his surprise he doesn't feel the urge to push her away, as he has recently. 'I really wish you hadn't worried,' she says.

'I couldn't help it. I knew what went on.'

'Oh, Charlie.' She sits back down, reaches for her wine and sips it.

Charlie takes a deep breath, steadying himself. He's not sure how she'll react to this. But they have grown closer again, and toasted the New Year together, and Charlie has made a private resolution to be more open and honest about his feelings instead of bottling stuff up. So, here goes. He licks his dry lips and takes another big inhalation. 'I don't want to do it anymore, Mum,' he blurts out.

'Do what? she asks, looking startled.

317

'The calls,' he says. 'The chats with Dad, I mean. I don't want to do them . . .'

She looks at him, and he knows what she's thinking because he can read the inside of *her* head. She thinks it's good for him to keep a connection; far healthier than being estranged. She's always wanted to protect him, to make him feel safe and loved, especially after that terrible day on the Mexican beach. But he's not that seven-year-old boy anymore with a plastic bucket, collecting sea presents for her. He's nearly eighteen and right now, Charlie knows best what's best for him.

'What's happened?' she asks, frowning. 'Why don't you want to talk to Dad?'

He rubs at his eyes. ''Cause I don't enjoy it. We've got nothing to talk about. And actually, I don't like him very much . . .'

'Oh, Charlie,' she exclaims. 'He's still your dad.'

'Yeah, I know,' he says, 'and I suppose I love him, deep down. I mean I'd never want anything bad to happen to him. I don't feel anger or anything like that. I just . . .' He shrugs, his gaze resting on the flickering flames. 'I just don't like him massively.'

They leave it at that, and he hugs her goodnight before heading back to the cabin and sleeping more soundly than he can ever remember.

In the morning, as they're packing the car, ready to leave, his mum says, 'This has been wonderful, Charlie.'

'Yeah, it has.' He smiles. 'What was your favourite part?' He catches himself sounding like the parent again and laughs.

'Oh, everything, Charlie. I can't decide. Just being with you really.' She pauses and closes the boot, then adds, 'I hope it hasn't been too dreadful, being stuck here with me.'

'It's been all right,' he says, teasing her.

She beams at him. 'D'you think you might come to Corsica with me this summer?'

He hesitates, looking back at the old stone cottage, and pushes back his dark hair. 'Erm, I'm not sure, Mum. Can I get back to you on that?'

She laughs. 'Yes, love. Of course you can. You can get back to me on that.'

CHAPTER FORTY-EIGHT

JAMES

It's not all squeezing a Jack Russell's anal gland, whatever Rhona might think. Yes, it's pets – but all kinds of things happen at our little practice. Take the tortoise, who I made a temporary splint for with balsa wood. He's not quite as mobile as he should be – not that he was racing around; I mean, he's a tortoise – and I keep thinking there must be something better I can do. It's bad enough, him being unable to hibernate this year, due to his accident. One winter, we can just about get away with. But we don't want it happening a second year. So I sit up late at home, when Esther's gone off to her room, researching options, making notes, trying to come up with a better solution.

I'd like to say it's keeping my mind off Lauren but of course it's not. Since I called, the morning she was leaving for Cornwall, there's been very little contact between us. *How was your trip? Did you have a good time?* That wouldn't do, I realised. She might not have even gone. All the planning she'd put into it, the anticipation and the money wasted. And I let her down on the day we

320

were meant to leave. Really, did I behave any better than Esther had, when she'd left me pacing about in a panic at the airport?

Esther hasn't even been that bad, as it turned out. It's not that I *wanted* to see her in the depths of despair, but she did seem to shake off the whole chicken episode remarkably quickly. 'I need to get a proper job, Dad,' she announced over dinner one evening, out of the blue. 'I'm a grown-up now and I want to get my grown-up life started.'

'What are you thinking of?' I asked.

'I don't know exactly. But I want to learn things and do something more worthwhile.'

This was great, of course – and just a week ago it would have been exactly what I wanted to hear. I tried to rouse the enthusiasm to discuss it with her, to chat about any little sparks of interest she might have. But I sounded like a school careers adviser who was biding their time until a better job came up. 'What kind of things are you interested in?' I asked. 'How d'you think you could use your skills?' Christ, I was talking as if I didn't know my own daughter. No wonder she flounced off.

I did send Lauren one message, after much deliberation: *So sorry about what happened. Can we get together and talk?*

Her reply, when it came several hours later, was to the point. *I don't think it's a good idea at the moment. Hope Esther's okay.*

She's doing fine, I replied, and that was that. Nothing more came, and messaging again seemed a bit pestery somehow. She'd made it clear that she didn't want to see me, and that was that.

What a bloody mess I'd made of everything. I hadn't even been able to give her her Christmas present of the antique earrings I'd spotted in a vintage place close to the practice. It would seem weird to post them so, instead, I just hide them away in a drawer.

I try to remind myself that my life is good and that I have a lot to be thankful for. Esther's okay, which is what matters. Meanwhile, I up my working hours to ridiculous levels. There's always admin to catch up on, plus the mammoth task of streamlining our records. One evening, after everyone else has gone home, I repaint the scuffed reception area.

A few weeks have gone by when it strikes me that I haven't seen Tony Lomax, with old Bob, for quite some time. I mention this to Fraser, in case he's been in and I've missed him. 'Last time was before New Year,' Fraser says.

'That time he told us about the attempted break-in?' I ask.

He nods. 'That's the one. And the time before that was about Bob's paws, I think?' I remember now that Tony had brought him in for an unnecessary appraisal of his digital pads, as he'd thought there might be 'a bit of abrasion there'. In fact they were perfectly fine, with barely any signs of wear and tear from the thousands of miles of pavements he must have covered over the years.

During quieter moments at the surgery I find myself wondering what Lauren's doing and if she took Kim to Cornwall, and if so, whether Kim had forced her into cold-water swimming, as I know she's a fan. Fraser, of course, is baffled as to why it's just fizzled out with Lauren and me.

'Just call her,' he says. 'What's wrong with you?'

'I don't want to pester her,' I say dismissively.

'For God's sake, how old are you?'

We're having a beer after work in a pub we haven't

been to for some time. It's been refurbished, its cosy old man's boozer vibe turned into something altogether more clinical. Everything seems to be made out of plasticky wood, and tinny Eighties music is barely audible. 'Same age as you,' I say, trying to lighten things. 'I don't think things change because we're in our fifties, you know.'

He shakes his head in exasperation. 'Just phone her, mate. You've screwed it up but you can still put it right.'

We leave the pub with me promising to do *something*, although I haven't specified what that might be, because I really don't know. But he's planted the thought, and next morning at work, before we're open, I'm about to message Lauren when the surgery line rings.

'Hello, can I speak to James Burton?' It's an elderly woman's voice. She sounds brusque, as if squaring up for a fight.

'Yes, speaking?'

'Oh. I didn't think you'd be the one answering calls.'

'Our receptionist isn't here yet,' I say. 'We don't open till eight-thirty—'

'Well, I've been left with a bit of a situation,' she cuts in. 'I can't manage it, not with my legs. He said to call you if anything ever happened so that's what I'm doing, all right? Can you help?'

CHAPTER FORTY-NINE

JAMES

'I'm sorry,' I start, 'but who is this?'

'Irene Craven.' She doesn't elaborate.

'And who said to call me?'

'Tony. Tony Lomax.' As if I'm incredibly dim not to have realised.

'Tony said to call me?' I ask.

'Yes, before he went into hospital. He said you'd sort things out . . .'

'Why's Tony in hospital? What's happened?'

'He had a stroke,' she replies. 'A bad stroke—'

'Oh, I'm so sorry!'

'I live across the road,' she continues. 'I took Bob in when Tony went off in the ambulance, thinking it'd just be a couple of days. But it's gone on and on, and I can't—'

'D'you know how he is?' I cut in. 'How he's doing?'

'I think he's a bit better now,' she says. 'He called me anyway so that's a good sign, isn't it?'

'Yes, I suppose it must be . . .'

'But he doesn't know when he's coming out,' she goes on, 'and I can't keep Bob here much longer. I can't manage the walks with my legs. I don't want to put him with a rescue centre or anything, but there's no one I can ask—'

'No, please don't do that,' I say quickly. 'I'll sort something out. Which hospital is Tony in?'

As she tells me I try to shake off a needle of guilt over that time I saw him, when he was all shaken up about the attempted burglary. Should I have spent more time with him? Perhaps tried to find out if he has anyone he could call upon, if it ever happens again? I have no idea. This is way beyond my remit. But I know he's a worrier and that he just needs to offload sometimes – in the way that Esther does, I suppose, with her therapist.

But I'm not a therapist. I'm a vet. So, having noted down Irene Craven's address, I decide that first I'll go round and take Bob off her hands. He can stay with me for the time being until Tony is well enough to come home. Esther can walk him during the day while I'm at work. It'll be good for her, I figure, being out in the fresh air, getting some exercise and having Bob for company. Plus, when I visit Tony I'll be able to show him some pictures of Bob in our care and report how well he's doing. Hopefully, that'll reassure him. It might even help his recovery.

It's the perfect plan, I decide, with the added bonus that hospital visits will also act as a distraction from the almighty fuck-up I've made of things with Lauren. I picture Tony alone in his flat, with only Bob for company. Am I that different really? Yes, I'm a fair bit younger but I've also spent an awfully long time on my own. It's well documented in my family how Polly 'ran away' to Peru in order to get away from me. 'It could've been worse,' Luc joked one night over drinks. 'If she'd wanted to put maximum distance between you she would have gone to New Zealand, eh, James?'

Trying to banish thoughts of myself at Tony's age (lonely cat man watching far too much TV on my own) I cycle home to pick up my car, and also to check on Esther and quickly explain the Bob situation to her. After all, she'll have to be a willing participant in this. I'll need to be able to count on her.

'So are you okay with that?' I ask.

'Mmm-hmm.' She's engrossed in something on her phone.

'I mean, you'd need to walk him in the day – would that be all right? Just until Tony's back home and well enough to take him out?'

'Will Walter be okay with Bob?' she asks distractedly.

'I think so. We'll have to see. I can't think of any other solution at the moment.'

She turns, finally, eyes bright and a big smile on her face. 'I'm just chatting to someone.'

By this she means messaging – no one talks on the phone anymore, I realise that – and something plummets inside me. Not Miles again. Here we go, I think, already bracing myself mentally. He's been simmering away in his bat cave, plotting how to win her back. 'Don't look like that,' Esther teases. 'It's not Miles, Dad.'

'Who is it, then?'

'Charlie.'

'You mean, Lauren's Charlie?'

'Who else?' she asks with a grin. 'I mean, what other Charlie would I be messaging?'

'I just didn't know you were still in touch,' I start.

'You know he sent me a sweet message after the chicken thing . . .'

'Yes, but I just thought that was a one-off.'

'No, Dad.' She looks at me, the unspoken subject of Lauren and me hovering like a cloud over us now. *Are you two on a break?* Esther had asked a couple of weeks ago. As if we were teenagers.

'It's not really happening at the moment,' I'd said. She'd tried to probe some more, perhaps not understanding that chickengate was the reason I hadn't gone to Cornwall, which had killed off the lovely thing we'd had. I didn't blame her exactly. But I wasn't prepared to delve into it with her.

Even so, the fact that she and Charlie are still in contact has slightly lifted my gloom as I drive over to Irene Craven's. I could grab at this as reason to send Lauren a message: *It was nice of Charlie to contact Esther. She was really happy to hear from him.* But should I even discuss the comings and goings of our kids? Would both of them resent it? They're human tripwires, highly tuned to parental interference or even comment. I thought the toddler stage was confusing, when you made them scrambled egg because they *loved* scrambled egg, then one day they pushed it away, scowling, as if you'd presented them with vomit on toast. One minute they'd be clamped to you like a baby monkey; the next they'd bristle with irritation when you happened to enter the room they were in.

But really, all that was a walk in the park compared to the workings of a young adult's mind.

I'm turning all of this over as I park up in Irene Craven's street. They're neatly kept terraces with tiny front patio gardens. Hers, it turns out, is home to countless ornamental creatures arranged on the flagstones: foxes, badgers and a not exactly lifelike, but admittedly striking iridescent metal stork.

I press the doorbell, happy now at the thought of Bob coming to us for a temporary stay. It'll be fun, I think, to have him around. He's an affectionate old boy, and it'll be something else to take my mind off the glaring void in my life where Lauren used to be.

The door opens and a tall, thin elderly woman in checked trousers and a peach sweater greets me with a look of disappointment, as if she'd expected something better. 'Mrs Craven? I'm James,' I start, aware now of the scramble of Bob approaching. He tumbles out of the door and fusses around my legs. 'Hello, boy!' I crouch down to greet him. At least someone seems happy to see me.

'I don't know what you're going to do with him,' Irene says, shaking her head.

'It'll be fine,' I say, straightening up. 'He can come and stay with me until Tony's home—'

'That's the thing,' Irene cuts in, frowning now. 'They called a little while ago. The hospital, I mean. Tony died this afternoon.'

CHAPTER FIFTY

LAUREN

I keep telling myself there are good things about not seeing James anymore. For one thing – although I'm not a pessimist normally – I used to find myself thinking, *Is this too good to be true, this being in love thing? Is it possible at fifty-one to not only have a holiday romance but for it to carry on back home when we have our own lives and jobs and families to keep on top of?*

Well, now I don't have to entertain such thoughts! Aren't I lucky being all on my own again?

I hadn't actually intended for this to happen, or even thought it through. Yes, I'd been bitterly disappointed about our little off-grid adventure and, in truth, I'd also felt a bit stupid over the intensity of my preparations – all those ingredients, meals and wine packed, pub meal booked, all that. But I'd also told myself that of course Esther had to come first and anyway, Charlie and I would have a wonderful time together.

I hadn't really thought beyond that. But after Cornwall it felt like everything had shifted. Our messages were short and to the point, then seemed to fall away. It felt too awkward somehow, and I decided that, rather than keep checking my phone like a lovesick fifteen-year-old, I'd roll up my sleeves and get on.

Fired up by our trip, I worked night after night on a cookbook proposal. Naturally, *A Corsican Kitchen* would be filled with recipes. But I also have hundreds of photographs from my trips to the island over the years, of the food markets, the boulangeries and charcuteries, the olive grove by my parents' place, the farm where a woman who's almost as old as the hills makes goat's cheese in the barn; the cafés with their perfect breakfasts of hot chocolate or excellent coffee in a handleless mug, served with the flakiest, butteriest croissants; the swathes of wild thyme and the orchards resplendent with clementines, apricots and almonds to be toasted and ground into the most wonderful tarts and puddings.

All of that could go into the book too, along with snippets from my mother's own handwritten recipe collections, the blue ink fading, the pages yellowing with age. I photographed pages and pages when I was there in the summer, which she found amusing: 'What d'you want with my scrawlings?' My heart quickens as I gather everything together; all my ideas, recipes, photos and love of the island bundled up into what, I'm sure, could be a wonderful book.

Of course I wish James was here and I could share it with him. But as time slips by, it only confirms that his life is already full to capacity and there's no room in it for us to be together.

And that's fine, I tell myself, as I sit up late researching literary agents and finally, with hope in my heart, send off my cookbook proposal.

Yes, it really is okay to be on my own again, I decide. It'll just take a bit of adjustment, that's all.

*

I used to think I led a very ordinary kind of life, doing my work but mainly focusing on Charlie, helping with his homework and answering his endless questions about how the solar system worked (until it became patently obvious that he knew far more about that than I did). Although my recipe work was taking off, I wasn't terribly confident. For a long time, at the back of my mind, I was still living with the fact that I'd spent so long with a man who'd neglected us and cheated on me; and more recently our son had started to push me away too, and soon he'd be gone and I'd be alone.

It scared me, if I'm honest. I wasn't sure about this next stage of my life – how it would look and feel. But since last summer things have happened.

For one thing, I fell in love. It might have been too good to be true, that lovely cocoon we were in on a beautiful Mediterranean island. But it's shown me that I *can* love someone. I can give myself like that, and will never again settle for a dreary man who springs straight off me after sex and starts going on about the fuse in his oven.

Other good things have happened too. Charlie and I grew closer again in Cornwall, which would never have happened if I'd taken James instead. I also know he reached out to Esther, and that they've been chatting a lot, because she has plenty of time on her hands at the moment. That's the phrase he'd used: 'reached out'. It made me smile, because he'd have scoffed at that not so long ago. I know he's felt pushed out by Remy, even though he'd rather put his hand in a fire than admit it to me. But my son has a sparkle back again and it's lovely to see. I haven't heard from Esther about doing more pictures – but maybe it's awkward for her now. Anyway, I'm sure she has plenty of friends who can help out.

So, yes, so many good things have been happening, and

if a wave of sadness rears up, I quickly quash it, keeping busy, busy, busy. After Cornwall I've been cold-water swimming with Kim. She was right; I can't think of anything that could be more exhilarating except . . . James pops into my mind again; specifically those many, many lovely nights we spent together. But they're consigned to the memory bank now.

I haven't even been to London since we broke up. I haven't had any reason to go there. But one grey winter's morning I check my emails and almost fall off my chair when I see a reply from a literary agent:

Dear Lauren,

Many thanks for sending us your proposal for A Corsican Kitchen. *The team and I really enjoyed it and wondered if you would be able to come to our office so we could talk it over and see where to go from here? If so, please let me know a convenient time for you.*

With best wishes,

Juliette Lloyd

I read it again to make sure I haven't got the wrong gist of it. But no, she wants to see me. My first thought is: I wish I could tell James. But a second later, I've jumped up from the kitchen chair and I'm charging through to Charlie's room, shouting, 'Charlie, good news!' And he jumps up too and we hug.

'I'm so proud of you,' he says, and without warning tears fill my eyes: tears over losing James but also at how my boy has somehow come back to me.

Three days later I wipe my sweaty hands on the front of my navy trousers and hope my outfit of blazer and a skinny-rib polo is appropriate for meeting a literary agent at a smart London address. It's crazy really because I've met dozens of clients face to face over the years: magazine editors, founders of online food platforms and even retail bigwigs who wanted to refresh their in-store magazines. It's never daunted me because they were just meetings, to discuss food, and what was there to be afraid of?

Plus, it would all feel pretty straightforward as they would commission me and I'd work to their brief. This – my very own cookbook – is different. The stakes feel much higher. Corsica is in my blood, after all, not to put too grand a point on it. As soon as I could use a knife safely I was next to Mum in the kitchen, standing on a little chair, chopping up herbs.

I grew up loving Corsican dishes. It set me on my career path and helped me to break free from Frank after Mexico and raise my son on my own. It's enabled me to build the life we have together. So, yes, it matters quite a lot.

Juliette Lloyd's office isn't too far from James's street, although her neighbourhood is posher. There's a beautiful Victorian pub on the corner with hanging baskets of winter pansies and purple hyacinths, and an attractive young couple in chunky sweaters are sitting at an outside table.

At the start of February the sky is blue, the air crisp and chilly. But still my hands are sweating with nerves. As I reach Juliette's townhouse in the middle of the terrace, I have to wipe them on my trousers again and hope no one's spotted me through the window, doing that.

Clearing my throat and thinking of what Charlie said – 'You can do anything you want, Mum' – I inhale deeply and knock on the glossy blue door.

CHAPTER FIFTY-ONE

JAMES

I miss Tony Lomax. There's a notable absence now he's not popping in on a regular basis with his packets of shortbread and concerns about Bob. After his stroke, he'd only been discovered because Irene Craven had seen Bob up at his living-room window, barking, which wasn't like him at all. Since we spoke again – touchingly, she'd wanted to know how Bob was doing – I've learnt that she'd knocked on his door to check if everything was okay. When Tony hadn't answered, and finding the door unlocked, she'd ventured in and discovered him lying on his kitchen floor.

I suspect now that Irene had felt guilty at being so offish when I'd gone round to collect Bob.

However, some good has come out of the sad situation. Esther and Bob are incredibly sweet together. I realise now that that's what her mother used to say about Esther and Miles. ('They're sweet, James! Surely you can see that?') But they really are, in a genuine way, with him padding around the house after her and nudging her wrist with his nose, wanting a walk or a treat. She only has to

pull on her jacket for him to be jumping about, tail spinning in delight. Esther was never an outdoorsy girl, not
really; she had to be cajoled along on those bracing seaside
walks. But now she's hardly in. And soon I realise something wonderful is happening.

Bob is helping to mend Esther's broken heart.

'He's always been a favourite of ours,' I tell her, meaning
all of us at the practice.

'Is it okay for vets to have favourites?' she asks.

'Yes, of course it is! We're not teachers.'

She laughs and kisses Bob's greying face. That's what
I've been trying to focus on lately; Esther and Bob, telling
myself how right and cosy it feels, the three of us here
together. I'm keeping busy, busy, busy – working full pelt,
then walking miles with Bob. Fitter than ever, he seems
to be ageing in reverse.

A few weeks later a surprise letter arrives at the practice, addressed to me. Tony might have seemed a bit
shambolic in his fraying sweaters and threadbare cords,
but he did have a will. His solicitor has written to say
that a substantial (actually eye-watering) amount has been
left in trust for our veterinary practice. By which he means
that it can be used – 'At your discretion' – to cover
veterinary care for those who would otherwise struggle
to afford it.

'So, he could have paid his bills after all?' Esther suggests
with a grin, when I tell her what's happened.

'Seems like it, yes.' I smile. 'But maybe that's how he
managed to build up all those savings. By being canny, I
mean.'

When I meet with the solicitor to figure how it'll work,
I learn that, while Tony's flat was rented, his savings were
substantial and the rest has been left to the animal rescue
centre he adopted Bob from as a pup.

So it's worked out, in some ways at least. Until Esther comes back from a walk one breezy afternoon, flushed with excitement. 'Dad, I've got a flat!'

'What?' I exclaim. 'I didn't think you were looking.'

'I can't stay here forever,' she says, looking so happy I wish I could take my reaction back. 'I'm twenty, Dad. I should be doing my own thing and leaving you in peace—'

'I don't mind you being here. I like it . . .'

'I know you do.' She grins. 'But all my friends are doing cool things and, y'know, not that it's not cool living with you . . .'

'So where's this flat?' I ask, trying not to sound hurt. 'And can you afford it?'

'Of course I can,' she retorts. 'I'm not as stupid as you think.'

'I've never thought you're stupid, Est. Of course I haven't. Quite the opposite.'

She smiles, pushes back her tangled hair and hugs me. 'Oh, Dad. I know it's not always been easy . . .'

'It's been fine, love.'

She looks up at me. 'You do realise I was never going to have a baby with Miles, don't you?'

I grimace. 'I was a bit worried there for a while.'

'Worried?' She chuckles. 'More like freaked out!'

I laugh, and as I drop Bob's food into his bowl I learn that her friend Jess, who's away studying at St Andrews, has been in touch. Concerned, apparently, about chickengate. A bit late in the day, I reflect, but decide not to comment as Esther is clearly thrilled to hear from her.

'. . . So we had a really good talk,' she tells me, 'the whole time I was out with Bob. And I told her about my situation here and that I was looking, and she knows someone who's subletting a room in Hackney and they

336

sent me pictures and it looks amazing and I said yes!' She beams triumphantly.

'You don't think you should see it in person?' I suggest.

'No, it's *fine*, Dad.' A flicker of an eye-roll. How foolish of me not to think it's a brilliant idea to move in without at least popping round for a cursory viewing. However, I'm happy for her; of course I am.

'I'll have flatmates,' she adds, beaming now.

'That'll be so great for you.' As I start to make dinner, another thought occurs to me. 'I think I might need to make another arrangement for Bob, then. If you're not going to be here, I mean. I can't leave him here all day on his own.'

Esther nods, twisting handfuls of hair and securing it all, by means of some kind of clip, into a messy bun. 'I've thought about that.'

'Have you?' I turn and look at her. 'What were you thinking?'

She gives me a bemused look, shrugging as if it's no concern of mine. 'Just a few thoughts, Dad. But don't worry. I'm sure we'll figure something out.'

CHAPTER FIFTY-TWO

LAUREN

I wish I could tell James how well it went, that meeting with Juliette Lloyd. How unintimidating and enthusiastic she was, telling me about her own childhood holiday in Corsica. She'd only been once but it had imprinted itself in her mind; the mountains, the pools, the scent of wild herbs and the sparkling sea. 'Looking at your proposal,' she said, 'was almost like being transported back there again.'

'I'm so glad,' I said. 'That's exactly what I wanted to get across. A feeling of actually being there, being able to smell and taste it . . .'

She smoothed back her neat brown bob and smiled. 'I'd like to represent you, if you feel our agency is a good fit for you.'

A good fit? Was she kidding? I wanted to jump for joy but instead I managed to sit there appearing professional while she detailed how things would go from here. She'd send out my proposal to a few editors she knows who would 'get' it. 'D'you think there's a good chance of it being published?' I asked.

'I can never promise,' she said, 'but let's put things in motion and we'll see. There's so much potential,' she adds, 'in marketing this. You could do cookery demonstrations and put together a video on your next trip to Corsica – taking your readers on a virtual tour of the food markets there.' *My readers*. I could barely contain myself. 'Would you be up for that?' Juliette asked.

'Oh yes,' I enthused.

She thanked me warmly for 'coming all this way' and I left on a cloud of happiness. All this way? It's nothing to me, I reflect now as I stroll across the nearby park, buzzing too much to head straight for the station and home. I need to walk it off and calm down a little. It's a beautiful winter's afternoon, sunny and bright, and I so want to share it with someone. So I find a bench and message Kim, who's thrilled for me, and Charlie, who calls immediately. Which is virtually unheard of for him.

'That's amazing, Mum. Well done!'

'Thanks, darling.'

'You're going to be an actual author. With an actual book!'

'Well, we'll see, love. It's a step in the right direction . . .'

'I'm so proud of you,' he says, with a catch in his voice. He's proud of *me*, his irritating mother who tries to slap sunscreen on him?

I get up and start to stroll back across the gently undulating park, thinking: maybe this really could be the start of something wonderful. Charlie will be leaving home in a few months' time, but that's fine. It's not the end. It's the beginning of something new, for both of us.

In the far distance I spot someone who looks familiar. His height, his build, even the colour of his jacket; it looks like James, I think. Even his walk is James's walk, and I'm remembering all the times we strolled across a park, or by the river at the edge of my village, his hand wrapped around mine. My heart is beating faster as I stop and watch him. I almost want to run over to check for sure.

But it can't be him, I tell myself. *Don't go and make a fool of yourself.* No, that's definitely not James, I realise now, because this man has a dog.

CHAPTER FIFTY-THREE

CHARLIE

'Can I tell you something, Dad?' Charlie butts in.

'What is it, son?' His dad frowns. They are FaceTiming, one of those duty chats that Charlie has put up with for far too long. As per usual his dad's been in full flow about his 'projects' and 'people'. All that boring shit.

'You only ever talk about yourself,' Charlie blurts out, trying to keep his emotions in check.

His dad's expression changes. He looks shocked, and it takes him a moment to compose himself. 'What are you on about?'

'Dad,' Charlie says, trying to keep his voice level because he's dreaded this moment, and has lost so many nights' sleep over it, 'we only have these chats so you can brag to me and tell me about all the amazing things you're doing.'

There's an awful stony pause that makes Charlie feel quite sick. 'Only to make conversation,' Frank says eventually. 'Only to keep things moving along when we're talking. You're not the easiest, y'know, Charlie. To communicate with, I mean. You're actually bloody difficult.'

'Am I?' Charlie asks. 'It's not deliberate.' *Esther doesn't find me hard to communicate with,* he thinks. They had a long conversation earlier today, about Bob, the dog who's living with her and her dad at the moment. She put some thoughts into Charlie's head, and he's waiting for the right time to bring the subject up with his mum. Not that she'll be unreasonable – he's pretty sure about that.

'Well, it feels that way,' his dad says curtly.

'Maybe it's just the way I am,' Charlie says, and without warning his voice cracks and tears well up in his eyes. *Don't cry. Don't show him that you're remotely emotional about this.* He blinks them away quickly, grateful that they aren't actually face to face.

'Are you all right?' His dad frowns.

'Yeah, I'm fine.'

'So, is that it then? That's what you wanted to tell me?'

As Charlie lets the moment hang, so many thoughts race through his head. He used to think that nothing ever happened in his life, apart from Young Stargazers and spending hours holed up in his room, looking through his telescope. And Remy would come over and they were so close, like brothers. Charlie was quite happy back then with his uneventful life.

But now there's loads going on. There's so much he could tell his dad, who's now looking impatient as he paces around on his Brooklyn roof. He could tell him about his mum working so hard and getting a book deal with a big publishing company. She's had her food columns and all her freelance jobs for years, working so hard, even on holiday when she should have been relaxing on the beach. Instead, she was often huddled over her laptop, bashing away at his grandparents' kitchen table. And now she's going to create her own cookbook! Charlie could tell his dad that, but he knows his eyes would glaze over.

(Funny how you can still detect the glazing thing over a distance of three and a half thousand miles!)

Charlie could also tell him about James, who his mum obviously loves so much and obviously wants to be with. And how he and Esther talked about that today. How they've come up with a plan that might or might not work, but it's worth a try, right? And then there's Esther, who his dad probably *would* be interested in because of her profile and Instagram following – even though he reckons influencers are 'stealing' all his photography jobs. He'd still be impressed, Charlie reckons.

But actually, that whole Instagram thing is the least interesting part about Esther. She's funny and scatty and actually incredibly kind and smart, *really* smart. She doesn't even know it. And there's no way Charlie could start to explain any of that to his dad, so he doesn't try.

Another thing he could tell his dad about is James's work, and how dedicated he is and how it spills over into his home life. That's why he's taken in this dog, Bob. All that time, this elderly man had been worried sick about what to do when Bob died. He lived in a flat with a shared garden so he couldn't go digging a great big hole to bury him out there. He didn't like the idea of dumping him in the woods somewhere and he didn't trust those cremation places. He said they were a rip-off and you'd never just get your own dog's ashes in a little pot.

All that worry over something he never actually had to face. We worry about things so much and they turn out to be nothing, Charlie decides. Like him, worrying about leaving his mum when he goes to university. And then deciding, when he was down in Cornwall with time to really think, that maybe he won't go to university this year after all. Remy's life has opened up by him doing exactly what he wanted to do, instead of what was

343

expected of him. His parents thought he was mad not to go to uni but all he wanted to do was his music.

Charlie thinks that maybe he'd like to do something else first, and study astrophysics later, when he's seen a bit more of life. There's a place on a remote Scottish island that's offering paid opportunities for young people to work on an archaeological dig. He'd never thought of doing anything like that before. But this island also happens to be the best place in Britain for observing the night sky. Better than Cornwall even. Charlie can feel the pull of it, tugging on his heart.

He's spinning away from the topic here, of what he really wanted to say to his dad today. His brain is shooting off like a comet.

'Charlie?' His dad's voice snaps him back to the present.

'Dad,' he starts, 'I've been thinking about this. I'm sorry but I don't want to have these calls with you anymore.'

A stunned pause follows. 'Some mood you're in today!' Frank blusters, finally.

'I'm not in a mood,' Charlie clarifies, 'and I don't mean forever. At least, I don't think I do. I just mean—'

'Okay, fine.' Frank's expression is neutral now. He's affecting indifference, Charlie thinks. Perhaps he does care at least a little, or maybe he doesn't like it that Charlie has taken control. 'That's it then. It's your decision,' he says gruffly. 'See you, then, son.' And the call ends.

Charlie sits for a long time in his room, breathing deeply, trying to steady his thoughts. And gradually, a sense of lightness comes over him. He's done it. He's finally said what he wanted to say, and he feels awful but also weirdly proud of himself. He won't tell his mum tonight because he doesn't want that to be the focus of their evening. Instead, he goes through and finds her at the kitchen table, working on her laptop.

'Mum?' he starts, pulling up the chair next to her.

'Yes, love?' She looks round at him.

'I, um . . . I hope you don't mind but . . .'

'What is it, Charlie?' she asks, closing her laptop.

He takes a deep breath and looks at her. *Just tell her*, he instructs himself. *Just get it all out.* What's the worst that can happen? She can only say no. But as he tells her about Bob, and how James can't keep him anymore, and how Bob would *love* it out here with them, with their garden and all the walks nearby, he senses that that won't happen. His mum is smiling, looking quite emotional, he realises now.

'James thinks it'd be a good idea, if you were okay with it. But no obligation,' Charlie adds quickly.

'Right,' she says, looking bemused.

'I know it might be difficult when I'm away, if you're in Corsica or wherever but maybe Kim and Lorenzo could look after him then?'

Did Charlie's dad know he'd always wanted a dog? Probably not. Because he never really knew him at all. But that doesn't matter, Charlie decides, because his mum always knew. 'Maybe one day,' she'd said. Even Esther knows him more than his own dad ever did.

'I don't go away often, do I?' his mum says now. 'I'm sure we could make it work . . .'

Charlie beams, his heart bursting with love for her. 'You mean it's a yes?'

She's grinning. 'I think I should give James a call to talk it over, don't you?'

'I think you should, Mum.' She reaches for her phone, her eyes shining with happiness. Before she's even made the call, Charlie leaves the room because he doesn't think she needs him listening in.

CHAPTER FIFTY-FOUR

FIVE MONTHS LATER
LAUREN

In the beginning it was just us two. That's the thing when you meet someone on holiday, away from your normal life. It's probably why it happens so often – *the holiday romance*. You're relaxed, away from all those responsibilities that demand so much of your energies back home.

Away from all that, you start to see things more vividly and fully appreciate the turquoise sea, a clear mountain pool, a searing blue sky. You're open to new things – experiences, maybe even a spot of canyoning, if you're into that! And falling in love. You're open to that too.

I fell in love with a man who makes my life wonderful. Of course, it wasn't all plain sailing. The transition from holiday to real life nearly ended us, even though neither of us had wanted to break up. But everything had become too tangled and complicated. At least, it had felt that way at the time. Thank goodness Esther decided to get involved – in a good way this time, by cooking up a plan with Charlie that Bob could come and live with me.

So really, it was her who brought James and I back

together. Or, more accurately, Esther, Charlie and Bob. A real team effort.

And now, a full year later, James and I are back in Corsica again. Although we're staying at the hotel where we spent our first night together, we're also spending plenty of time at my parents' place. James has been working on the garden today, while Mum and I have rustled up a couple of salads to go with the leftover quiche I made yesterday, which we're having for lunch. When I peep into Dad's study he's battering away at his keyboard with the force required for a manual typewriter in 1982. Earlier today, I happened to mention to him that 'I'm getting to grips with how the book publishing industry works, Dad.'

'That's an industry now, is it?' he asked with a bemused glint in his grey eyes. In his view, the word 'industry' is reserved for things like ship building and the smelting of iron. I also mentioned that I might be doing some cookery workshops to promote my book. 'Workshops?' he scoffed. 'You'll need your toolbox for that!'

Now Dad emerges into the garden, blinking like a mole in the sunshine, when lunch is ready. I glance at James and smile. He has brought a book with him; a huge textbook. It's sitting face down and open on the bench. *The Large Animal Veterinary Handbook*, it's called. He's keen to refresh his knowledge on farm animals because, as he put it, it's a very long time since he was at vet school.

'I could set up a practice near you,' he's suggested. We're talking about Fraser taking over the London practice and James moving in with me.

'But I thought you were a city vet?' I smiled.

'I'm adaptable,' he'd laughed.

'I'm sure you'd still get the odd tortoise out there,' I remarked, impressed by the solution he came up with, eventually, for a splint. Inspired by both Charlie and Esther's childhood love of Lego, James fashioned one with a Lego wheel at the foot, and now his patient apparently moves around the garden without any trouble at all.

When we'd booked our flights, I'd hoped that Charlie would be persuaded to join us too. Not that I was going to beg him. But I know he's always loved it out here, and lately we've felt a lot closer again. I'd already made a mental note not to nag him about sunscreen, and I certainly wouldn't expect him to hang out with us all the time.

Perhaps, I'd thought, we could do it differently this time. Maybe he and James could do some cycling together, or we'd travel around the island for a couple of days, and leave him to do his own thing. I was open to suggestions because I'd realised, finally, that I can't expect everything to stay the way it's always been. Charlie is an adult, after all.

At first, he seemed open to these suggestions. I actually thought he was on the brink of saying yes. But he was just trying to let me down gently, I soon discovered. He didn't want me to feel hurt. It turned out, when I went to book our flights, that Charlie wouldn't be coming to Corsica this summer after all.

Apparently he had 'other plans'.

CHAPTER FIFTY-FIVE

CHARLIE

He hadn't expected her to agree to come, but people keep surprising him. Okay, it wasn't a huge surprise that his mum had agreed to have Bob – but he had been slightly shocked that she'd been okay about him deferring his university place to study astrophysics.

Why had that surprised him? He'd thought she might think it was weird, that he'd be 'wasting' a year, or was delaying things because he wasn't ready to leave home.

It wasn't that at all. It was just, he wanted to do something else first.

When Charlie had been offered the place on the archaeological dig, it turned out that they were still short of participants. Maybe being stuck on a Hebridean island for six months wasn't many young people's idea of fun. Were they mad? It was amazing.

Esther isn't staying for the full six months as she has loads of other stuff going on. She and her new flatmates are planning an Interrail trip around Europe, and then she'll be getting her head around applying to university to study history. Her A-level grades were actually good enough. She'd just been swept along by the whirl of excitement after the reality show, and almost forgotten that other things were possible too.

Better things, actually. Charlie knew she could do it, and that getting involved in the dig would look great on her applications for courses.

Not that that's why she's come. She's come because they're friends. Best friends, really.

Their accommodation is in basic prefab huts, and there's a big communal kitchen and lounge where everyone hangs out. As well as working on the site – a swathe of hillside close to the shore – there's also lots of cataloguing and research to be done. But most of the work is dirty, and Charlie was amazed at first how Esther just got stuck in, working as hard as anyone.

She seemed different, he thought when she arrived on the ferry. She looked different too. For one thing, her hair didn't look quite as thick as it used to be. He decided not to mention it, but one evening, as they all sat around the open fire with a few beers, she caught him looking at her and said, 'Yes, Charlie. I had hair extensions and they're gone now. Far too high-maintenance.'

Day after day they work on the site, with shovels and trowels and, for the finer work, small brushes to sweep the earth away from their finds. Another thing that amazed Charlie about Esther is that she arrived *not* with a collection of suitcases but just one small rucksack, neatly packed, with proper walking shoes. His mum was amazed when he told her. Actually, she was amazed that Esther had gone there at all. 'Charlie,' she ventured last time they spoke, 'are you and Esther, um . . .'

'Together? No, Mum,' he retorted. 'She's three years older than me.'

He knew she was thinking about the Esther–Miles age

gap, and they laughed. 'We're just friends,' he said simply, although there's no 'just' about it.

It really is as simple as that, Charlie thinks now. He liked it when she said, 'I'm just Esther to you, aren't I? I'm not "Esther Burton".'

He's thinking about that as she knocks on the door of his room, scrub-faced, shiny-cheeked and ready to start the day. It's Sunday; a day off from the dig. 'Ready?' she says.

'I'm ready,' Charlie says and smiles, smiles, smiles at the thought of the day ahead.

*

But actually it turns out completely different to how he'd expected. When Charlie arrived here he'd been told that the weather can change in a blink, and you can be sunbathing one minute and hammered by hailstones the next. Which is why he'd told Esther to bring waterproof gear and warm woollies even though it's the height of summer.

On the beach now, they've been huddled in thick sweaters, but gradually the clouds part and the day starts to brighten. Esther pulls her phone from her pocket. 'Checking the weather?' Charlie teases her. 'You can just look at the sky, y'know . . .'

'No,' she retorts. 'It's just, I can actually get a signal here.'

'Can you?' he asks in surprise. Normally he doesn't bother bringing his phone out here on the island because it's pretty much off-grid. For some reason his granddad pops into his mind. He says he 'doesn't believe' in mobile phones.

'They're not a religion,' Charlie teased him last time he was in Corsica. That was the time he'd hid under a

351

towel on the beach like a stupid twelve-year-old and yelled at his mum. Okay, she *was* being annoying – but she was only trying to stop him getting burned. But he'd been all out of sorts that whole summer.

It wasn't that he'd been jealous of Remy being in Paris. It was that he'd known their friendship had changed forever. Remy had Freya now, and it was as if that thing between him and Charlie had never happened.

Just one kiss, it had been, well over a year ago now. They'd sat up late watching a movie at Charlie's and both been a bit drunk. They'd laughed and been a bit embarrassed afterwards, and it had never been mentioned again.

Charlie wasn't sure about what was going on in his head. However, he *had* known that he needed to push his mum away during that time, just to get some space to think. It made him feel terrible, this cycle of being horrible to her, then feeling guilty, then feeling mad at her for 'making' him feel guilty . . . God! Wasn't it exhausting sometimes, being alive? It was easier to just keep out of her way. But what a jerk he was last summer. Not now, he hopes. He's grown up a lot since then.

Charlie does have his phone today because he thought he'd take some pictures on their day off, to send to his mum in Corsica. To show he's surviving, and isn't sunburned. He smiles at the idea. He's doing more than surviving. Here on this island, with a billion stars above his head, he's really living.

He looks down at his phone now. There's a message from Remy, out of the blue. *I miss you mate*, is all it says.

Charlie tries not to react but he knows Esther can see it in his face. She's perceptive like that. And she knows not to say anything right away. They just sit there, the two of them with no one else around. It's just them and the steady whoosh of the waves until finally she says, 'Was that Remy?'

Charlie nods. The look Esther gives him tells him she understands. She never probes for details. She just lets him *be*.

He smiles, aware of a warm glow inside him as he and Remy message back and forth for a few minutes. The sun has come out now and he and Esther tug off their sweaters. Charlie is wearing a T-shirt under his; Esther a ribbed vest. 'I've got an idea,' he says.

'What?' She grins, looking thrilled at whatever it is he's going to suggest. He loves that about her; that she gets so excited about stuff, like a little kid.

'How much food have we got with us?' he asks.

'I've got some crisps, maybe half a sandwich left . . .' She starts burrowing into her bag and produces half a clingfilm-wrapped sandwich, squashed flat, plus a bag of Quavers and about a third of a bar of chocolate. 'Why?'

In Charlie's own rucksack he finds a slightly bashed KitKat, a packet of Hula Hoops and a banana. 'I was thinking we could stay here until it's dark,' he says.

She gives him a quizzical look. 'Okay. Why not?' She looks down at the food they've laid out on the silvery sand. 'There's enough to keep us going, I think.'

'Yeah, definitely.' They fall into a comfortable silence again until she asks, 'So, how's Remy?'

'He's doing good,' Charlie says, trying to look neutral but unable to stop the smile spreading across his face.

They sit for ages then, watching the sea, the birds and the occasional seal popping its dark head above the water. The sky turns deep blue, then streaks with pink and gold. They chat about the dig, and the new friends they've made, as it darkens some more until eventually it's full of stars. The sliver of moon glows brightly.

'It's nice he was thinking about you,' Esther says.

Charlie nods.

'He might even be looking at the moon too,' she adds.

'Yeah, he might be.' That's so weird, Charlie thinks, because that's what he was thinking too. He thinks Esther knows this because she puts an arm around his shoulders and they sit there together, looking up at the glinting stars.

'I'm glad Mum met your dad,' Charlie says.

'I'm glad Dad met your mum.' They laugh and she leans her head against him. Without thinking, Charlie reaches for a tiny shell. He examines it for a moment, then slips it into his jeans pocket, like he did when he was little. All those beach finds he presented to his mum.

'Are you keeping that?' Esther asks.

'Yeah.'

'For a souvenir?' she says.

He nods. 'Kind of.'

They sit in silence for a while watching the waves swish against the sandy shore. 'I wish I'd known you when I was younger,' Esther says suddenly. 'What kind of adolescent were you?'

Charlie laughs, surprised by her question. But then she's always surprising him. 'I was still close to Mum then. We'd go to the cinema, have pizza – that kind of stuff.'

'Cinema and pizza with your mum? What kind of behaviour is that?' she teases.

'I know. We were really close,' he says, laughing at her reaction.

'No moody sulks or slamming doors?'

Charlie grins and shakes his head. 'Not that I can remember. I was a terrible adolescent! What about you?'

'Oh, I was a really good one,' Esther says. 'My parents broke up around then so I could use it as an excuse to be an absolute horror.'

He looks at her, wondering how to broach this. 'Did it affect you, d'you think? Them breaking up, I mean?'

'Maybe. I'm not sure. I think a lot of it was just in me, to be honest. But last year I had a therapist, a woman called Chrissie I used to see.'

'You don't see her anymore?' Charlie asks.

'No.' Esther tosses a small, flat pebble into the sea. 'I was basically paying sixty quid an hour to be told to write a gratitude journal.'

Charlie smiles. 'I think you sound like you were an excellent adolescent.'

'Why, thank you, darling,' she says in a jokey voice.

He looks at her with her red hair blowing around her face, thinking, if he had a gratitude journal he could fill it a million times over. 'I love you,' he says, before he can stop himself.

'I love you too, Charlie. You're my best friend.'

'And you're mine,' he says, meaning it. They hug then, in the dark, on the deserted beach.

Esther pulls back, smiling broadly. 'I want to get in the sea. Do you?'

She knows all about his thing, his fear of it. But he doesn't feel bullied or embarrassed at all. He looks at her and then at the sea, sparkling in the moonlight. 'Charlie, come in the sea with me,' Esther says.

He turns his gaze to the vast expanse of shimmering water. This isn't Mexico with his mum and dad. It's a tiny Hebridean island with Esther and they're here to work, unearthing tiny fragments of ancient pottery. That day in Mexico used to be vivid in Charlie's mind – like a film he saw only yesterday. But it's fading now, into the past.

'You *can* swim, can't you?' Esther says with an encouraging smile.

Charlie nods. His stomach is swirling, not in fear but in excitement about his life opening up. Living here until winter and being involved in the dig, making friends, discovering fragments of things that people drank from and cooked with thousands of years ago.

It's mind-boggling. Even more, almost, than the stars above. Being here on the island, Charlie feels as if his head could explode – in a good way.

'Come on then!' Esther has jumped up and pulled off her jeans. She's standing there in her knickers and vest.

Charlie pulls off his T-shirt and jeans so he's just in his boxers. He looks at her, filled with happiness. He doesn't even feel the cold. The sky above is glittering with a million stars.

She grins at him as if challenging him to do this. Then – 'Race you!' Esther yells, and something about her exuberance makes him jump up and think, fuck it, what's he been so scared about? And they kick up sand with their bare feet as they charge towards the sea.

CHAPTER FIFTY-SIX

LAUREN

This time in Corsica is probably the best time. I know we all think of the most recent time as the best time, but it really is. Even though Charlie isn't here. But I know he's having his own adventure and that makes it okay. In fact it makes it better than that. I can tell he's happy, from the pictures he's sent of him and Esther on that Hebridean island, the two of them all muddy and messed up from working on the dig all day.

And it makes me happy to think of them together.

It's wonderful here too, in a way that I've never experienced before. Being with James, I mean. The two of us together, growing closer and closer all the time. I love just being with him, doing our own thing, and the way he is with Mum and Dad. He just fits right in, and he 'gets' Dad in the way that few people do.

'I like the way he turns an apology into an insult,' he says as we find ourselves alone in my parents' kitchen.

'What d'you mean?' I ask.

'That thing with Minnie and the little terrier.' He's referring to a moment last night, when the four of us

357

went out to Camille's restaurant. We'd taken Minnie along too because Camille always makes a big fuss of her. But there'd also been a small brown and white terrier at the restaurant and Minnie had been a bit barky and not especially friendly, I have to say.

'Sorry, she's not good with little rat-like dogs,' Dad had announced loudly, clutching his glass of red wine.

'You know what he's like,' I say, laughing – because by now, James actually does know him, and Mum too. He knows Dad has never learnt French beyond the basic phrases. He can order a croque monsieur, have a new battery put in his ancient car and call a plumber. But he loves it here, if he'd only admit it: the climate, the wine, the food and, of course, my mum.

He has a small collection of friends too: elderly men who get together in the local bar and watch football on the blaring TV. My parents are happy, and I am too, especially when I check my phone to see a message from Charlie. 'James,' I call out, 'Charlie says they're coming here.'

'What? Who's coming?'

'Esther and Charlie,' I exclaim. 'They've booked flights. They're coming tomorrow!'

'I thought they were meant to be on their dig?' he says, but I know he's delighted.

'They just fancy a few days in the sun, he says.' I look at James, who's slicing figs for the sweet pie I'm planning to make for dinner. This is a dish that will definitely go into my book.

'We're going to have a couple of extras for dinner tomorrow,' he tells Mum as she wanders in.

So they come, and of course Dad rouses himself and is actually enthralled by the young people around our table as we all tuck in. Minnie meanders around, looking for scraps, and I think how lucky I am to be here, on this beautiful island with the people I love the most, with Bob being looked after at home by Kim and Lorenzo. The oldest collie in London may no longer be in London, but he's still going strong, and when we come home he bounds towards me, ears flapping, delighted to see us all.

If I had a gratitude journal it would be filled to the brim, and as the months go by, I find myself missing Charlie but also glad he's living his own life on the island. It was time for him to spread his wings.

Then one weekend in October, when the garden has turned golden, he comes home on a visit on the same day a parcel arrives for me. James and Charlie watch as I tear it open, and lift out a glossy hardback book.

I open it, and focus on the words on the opening page:
A Corsican Kitchen by Lauren Summer

'This looks great, Mum,' Charlie says as James hugs me and Bob settles at my side.

Together we turn the page to Chapter One.

ACKNOWLEDGEMENTS

Huge thanks as ever to my wonderful agent Caroline Sheldon, and to my editor Cara Chimirri, publicist Becci Mansell, copy editor supremo Helena Newton and the entire brilliant Avon team. Thank you Jenno and Kath for our many holiday capers – you have given me a billion books' worth of fun and adventures! Thank you dear Marie, Riggsy, Cathy, Liam, Michelle, Tania, Jennifer, Mickey and the Curries for our decades of friendship. Big thanks to Elise Allen's coaching group – Anne, Annie, Christobel and Mif, I love our get-togethers. Special thanks to Sue Baker for helping me with vet-related info – you're always so supportive and it's hugely appreciated. Thank you Mandy Pearce for lending me the name 'Minnie' for the dog in this novel, and to Lisa W for (unwittingly!) giving me lots of story ideas which I find myself storing away for future use. Special love and hugs to Elisabet Corlin. As ever thank you to Jimmy – this time for encouraging me to sneak off to a hotel in Perth to tackle the final chapters, and to Sam, Dexter and Erin for always lifting my heart. You are the best.

Meet Jen. Flight attendant.
Mum to a grown-up daughter.
Permanently single . . .

'The voice
of modern
woman'
*MARIE
CLAIRE*

'Warm,
funny and
poignant'
*DAILY
MAIL*

FIONA GIBSON

The

WOMAN

WHO TOOK A

CHANCE

Life really can begin again...

A heart-warming and hilarious novel that proves
age is just a number and it's never too late for a
second chance!

Suzy Medley is having a bad day . . .

. . . when a shabby terrier turns up at her door . . .

FIONA GIBSON

The
DOG
SHARE

Two strangers.

One dog.

It's complicated!

Can one unruly dog change her life forever?

Sometimes life can be bittersweet . . .

FIONA GIBSON

WHEN LIFE gives you LEMONS

...just add gin and tonic!

When life gives you lemons, lemonade just won't cut it. Bring on the gin!

When the kids are away ...

'Warm, funny and poignant' *Daily Mail*

THE MUM WHO GOT HER LIFE BACK

An empty nest has
never been so much fun!

Fiona Gibson

**The laugh-out-loud *Sunday Times* bestseller is back
and funnier than ever!**

Everyone has a last straw . . .

An unmissable novel, perfect for fans of Milly Johnson
and Jill Mansell.

What happens when The One That Got Away shows up again . . . thirty years later?

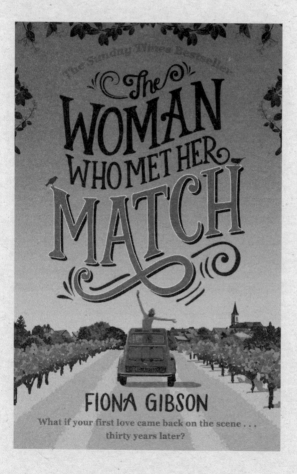

An unmissable novel from the voice of the modern woman!

Forget about having it all. Sometimes you just
want to leave it all behind.

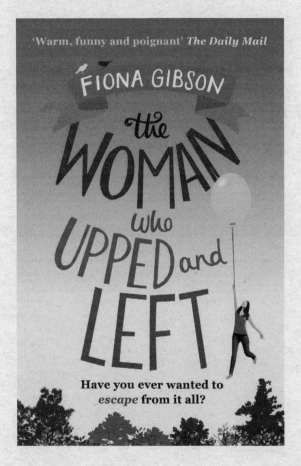

'Warm, funny and poignant' *The Daily Mail*

FIONA GIBSON

the WOMAN who UPPED and LEFT

Have you ever wanted to
escape from it all?

A warm, funny and honest read that's perfect for when
you've just had enough.